SCOUT IS NOT A BAND KID

JADE ARMSTRONG

This book is dedicated to Annabel Scott.

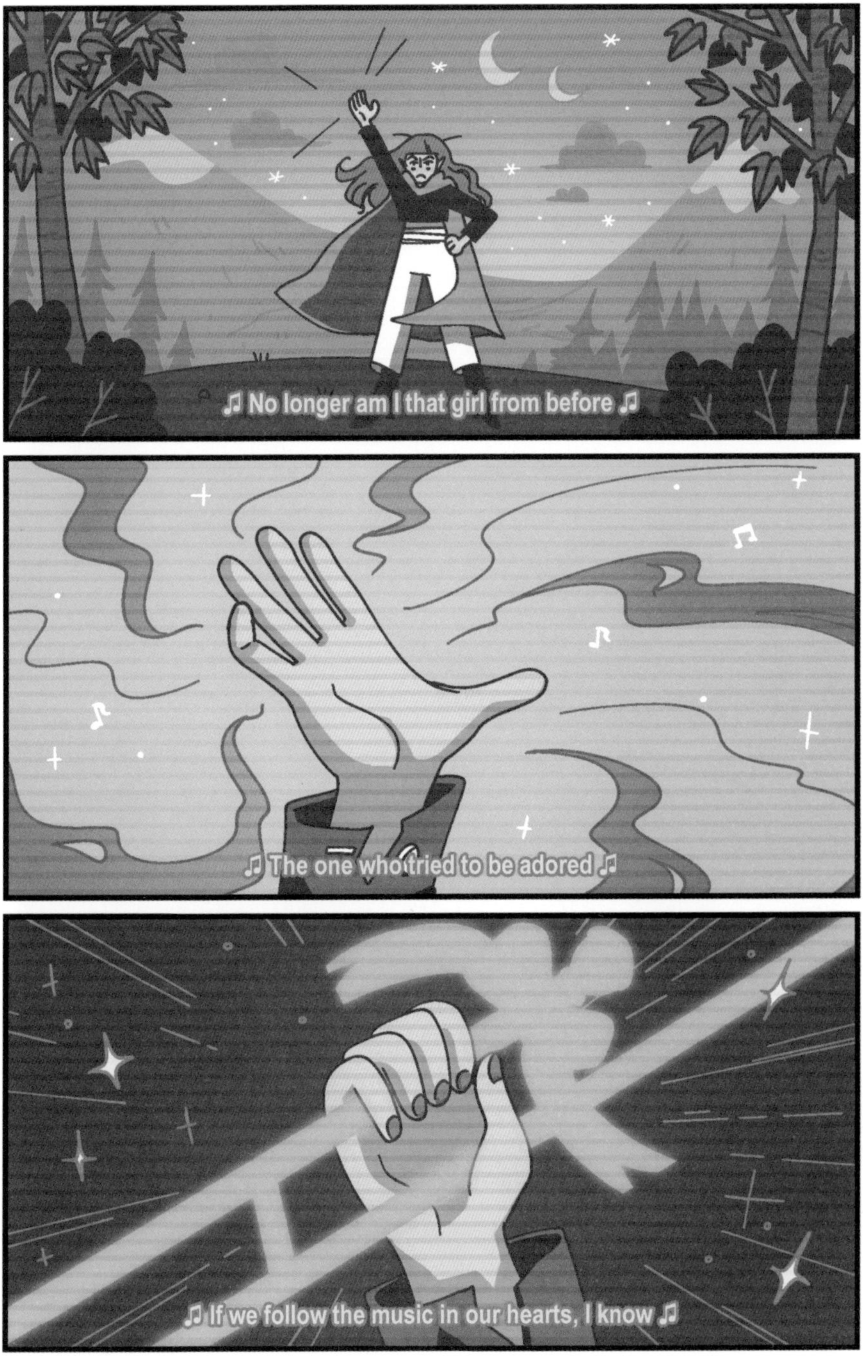
♫ No longer am I that girl from before ♫
♫ The one who tried to be adored ♫
♫ If we follow the music in our hearts, I know ♫

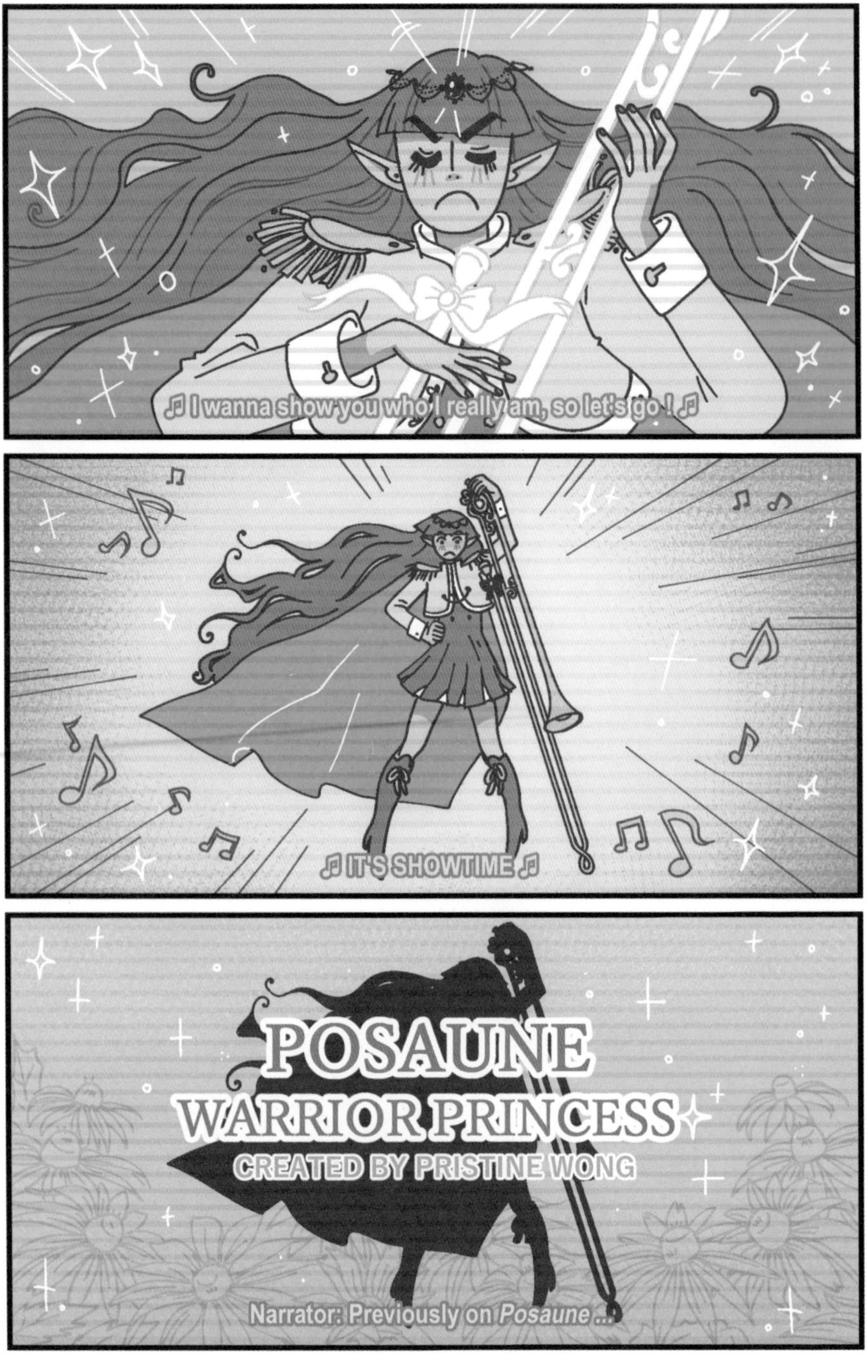
♬ I wanna show you who I really am, so let's go ! ♬
♬ IT'S SHOWTIME ♬
POSAUNE
WARRIOR PRINCESS
CREATED BY PRISTINE WONG
Narrator: Previously on *Posaune* ...

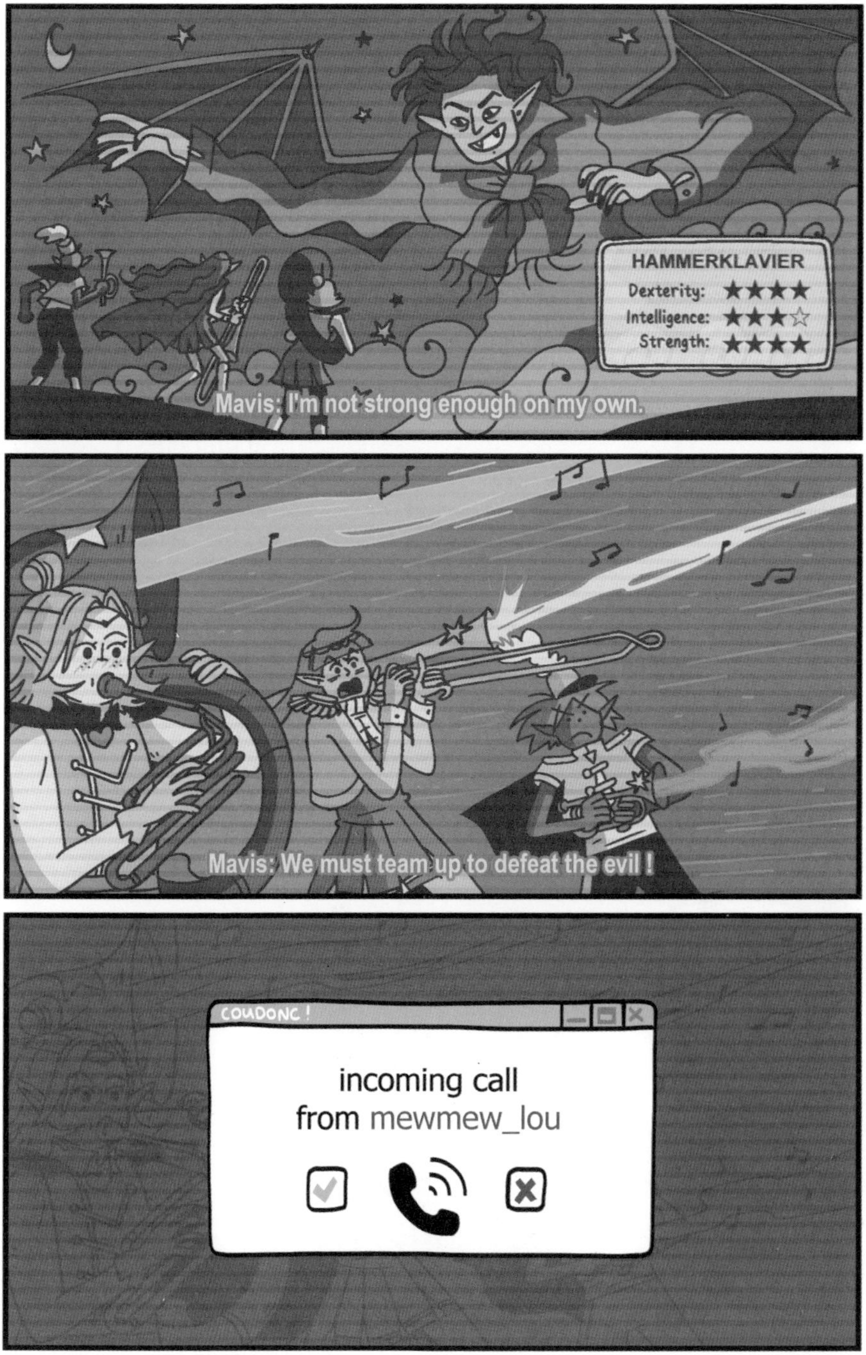
HAMMERKLAVIER
Dexterity: ★★★★
Intelligence: ★★★☆
Strength: ★★★★
Mavis: I'm not strong enough on my own.
Mavis: We must team up to defeat the evil !
COUDONC !
incoming call
from mewmew_lou

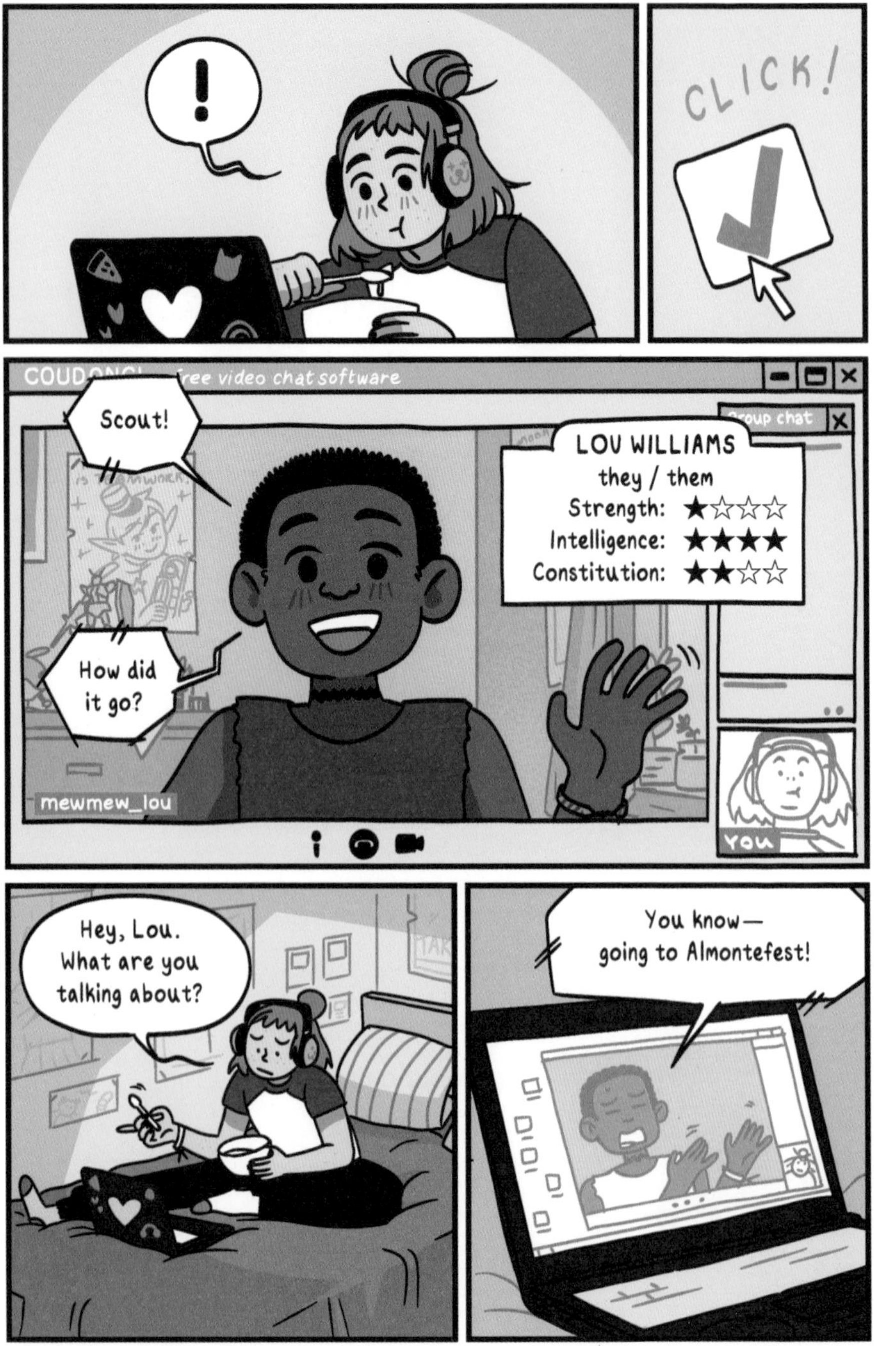
!
CLICK!
ree video chat software
Scout!
LOU WILLIAMS
they / them
Strength: ★☆☆☆
Intelligence: ★★★★
Constitution: ★★☆☆
How did it go?
mewmew_lou
YOU
Hey, Lou. What are you talking about?
You know— going to Almontefest!

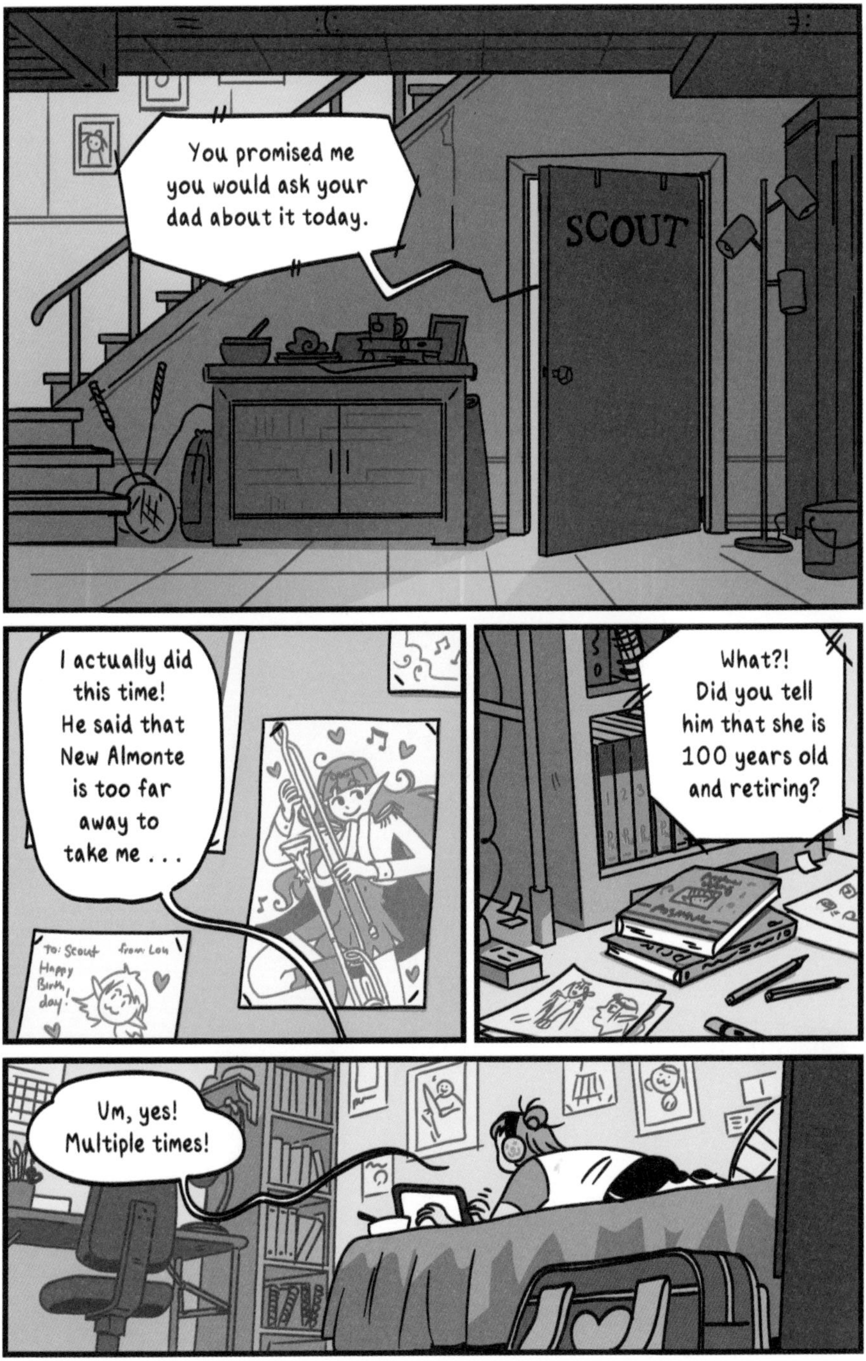
SCOUT
You promised me you would ask your dad about it today.
I actually did this time! He said that New Almonte is too far away to take me . . .
To: Scout from: Lou Happy Birthday!
What?! Did you tell him that she is 100 years old and retiring?
Um, yes! Multiple times!

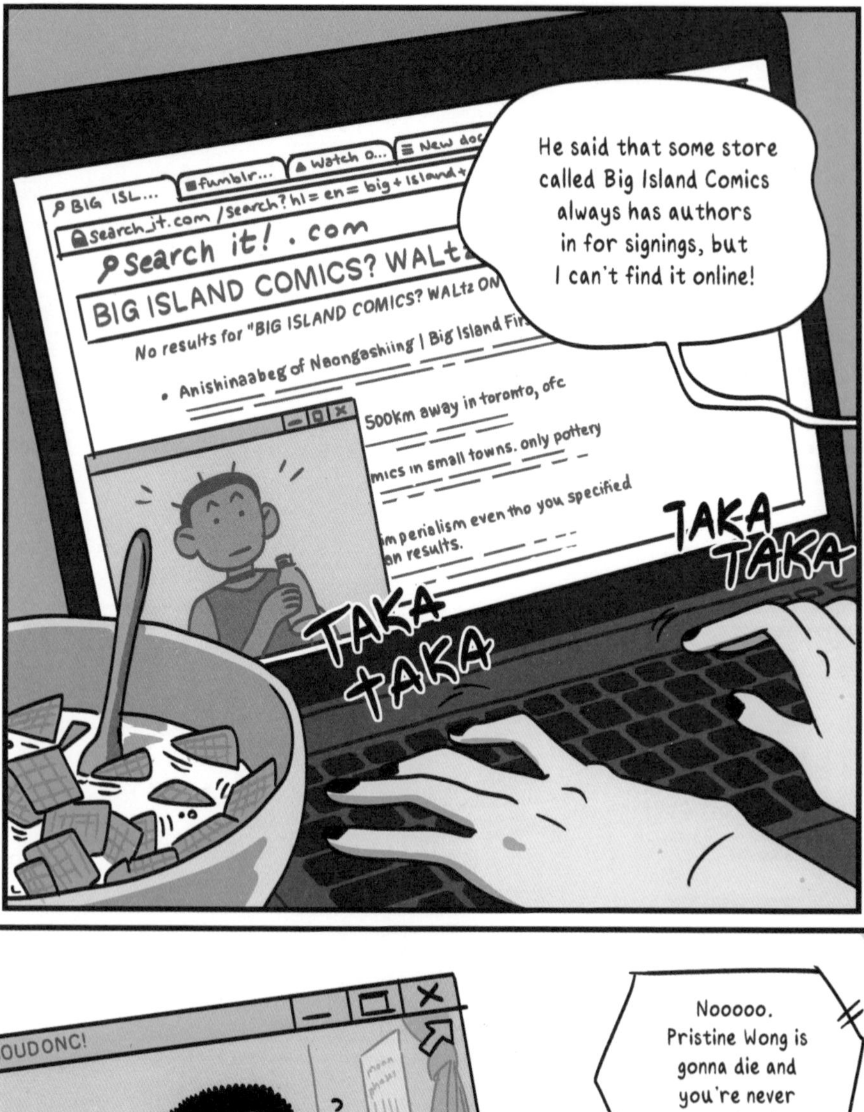
BIG ISL...
fumblr...
Watch o...
New doc
search_it.com /search?hl=en=big+island+
Search it! .com
BIG ISLAND COMICS? WALtz ON
No results for "BIG ISLAND COMICS? WALtz ON
Anishinaabeg of Neongashiing | Big Island Fir
500km away in toronto, ofc
mics in small towns. only pottery
imperialism even tho you specified
an results.
He said that some store called Big Island Comics always has authors in for signings, but I can't find it online!
TAKA TAKA
TAKA TAKA

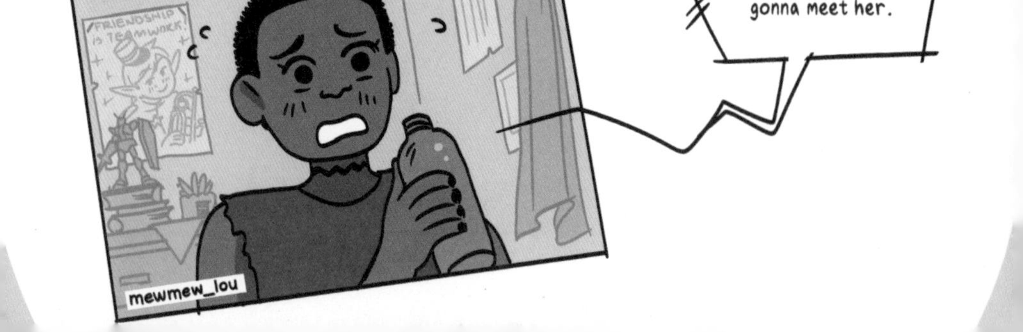
COUDONC!
FRIENDSHIP is TEAMWORK!
mewmew_lou
Nooooo. Pristine Wong is gonna die and you're never gonna meet her.

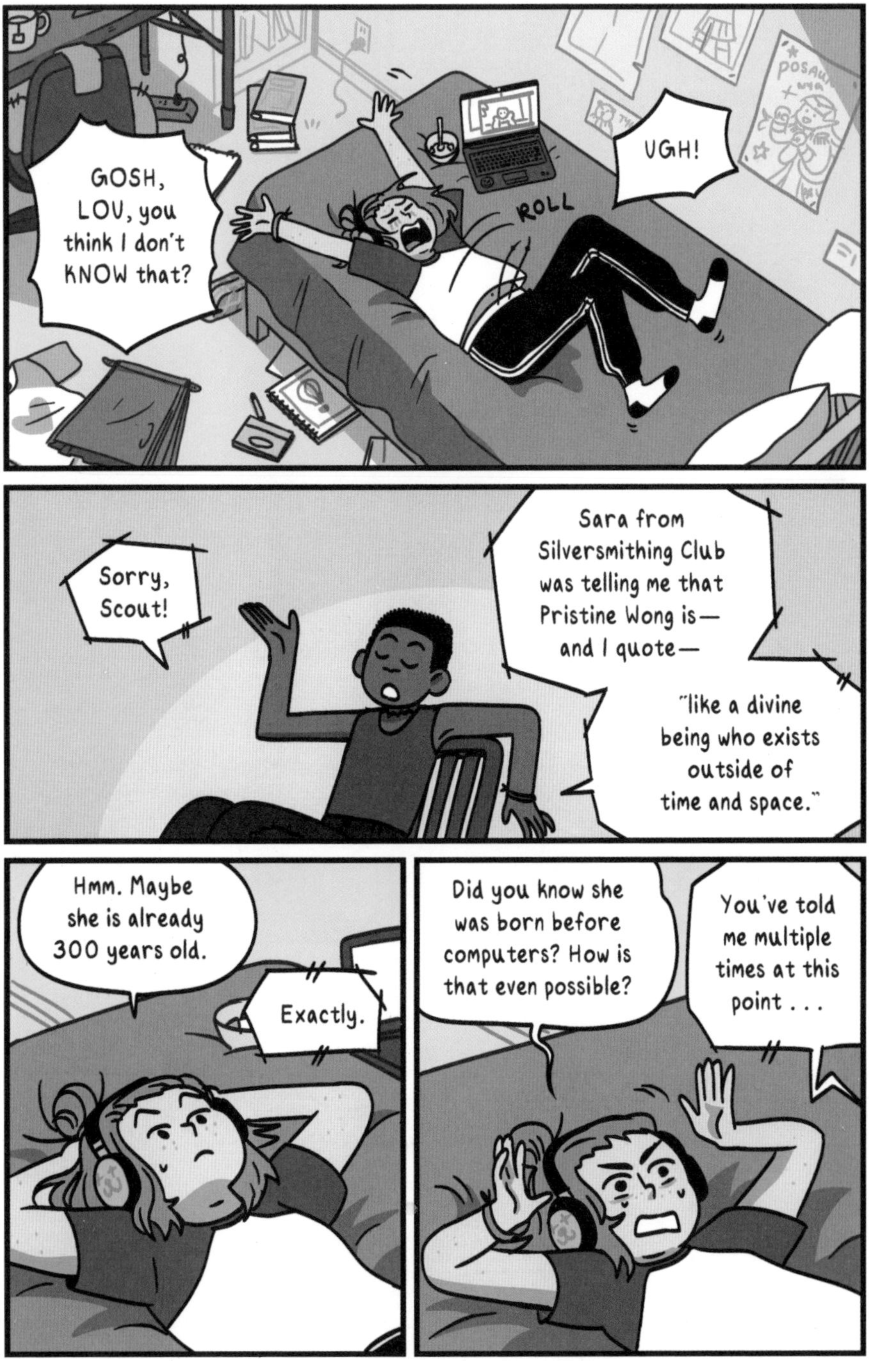
GOSH, LOU, you think I don't KNOW that?
ROLL
UGH!
Sorry, Scout!
Sara from Silversmithing Club was telling me that Pristine Wong is— and I quote—
"like a divine being who exists outside of time and space."
Hmm. Maybe she is already 300 years old.
Exactly.
Did you know she was born before computers? How is that even possible?
You've told me multiple times at this point . . .

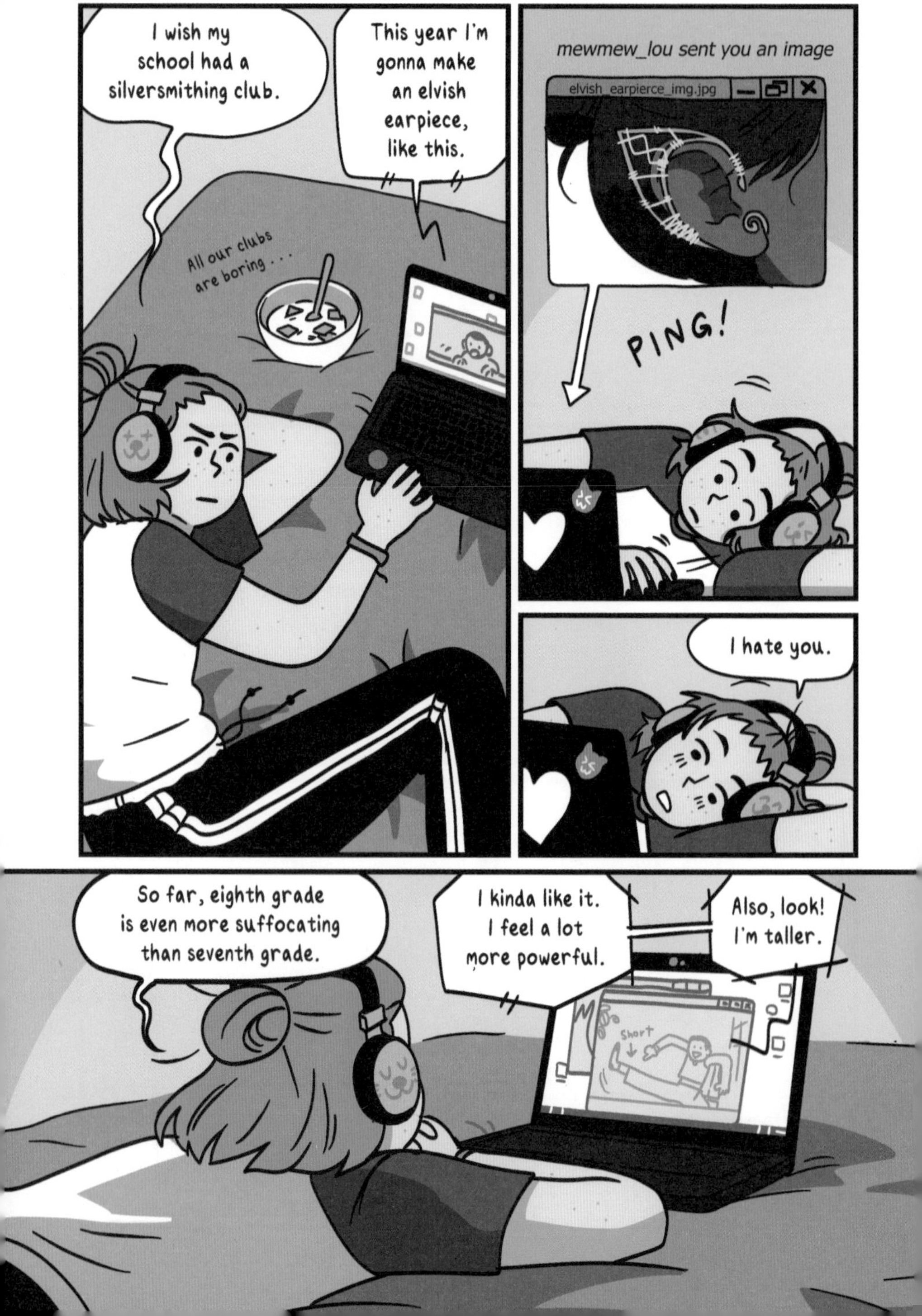
I wish my school had a silversmithing club.
All our clubs are boring . . .
This year I'm gonna make an elvish earpiece, like this.
mewmew_lou sent you an image
elvish_earpierce_img.jpg
PING!
I hate you.
So far, eighth grade is even more suffocating than seventh grade.
I kinda like it. I feel a lot more powerful.
Also, look! I'm taller.
Short

*Original Character

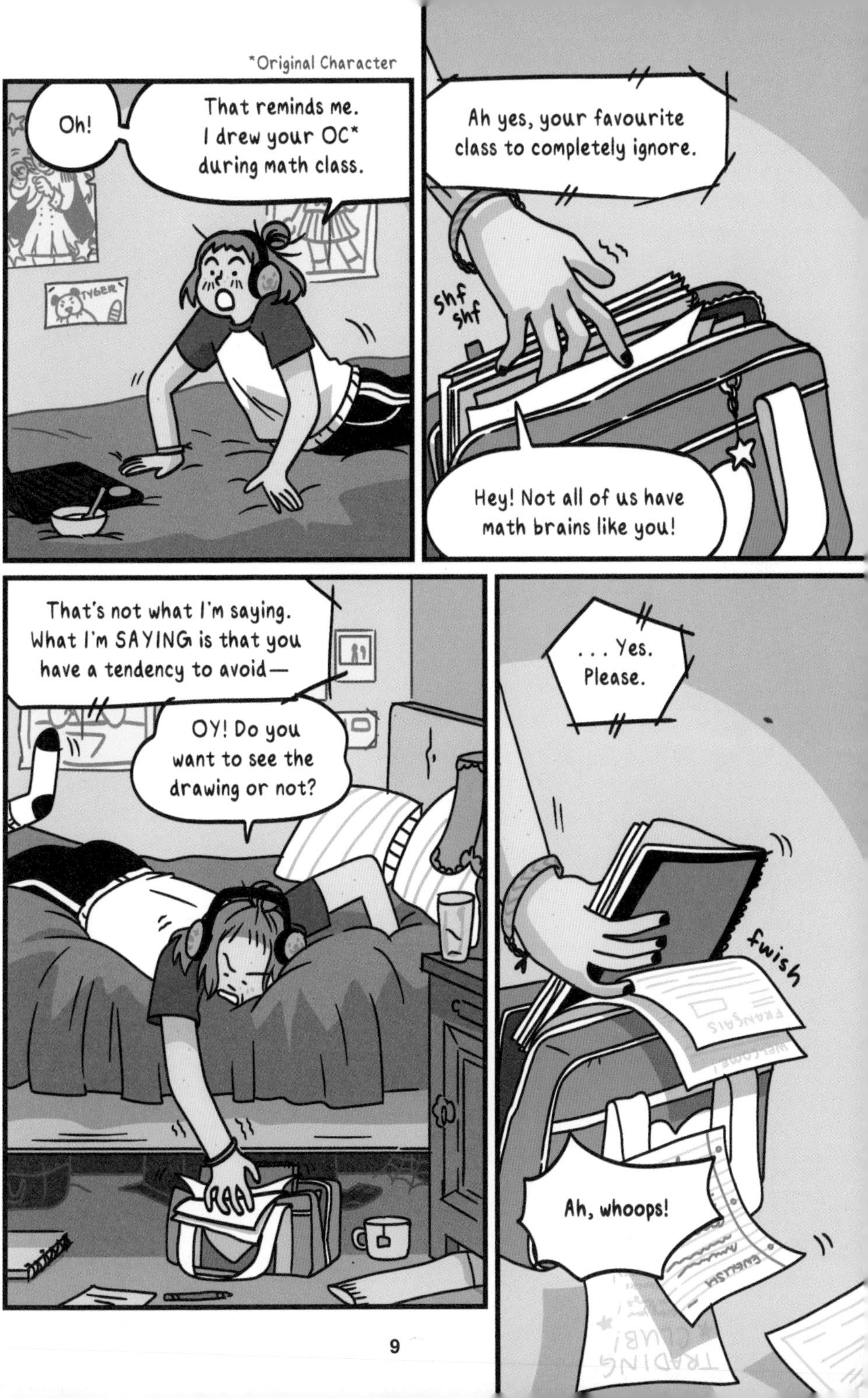
Oh!
That reminds me. I drew your OC* during math class.
TYGER
Ah yes, your favourite class to completely ignore.
shf shf
Hey! Not all of us have math brains like you!
That's not what I'm saying. What I'm SAYING is that you have a tendency to avoid—
OY! Do you want to see the drawing or not?
. . . Yes. Please.
fwish
Ah, whoops!

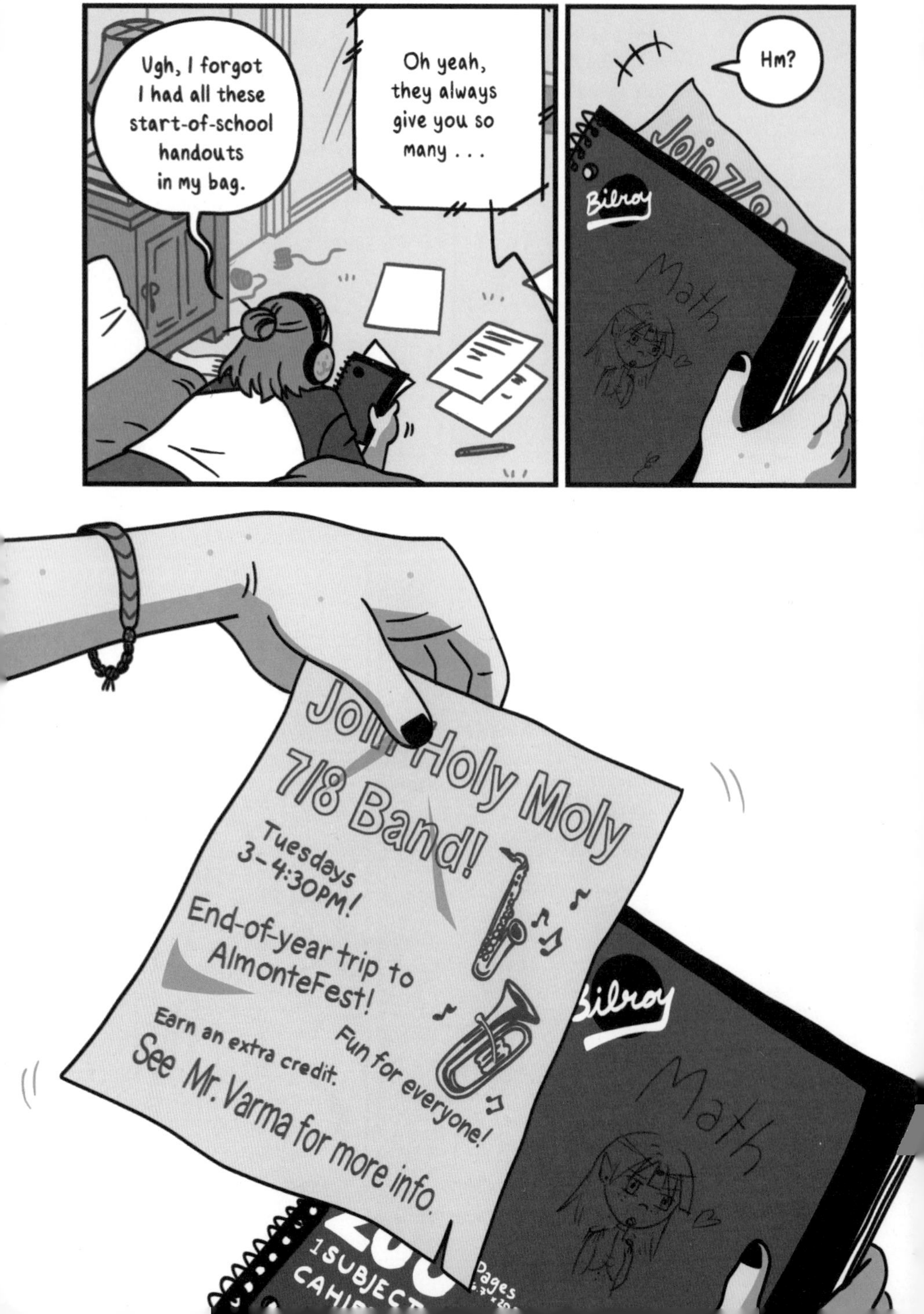
Ugh, I forgot I had all these start-of-school handouts in my bag.
Oh yeah, they always give you so many . . .
Bilroy
Math
Hm?
Holy Moly
7/8 Band!
Tuesdays 3–4:30PM!
End-of-year trip to AlmonteFest!
Fun for everyone!
Earn an extra credit.
See Mr. Varma for more info.
Bilroy
Math
1SUBJECT
Pages

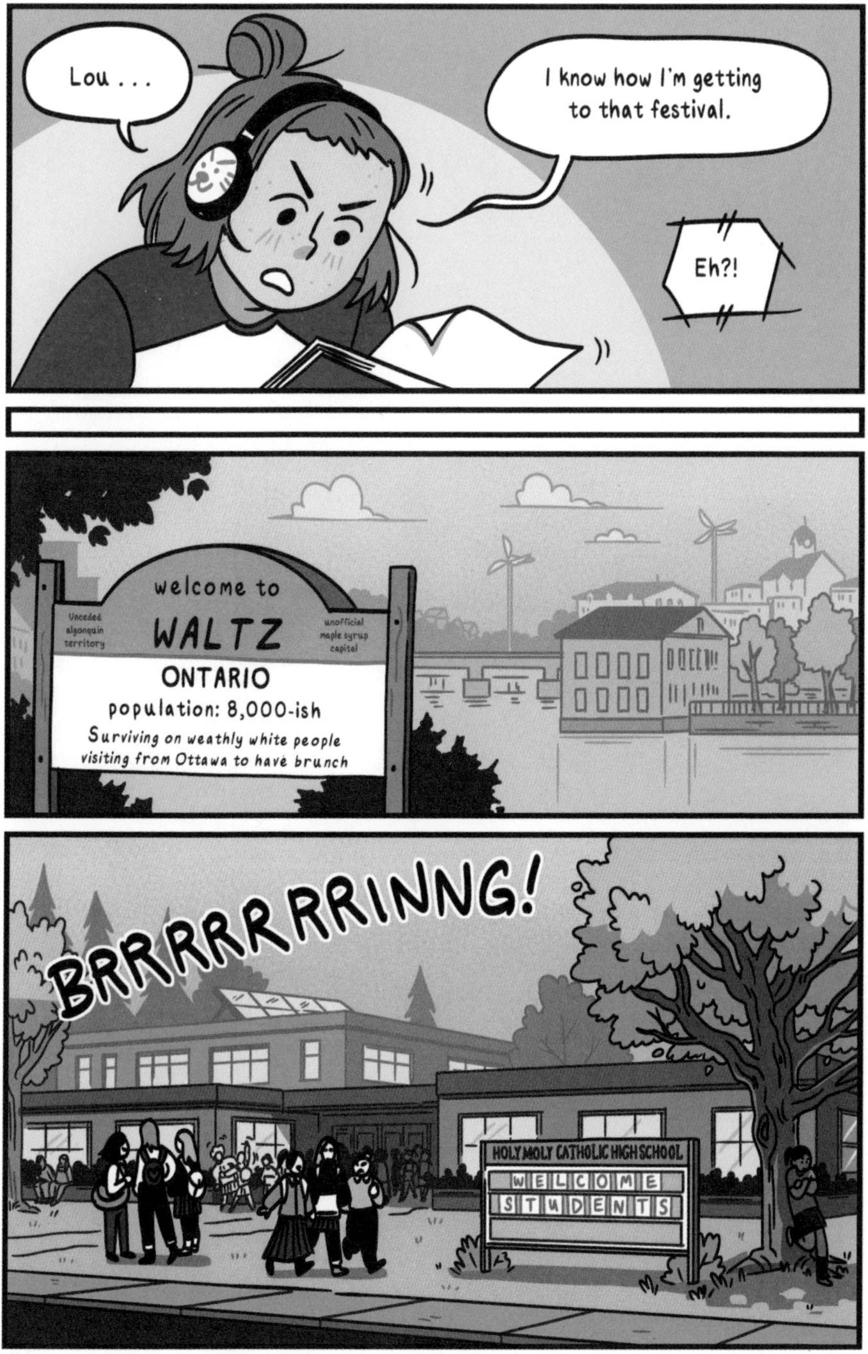
Lou . . .
I know how I'm getting to that festival.
Eh?!
welcome to
Uneeded algonquin territory
WALTZ
unofficial maple syrup capital
ONTARIO
population: 8,000-ish
Surviving on weathly white people visiting from Ottawa to have brunch
BRRRRRRRINNG!
HOLY MOLY CATHOLIC HIGH SCHOOL
WELCOME
STUDENTS

Chapter 1

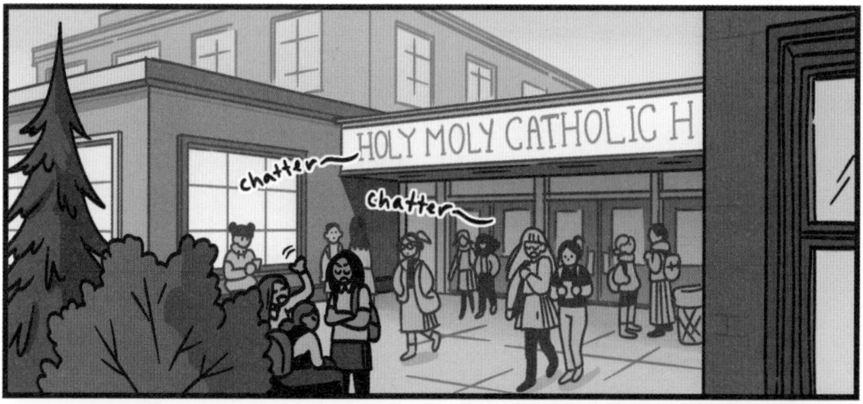
HOLY MOLY CATHOLIC H
chatter~
chatter~

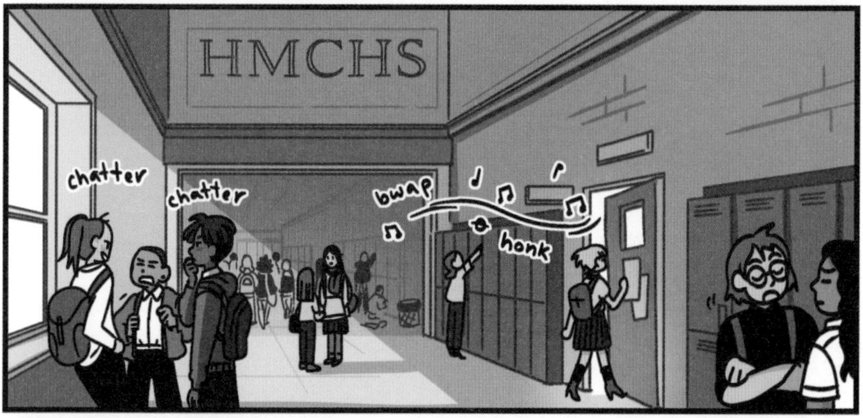
HMCHS
chatter
chatter
bwap
honk

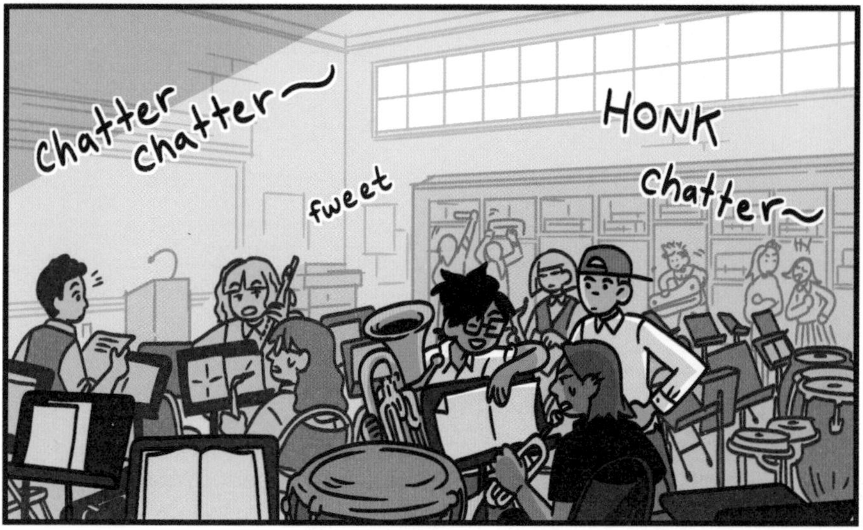
chatter
chatter~
HONK
fweet
chatter~

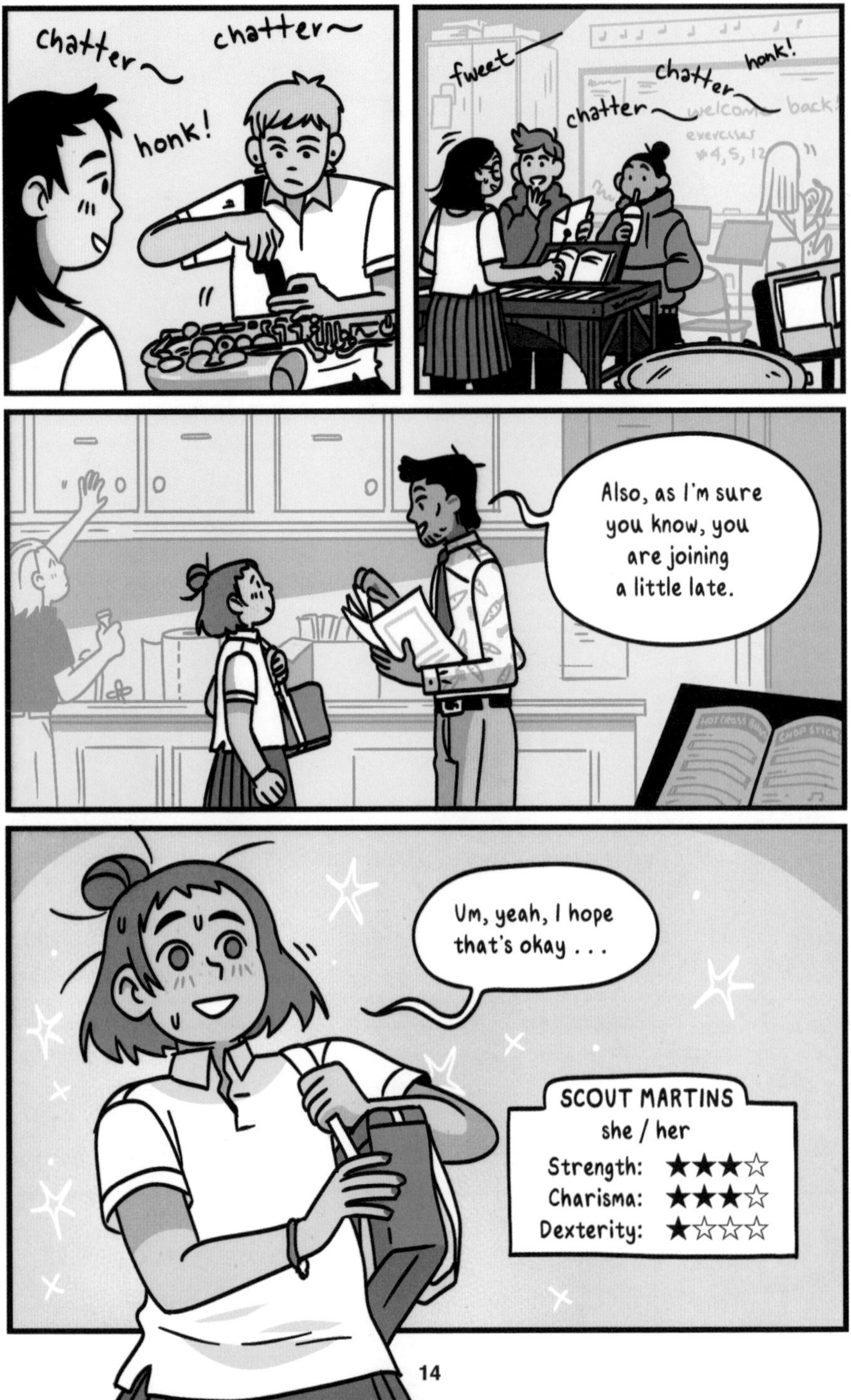
chatter~
chatter~
honk!
fweet
chatter~
chatter~
honk!
welcome back!
exercises #4, 5, 12
Also, as I'm sure you know, you are joining a little late.
HOT CROSS BUNS
CHOPSTICKS
Um, yeah, I hope that's okay . . .
SCOUT MARTINS
she / her
Strength: ★★★☆
Charisma: ★★★☆
Dexterity: ★☆☆☆

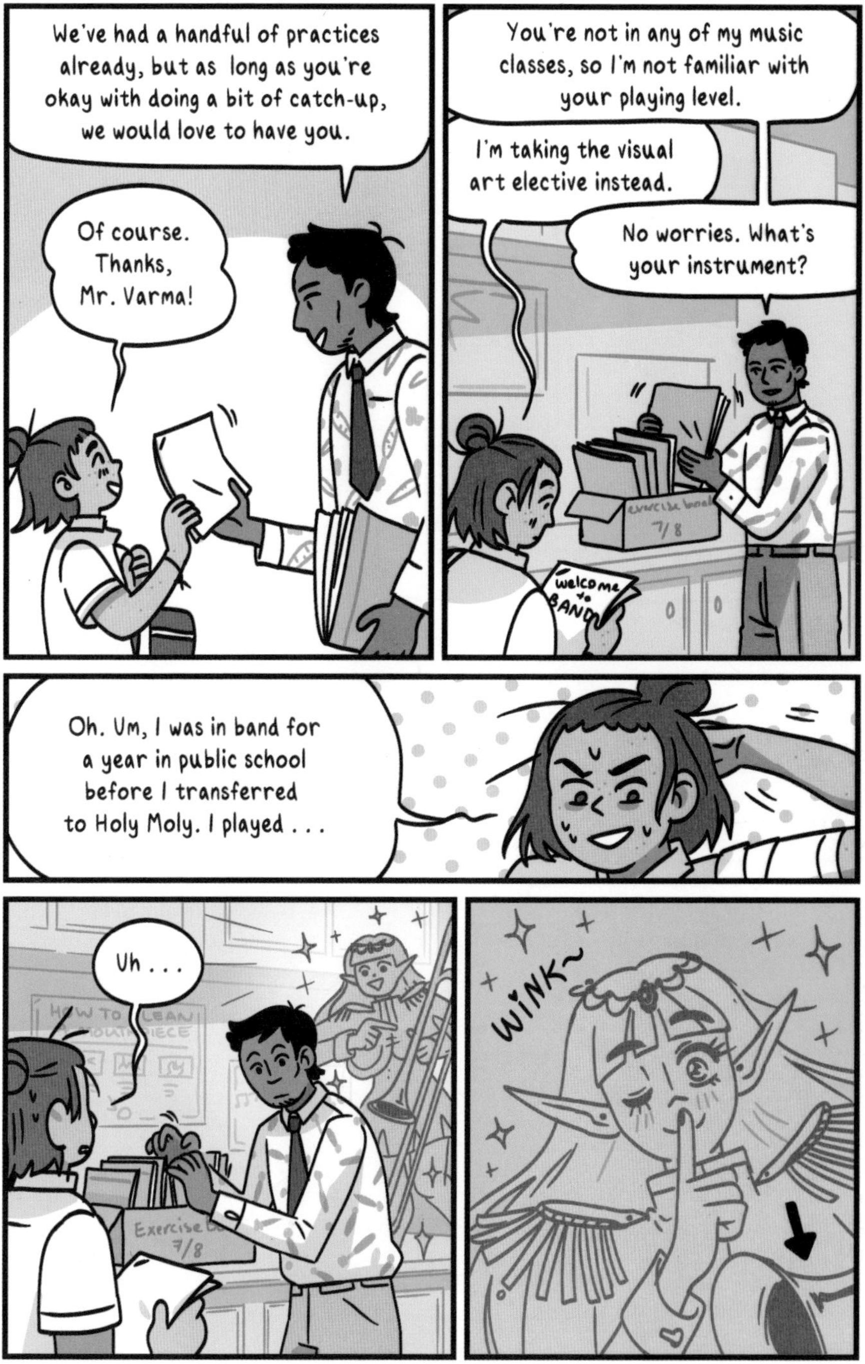
We've had a handful of practices already, but as long as you're okay with doing a bit of catch-up, we would love to have you.
Of course. Thanks, Mr. Varma!
You're not in any of my music classes, so I'm not familiar with your playing level.
I'm taking the visual art elective instead.
No worries. What's your instrument?
Welcome to BAND
Oh. Um, I was in band for a year in public school before I transferred to Holy Moly. I played . . .
Uh . . .
Exercise Books 7/8
WINK~

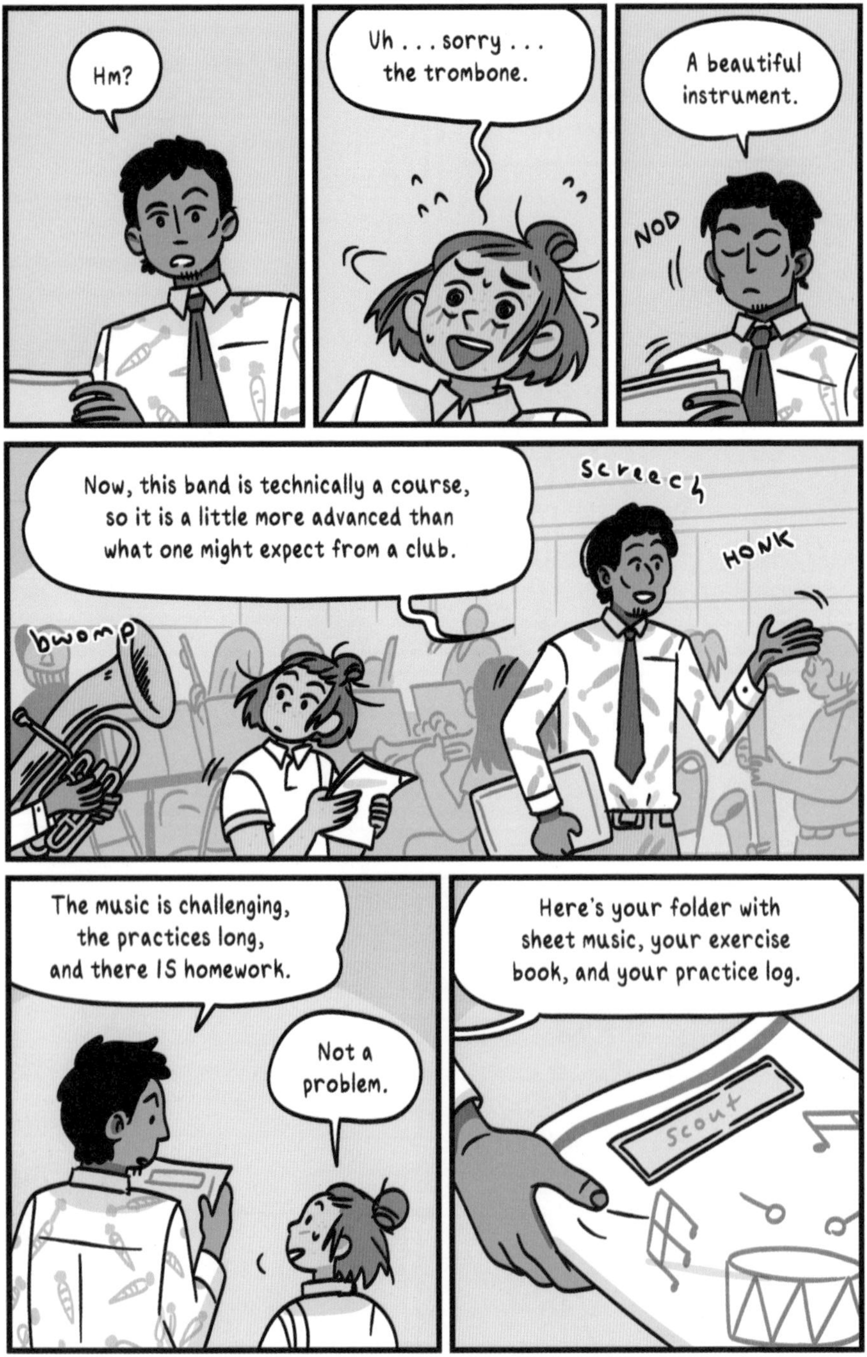
Hm?
Uh . . . sorry . . . the trombone.
A beautiful instrument.
NOD
Now, this band is technically a course, so it is a little more advanced than what one might expect from a club.
Screech
HONK
bwomp
The music is challenging, the practices long, and there IS homework.
Not a problem.
Here's your folder with sheet music, your exercise book, and your practice log.
Scout

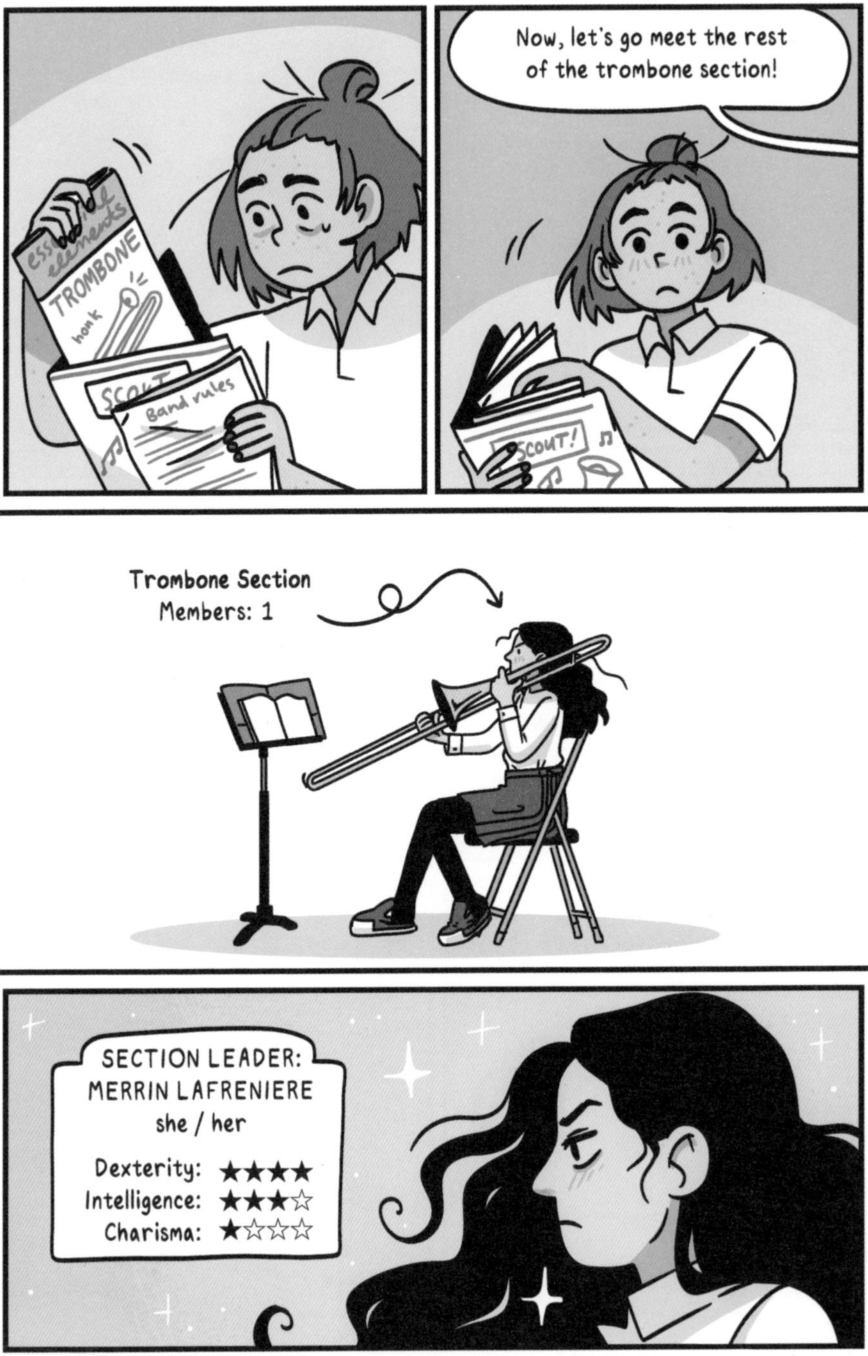
TROMBONE
honk
Band rules
Now, let's go meet the rest of the trombone section!
SCOUT!
Trombone Section
Members: 1
SECTION LEADER:
MERRIN LAFRENIERE
she / her
Dexterity: ★★★★
Intelligence: ★★★☆
Charisma: ★☆☆☆

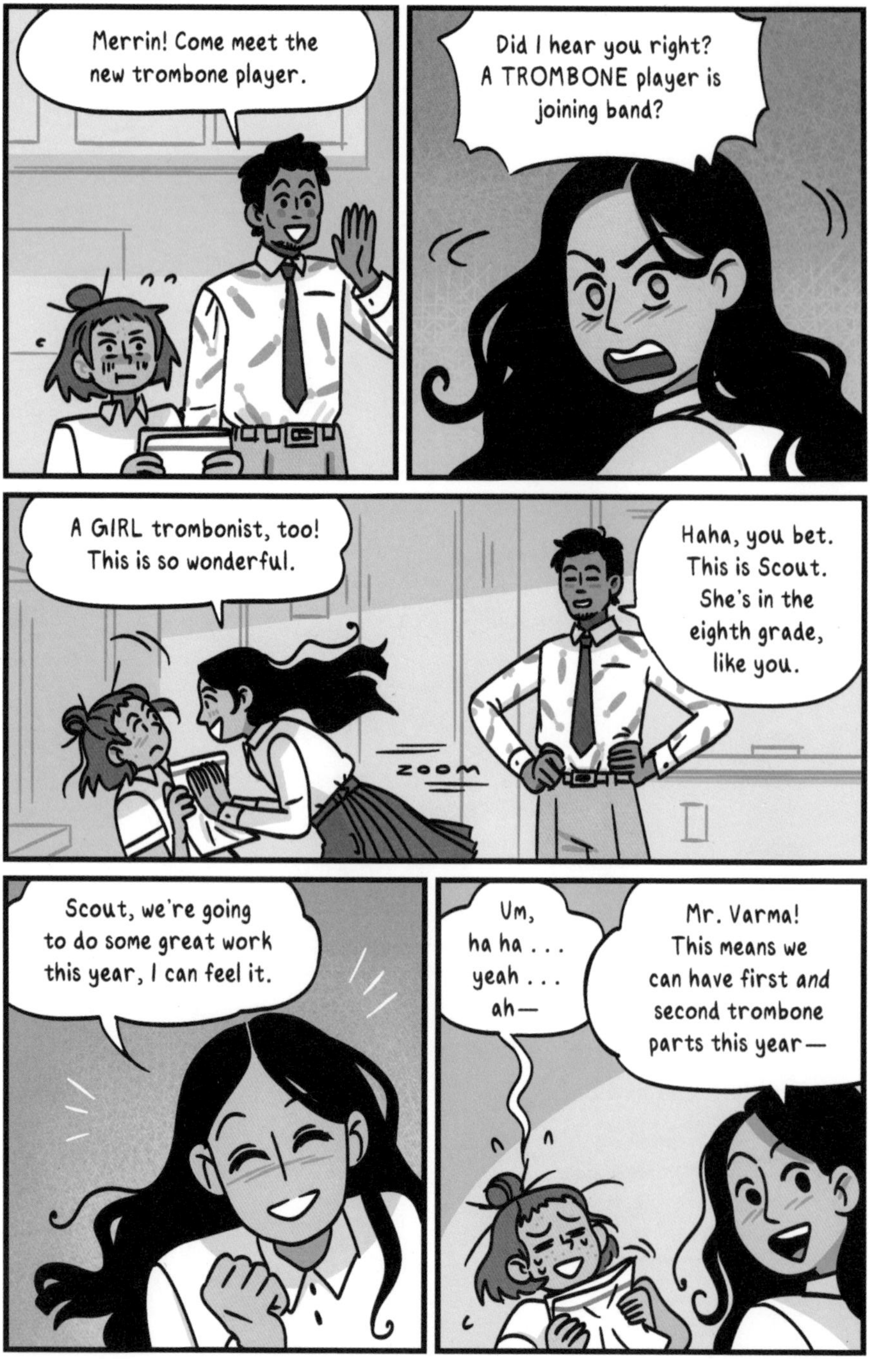
Merrin! Come meet the new trombone player.
Did I hear you right? A TROMBONE player is joining band?
A GIRL trombonist, too! This is so wonderful.
Haha, you bet. This is Scout. She's in the eighth grade, like you.
ZOOM
Scout, we're going to do some great work this year, I can feel it.
Um, ha ha . . . yeah . . . ah—
Mr. Varma! This means we can have first and second trombone parts this year—

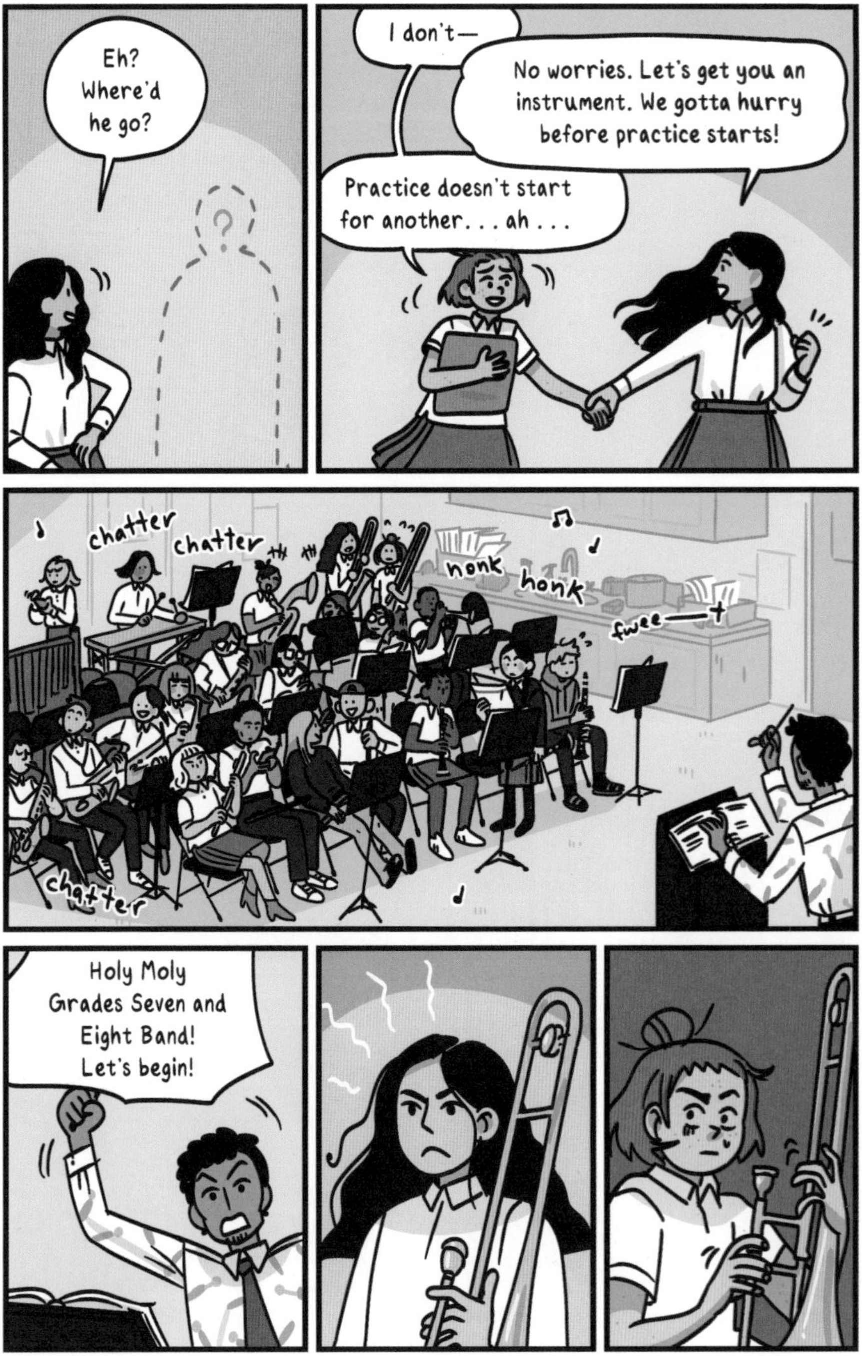
Eh?
Where'd he go?
I don't—
No worries. Let's get you an instrument. We gotta hurry before practice starts!
Practice doesn't start for another. . . ah . . .
chatter
chatter
honk
honk
fwee—t
chatter
Holy Moly Grades Seven and Eight Band! Let's begin!

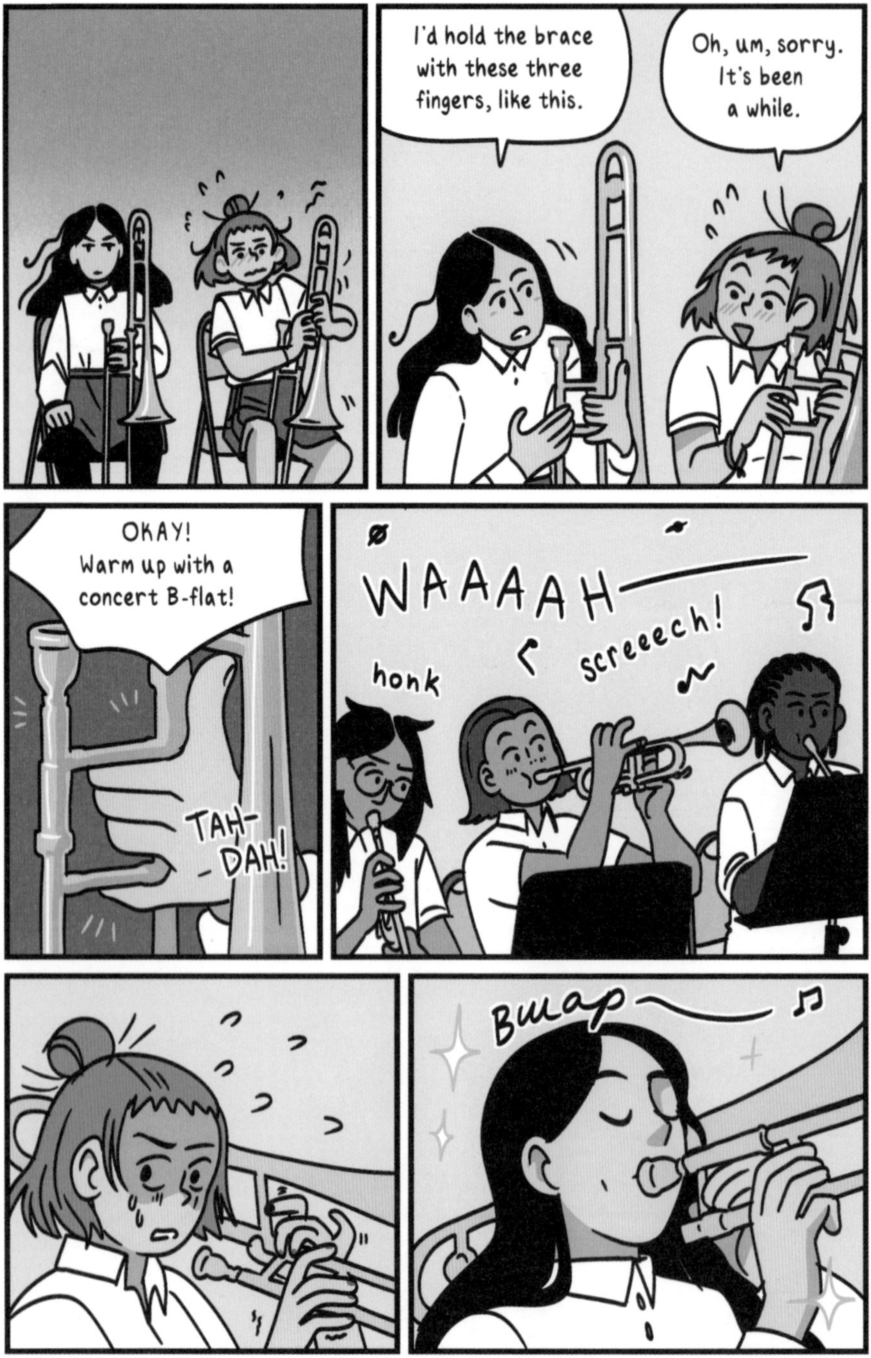

I'd hold the brace with these three fingers, like this.
Oh, um, sorry. It's been a while.
OKAY! Warm up with a concert B-flat!
TAH-DAH!
WAAAAH
honk
screeech!
Bwap

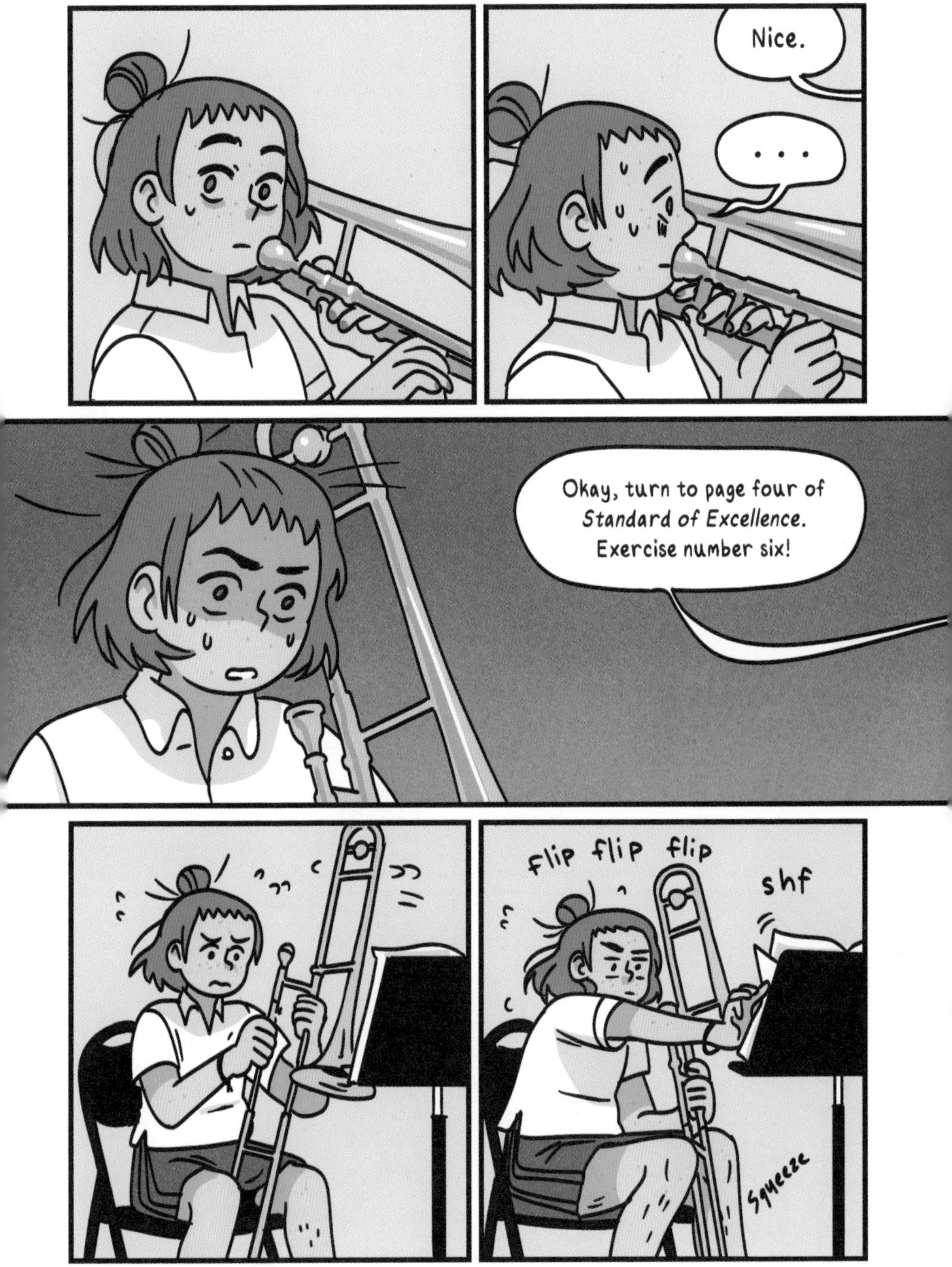

Nice.
. . .
Okay, turn to page four of *Standard of Excellence*. Exercise number six!
flip flip flip
shf
squeeze

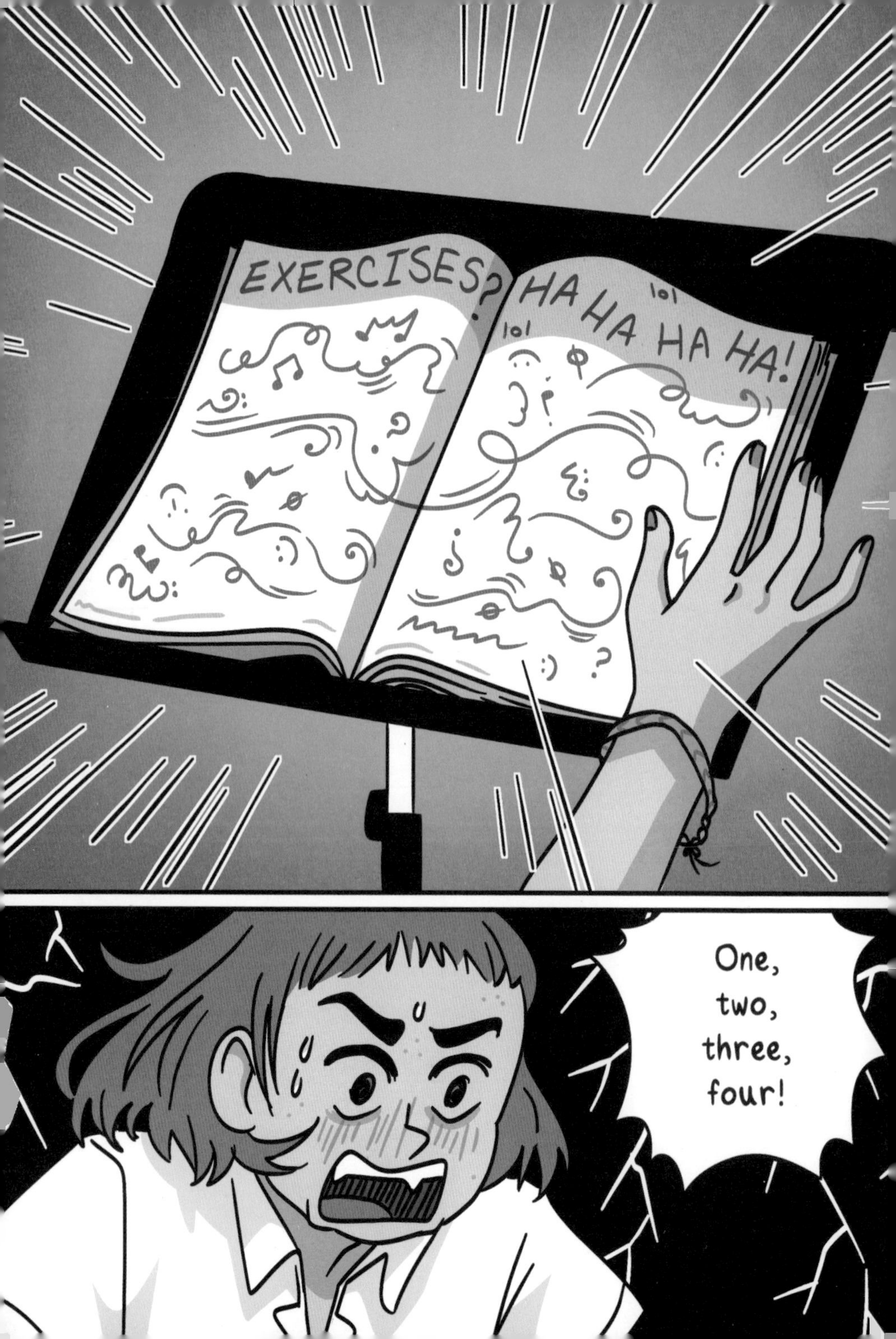
EXERCISES?
HA HA HA HA!
One, two, three, four!

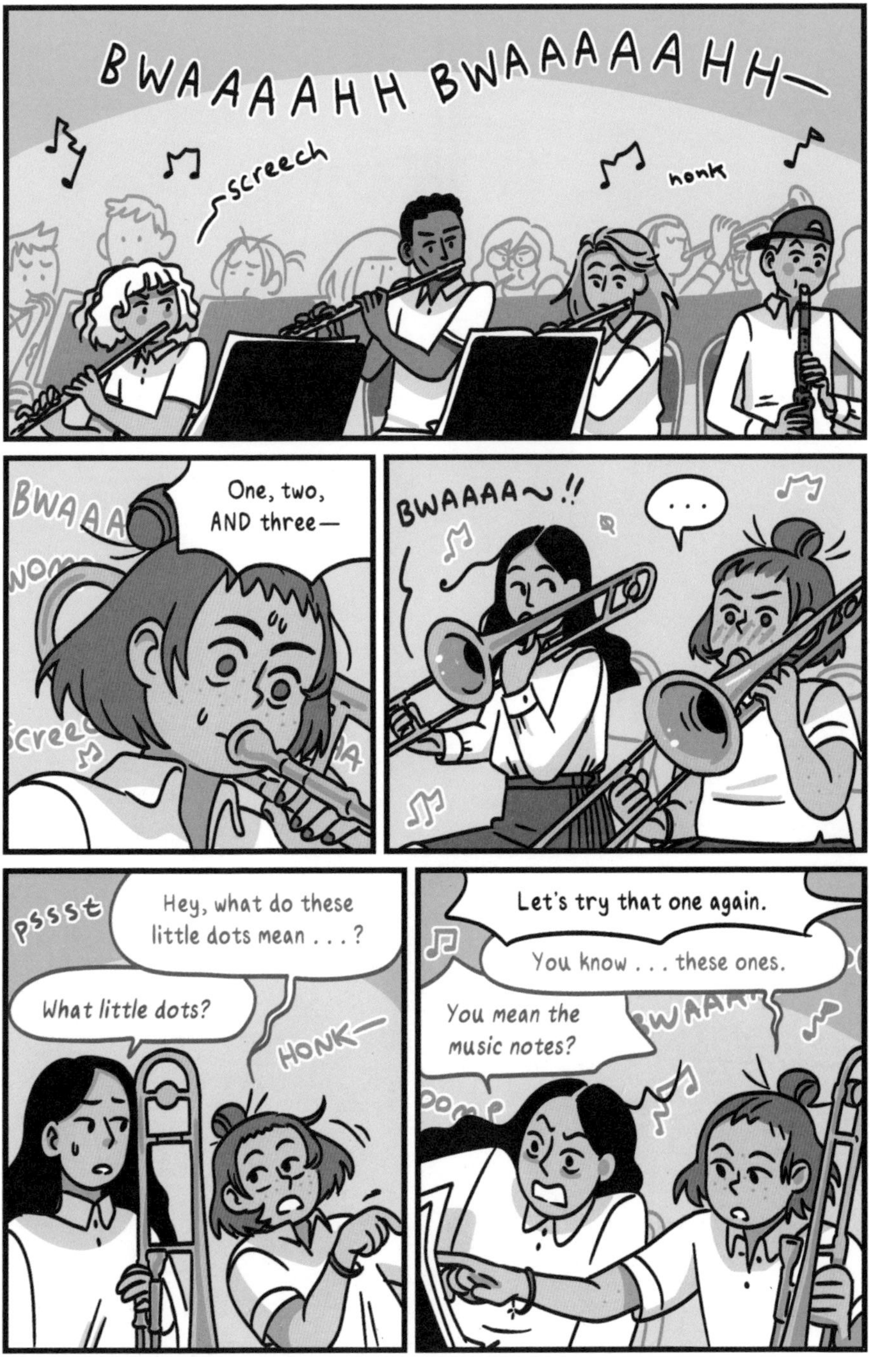
BWAAAAAHH BWAAAAAAHH—
screech
honk
One, two, AND three—
BWAAA
BWAAAA~!!
. . .
pssst
Hey, what do these little dots mean . . . ?
What little dots?
HONK—
Let's try that one again.
You know . . . these ones.
You mean the music notes?

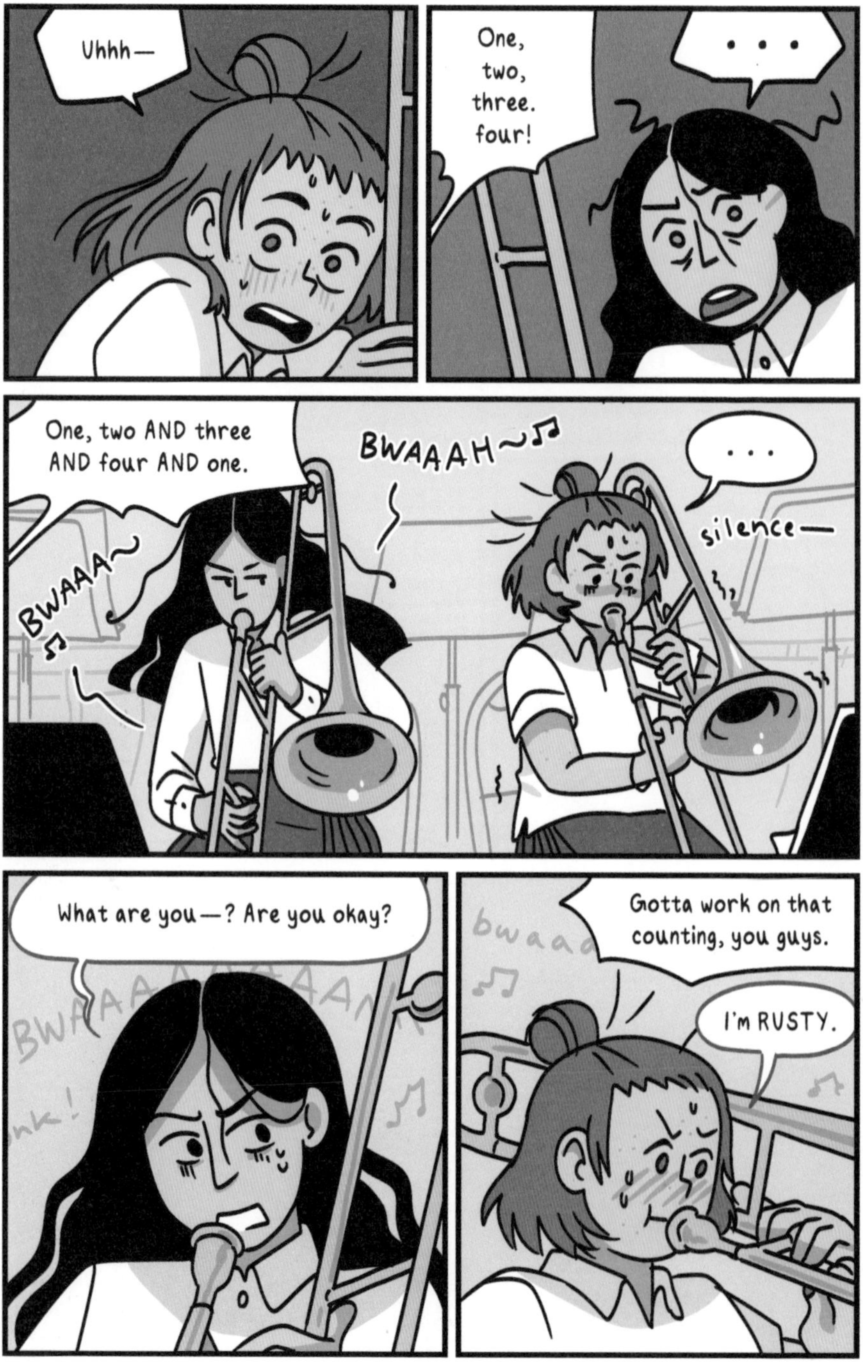
Uhhh—
One, two, three. four!
. . .
One, two AND three AND four AND one.
BWAAA~
BWAAAH~
. . .
silence—
What are you—? Are you okay?
Gotta work on that counting, you guys.
I'm RUSTY.

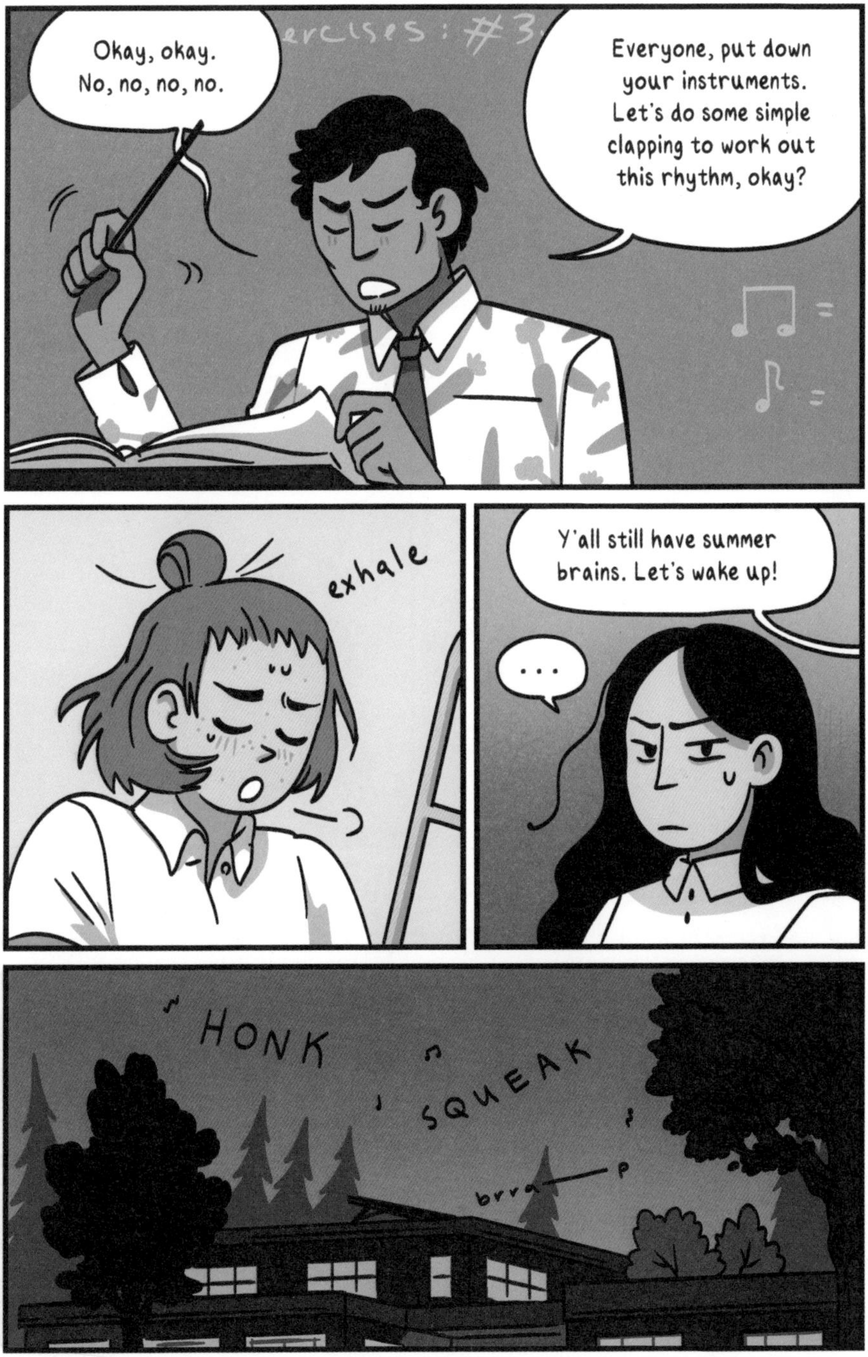

ercises: #3
Okay, okay. No, no, no, no.
Everyone, put down your instruments. Let's do some simple clapping to work out this rhythm, okay?
exhale
Y'all still have summer brains. Let's wake up!
...
HONK
SQUEAK
brra—p

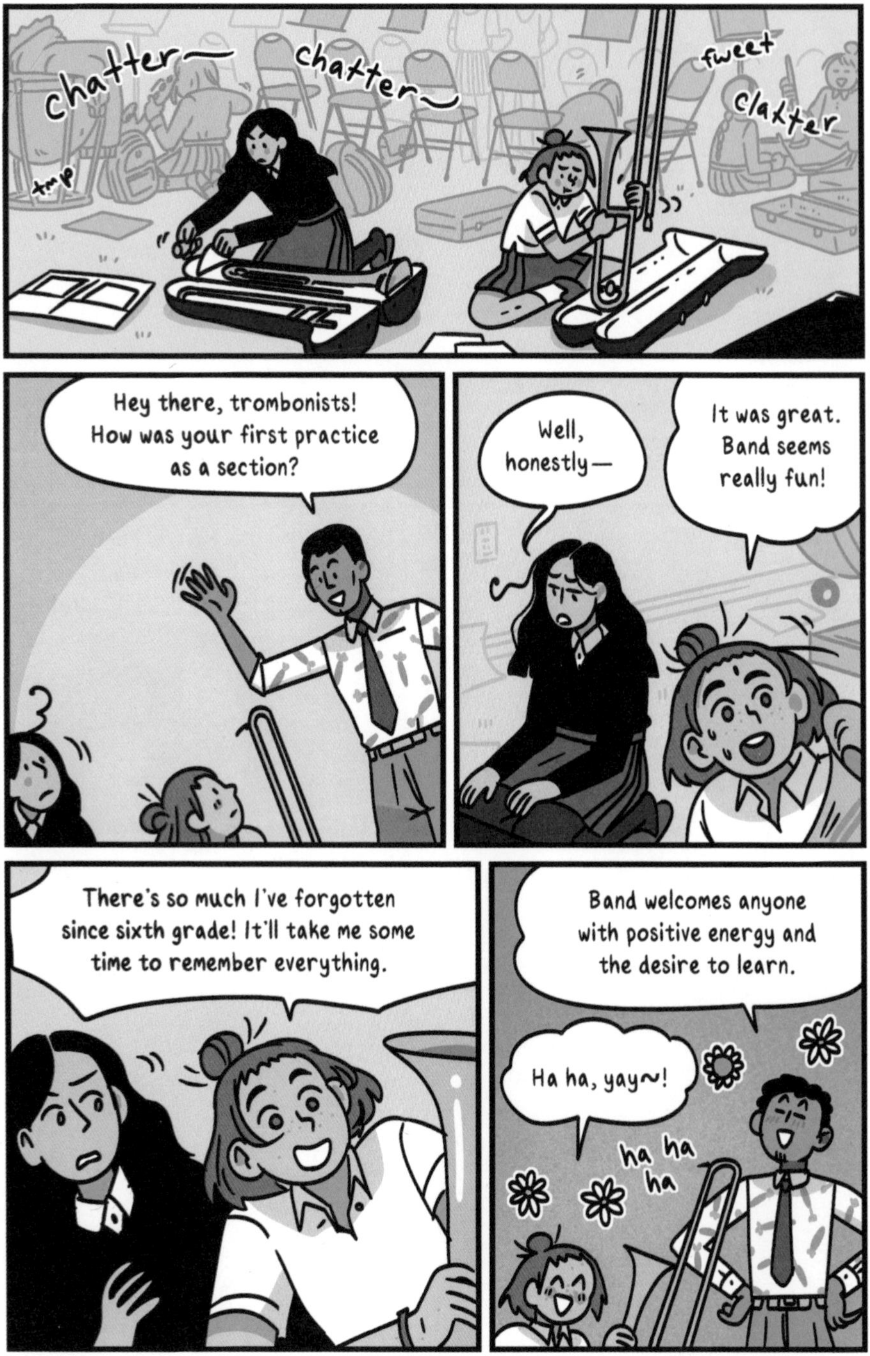
chatter—
chatter~
tmp
fweet
clatter
Hey there, trombonists! How was your first practice as a section?
Well, honestly—
It was great. Band seems really fun!
There's so much I've forgotten since sixth grade! It'll take me some time to remember everything.
Band welcomes anyone with positive energy and the desire to learn.
Ha ha, yay~!
ha ha ha

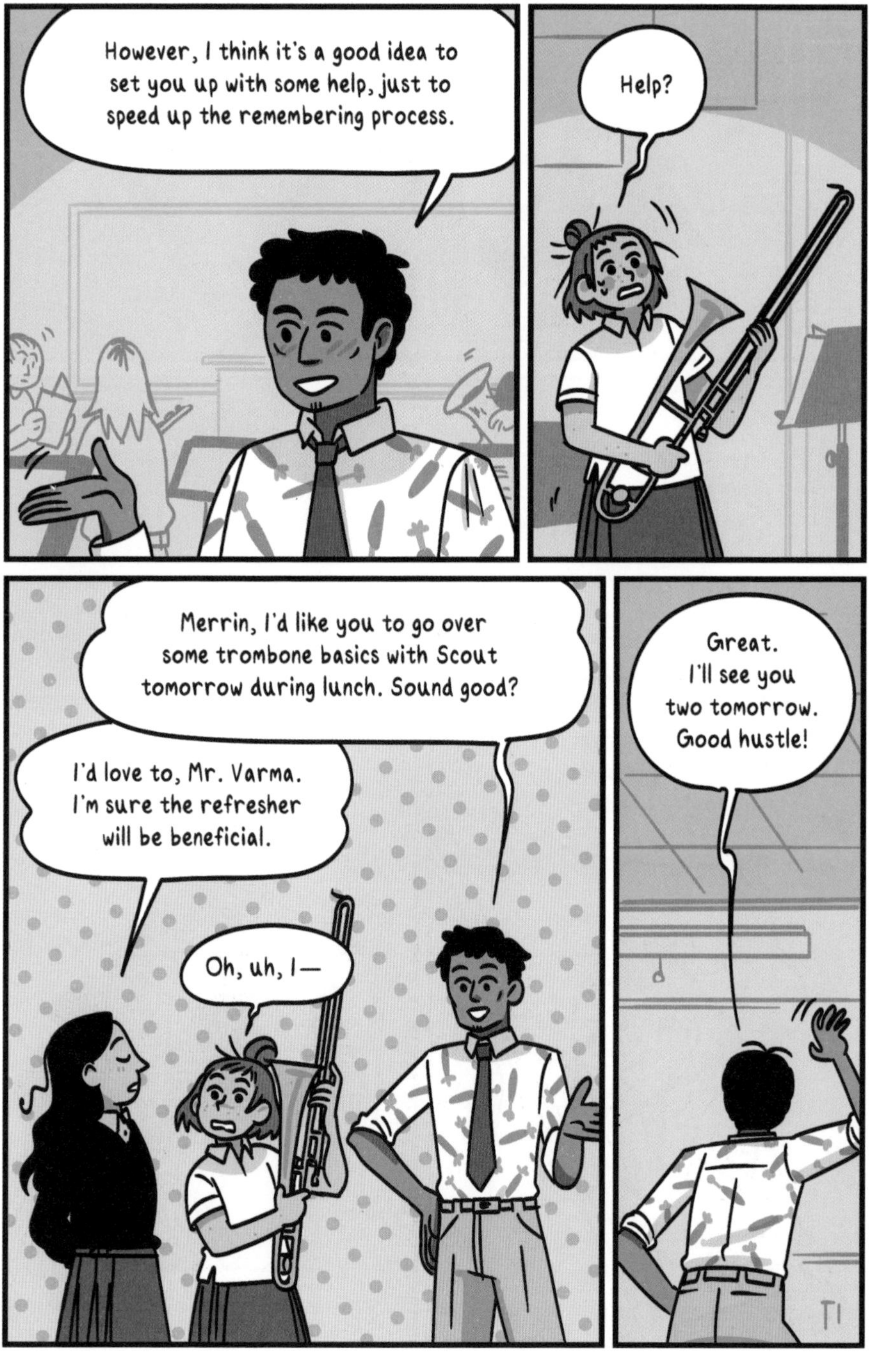
However, I think it's a good idea to set you up with some help, just to speed up the remembering process.
Help?
Merrin, I'd like you to go over some trombone basics with Scout tomorrow during lunch. Sound good?
I'd love to, Mr. Varma. I'm sure the refresher will be beneficial.
Oh, uh, I—
Great. I'll see you two tomorrow. Good hustle!

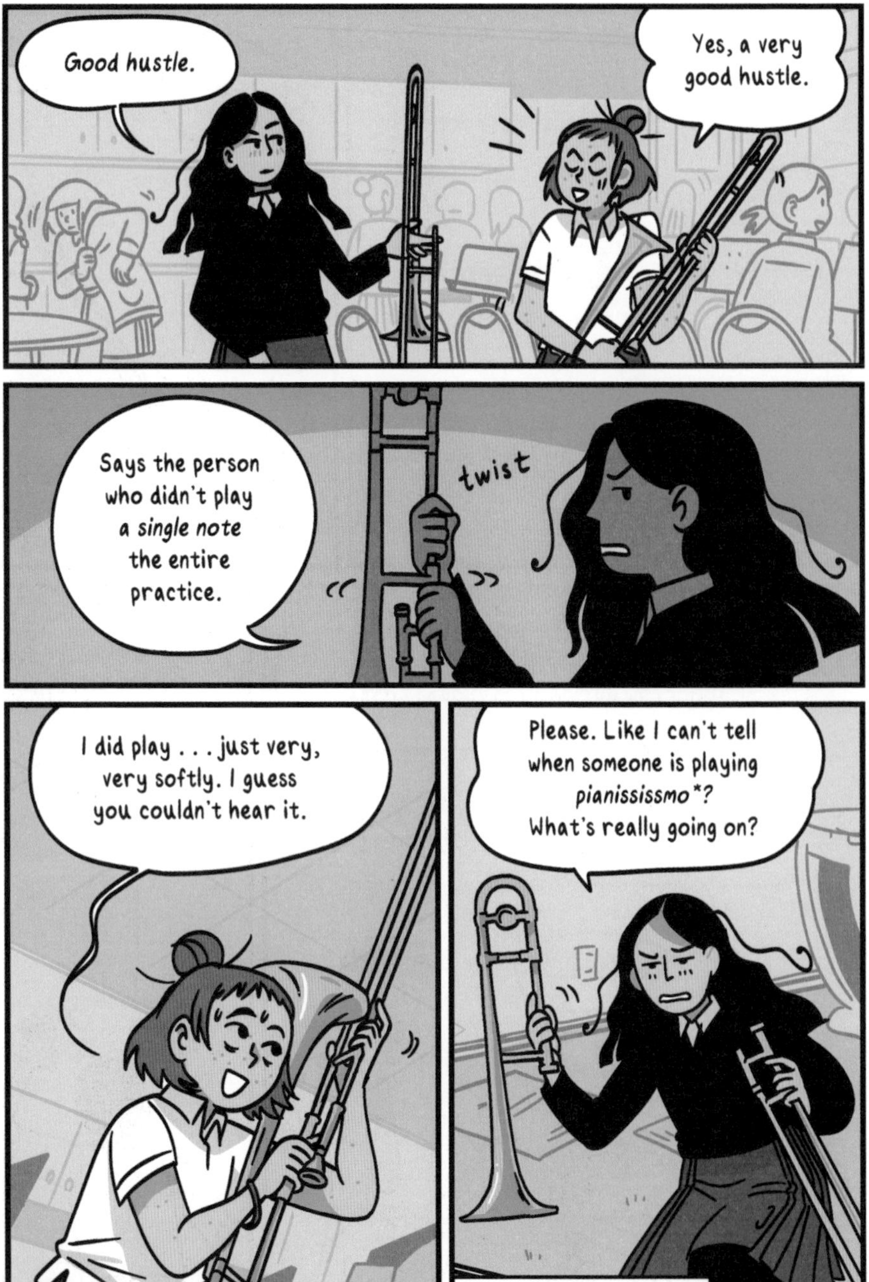
Good hustle.
Yes, a very good hustle.
Says the person who didn't play a *single note* the entire practice.
twist
I did play . . . just very, very softly. I guess you couldn't hear it.
Please. Like I can't tell when someone is playing *pianississmo**? What's really going on?
* piano p soft
pianissimo pp very soft
pianississimo ppp very very soft

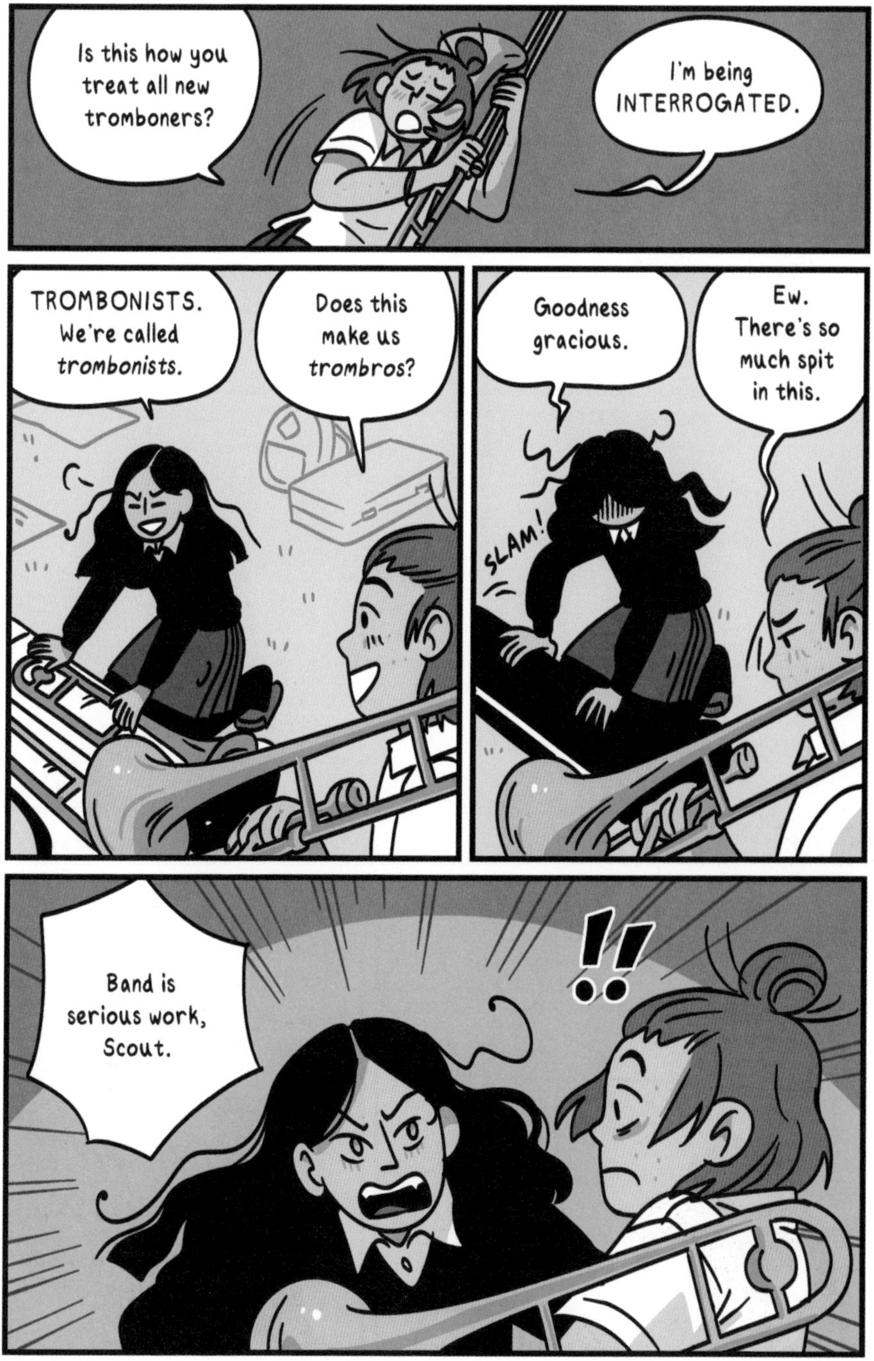
Is this how you treat all new tromboners?
I'm being INTERROGATED.
TROMBONISTS. We're called *trombonists.*
Does this make us *trombros?*
Goodness gracious.
Ew. There's so much spit in this.
SLAM!
Band is serious work, Scout.
!!

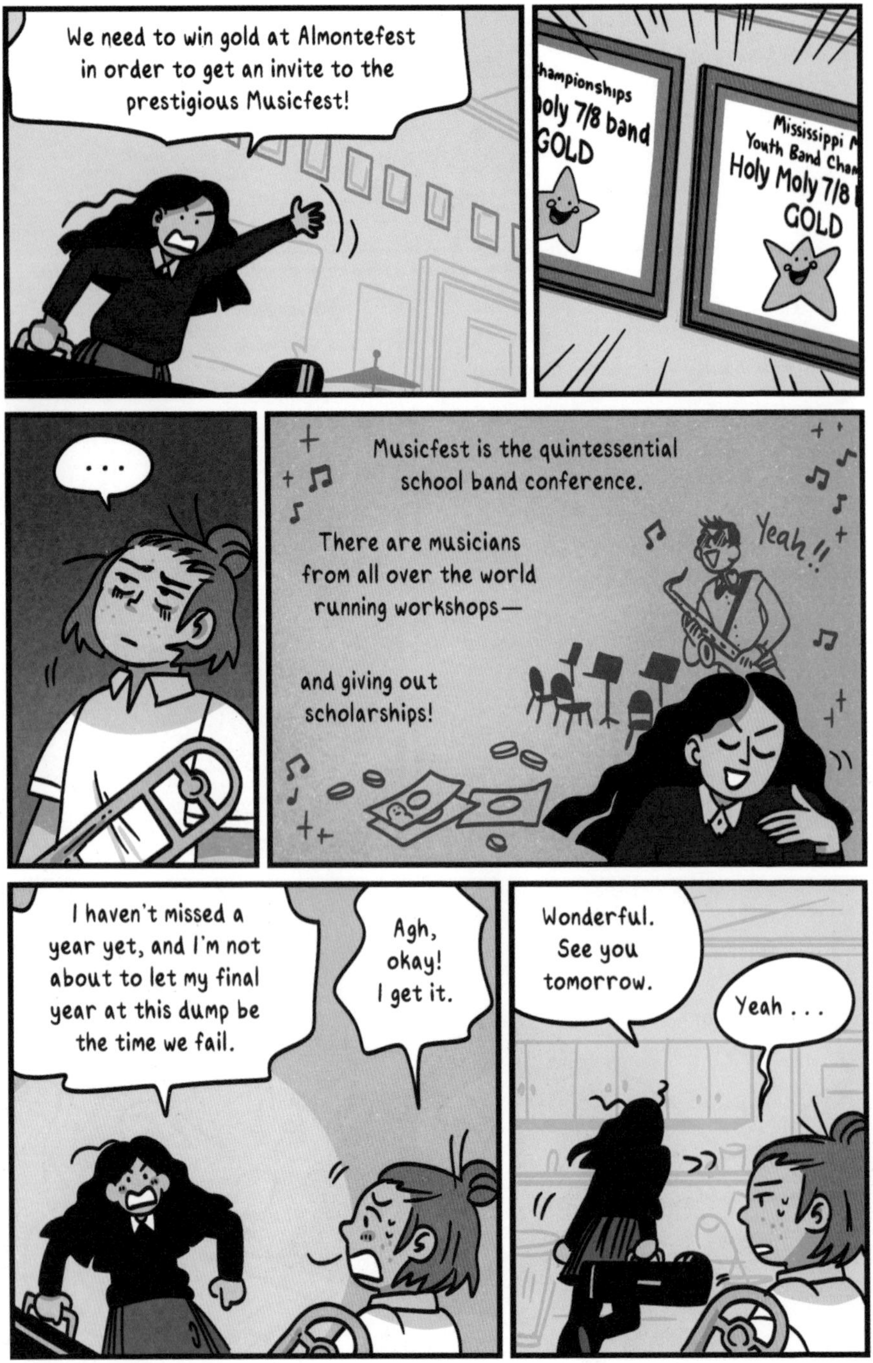
We need to win gold at Almontefest in order to get an invite to the prestigious Musicfest!
hampionships
oly 7/8 band
GOLD
Mississippi M
Youth Band Cha
Holy Moly 7/8
GOLD
. . .
Musicfest is the quintessential school band conference.
There are musicians from all over the world running workshops—
Yeah!!
and giving out scholarships!
I haven't missed a year yet, and I'm not about to let my final year at this dump be the time we fail.
Agh, okay! I get it.
Wonderful. See you tomorrow.
Yeah . . .

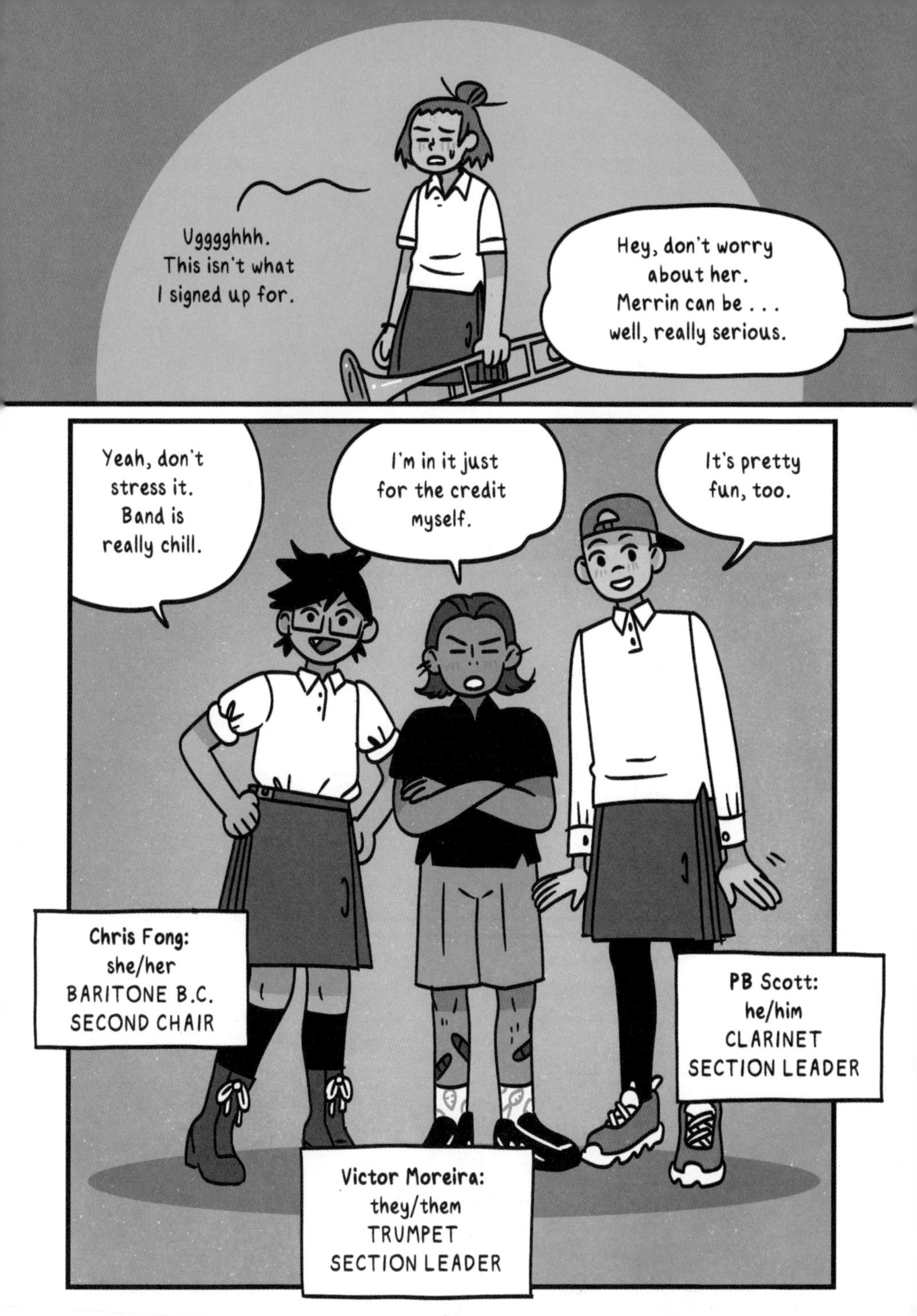
Ugggghhh.
This isn't what
I signed up for.
Hey, don't worry
about her.
Merrin can be . . .
well, really serious.
Yeah, don't
stress it.
Band is
really chill.
I'm in it just
for the credit
myself.
It's pretty
fun, too.
Chris Fong:
she/her
BARITONE B.C.
SECOND CHAIR
Victor Moreira:
they/them
TRUMPET
SECTION LEADER
PB Scott:
he/him
CLARINET
SECTION LEADER

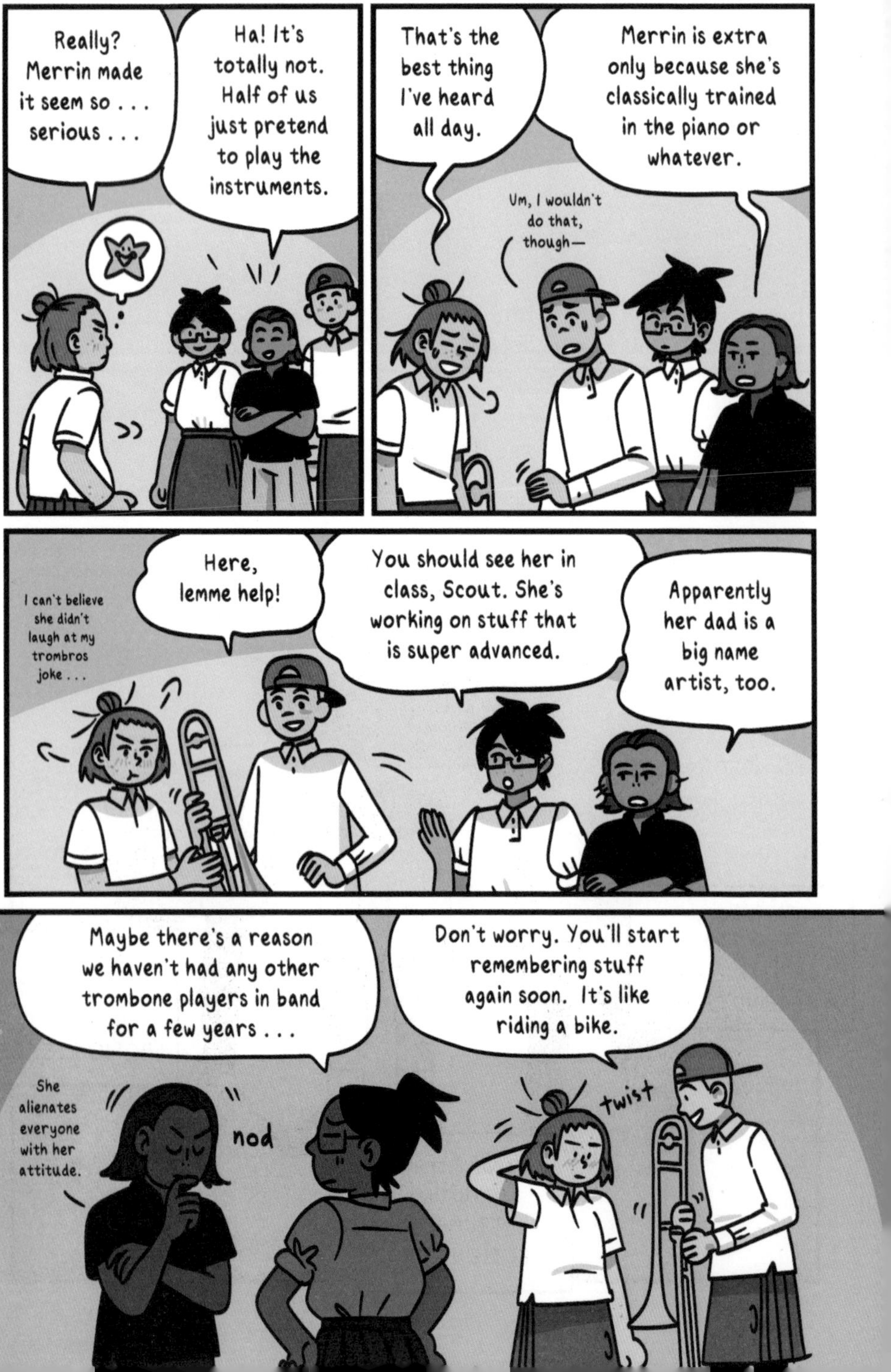
Really? Merrin made it seem so . . . serious . . .
Ha! It's totally not. Half of us just pretend to play the instruments.
That's the best thing I've heard all day.
Merrin is extra only because she's classically trained in the piano or whatever.
Um, I wouldn't do that, though—
I can't believe she didn't laugh at my trombros joke . . .
Here, lemme help!
You should see her in class, Scout. She's working on stuff that is super advanced.
Apparently her dad is a big name artist, too.
Maybe there's a reason we haven't had any other trombone players in band for a few years . . .
Don't worry. You'll start remembering stuff again soon. It's like riding a bike.
She alienates everyone with her attitude.
nod
twist

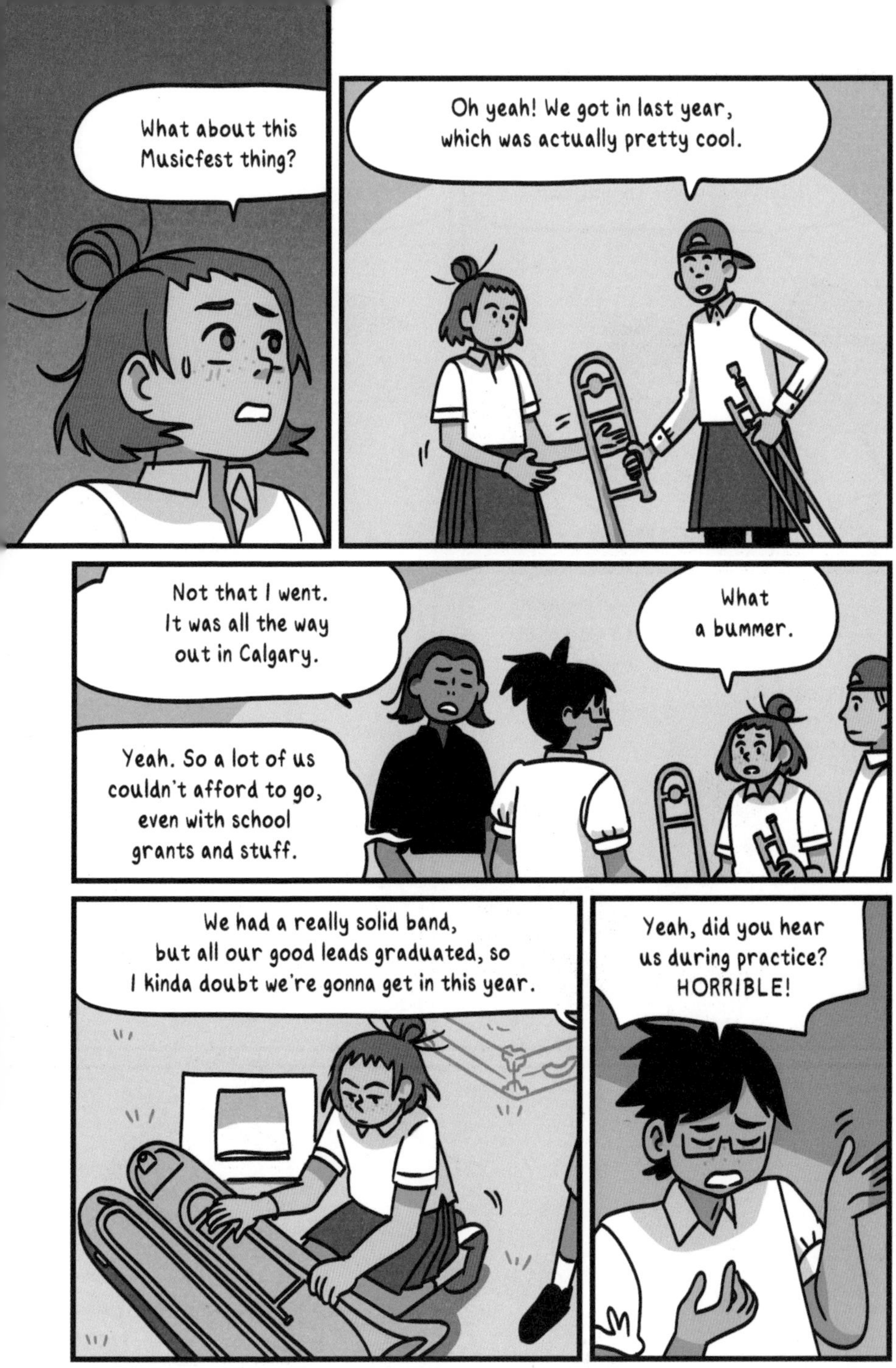

What about this Musicfest thing?
Oh yeah! We got in last year, which was actually pretty cool.
Not that I went. It was all the way out in Calgary.
Yeah. So a lot of us couldn't afford to go, even with school grants and stuff.
What a bummer.
We had a really solid band, but all our good leads graduated, so I kinda doubt we're gonna get in this year.
Yeah, did you hear us during practice? HORRIBLE!

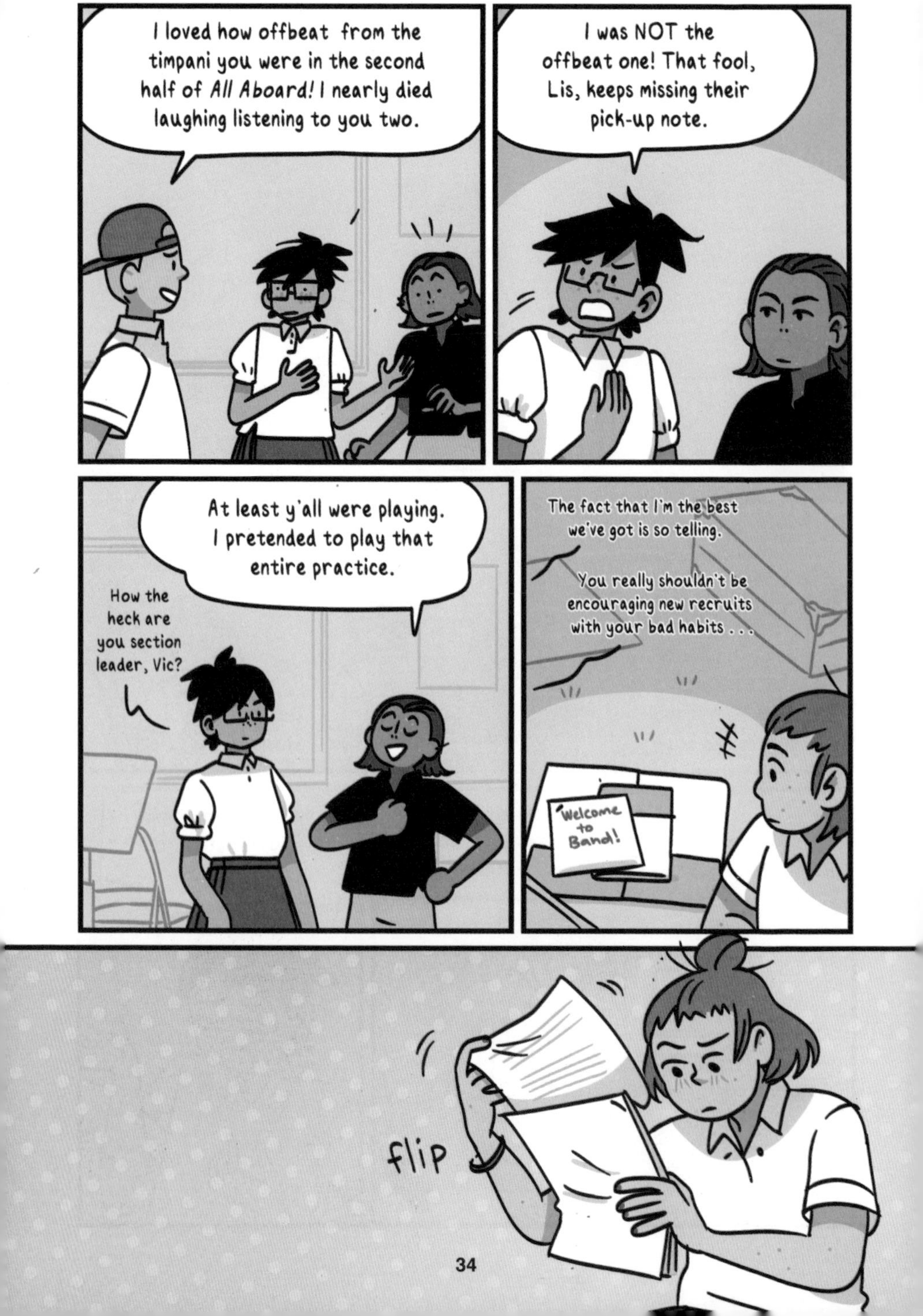
I loved how offbeat from the timpani you were in the second half of *All Aboard!* I nearly died laughing listening to you two.
I was NOT the offbeat one! That fool, Lis, keeps missing their pick-up note.
At least y'all were playing. I pretended to play that entire practice.
How the heck are you section leader, Vic?
The fact that I'm the best we've got is so telling.
You really shouldn't be encouraging new recruits with your bad habits . . .
Welcome to Band!
flip

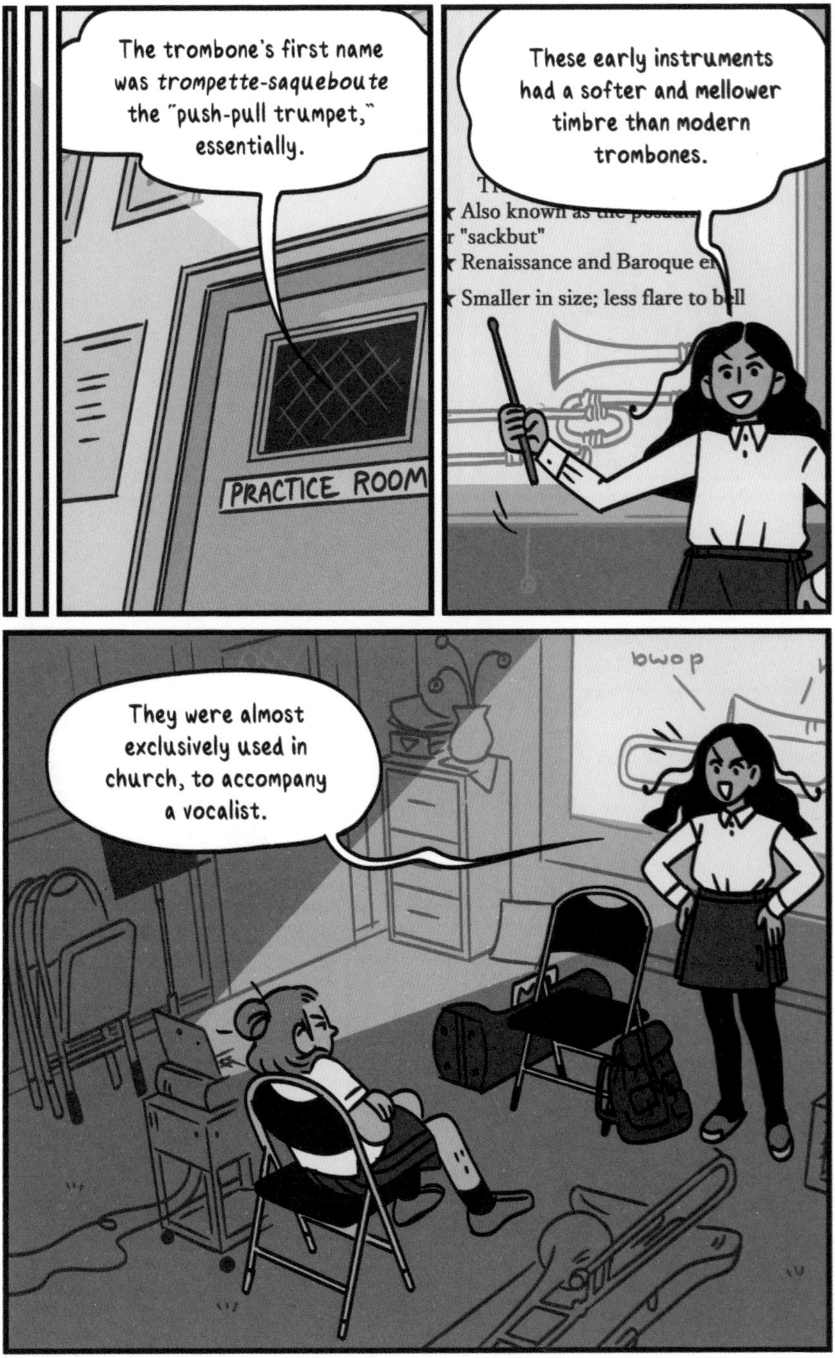

The trombone's first name was *trompette-saqueboute* the "push-pull trumpet," essentially.
PRACTICE ROOM
These early instruments had a softer and mellower timbre than modern trombones.
Also known as the posaune
"sackbut"
Renaissance and Baroque era
Smaller in size; less flare to bell
They were almost exclusively used in church, to accompany a vocalist.
bwop

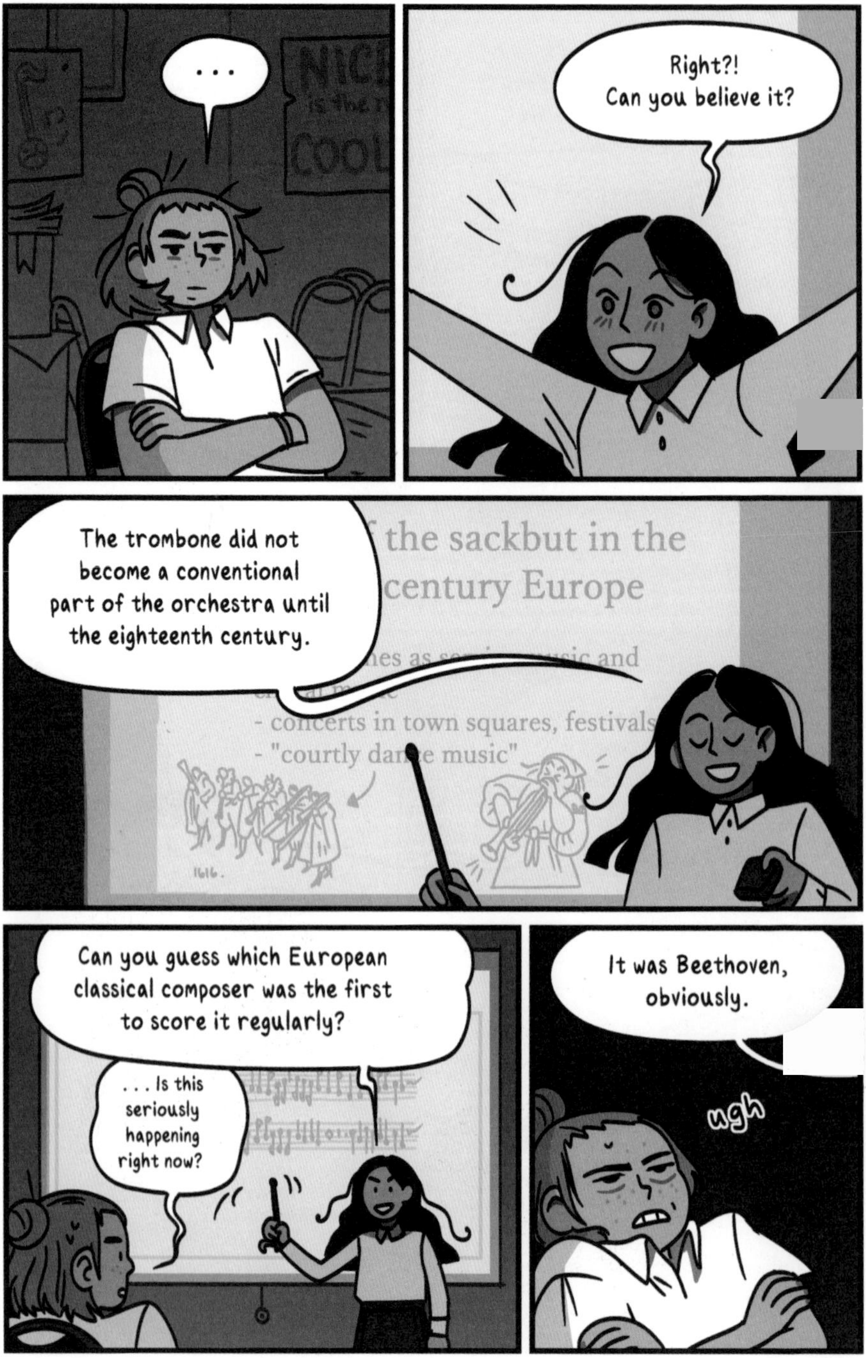
. . .
Right?!
Can you believe it?
the sackbut in the
century Europe
The trombone did not become a conventional part of the orchestra until the eighteenth century.
- concerts in town squares, festivals
1616.
Can you guess which European classical composer was the first to score it regularly?
. . . Is this seriously happening right now?
It was Beethoven, obviously.
ugh

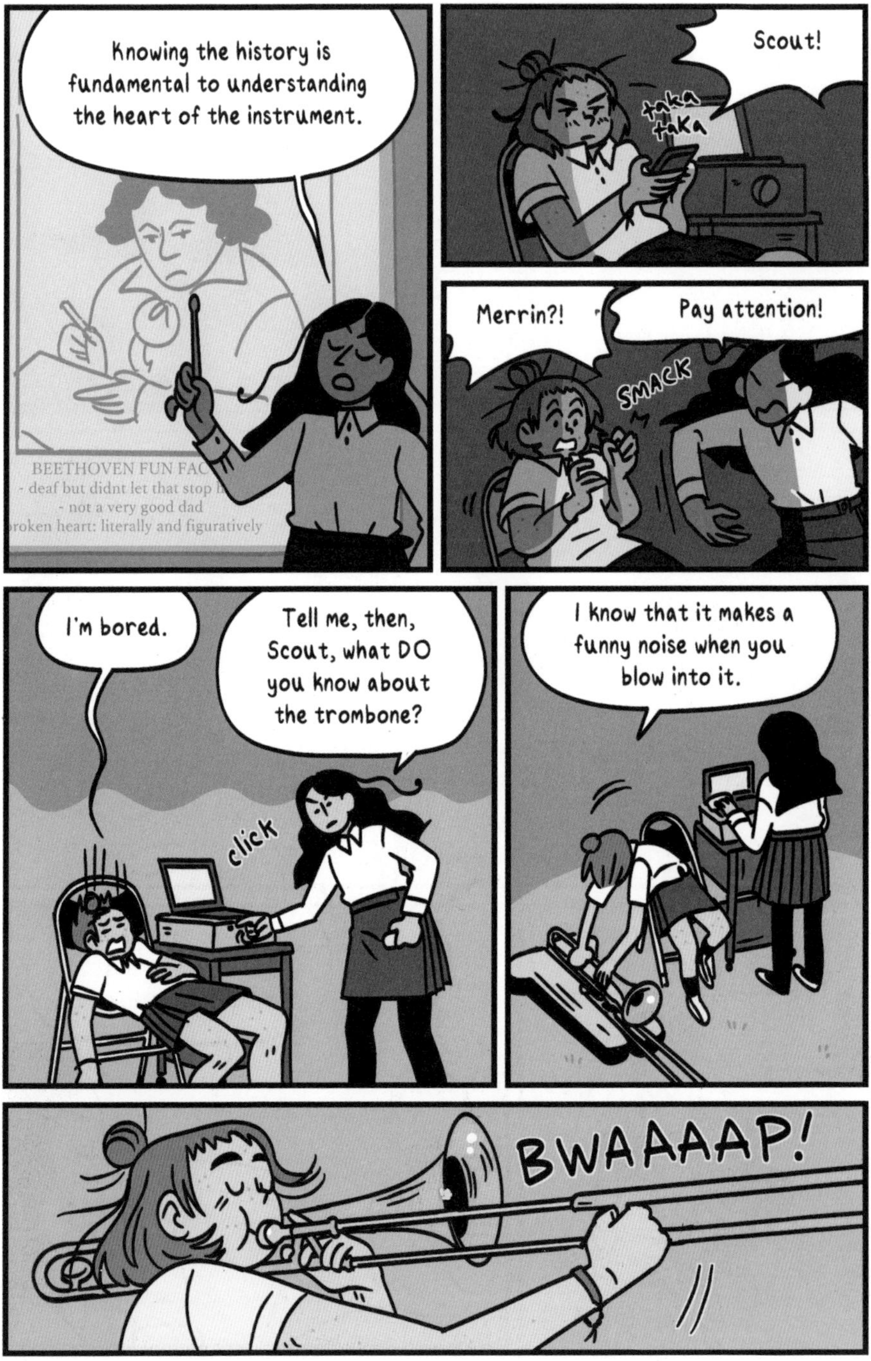
Knowing the history is fundamental to understanding the heart of the instrument.
BEETHOVEN FUN FAC
- deaf but didnt let that stop h
- not a very good dad
roken heart: literally and figuratively
Scout!
taka taka
Merrin?!
Pay attention!
SMACK
I'm bored.
Tell me, then, Scout, what DO you know about the trombone?
click
I know that it makes a funny noise when you blow into it.
BWAAAAP!

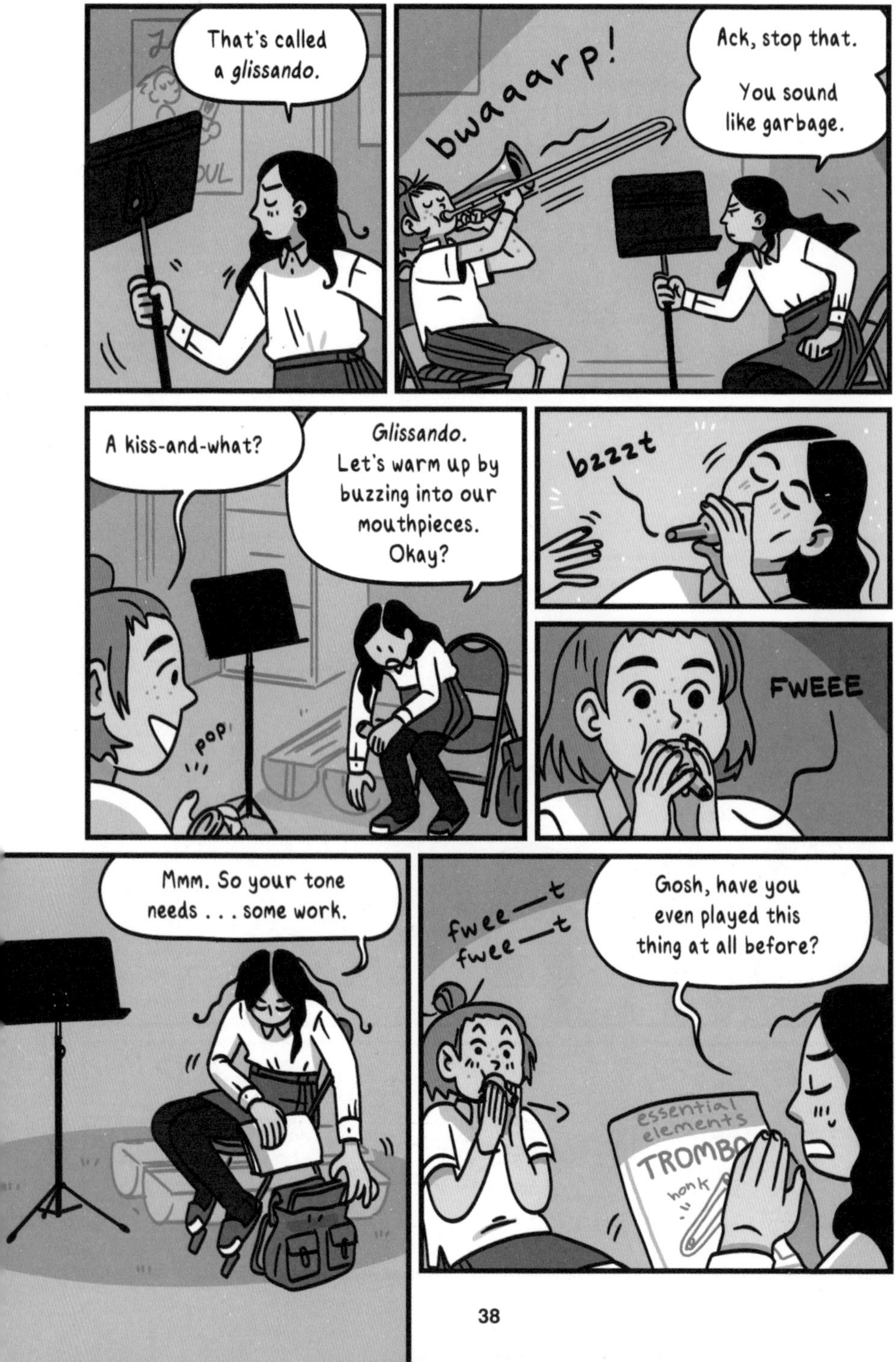
That's called a glissando.
bwaaarp!
Ack, stop that.
You sound like garbage.
A kiss-and-what?
Glissando. Let's warm up by buzzing into our mouthpieces. Okay?
pop
bzzzt
FWEEE
Mmm. So your tone needs . . . some work.
fwee—t fwee—t
Gosh, have you even played this thing at all before?
essential elements
TROMBO
honk

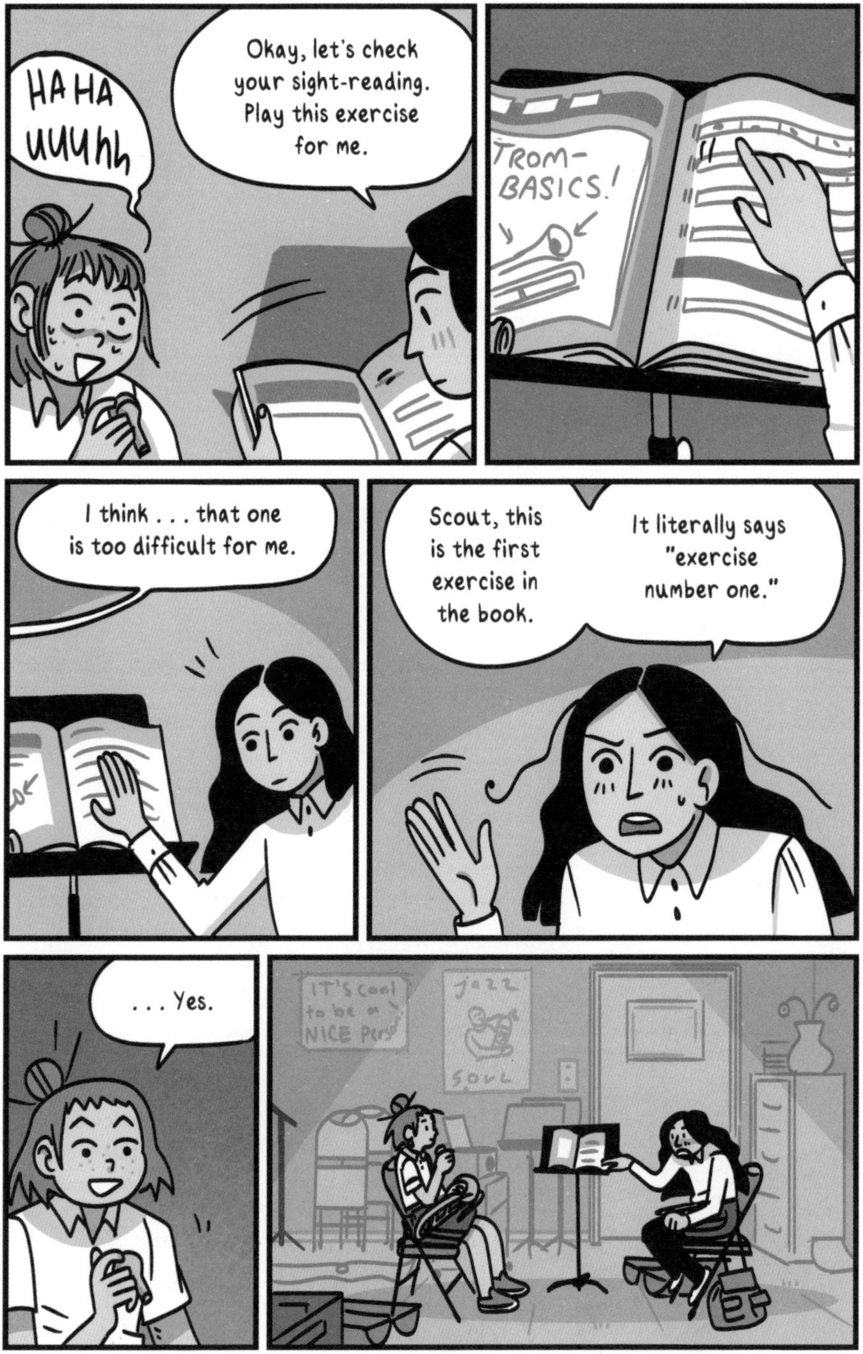
HA HA uuuhh
Okay, let's check your sight-reading. Play this exercise for me.
TROM-BASICS!
I think . . . that one is too difficult for me.
Scout, this is the first exercise in the book.
It literally says "exercise number one."
. . . Yes.
IT'S cool to be a NICE Person
Jazz
SOUL

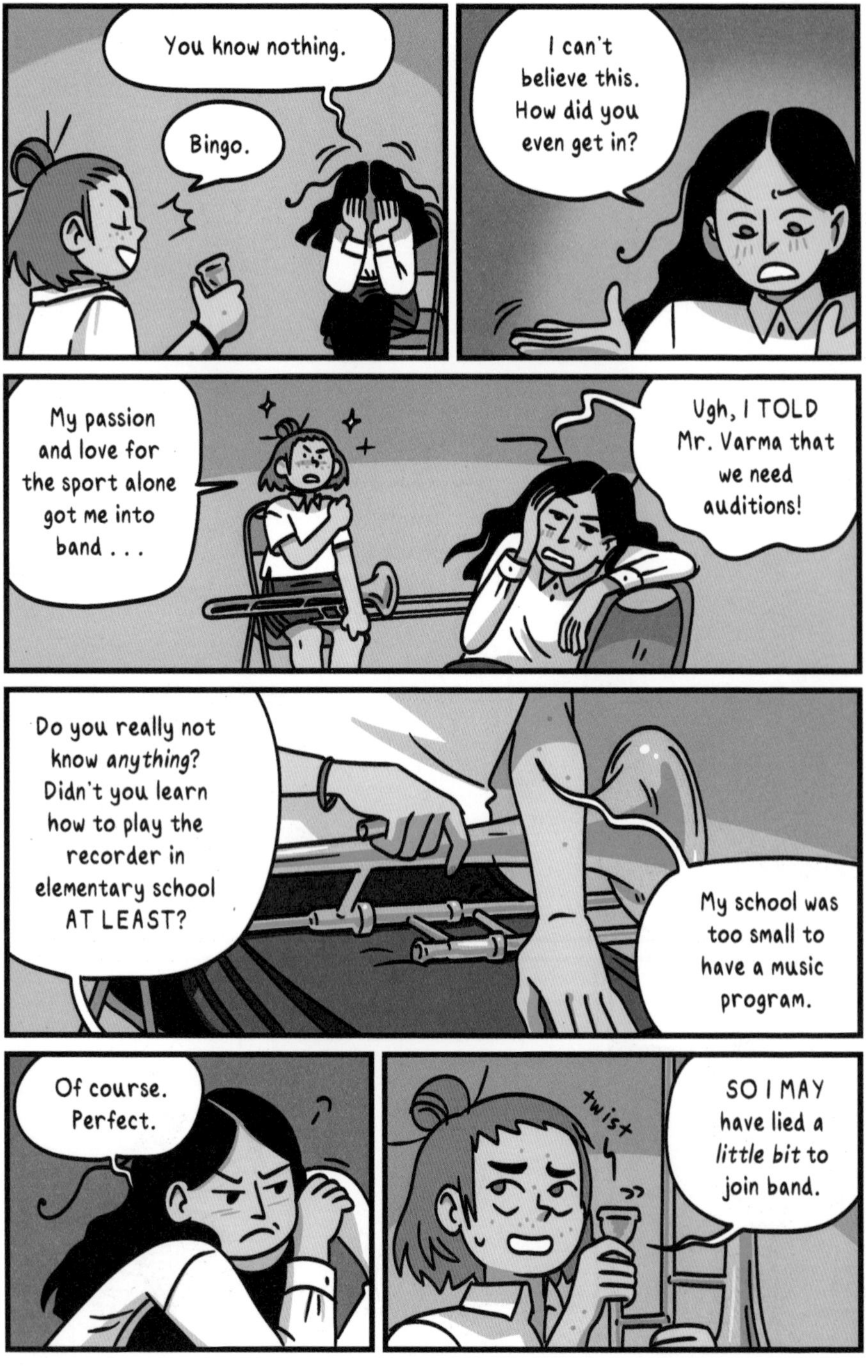
You know nothing.
Bingo.
I can't believe this. How did you even get in?
My passion and love for the sport alone got me into band . . .
Ugh, I TOLD Mr. Varma that we need auditions!
Do you really not know *anything*? Didn't you learn how to play the recorder in elementary school AT LEAST?
My school was too small to have a music program.
Of course. Perfect.
twist
SO I MAY have lied a *little bit* to join band.

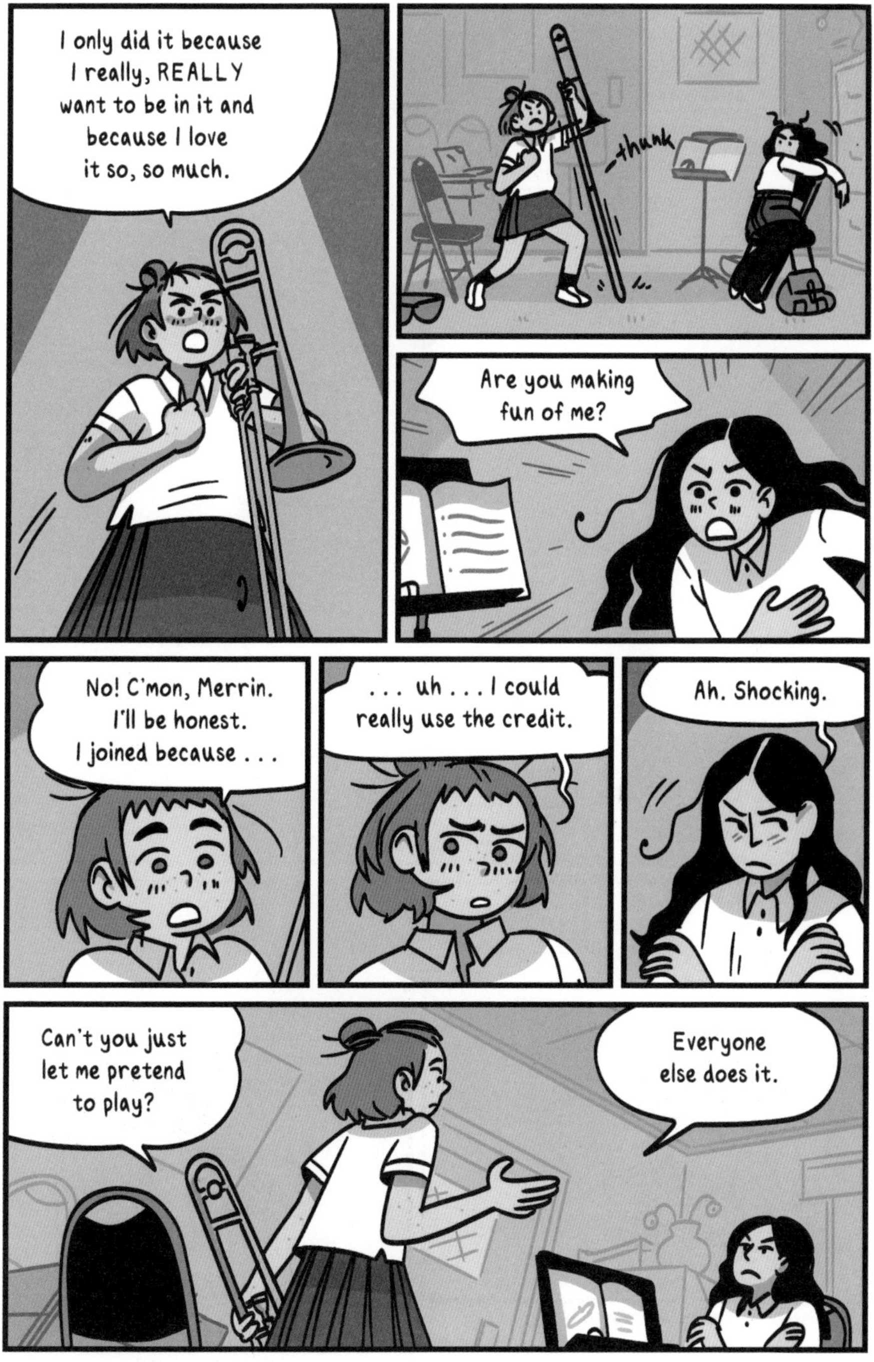
I only did it because I really, REALLY want to be in it and because I love it so, so much.
-thunk
Are you making fun of me?
No! C'mon, Merrin. I'll be honest. I joined because . . .
. . . uh . . . I could really use the credit.
Ah. Shocking.
Can't you just let me pretend to play?
Everyone else does it.

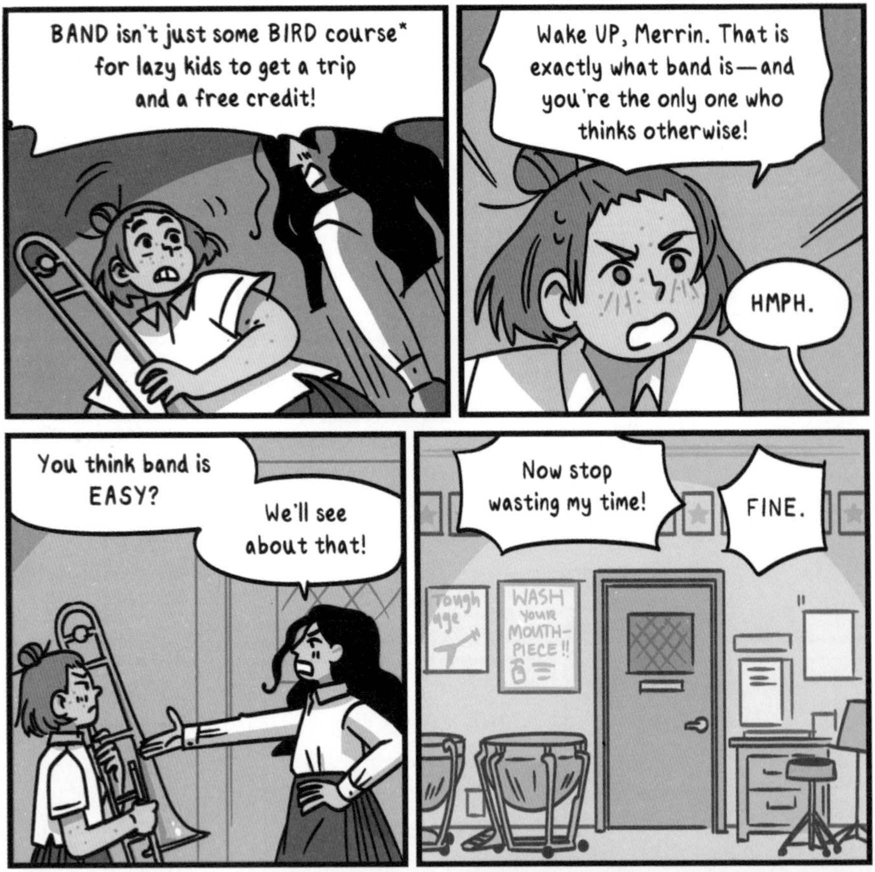
BAND isn't just some BIRD course* for lazy kids to get a trip and a free credit!
Wake UP, Merrin. That is exactly what band is—and you're the only one who thinks otherwise!
HMPH.
You think band is EASY?
We'll see about that!
Now stop wasting my time!
FINE.
Tough
WASH your MOUTH-PIECE!!

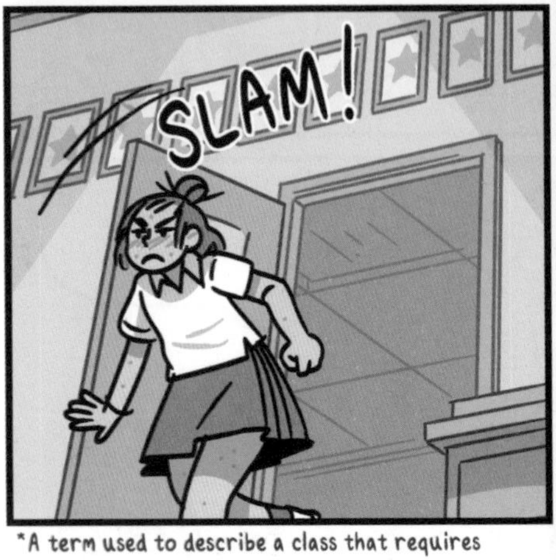
SLAM!

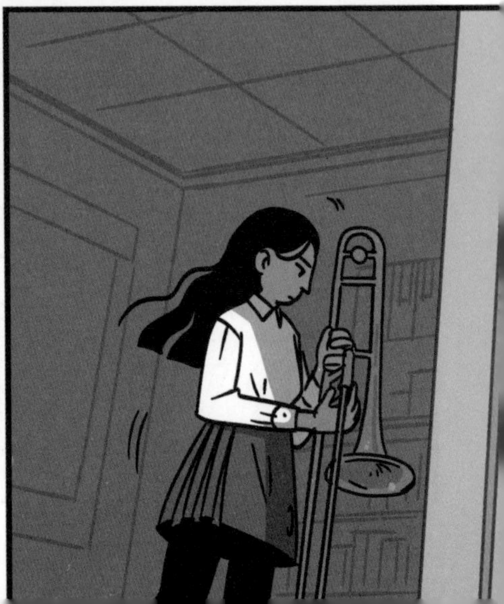

*A term used to describe a class that requires little work. An easy pass!

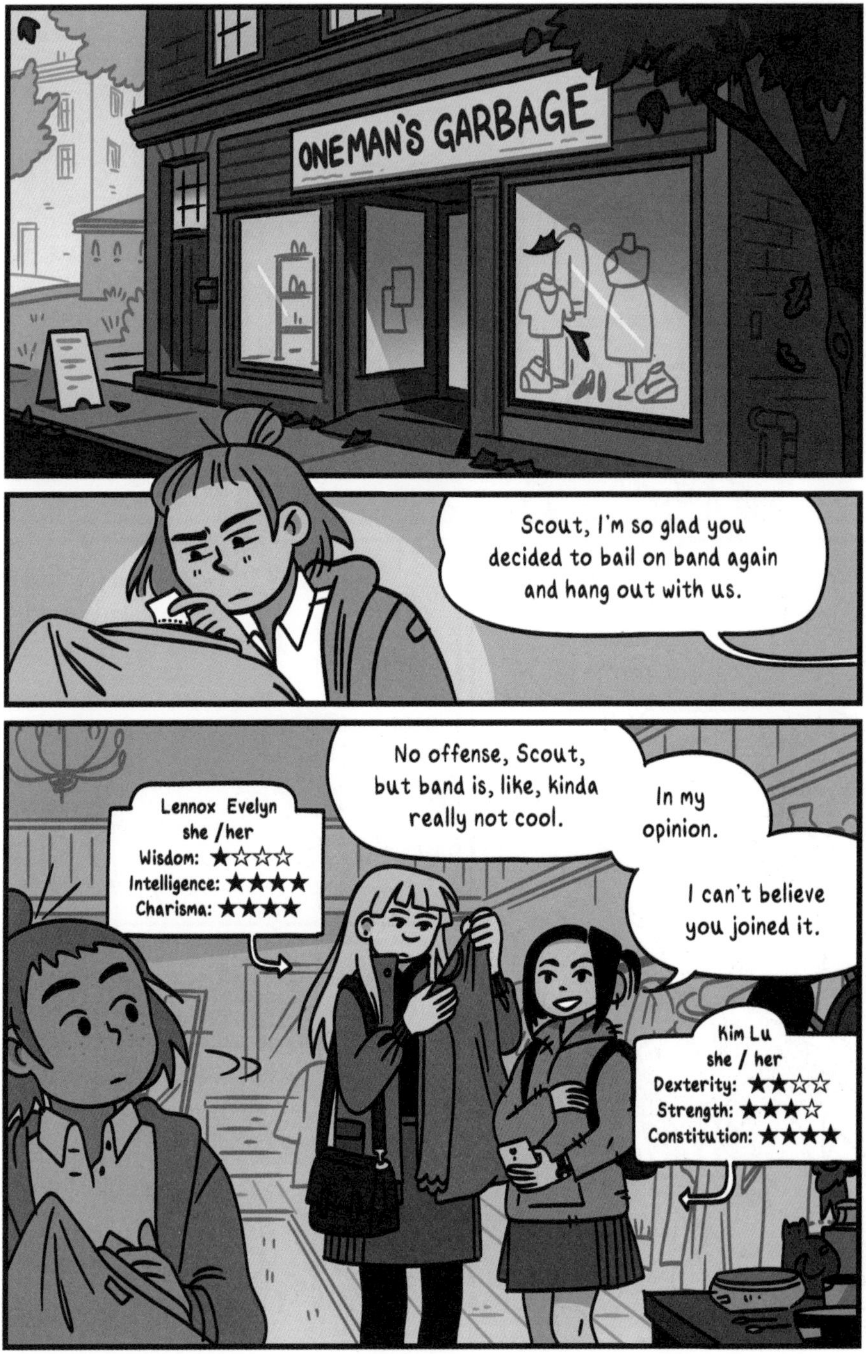
ONEMAN'S GARBAGE
Scout, I'm so glad you decided to bail on band again and hang out with us.
Lennox Evelyn she /her Wisdom: ★☆☆☆ Intelligence: ★★★★ Charisma: ★★★★
No offense, Scout, but band is, like, kinda really not cool.
In my opinion.
I can't believe you joined it.
Kim Lu she / her Dexterity: ★★☆☆ Strength: ★★★☆ Constitution: ★★★★

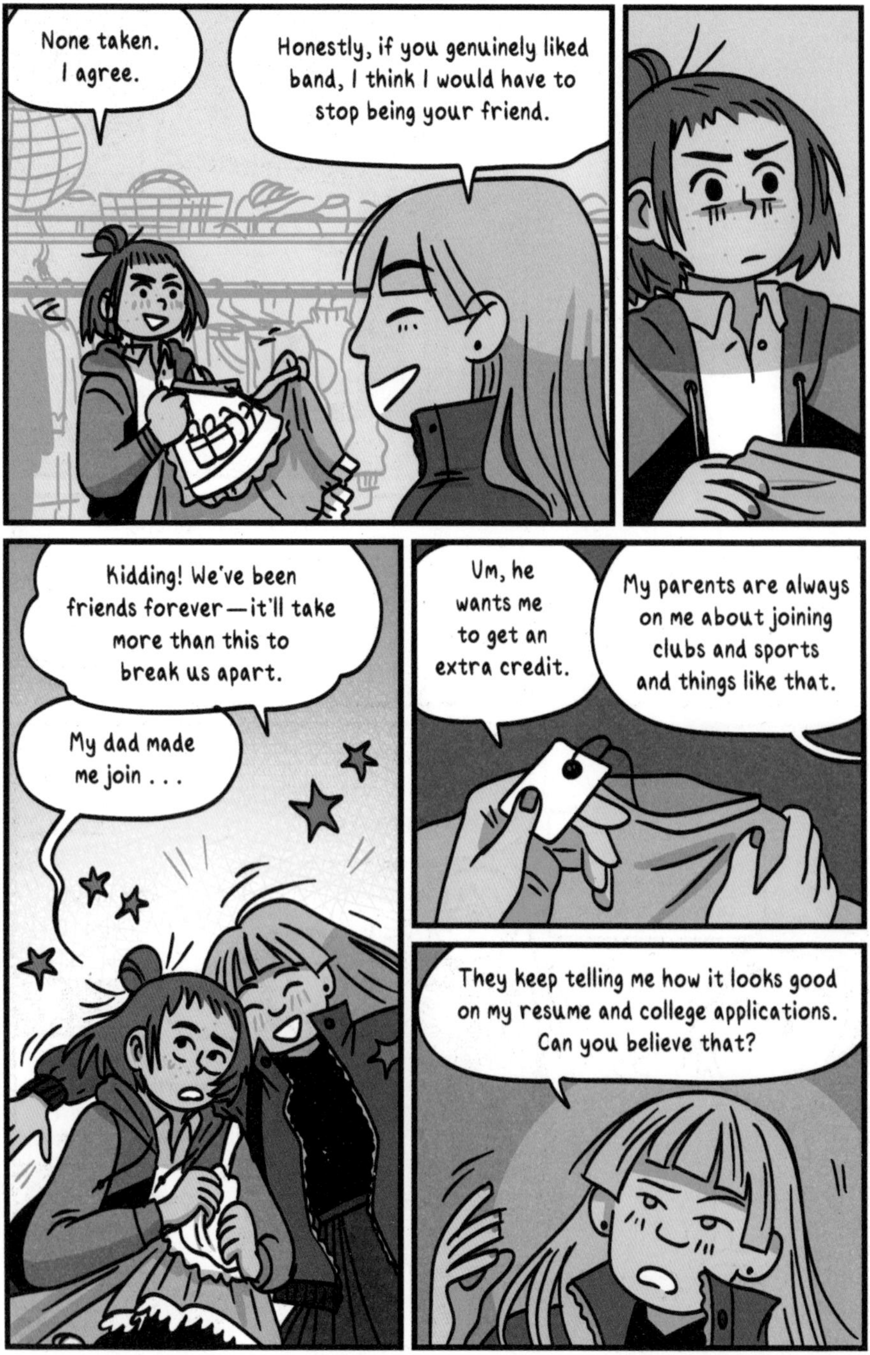

None taken. I agree.
Honestly, if you genuinely liked band, I think I would have to stop being your friend.
Kidding! We've been friends forever—it'll take more than this to break us apart.
My dad made me join . . .
Um, he wants me to get an extra credit.
My parents are always on me about joining clubs and sports and things like that.
They keep telling me how it looks good on my resume and college applications. Can you believe that?

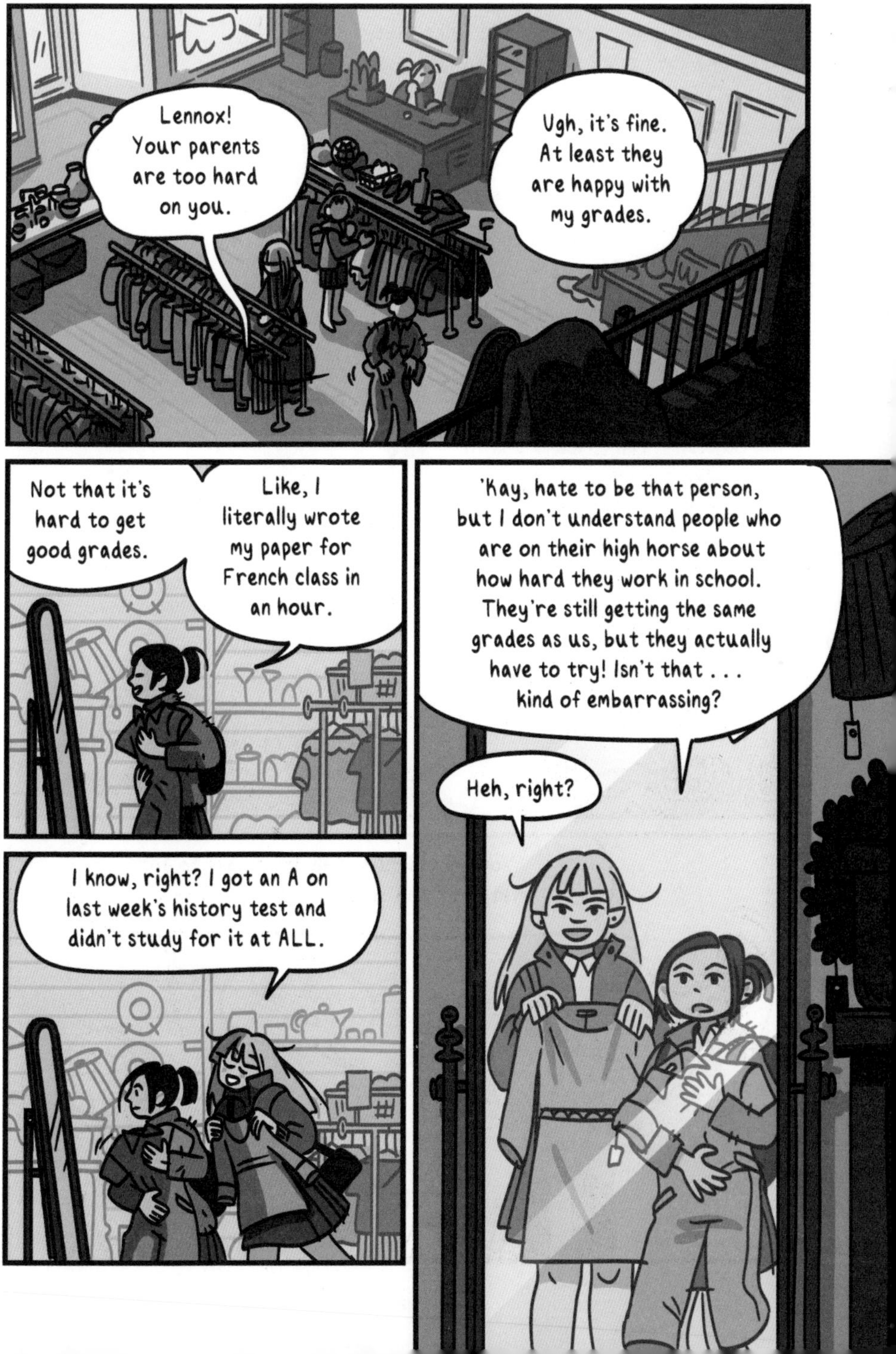
Lennox! Your parents are too hard on you.
Ugh, it's fine. At least they are happy with my grades.
Not that it's hard to get good grades.
Like, I literally wrote my paper for French class in an hour.
I know, right? I got an A on last week's history test and didn't study for it at ALL.
'Kay, hate to be that person, but I don't understand people who are on their high horse about how hard they work in school. They're still getting the same grades as us, but they actually have to try! Isn't that . . . kind of embarrassing?
Heh, right?

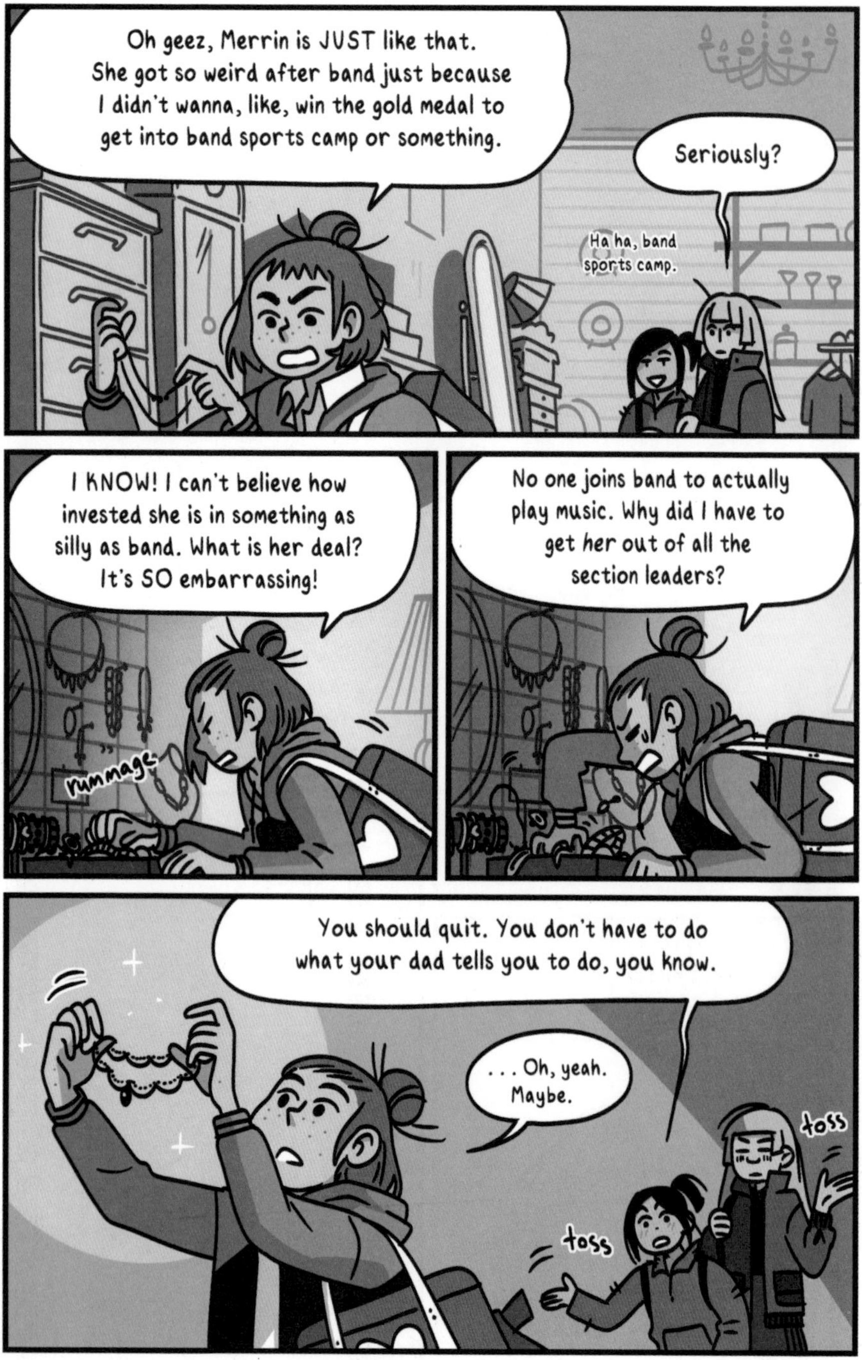
Oh geez, Merrin is JUST like that. She got so weird after band just because I didn't wanna, like, win the gold medal to get into band sports camp or something.
Ha ha, band sports camp.
Seriously?
I KNOW! I can't believe how invested she is in something as silly as band. What is her deal? It's SO embarrassing!
rummage
No one joins band to actually play music. Why did I have to get *her* out of all the section leaders?
You should quit. You don't have to do what your dad tells you to do, you know.
. . . Oh, yeah. Maybe.
toss
toss

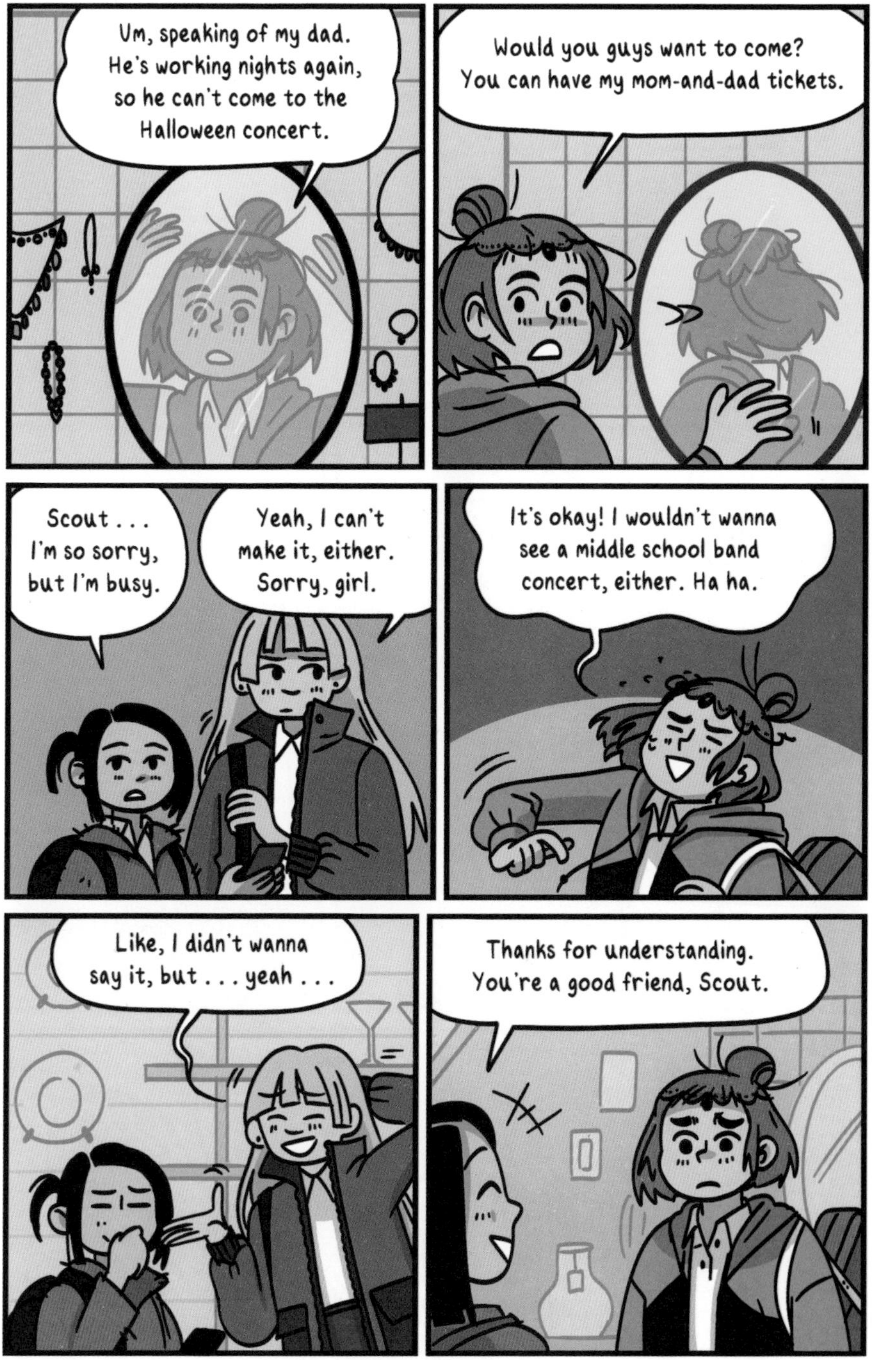

Um, speaking of my dad. He's working nights again, so he can't come to the Halloween concert.
Would you guys want to come? You can have my mom-and-dad tickets.
Scout . . . I'm so sorry, but I'm busy.
Yeah, I can't make it, either. Sorry, girl.
It's okay! I wouldn't wanna see a middle school band concert, either. Ha ha.
Like, I didn't wanna say it, but . . . yeah . . .
Thanks for understanding. You're a good friend, Scout.

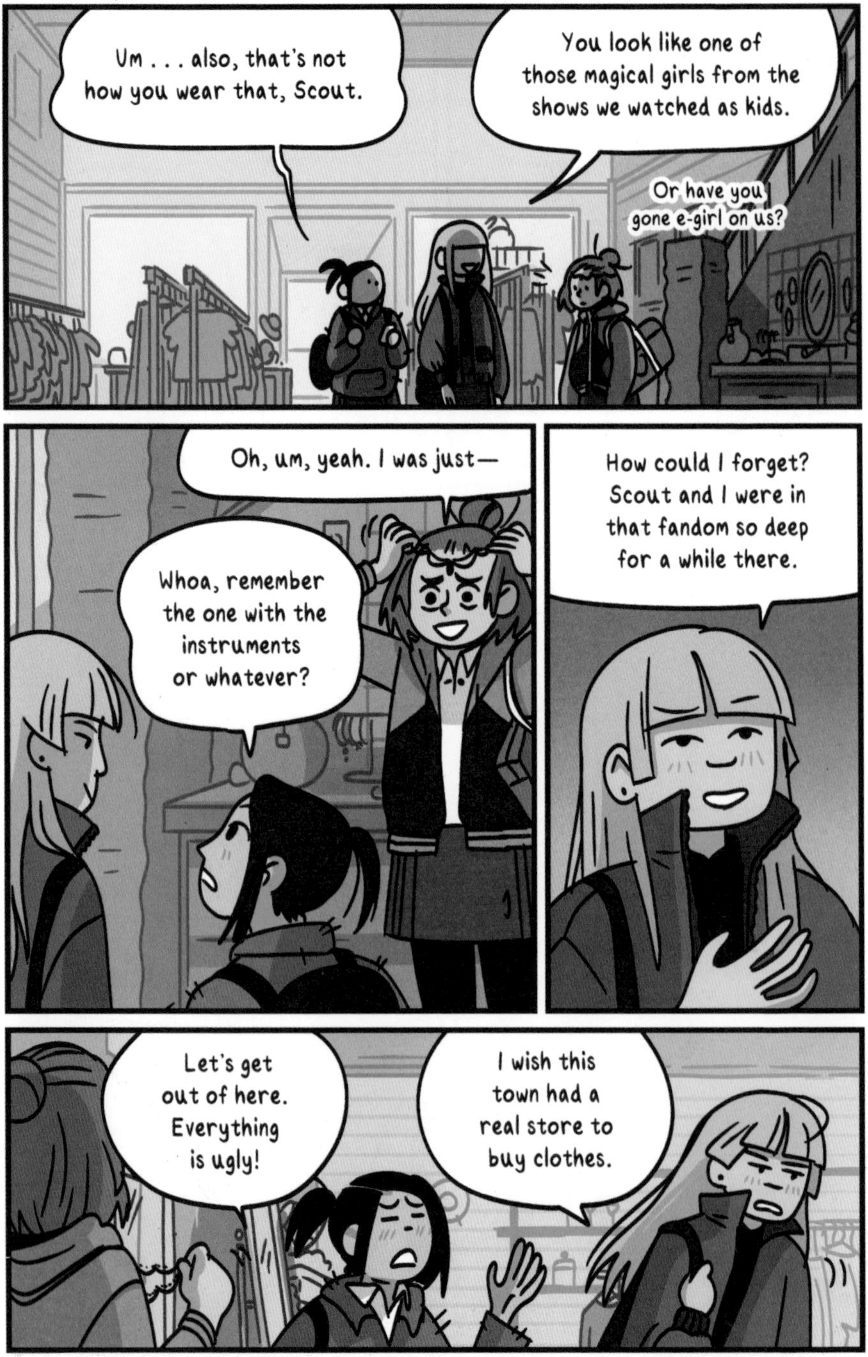
Um . . . also, that's not how you wear that, Scout.
You look like one of those magical girls from the shows we watched as kids.
Or have you gone e-girl on us?
Oh, um, yeah. I was just—
Whoa, remember the one with the instruments or whatever?
How could I forget? Scout and I were in that fandom so deep for a while there.
Let's get out of here. Everything is ugly!
I wish this town had a real store to buy clothes.

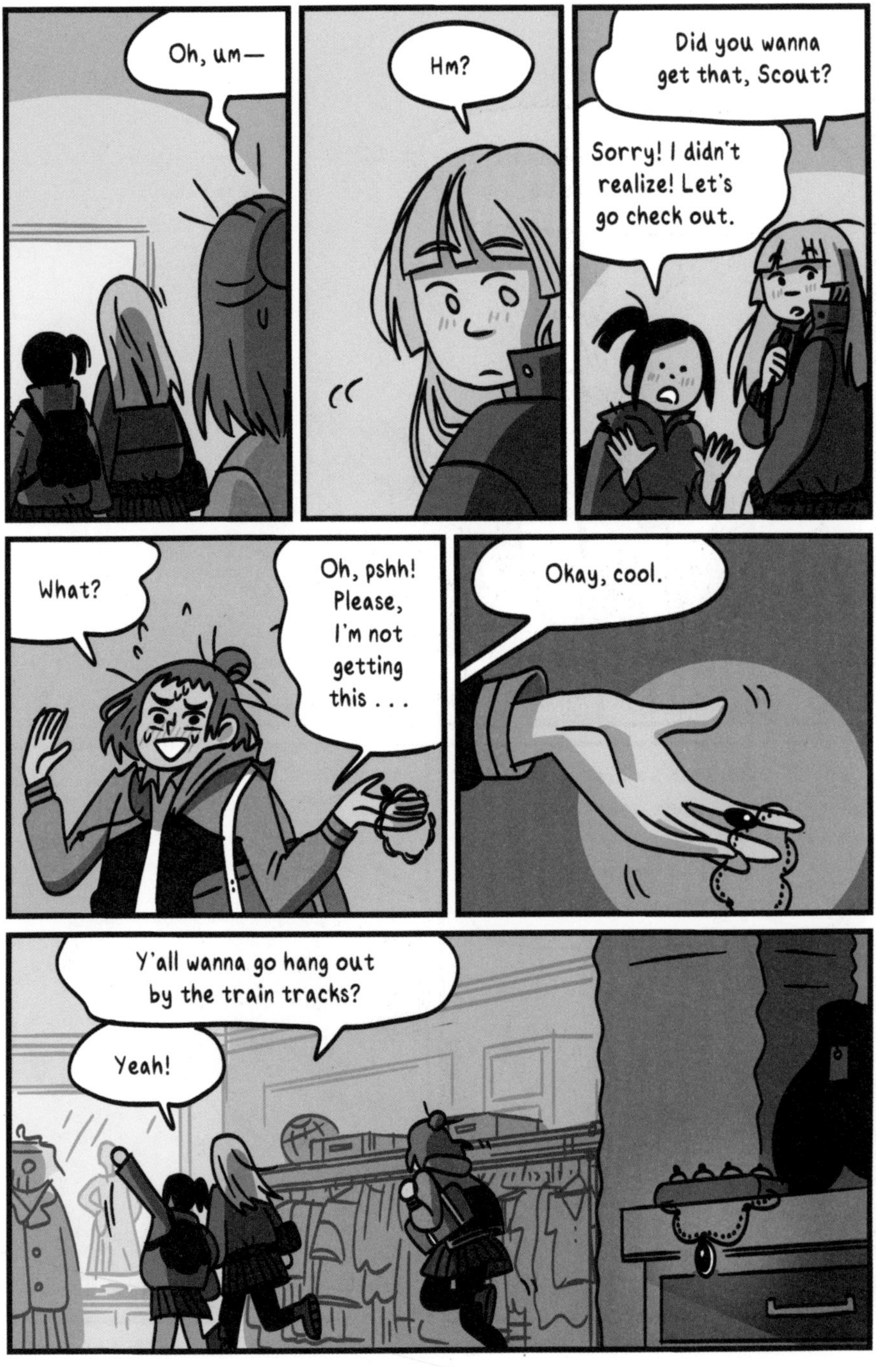
Oh, um—
Hm?
Did you wanna get that, Scout?
Sorry! I didn't realize! Let's go check out.
What?
Oh, pshh! Please, I'm not getting this . . .
Okay, cool.
Y'all wanna go hang out by the train tracks?
Yeah!

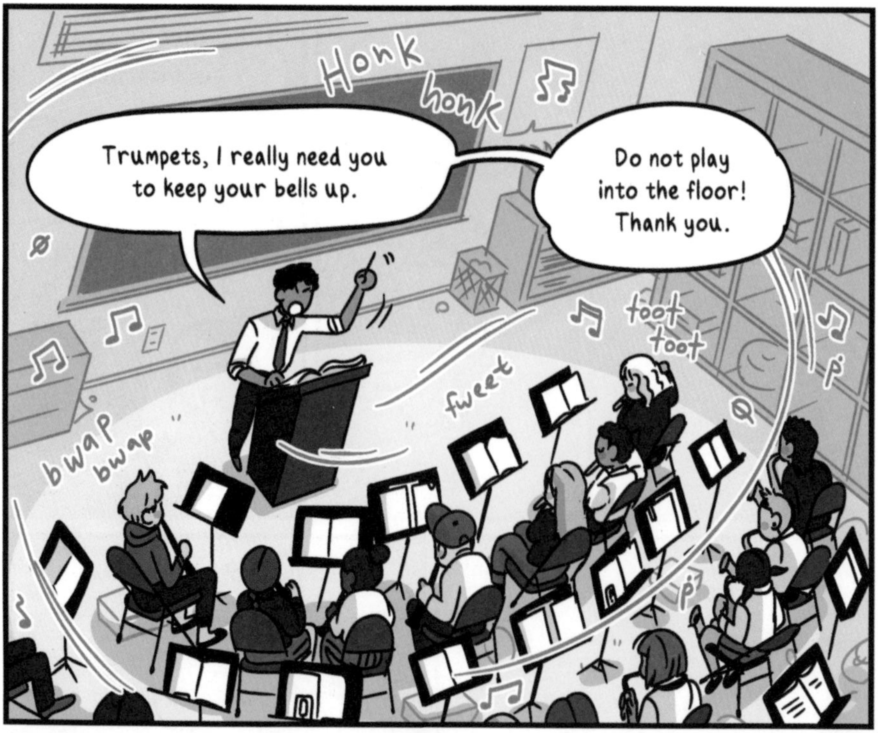
Honk
honk
Trumpets, I really need you to keep your bells up.
Do not play into the floor! Thank you.
toot toot
fweet
bwap bwap

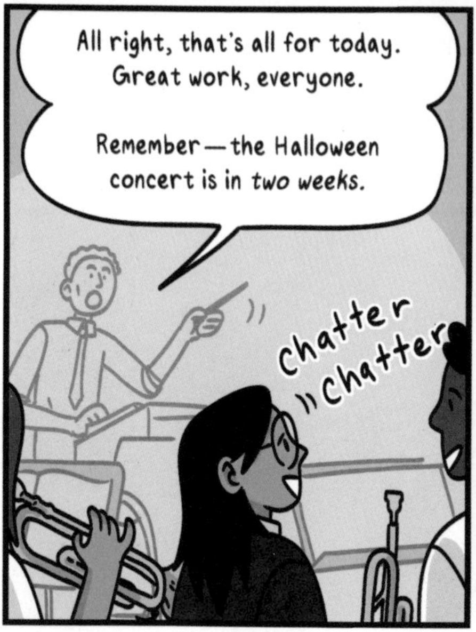
All right, that's all for today. Great work, everyone.
Remember—the Halloween concert is in *two weeks.*
chatter chatter

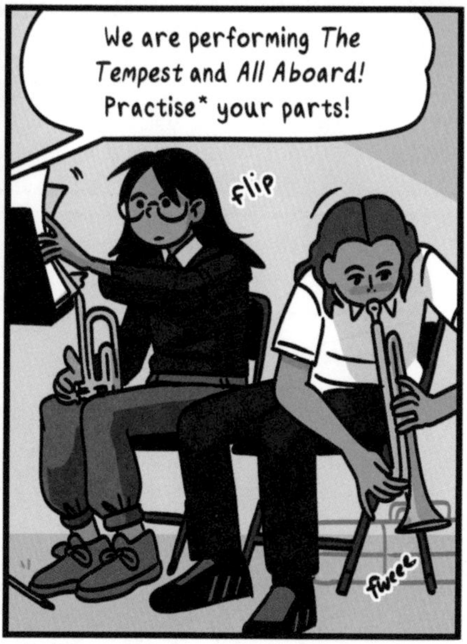
We are performing *The Tempest* and *All Aboard!* Practise* your parts!
flip
fweee

*In Canadian English, *practise* is a verb and *practice* is a noun.

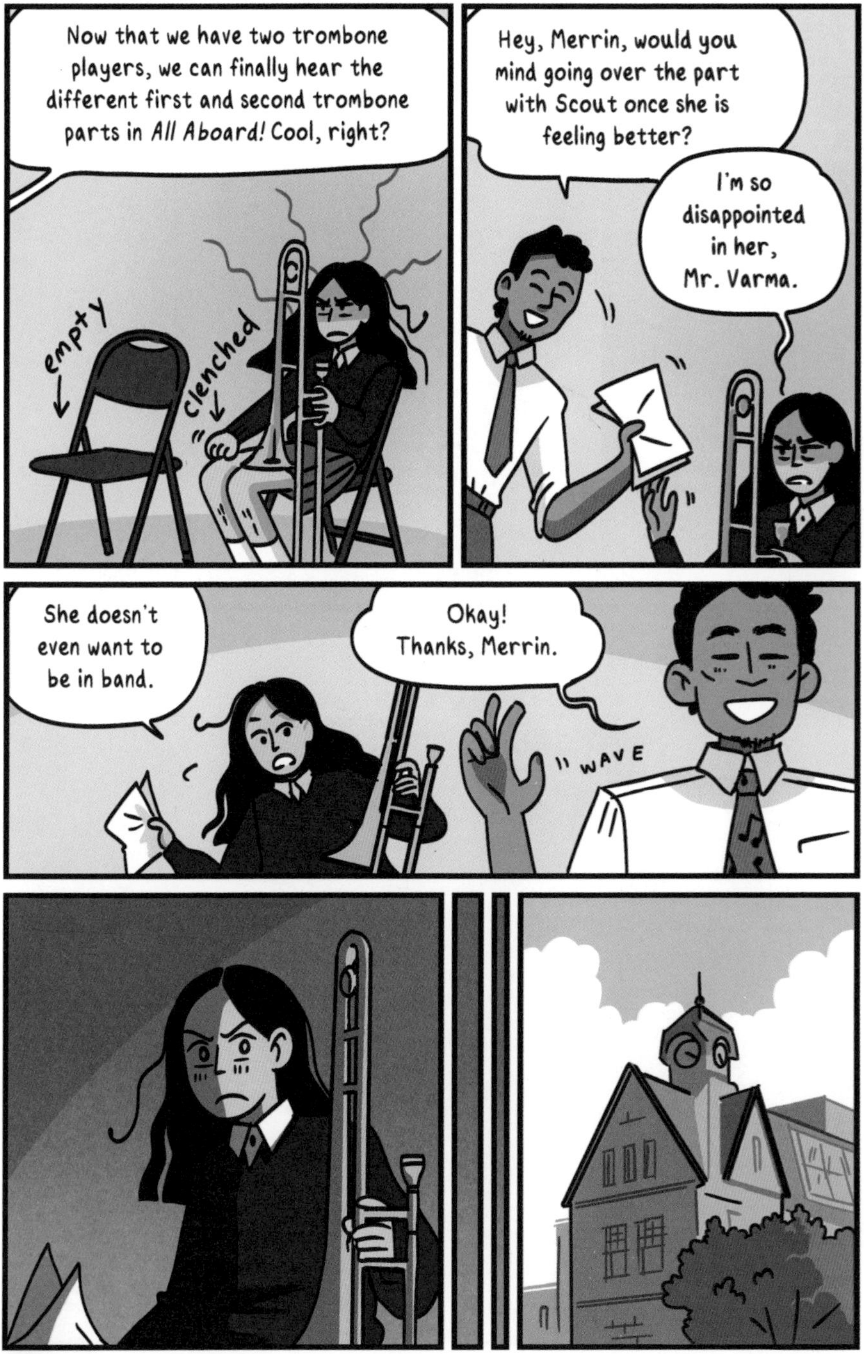
Now that we have two trombone players, we can finally hear the different first and second trombone parts in *All Aboard!* Cool, right?
empty
clenched
Hey, Merrin, would you mind going over the part with Scout once she is feeling better?
I'm so disappointed in her, Mr. Varma.
She doesn't even want to be in band.
Okay! Thanks, Merrin.
WAVE

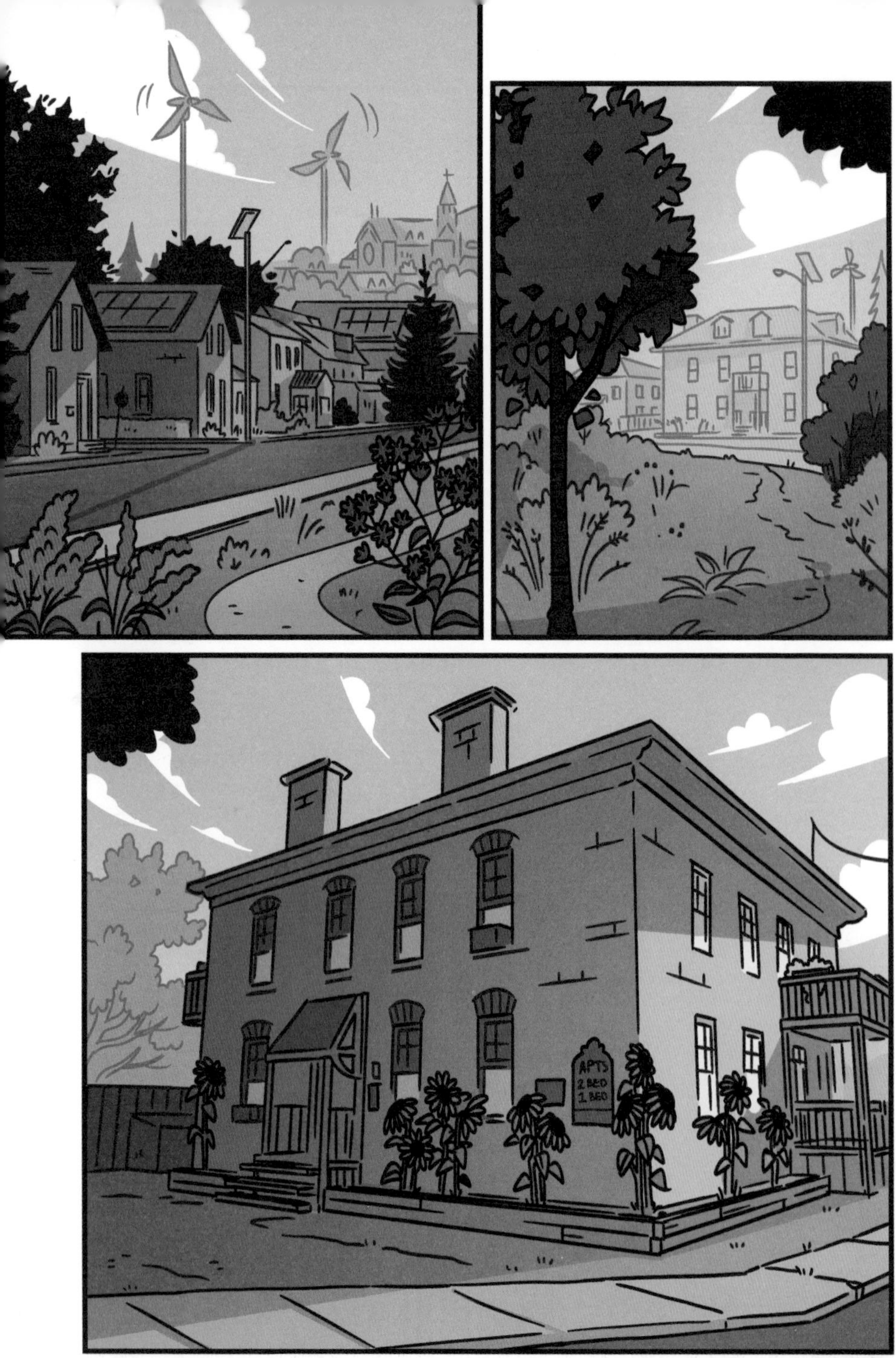
APTS
2 BED
1 BED

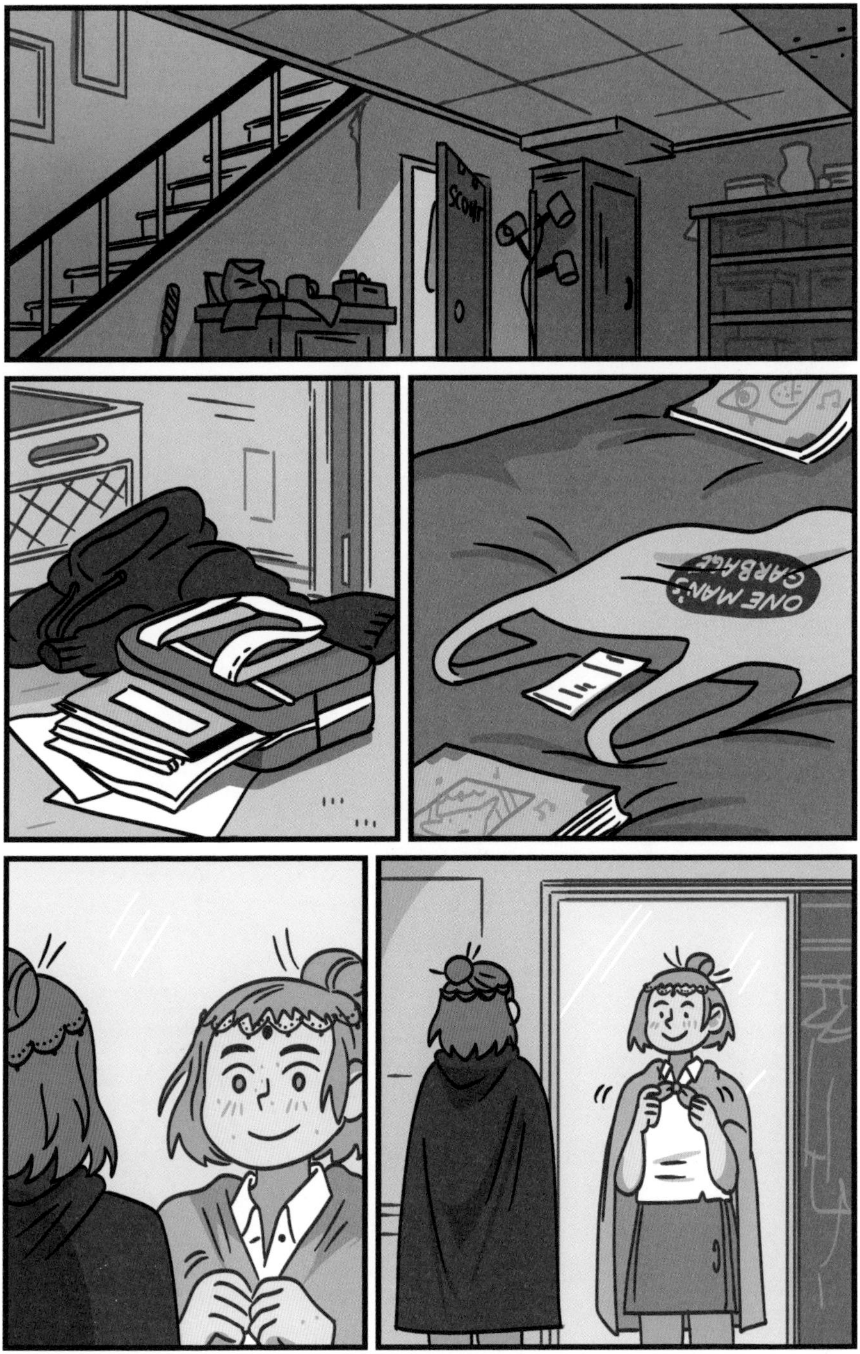
SCOUT
ONE MAN'S GARBAGE

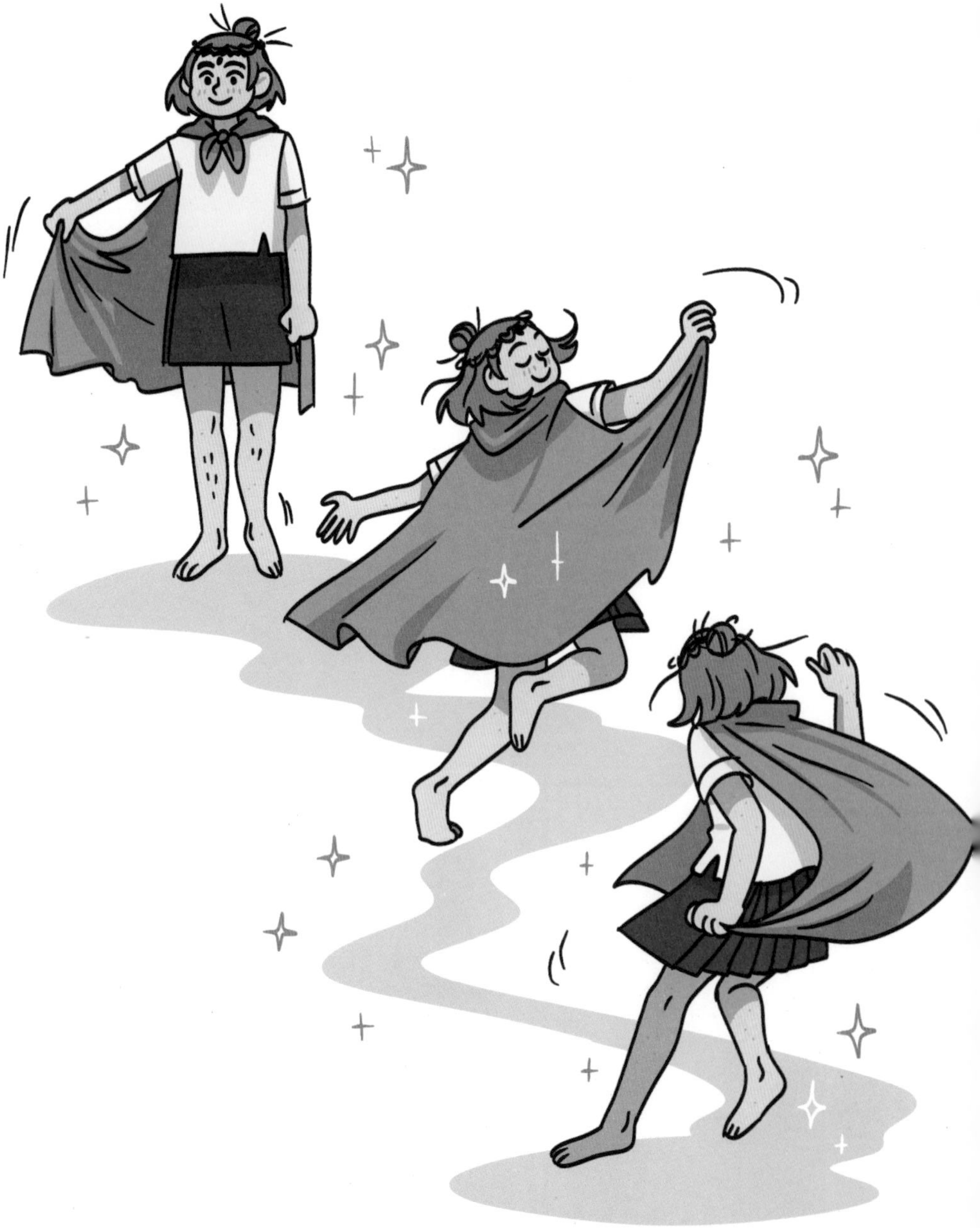

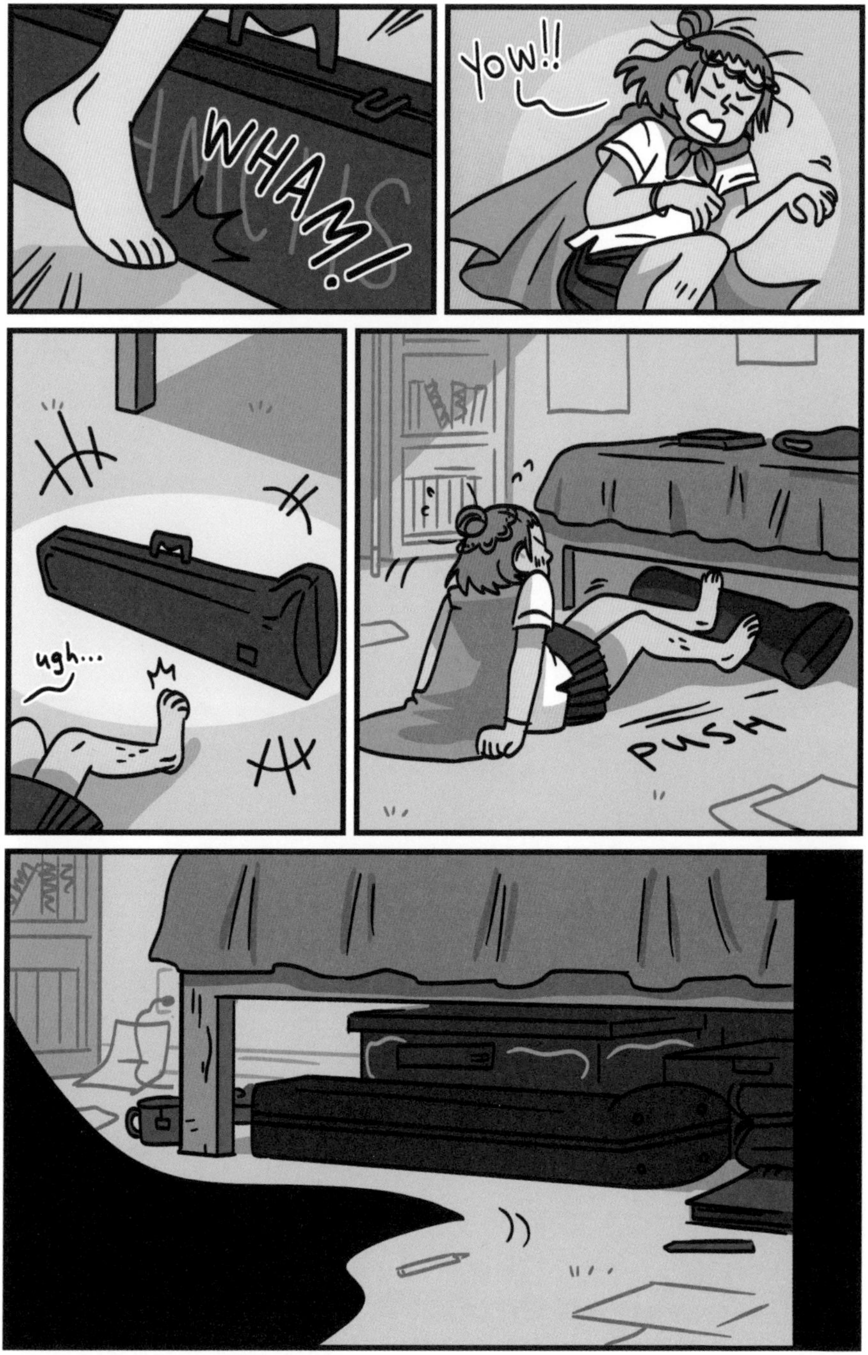
WHAM!
YOW!!
ugh...
PUSH

Chapter 2

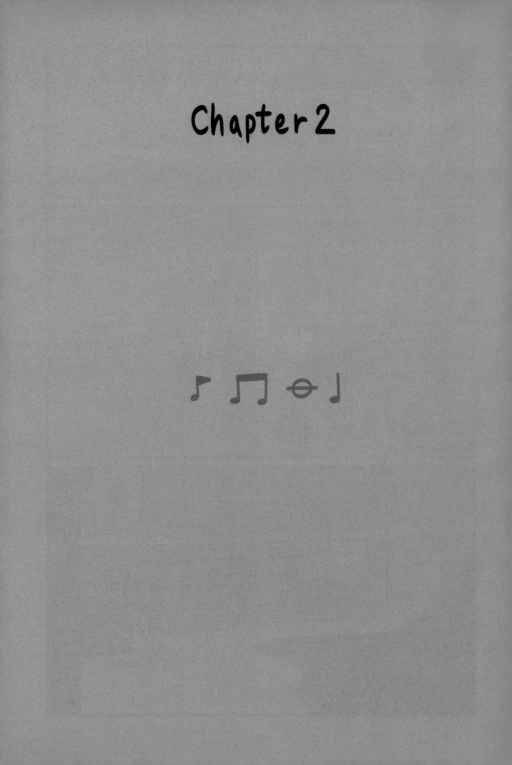

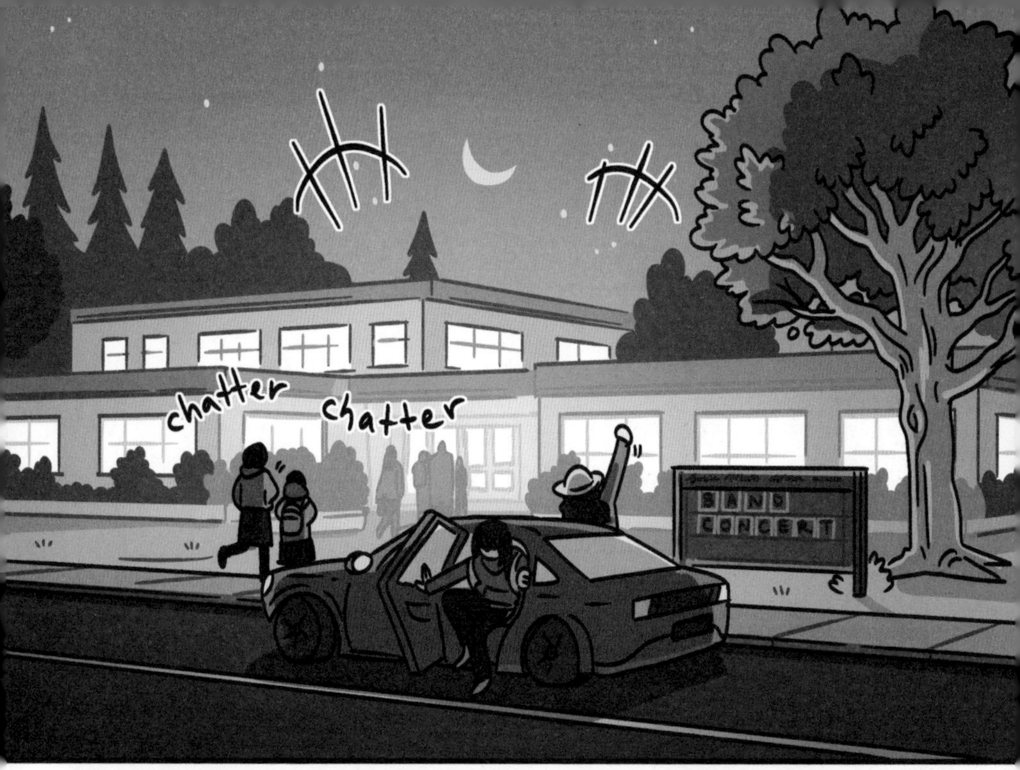
chatter
chatter
BAND CONCERT

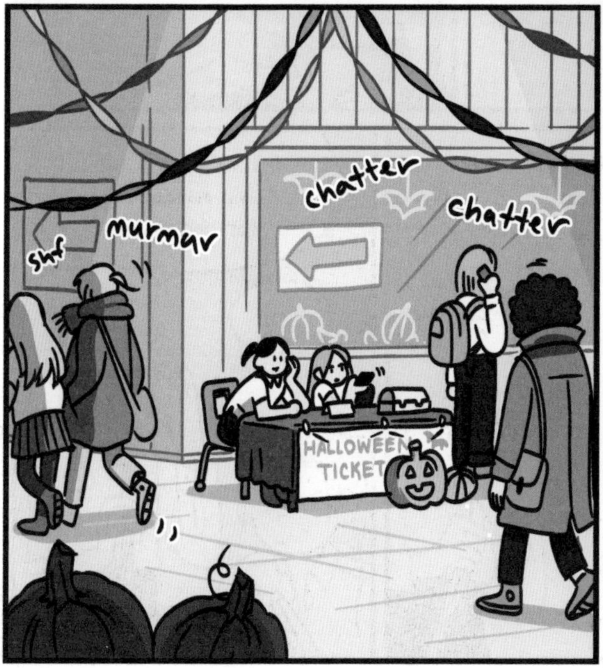
chatter
chatter
shf
murmur
HALLOWEEN TICKET

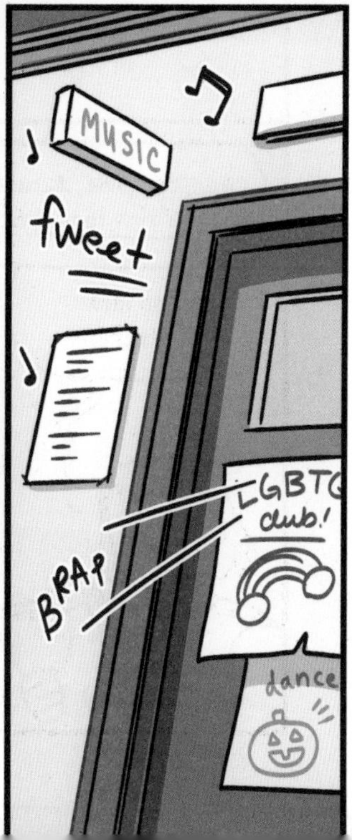
MUSIC
fweet
LGBTQ club!
BRAP
dance

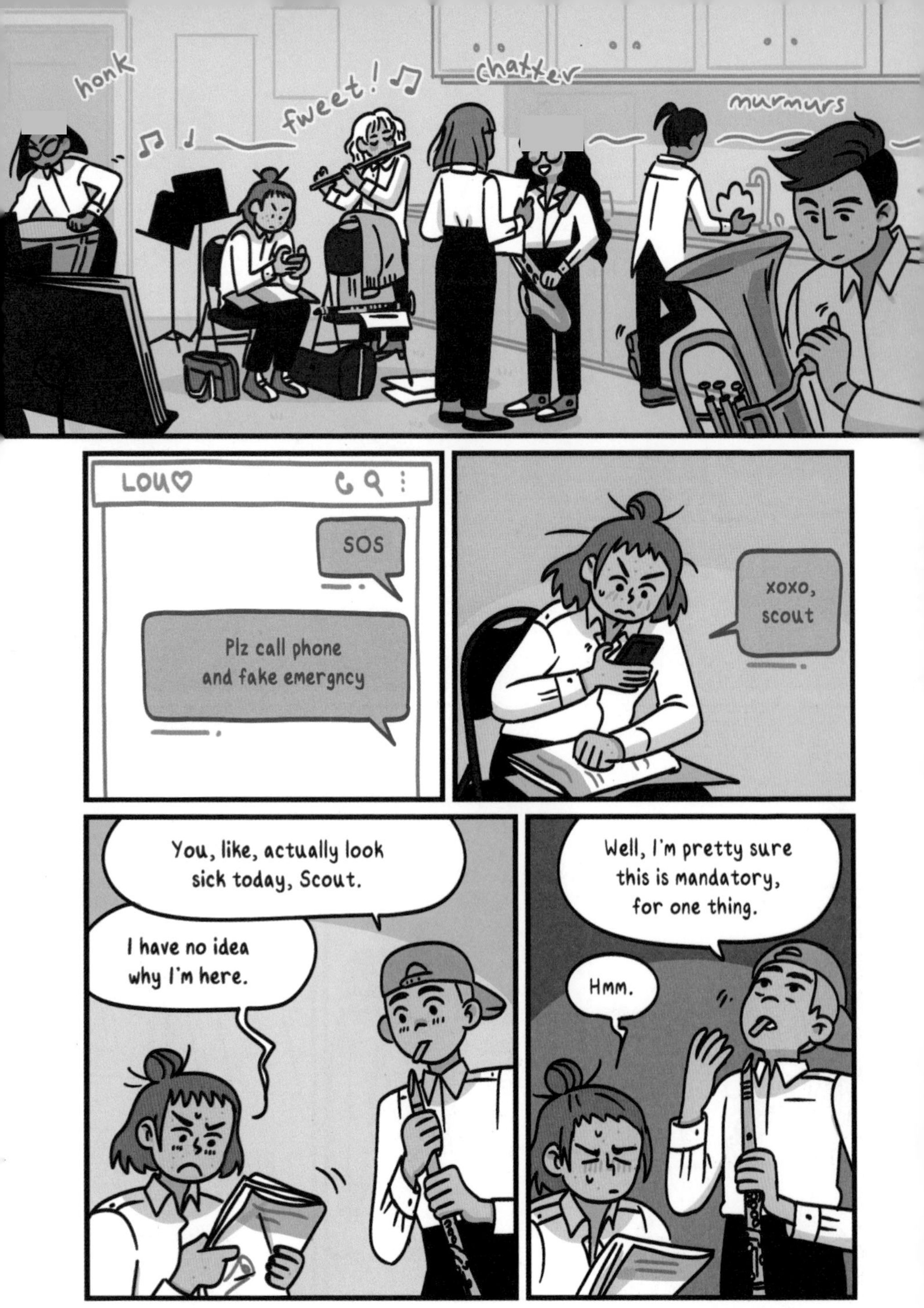
honk
fweet!
chatter
murmurs
LOU♡
SOS
Plz call phone and fake emergncy
xoxo, scout
You, like, actually look sick today, Scout.
I have no idea why I'm here.
Well, I'm pretty sure this is mandatory, for one thing.
Hmm.

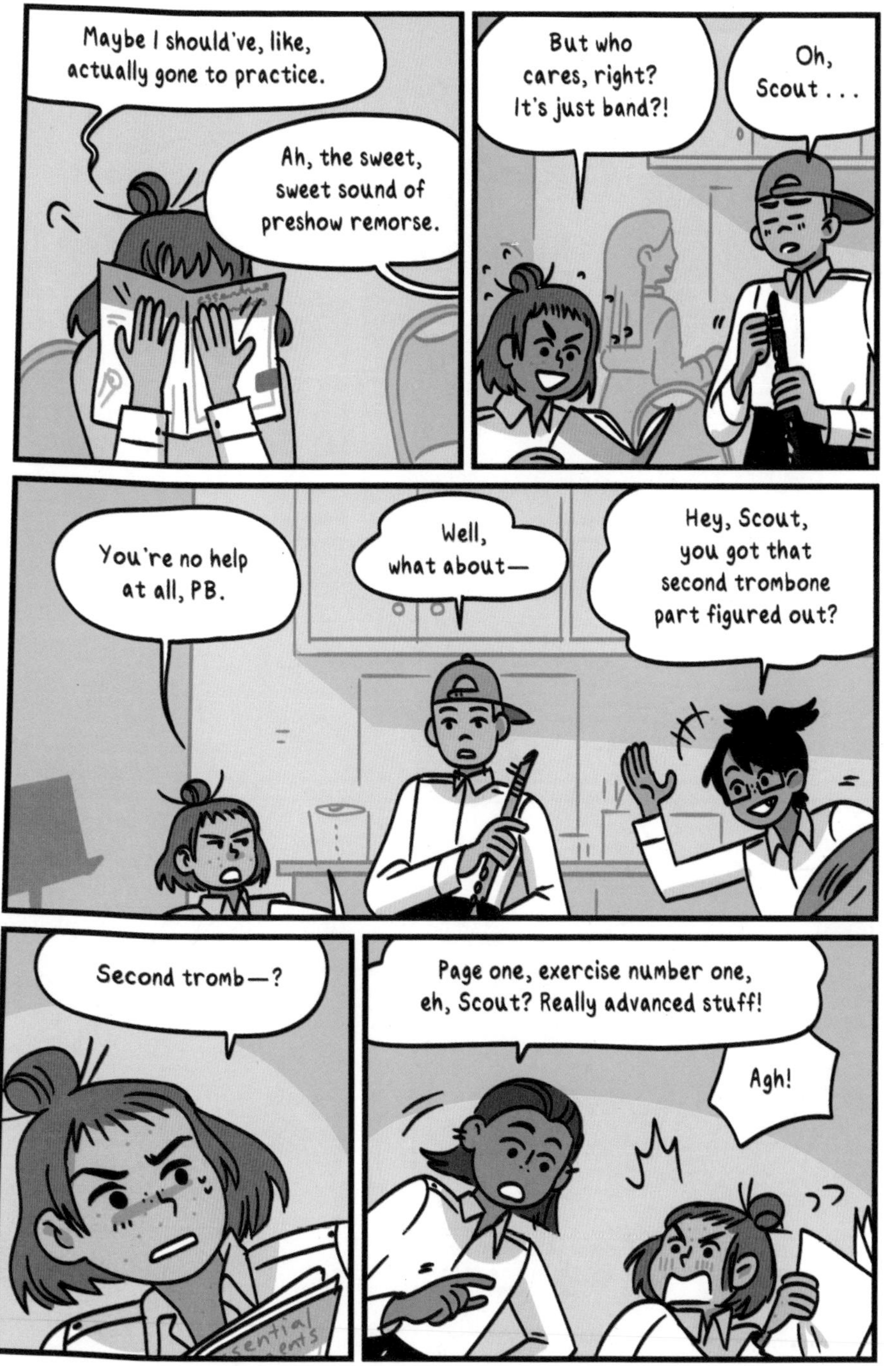
Maybe I should've, like, actually gone to practice.
Ah, the sweet, sweet sound of preshow remorse.
But who cares, right? It's just band?!
Oh, Scout . . .
You're no help at all, PB.
Well, what about—
Hey, Scout, you got that second trombone part figured out?
Second tromb—?
Page one, exercise number one, eh, Scout? Really advanced stuff!
Agh!

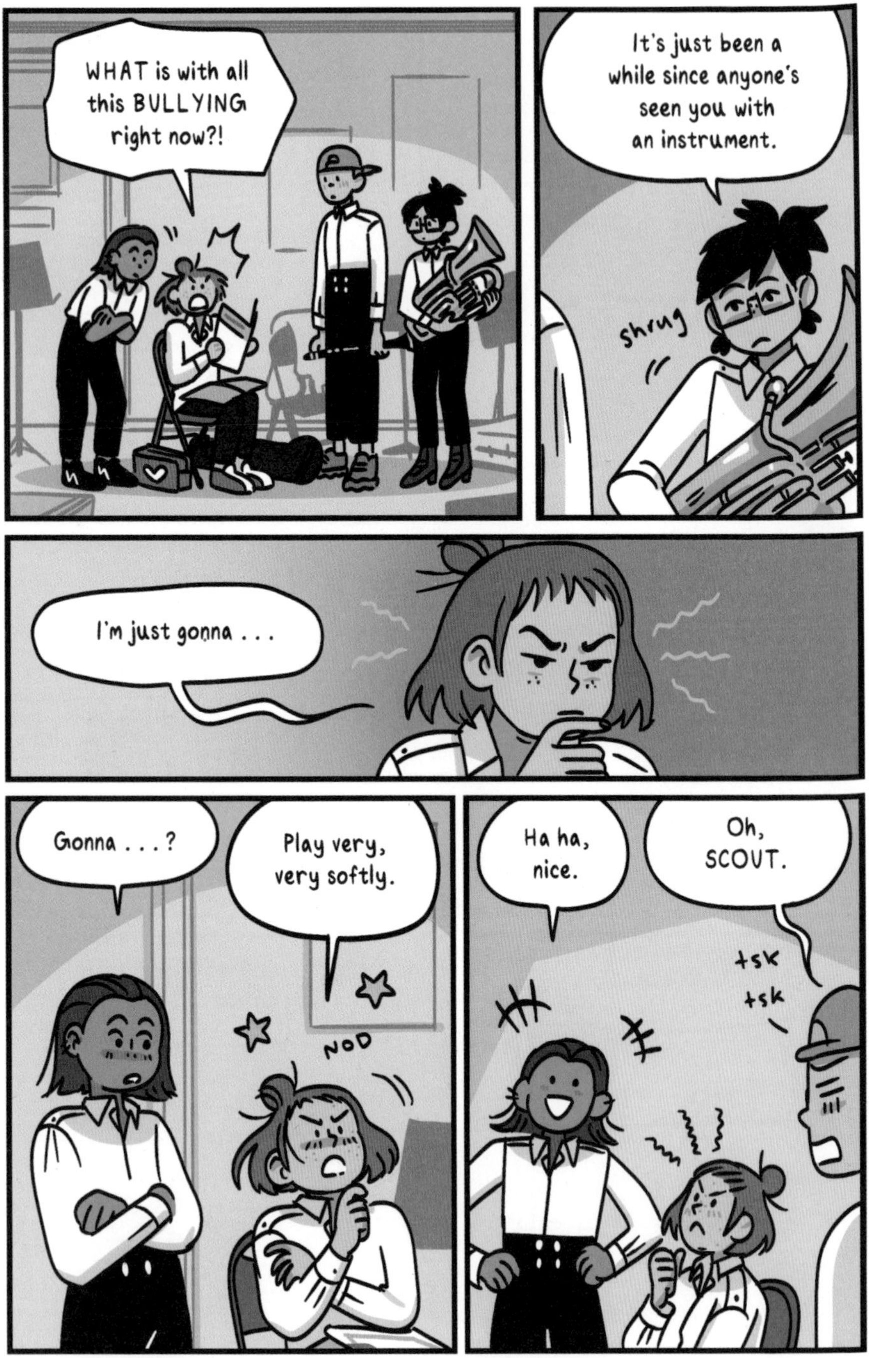
WHAT is with all this BULLYING right now?!
It's just been a while since anyone's seen you with an instrument.
shrug
I'm just gonna . . .
Gonna . . . ?
Play very, very softly.
NOD
Ha ha, nice.
Oh, SCOUT.
tsk
tsk

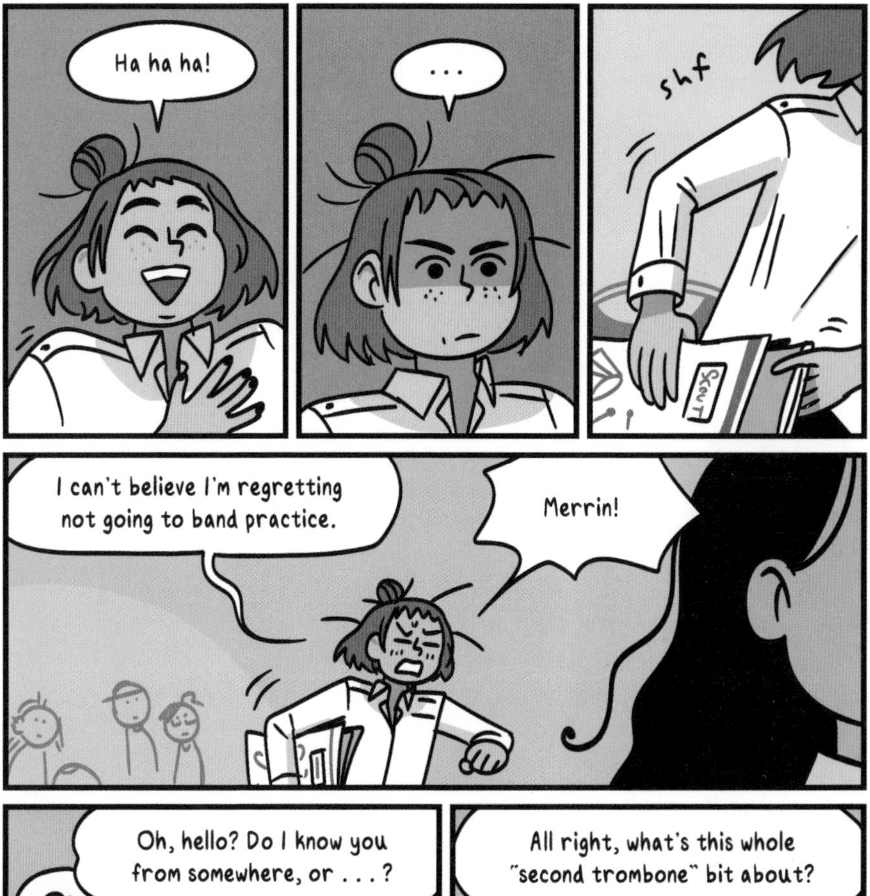
Ha ha ha!
. . .
shf
SCOUT
I can't believe I'm regretting not going to band practice.
Merrin!
Oh, hello? Do I know you from somewhere, or . . . ?
All right, what's this whole "second trombone" bit about?

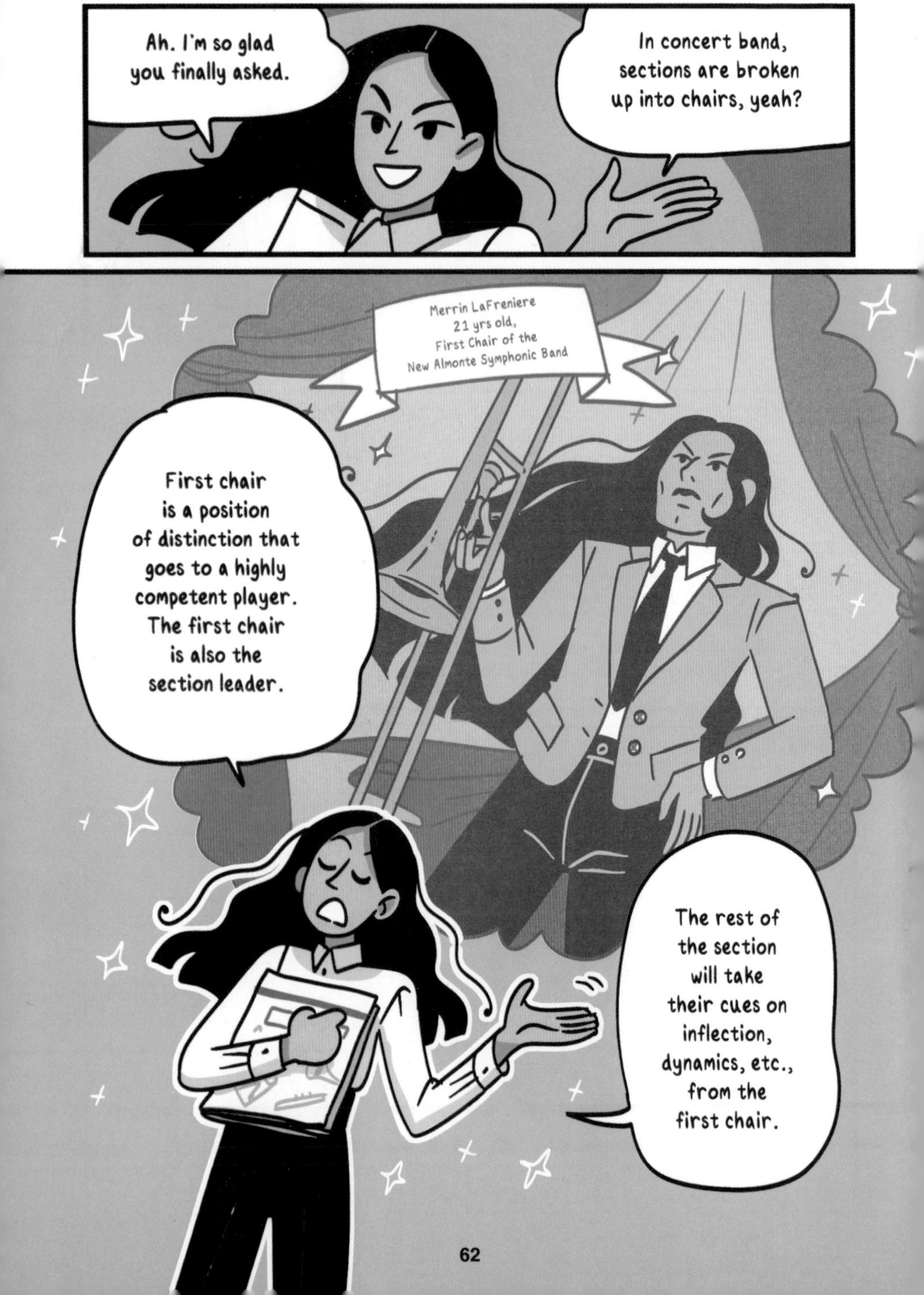
Ah. I'm so glad you finally asked.
In concert band, sections are broken up into chairs, yeah?
Merrin LaFreniere 21 yrs old, First Chair of the New Almonte Symphonic Band
First chair is a position of distinction that goes to a highly competent player. The first chair is also the section leader.
The rest of the section will take their cues on inflection, dynamics, etc., from the first chair.

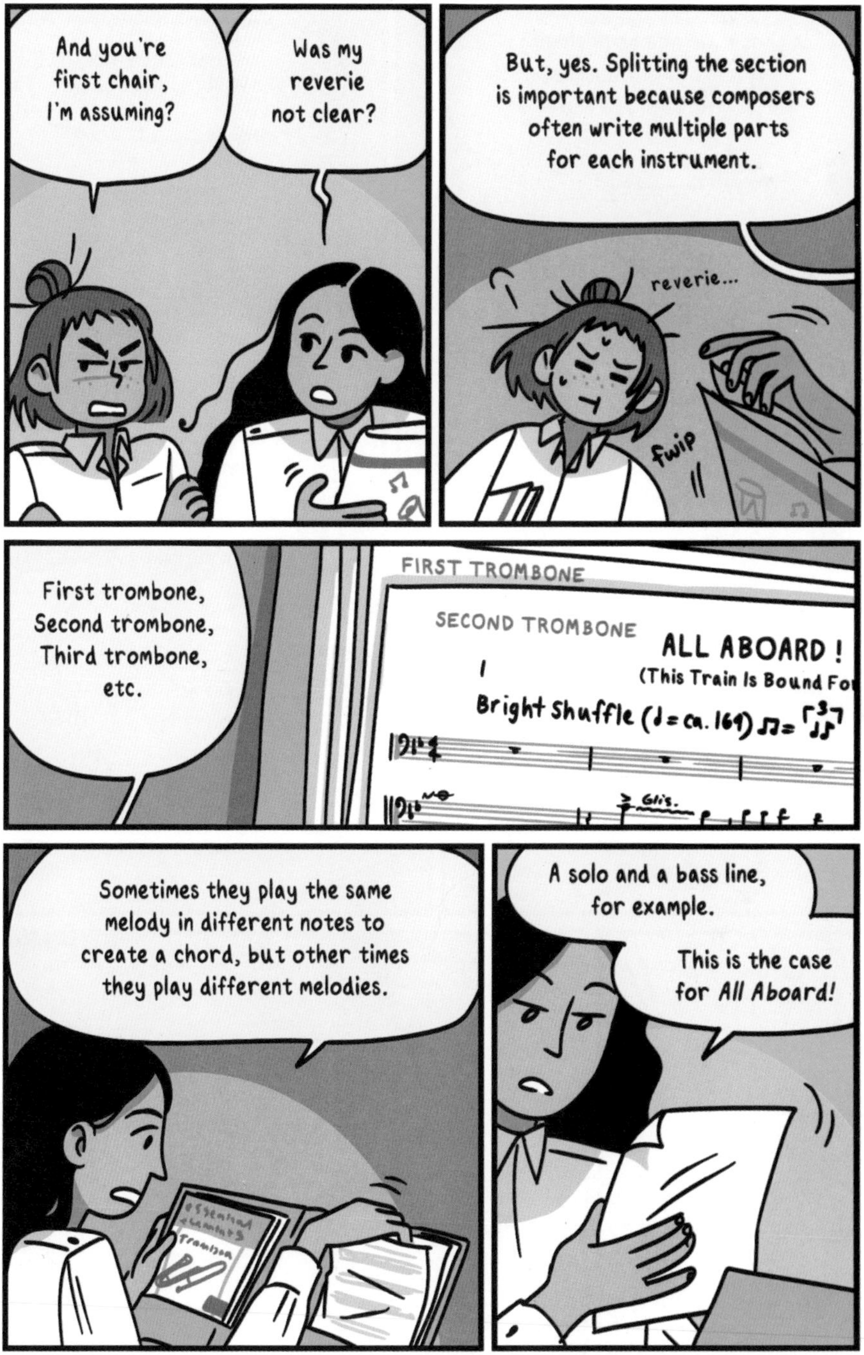

And you're first chair, I'm assuming?
Was my reverie not clear?
But, yes. Splitting the section is important because composers often write multiple parts for each instrument.
reverie...
fwip
First trombone, Second trombone, Third trombone, etc.
FIRST TROMBONE
SECOND TROMBONE
ALL ABOARD!
(This Train Is Bound Fo
Bright Shuffle
Gliss.
Sometimes they play the same melody in different notes to create a chord, but other times they play different melodies.
A solo and a bass line, for example.
This is the case for *All Aboard!*

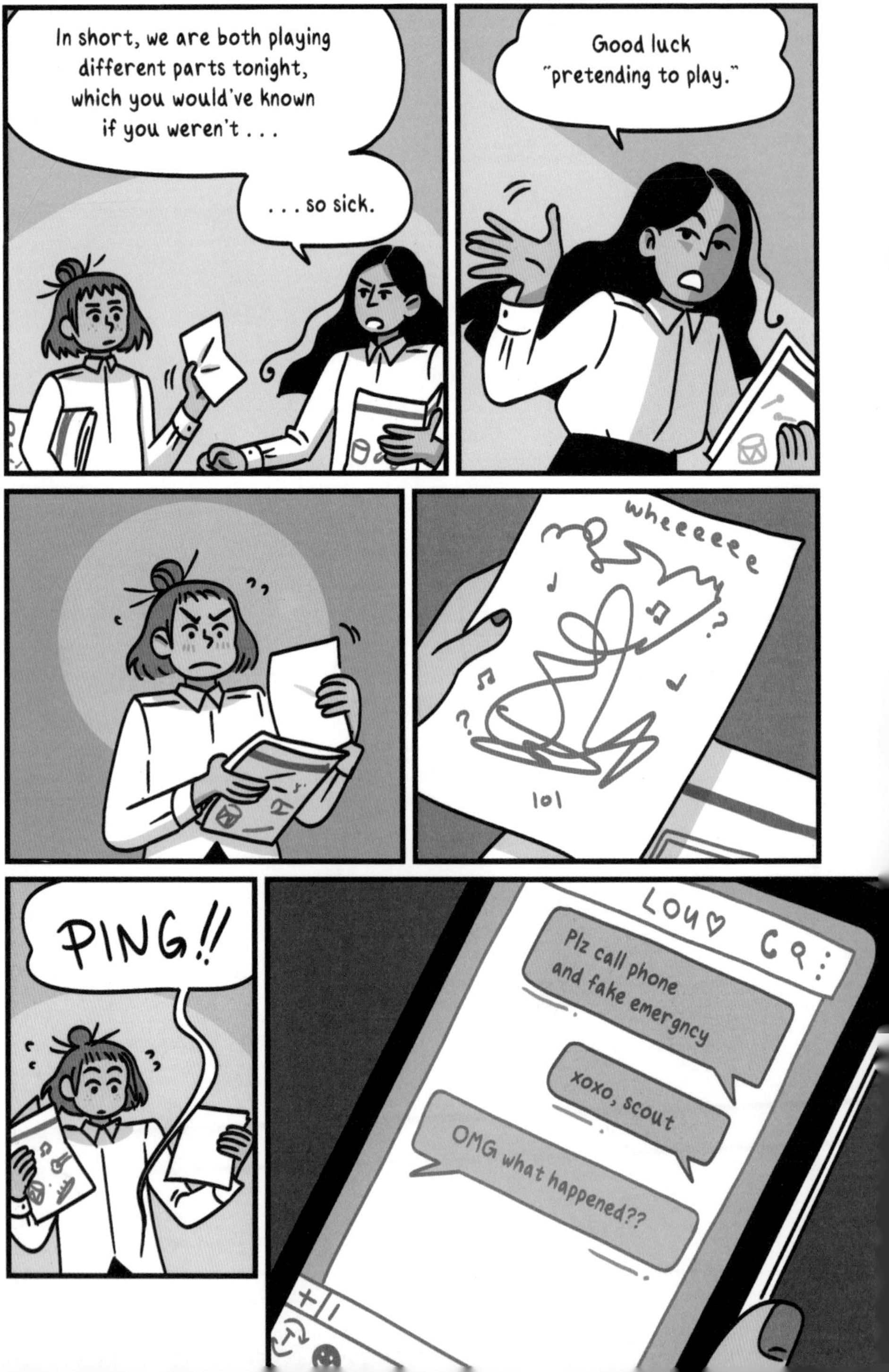
In short, we are both playing different parts tonight, which you would've known if you weren't . . .
. . . so sick.
Good luck "pretending to play."
wheeeeee
lol
PING!!
Lou♡
Plz call phone and fake emergncy
xoxo, scout
OMG what happened??

*In Canadian English, *gray* is spelt *grey*.

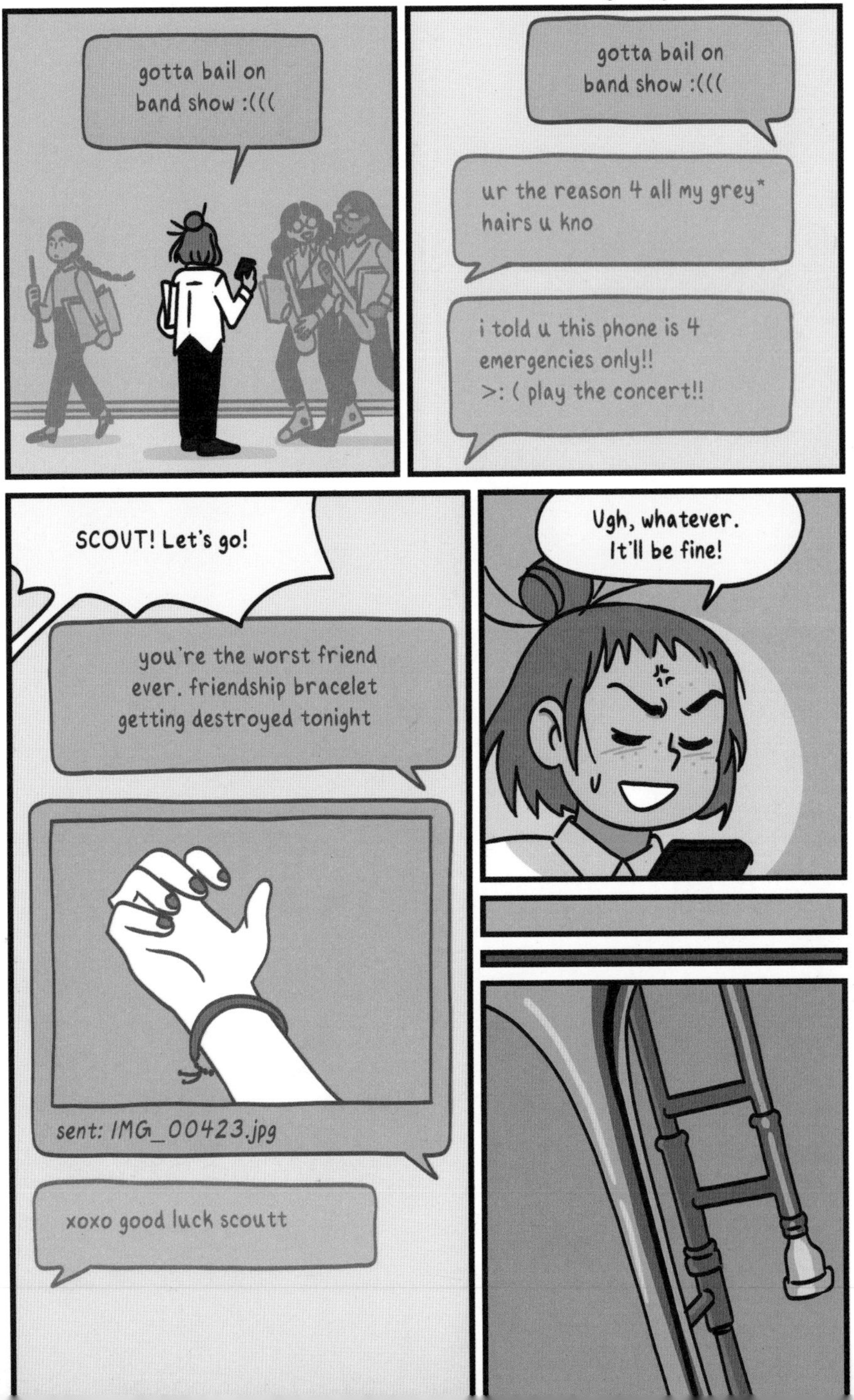
gotta bail on band show :(((
gotta bail on band show :(((
ur the reason 4 all my grey* hairs u kno
i told u this phone is 4 emergencies only!! >: (play the concert!!
SCOUT! Let's go!
you're the worst friend ever. friendship bracelet getting destroyed tonight
sent: IMG_00423.jpg
xoxo good luck scoutt
Ugh, whatever. It'll be fine!

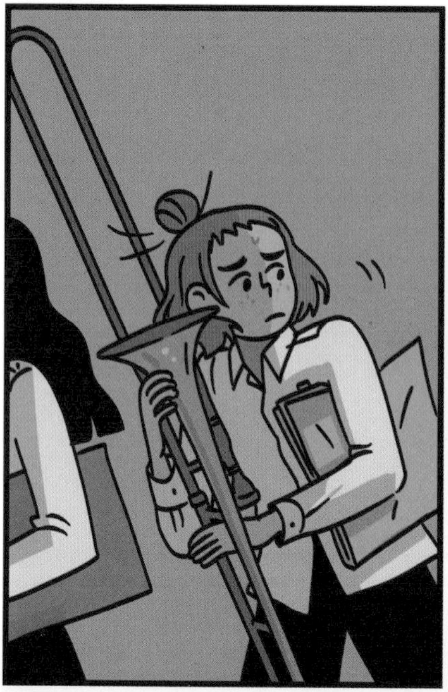

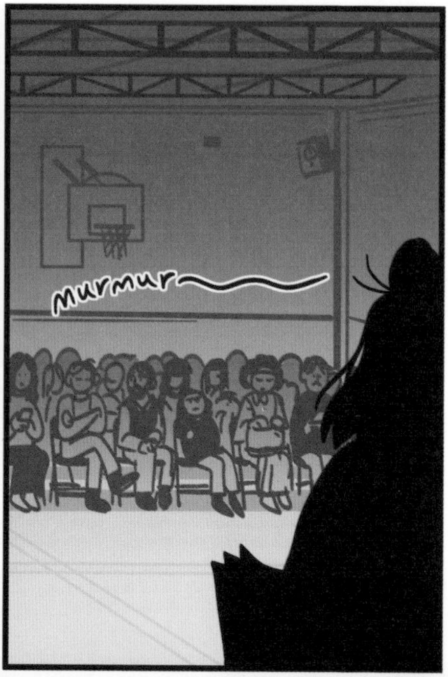
murmur

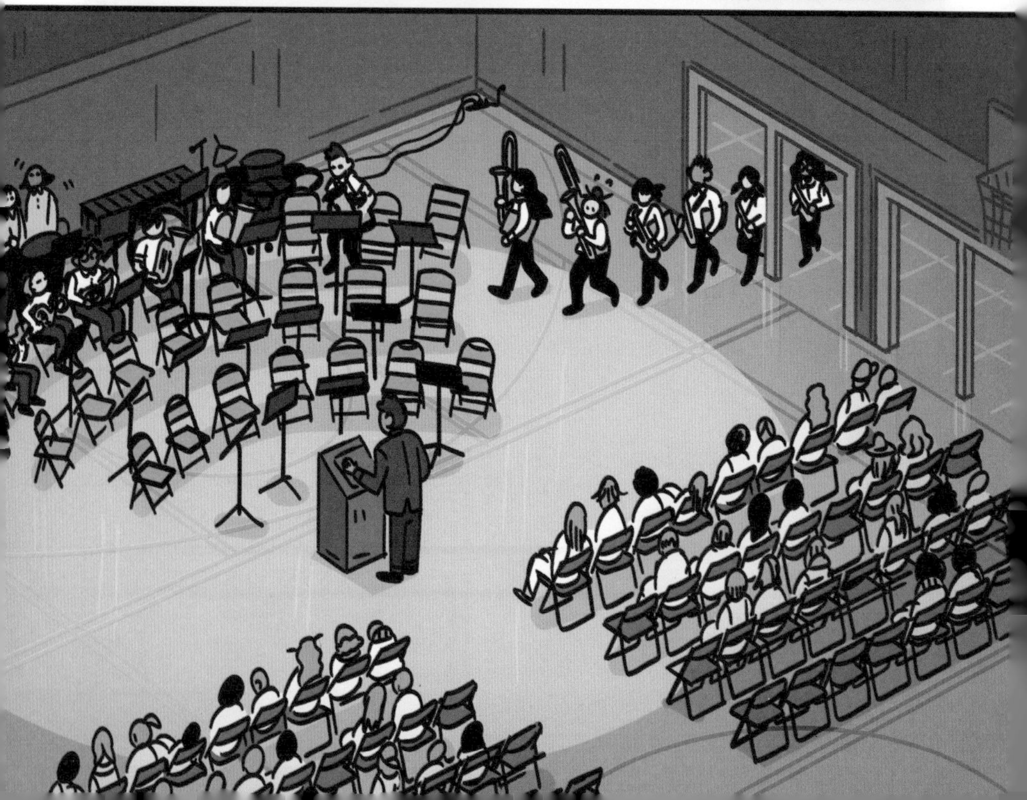

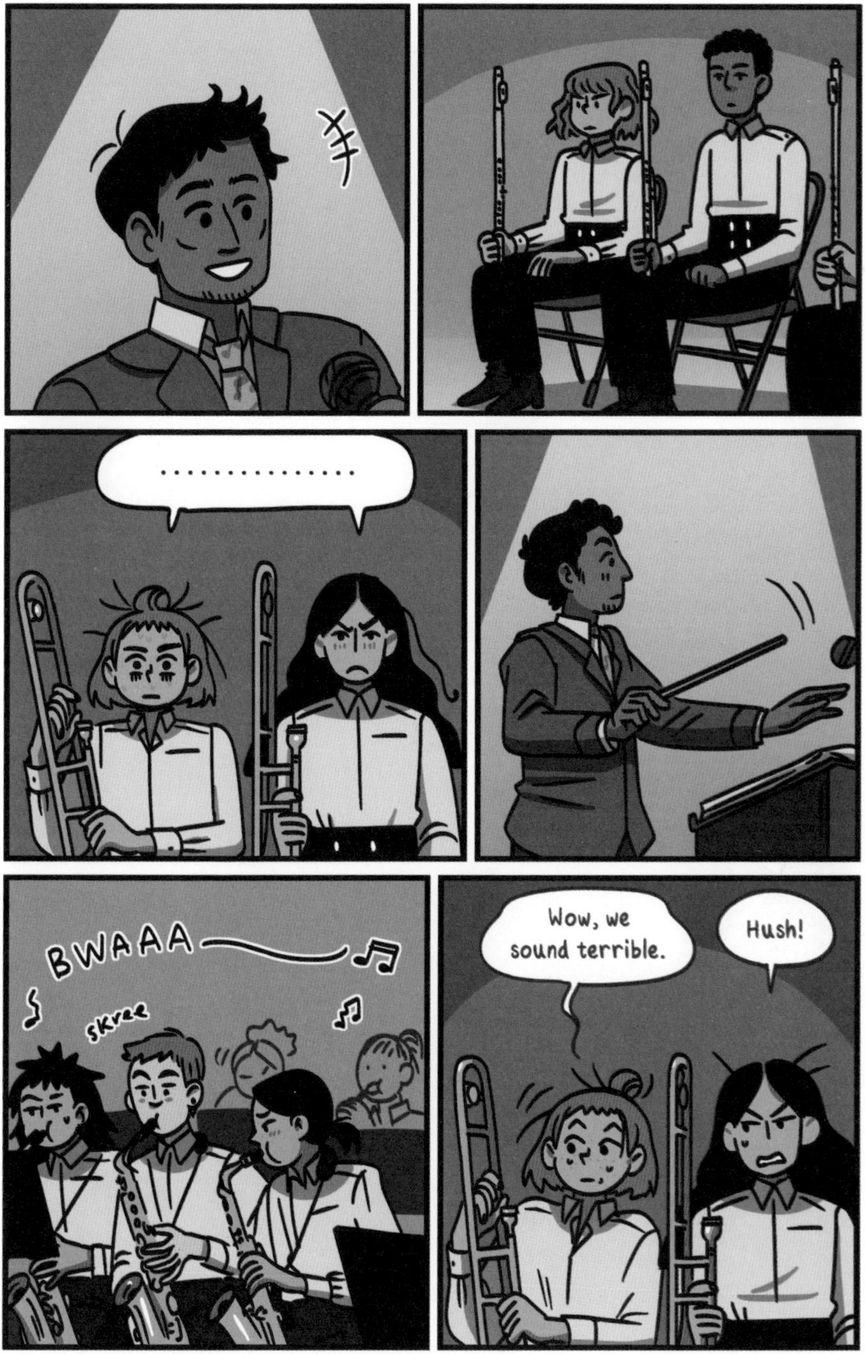
....
BWAAA
skree
Wow, we sound terrible.
Hush!

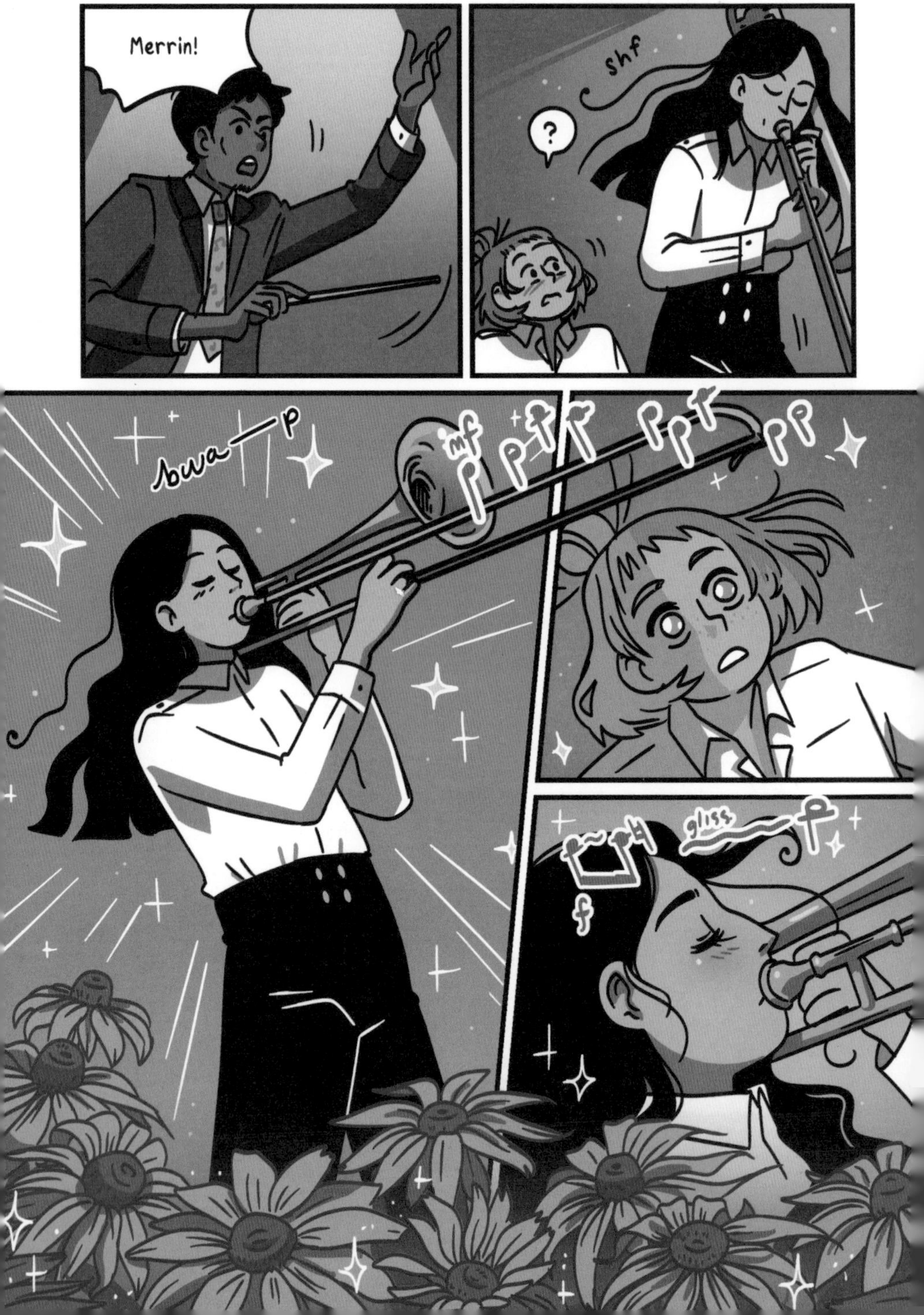
Merrin!
shf
?
bwa—p
mf
gliss
f

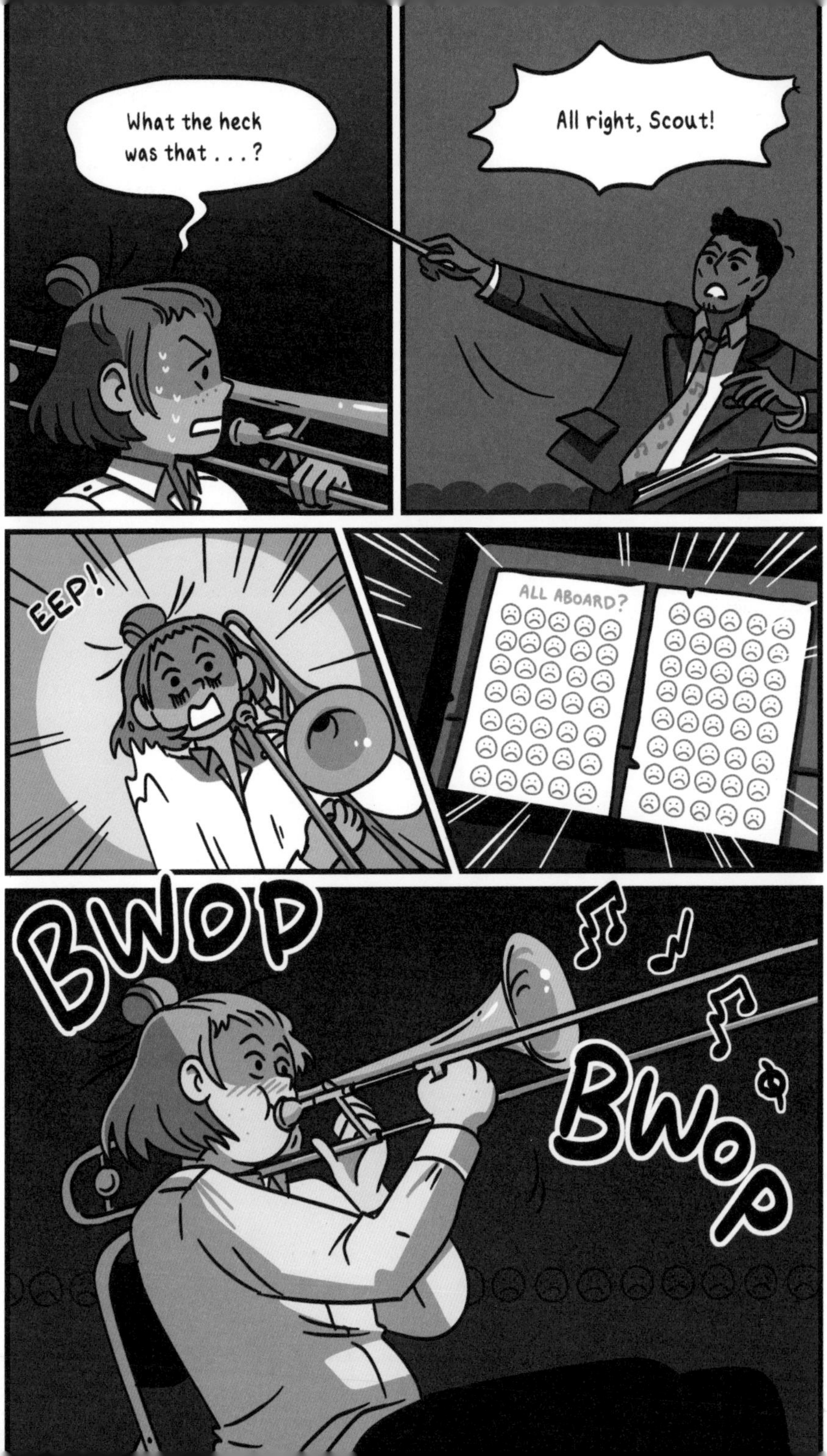
What the heck was that . . . ?
All right, Scout!
EEP!
ALL ABOARD?
BWOP
BWOP

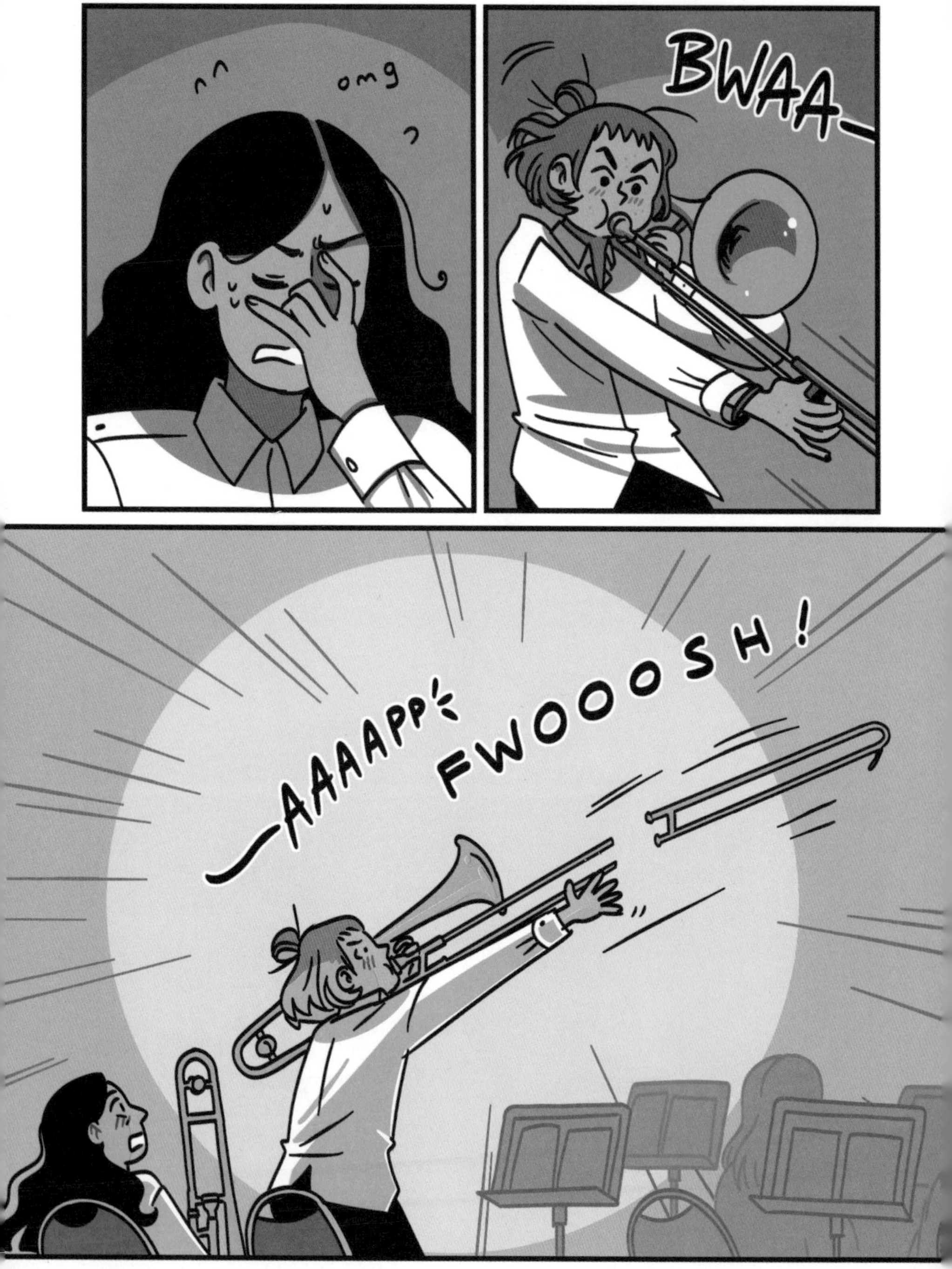
omg
BWAA-
-AAAAPP
FWOOOOSH!

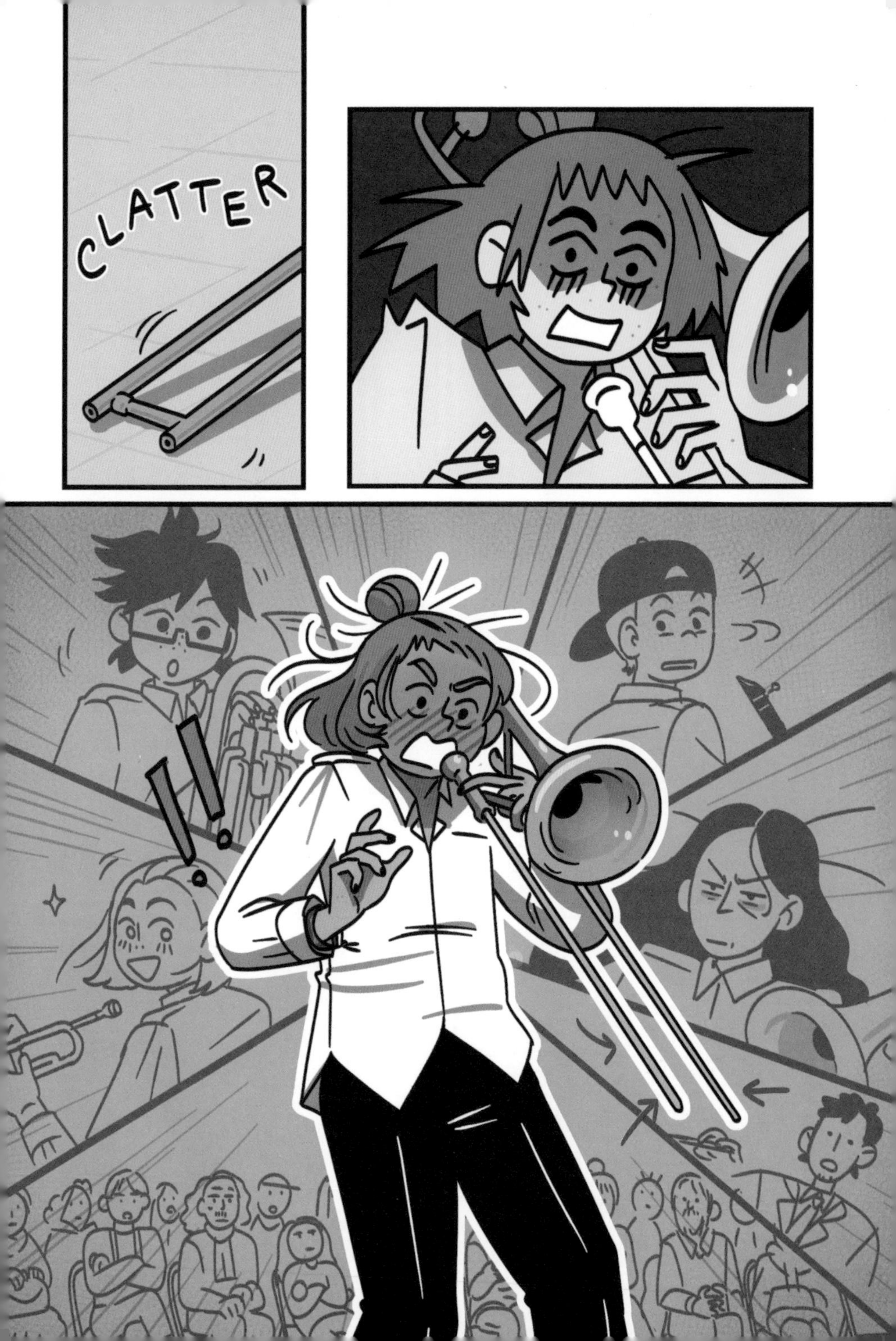
CLATTER
!!

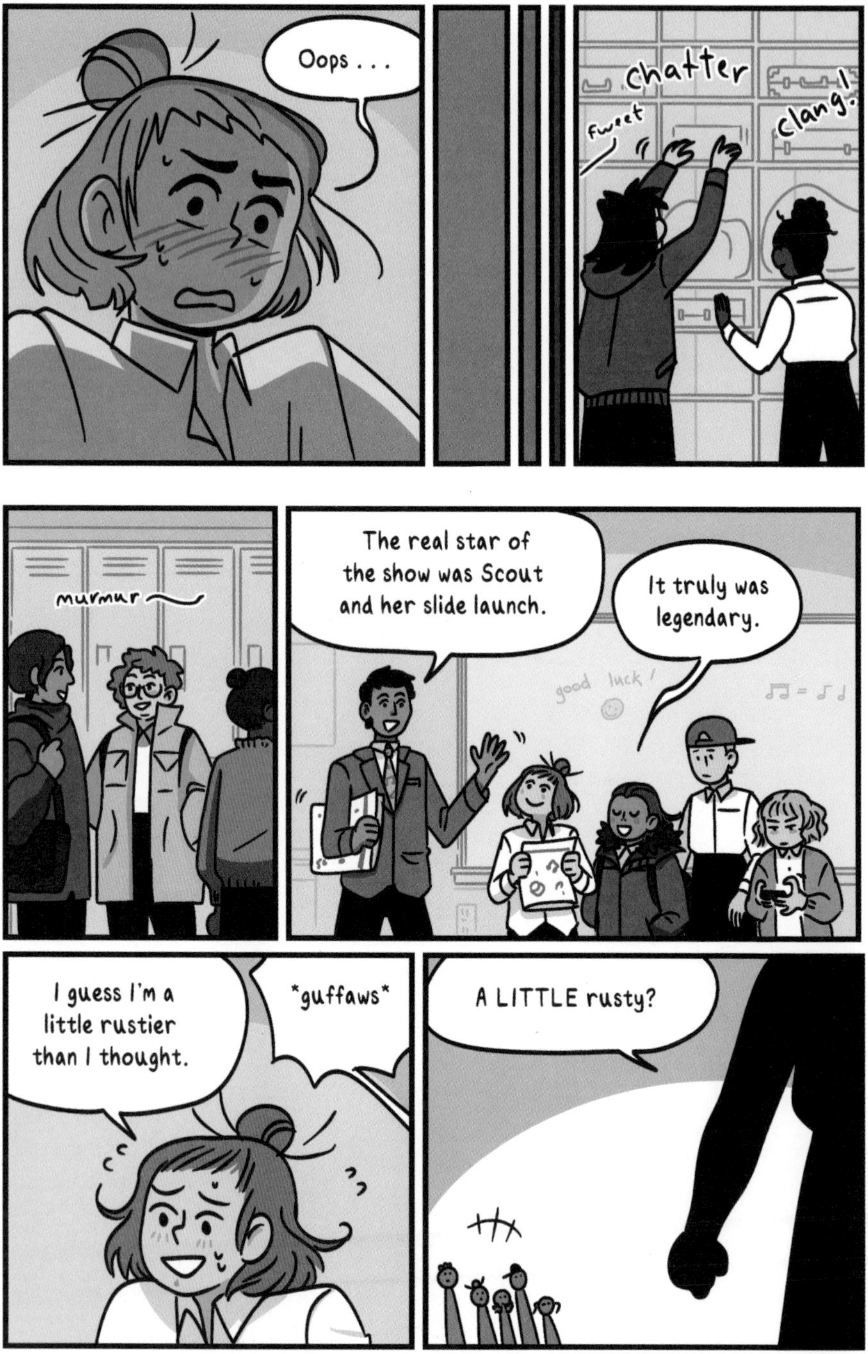
Oops . . .
Chatter
Fweet
Clang!
murmur
The real star of the show was Scout and her slide launch.
It truly was legendary.
good luck!
I guess I'm a little rustier than I thought.
guffaws
A LITTLE rusty?

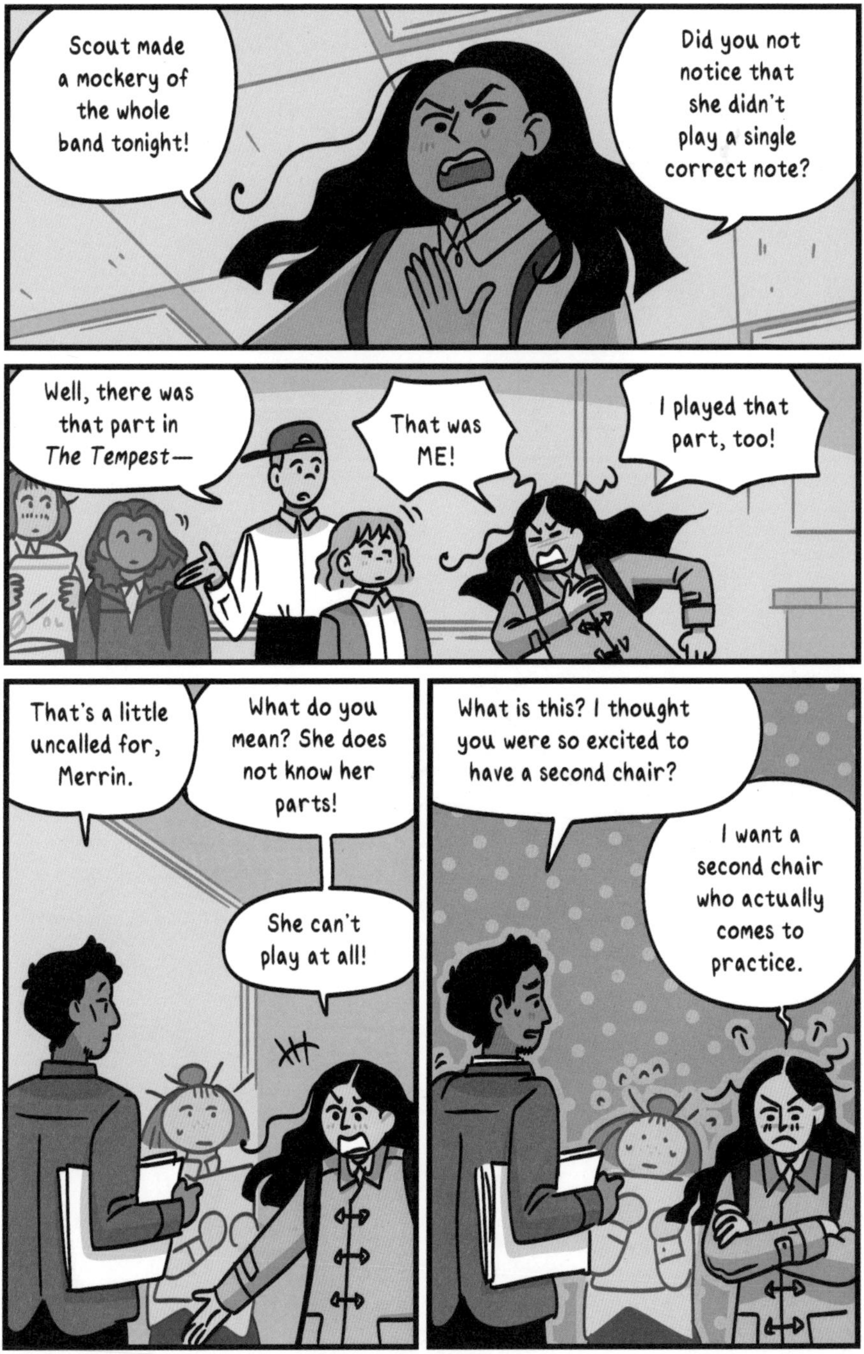

Scout made a mockery of the whole band tonight!
Did you not notice that she didn't play a single correct note?
Well, there was that part in *The Tempest*—
That was ME!
I played that part, too!
That's a little uncalled for, Merrin.
What do you mean? She does not know her parts!
She can't play at all!
What is this? I thought you were so excited to have a second chair?
I want a second chair who actually comes to practice.

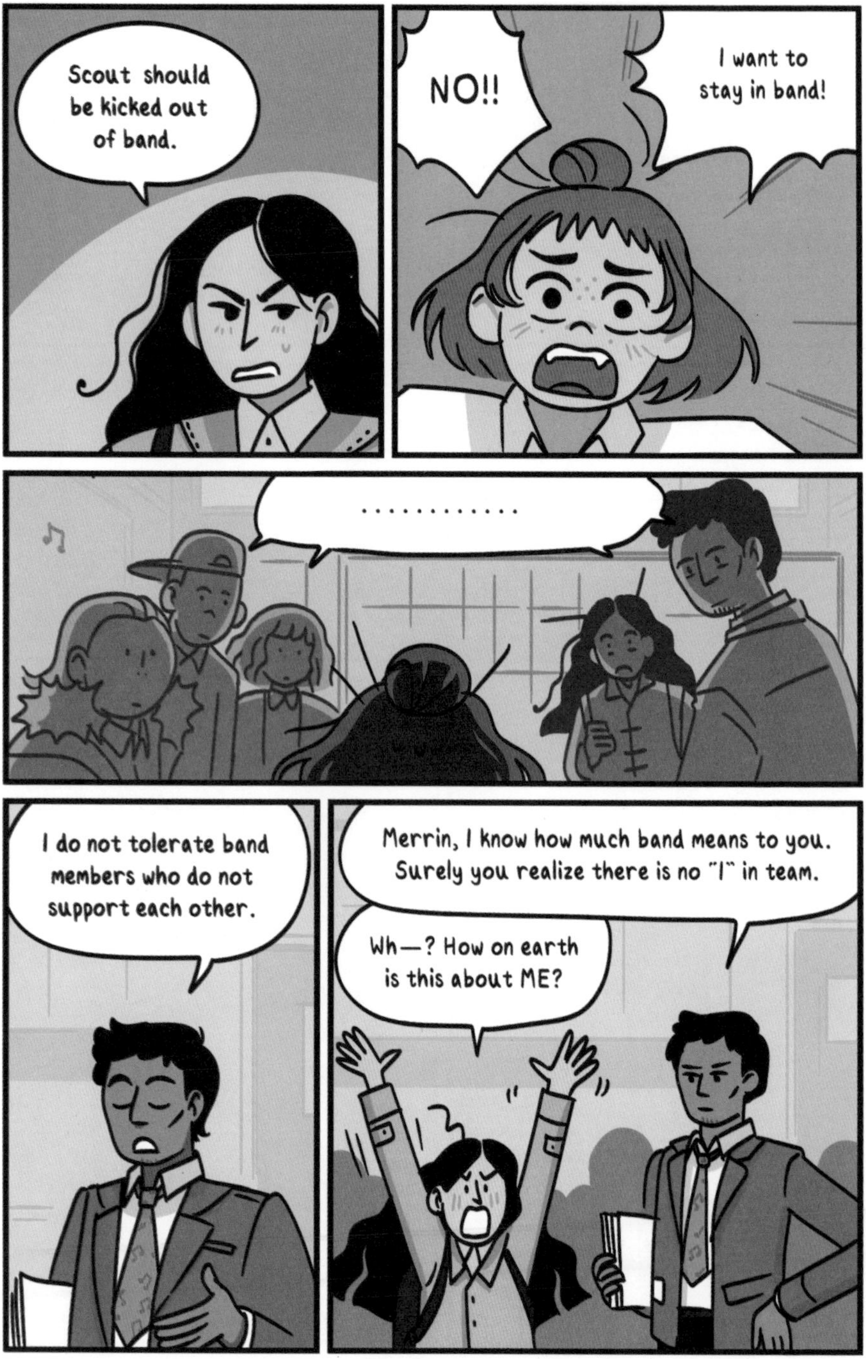
Scout should be kicked out of band.
NO!!
I want to stay in band!
. . . .
I do not tolerate band members who do not support each other.
Merrin, I know how much band means to you. Surely you realize there is no "I" in team.
Wh—? How on earth is this about ME?

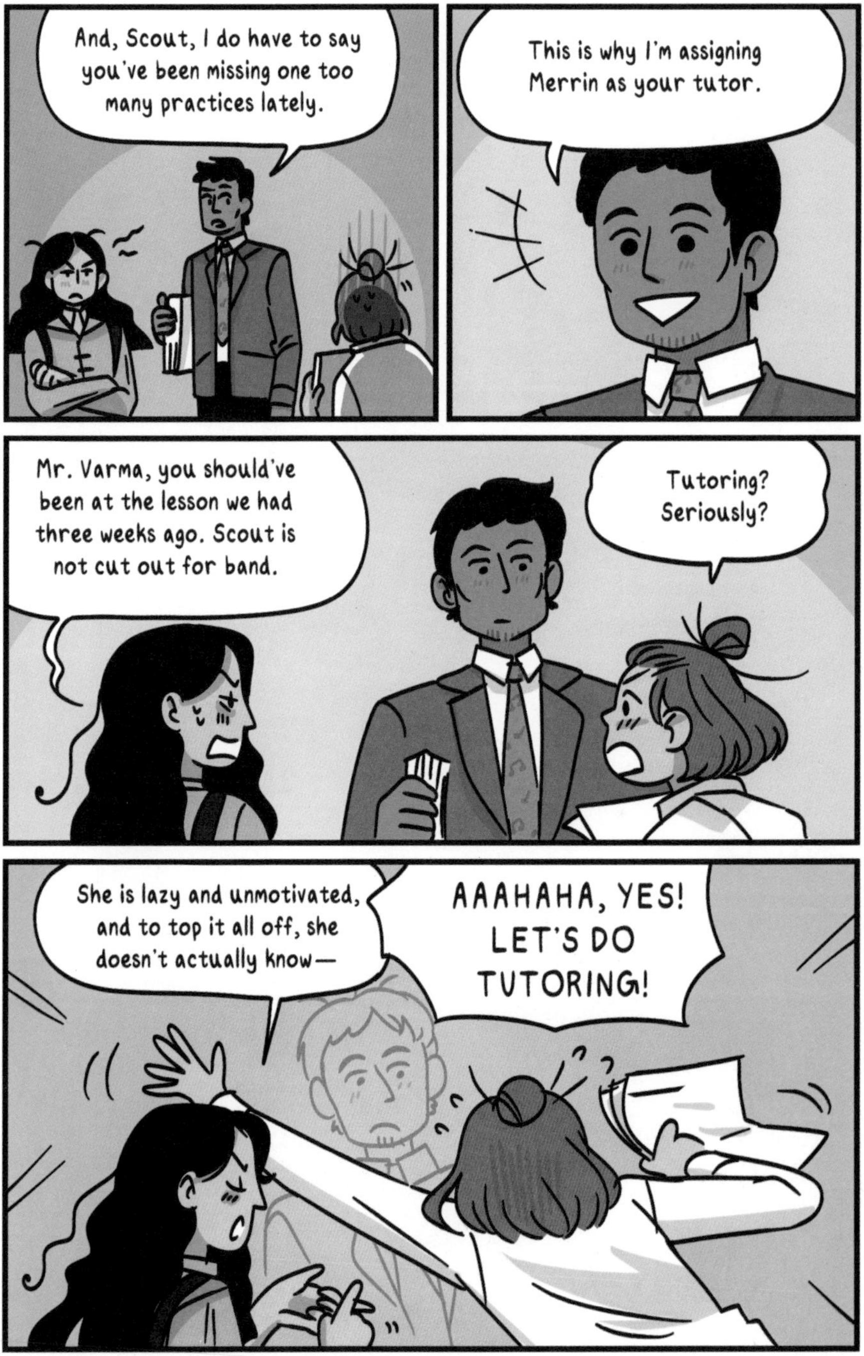
And, Scout, I do have to say you've been missing one too many practices lately.
This is why I'm assigning Merrin as your tutor.
Mr. Varma, you should've been at the lesson we had three weeks ago. Scout is not cut out for band.
Tutoring? Seriously?
She is lazy and unmotivated, and to top it all off, she doesn't actually know—
AAAHAHA, YES! LET'S DO TUTORING!

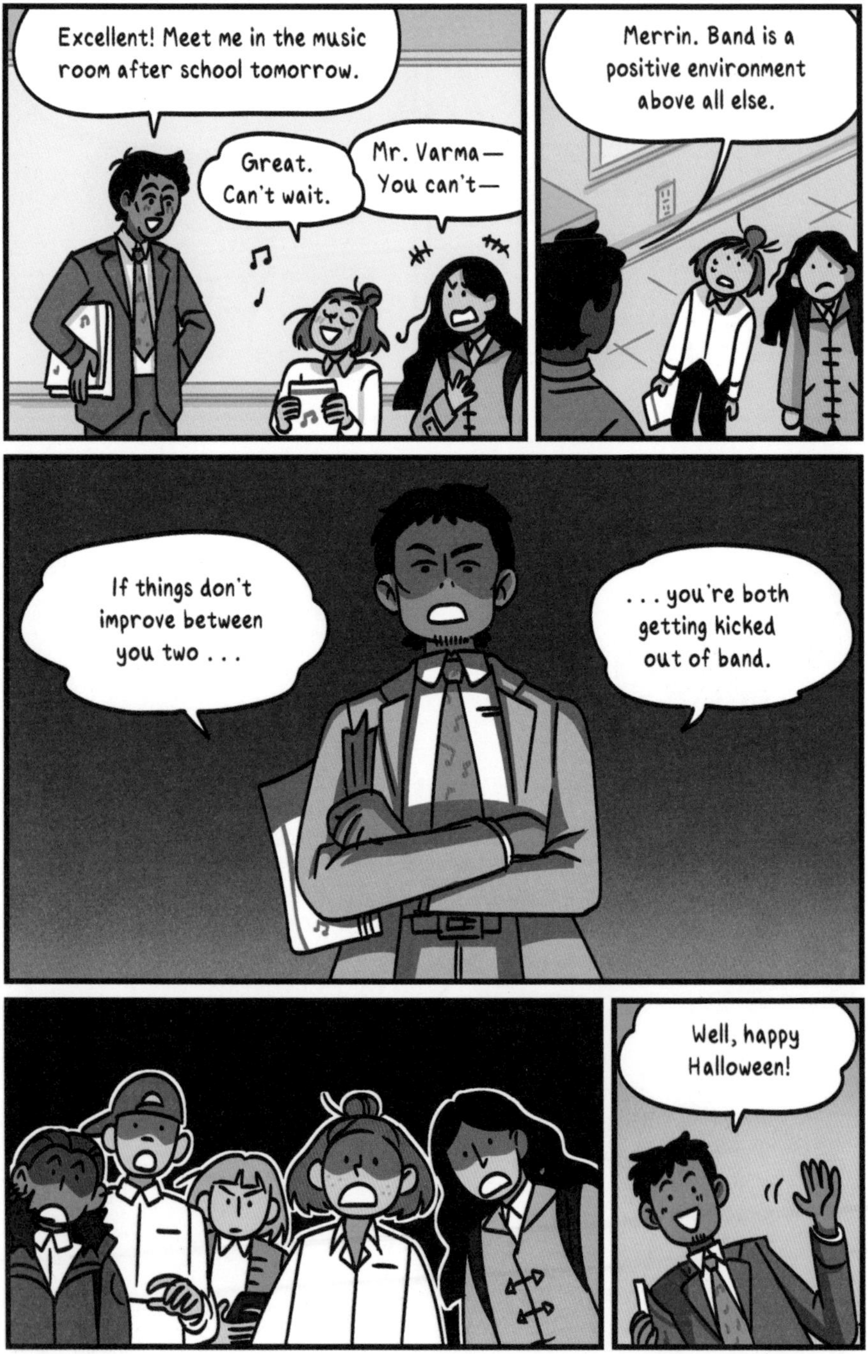

Excellent! Meet me in the music room after school tomorrow.
Great. Can't wait.
Mr. Varma— You can't—
Merrin. Band is a positive environment above all else.
If things don't improve between you two . . .
. . . you're both getting kicked out of band.
Well, happy Halloween!

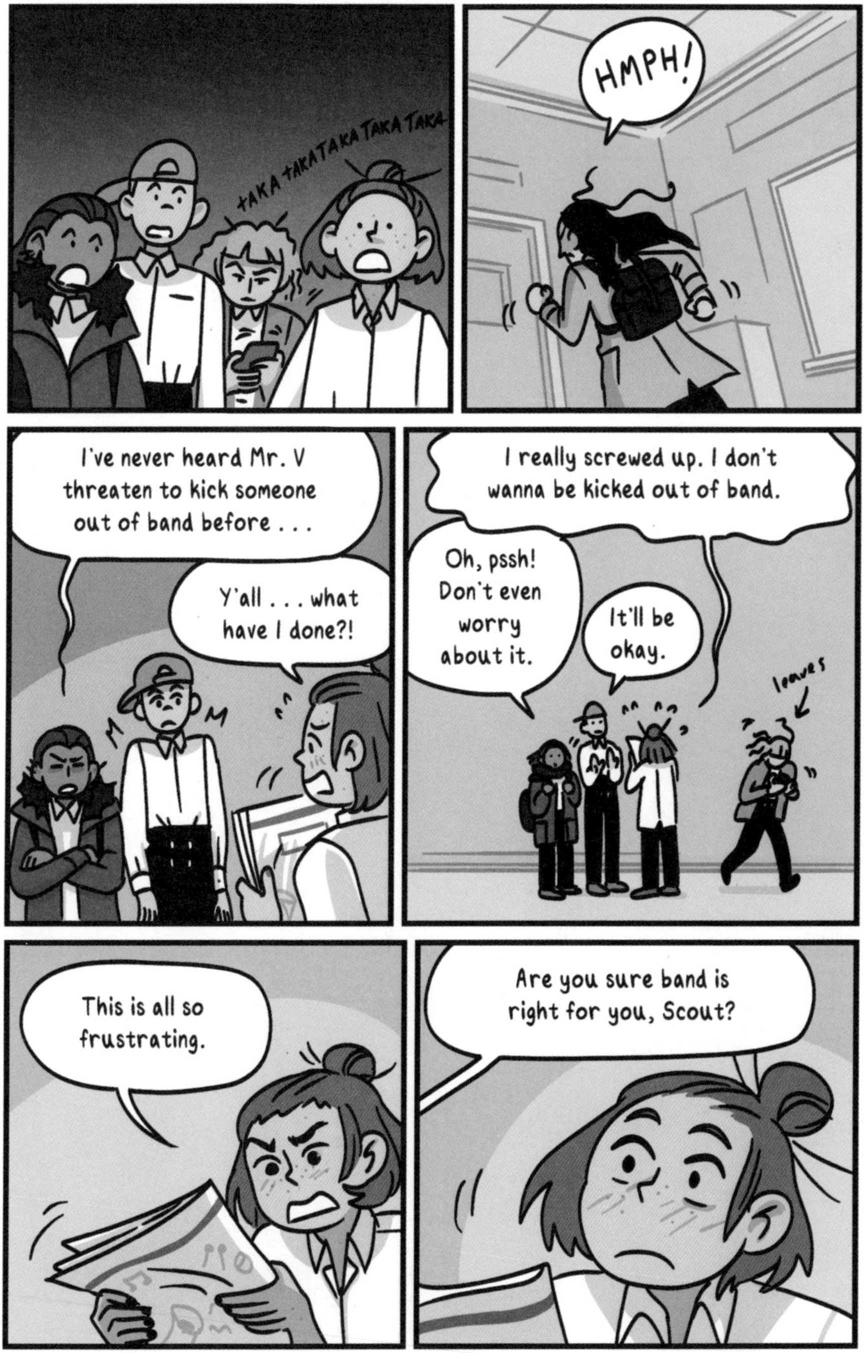
TAKA TAKA TAKA TAKA TAKA TAKA
HMPH!
I've never heard Mr. V threaten to kick someone out of band before . . .
Y'all . . . what have I done?!
I really screwed up. I don't wanna be kicked out of band.
Oh, pssh! Don't even worry about it.
It'll be okay.
leaves
This is all so frustrating.
Are you sure band is right for you, Scout?

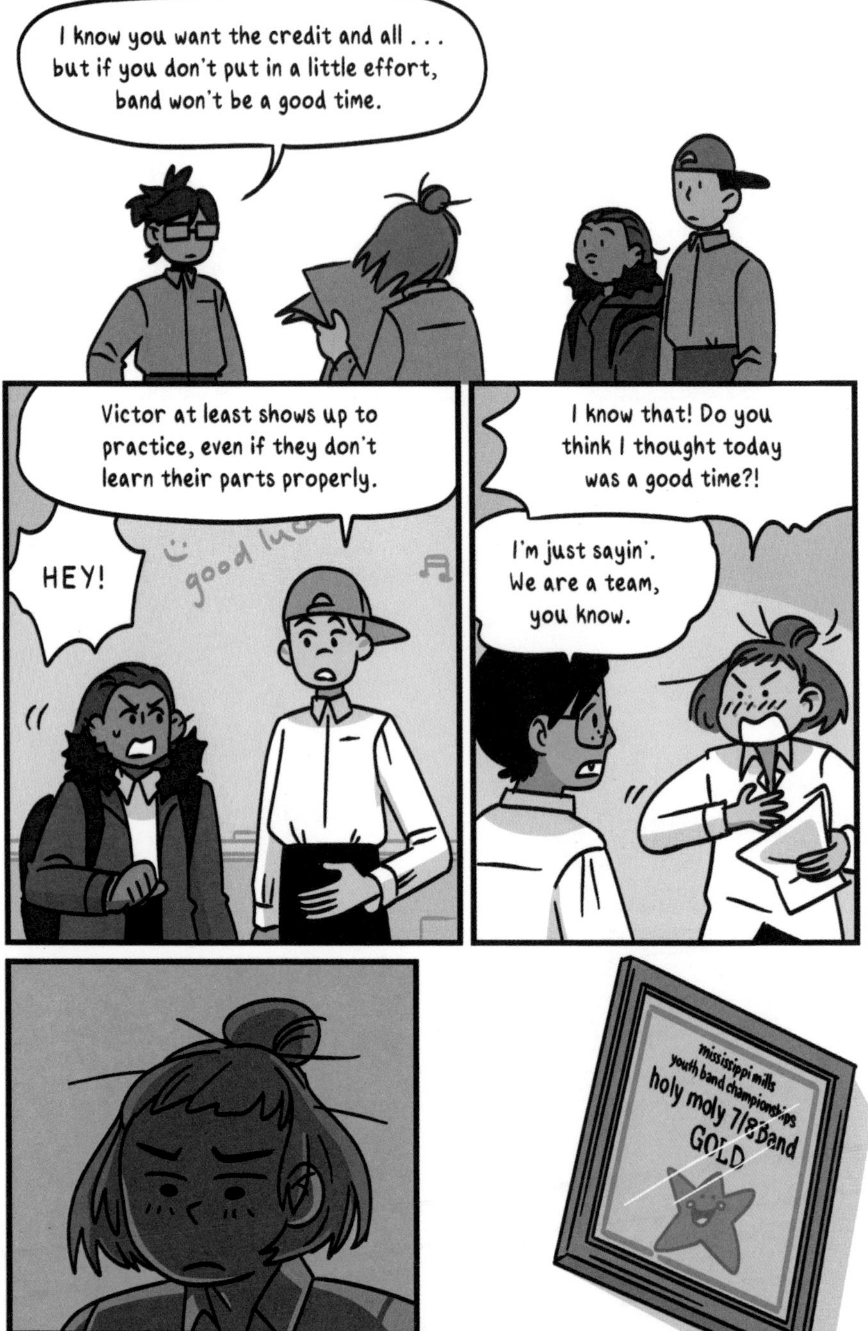

I know you want the credit and all . . . but if you don't put in a little effort, band won't be a good time.
Victor at least shows up to practice, even if they don't learn their parts properly.
HEY!
I know that! Do you think I thought today was a good time?!
I'm just sayin'. We are a team, you know.
mississippi mills
youth band championships
holy moly 7/8 Band
GOLD

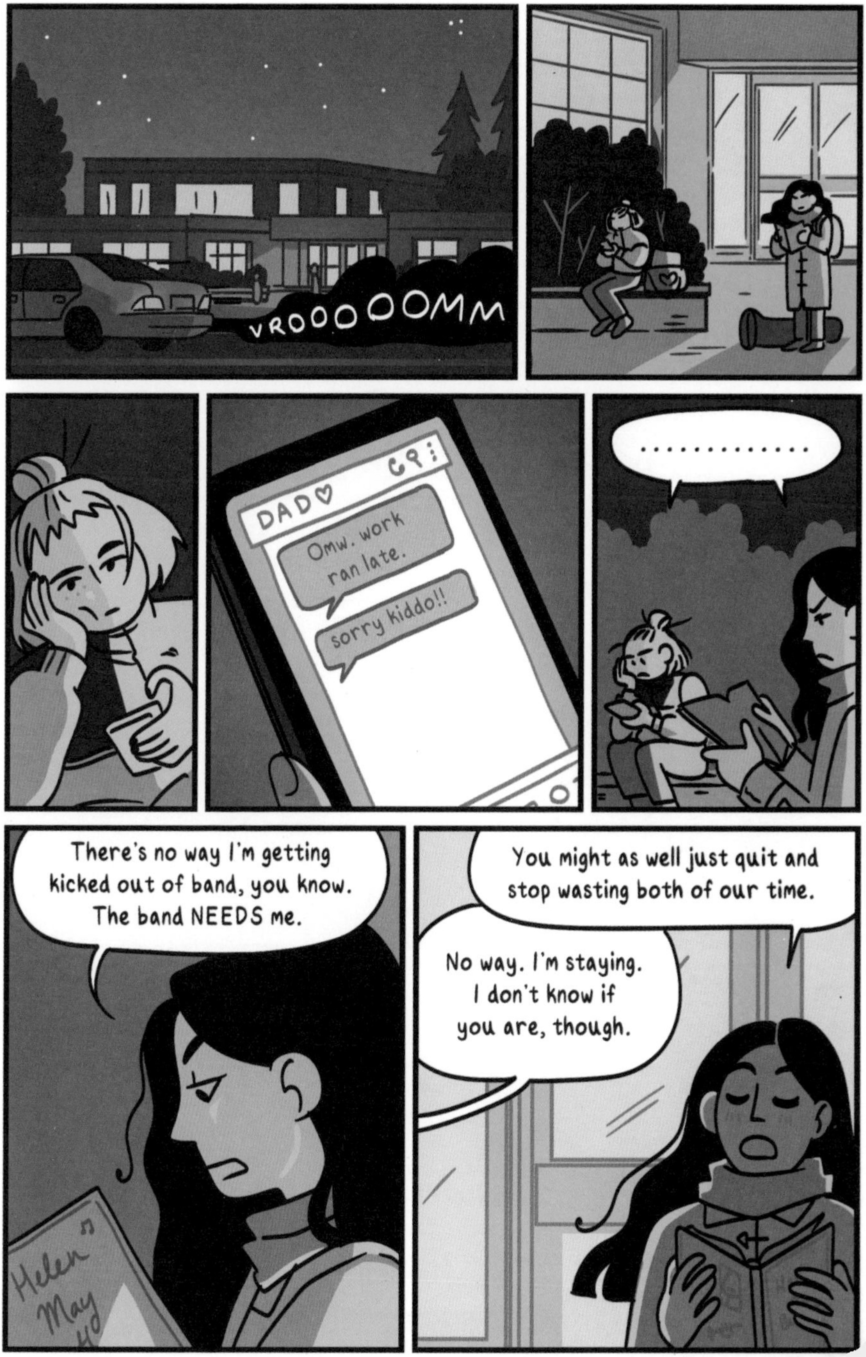
VROOOOOMM
DAD♡
Omw. work ran late.
sorry kiddo!!
....
There's no way I'm getting kicked out of band, you know. The band NEEDS me.
Helen May
You might as well just quit and stop wasting both of our time.
No way. I'm staying. I don't know if you are, though.

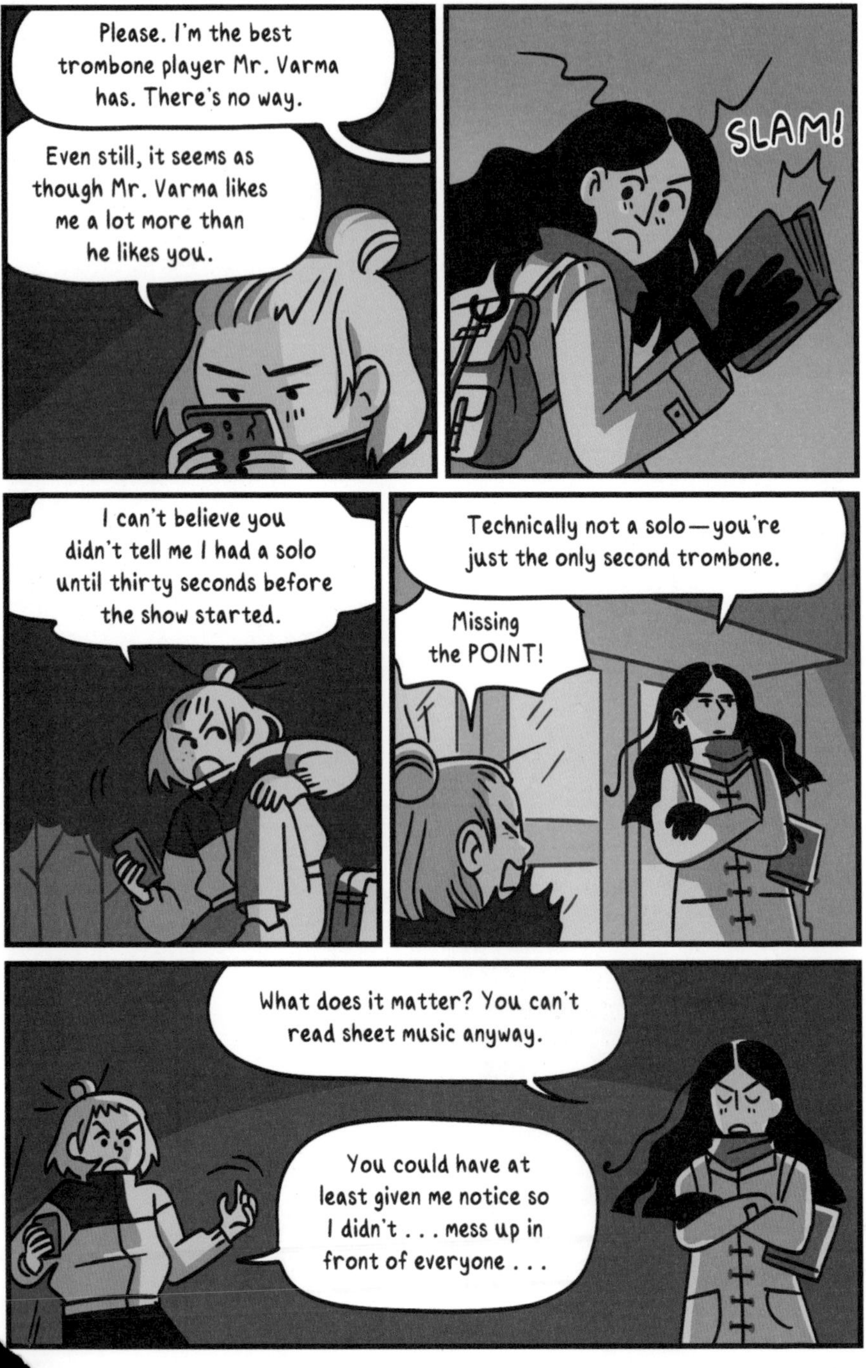
Please. I'm the best trombone player Mr. Varma has. There's no way.
Even still, it seems as though Mr. Varma likes me a lot more than he likes you.
SLAM!
I can't believe you didn't tell me I had a solo until thirty seconds before the show started.
Technically not a solo—you're just the only second trombone.
Missing the POINT!
What does it matter? You can't read sheet music anyway.
You could have at least given me notice so I didn't . . . mess up in front of everyone . . .

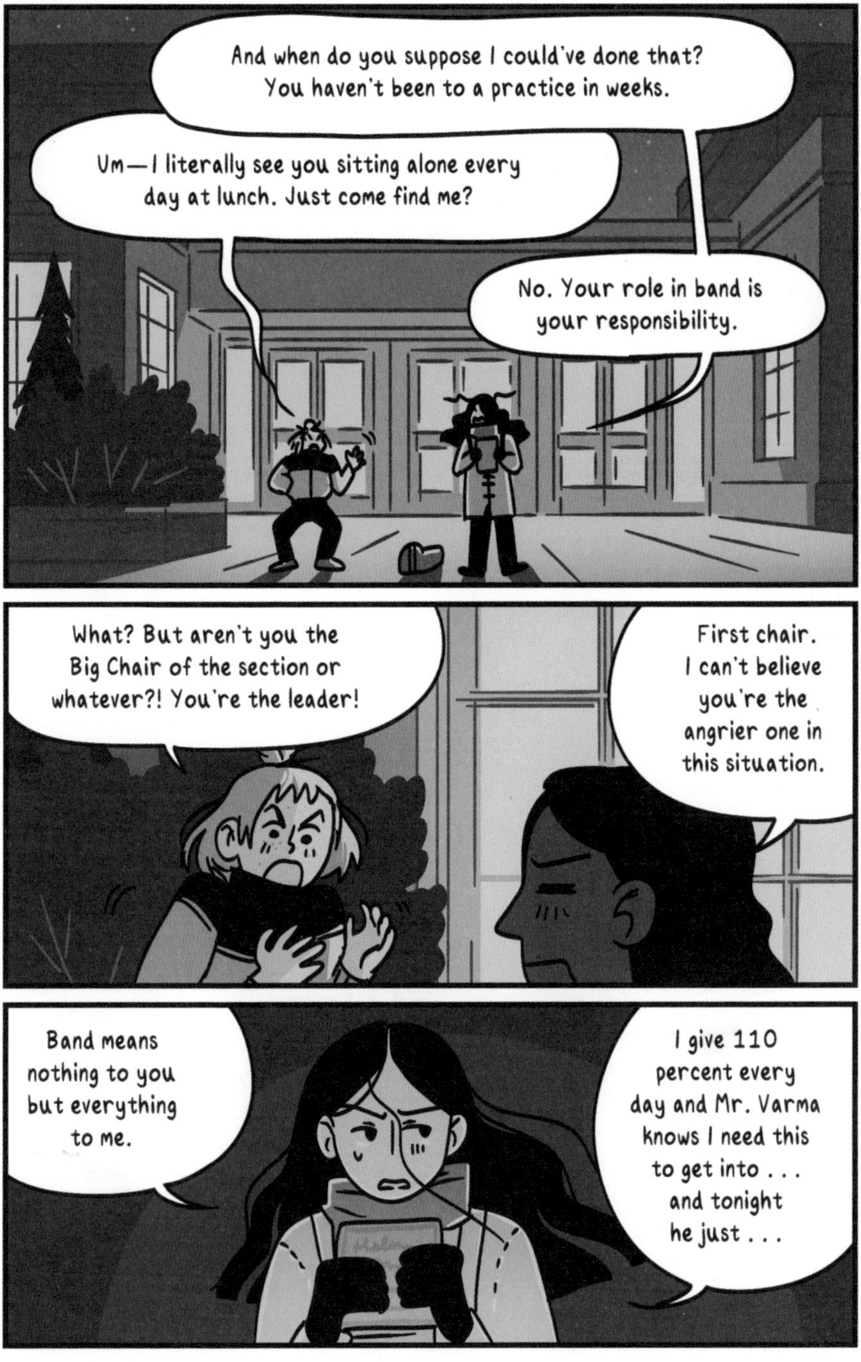

And when do you suppose I could've done that? You haven't been to a practice in weeks.
Um—I literally see you sitting alone every day at lunch. Just come find me?
No. Your role in band is your responsibility.
What? But aren't you the Big Chair of the section or whatever?! You're the leader!
First chair. I can't believe you're the angrier one in this situation.
Band means nothing to you but everything to me.
I give 110 percent every day and Mr. Varma knows I need this to get into . . . and tonight he just . . .

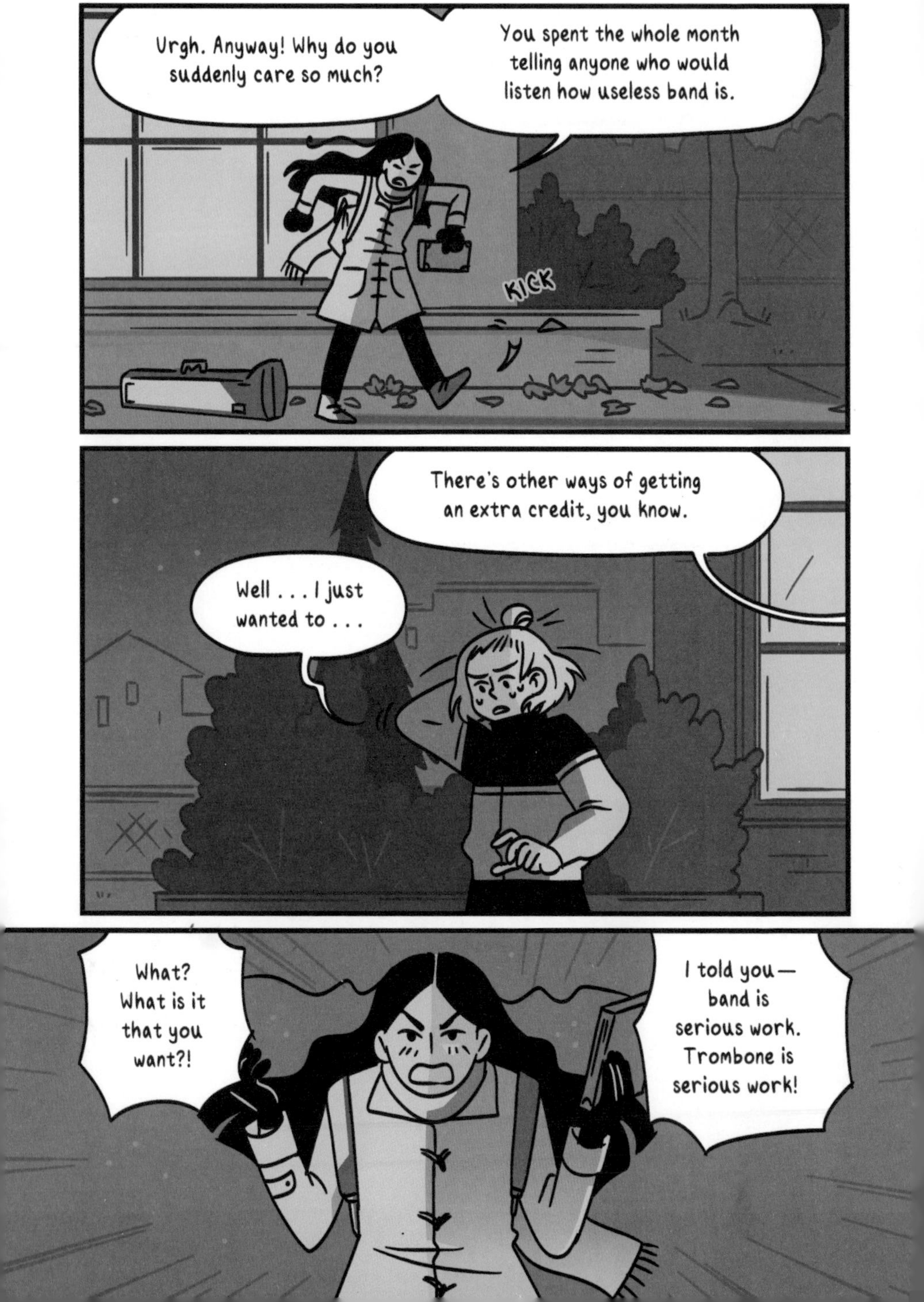
Urgh. Anyway! Why do you suddenly care so much?
You spent the whole month telling anyone who would listen how useless band is.
KICK
There's other ways of getting an extra credit, you know.
Well . . . I just wanted to . . .
What? What is it that you want?!
I told you— band is serious work. Trombone is serious work!

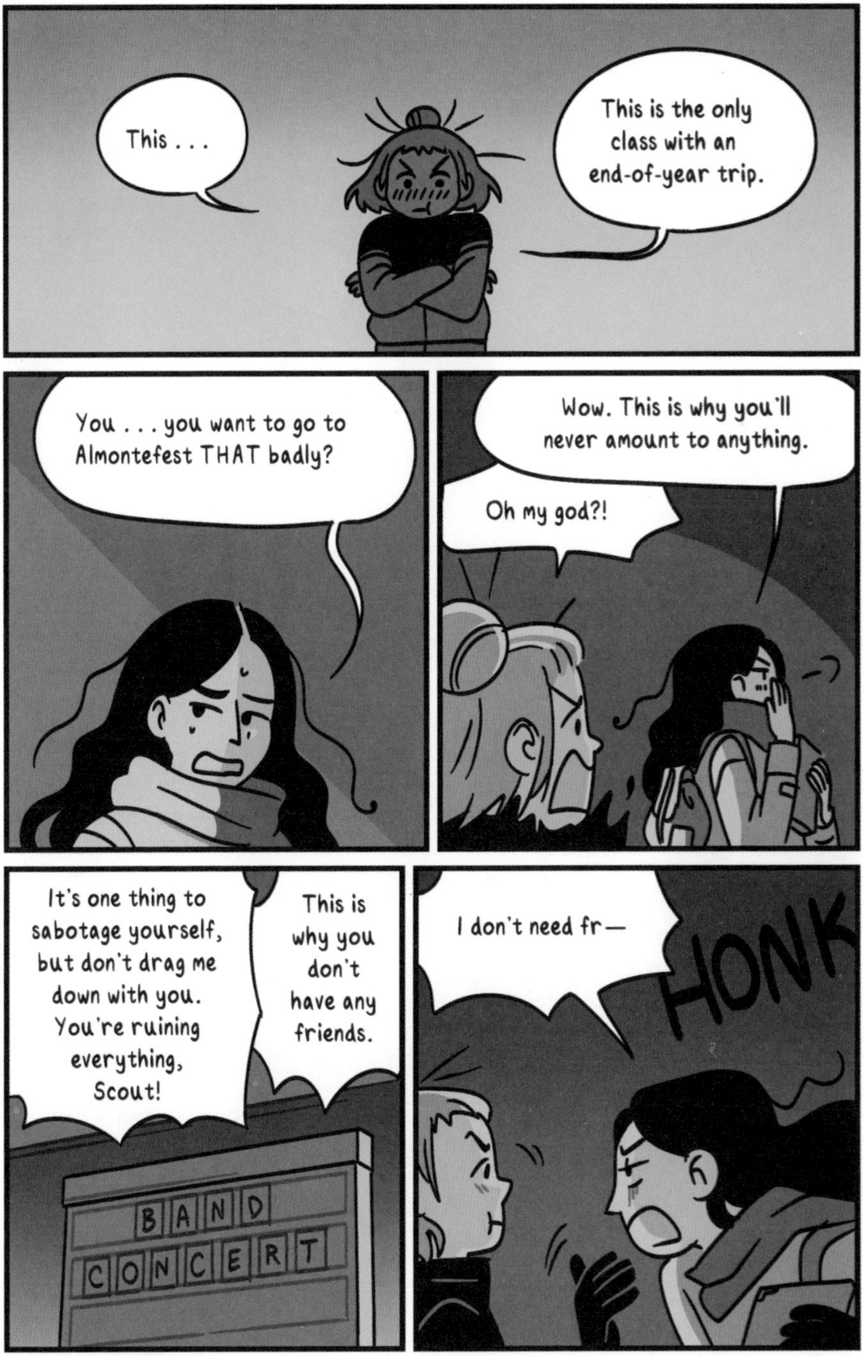
This . . .
This is the only class with an end-of-year trip.
You . . . you want to go to Almontefest THAT badly?
Wow. This is why you'll never amount to anything.
Oh my god?!
It's one thing to sabotage yourself, but don't drag me down with you. You're ruining everything, Scout!
This is why you don't have any friends.
BAND CONCERT
I don't need fr—
HONK

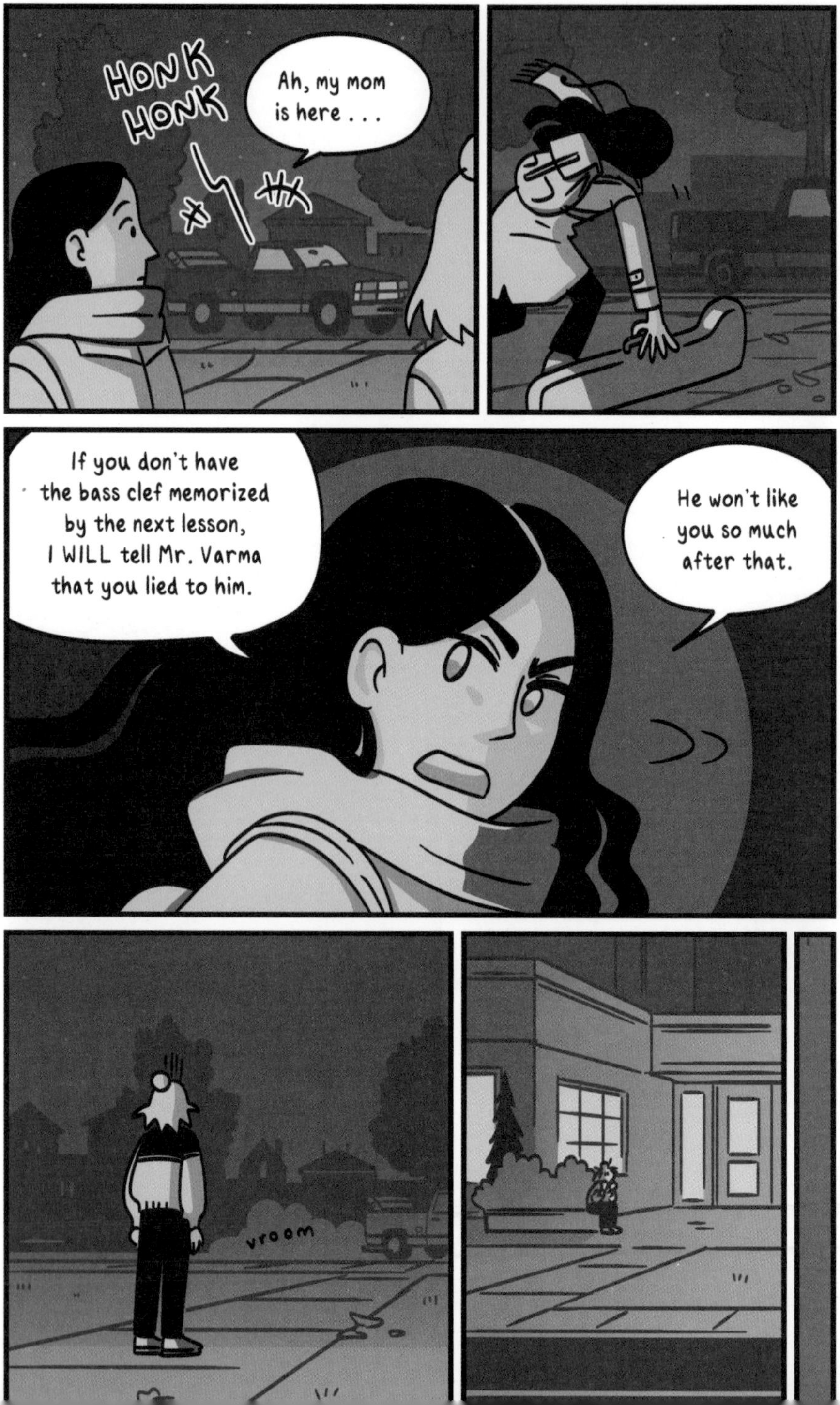
HONK HONK
Ah, my mom is here . . .
If you don't have the bass clef memorized by the next lesson, I WILL tell Mr. Varma that you lied to him.
He won't like you so much after that.
vroom

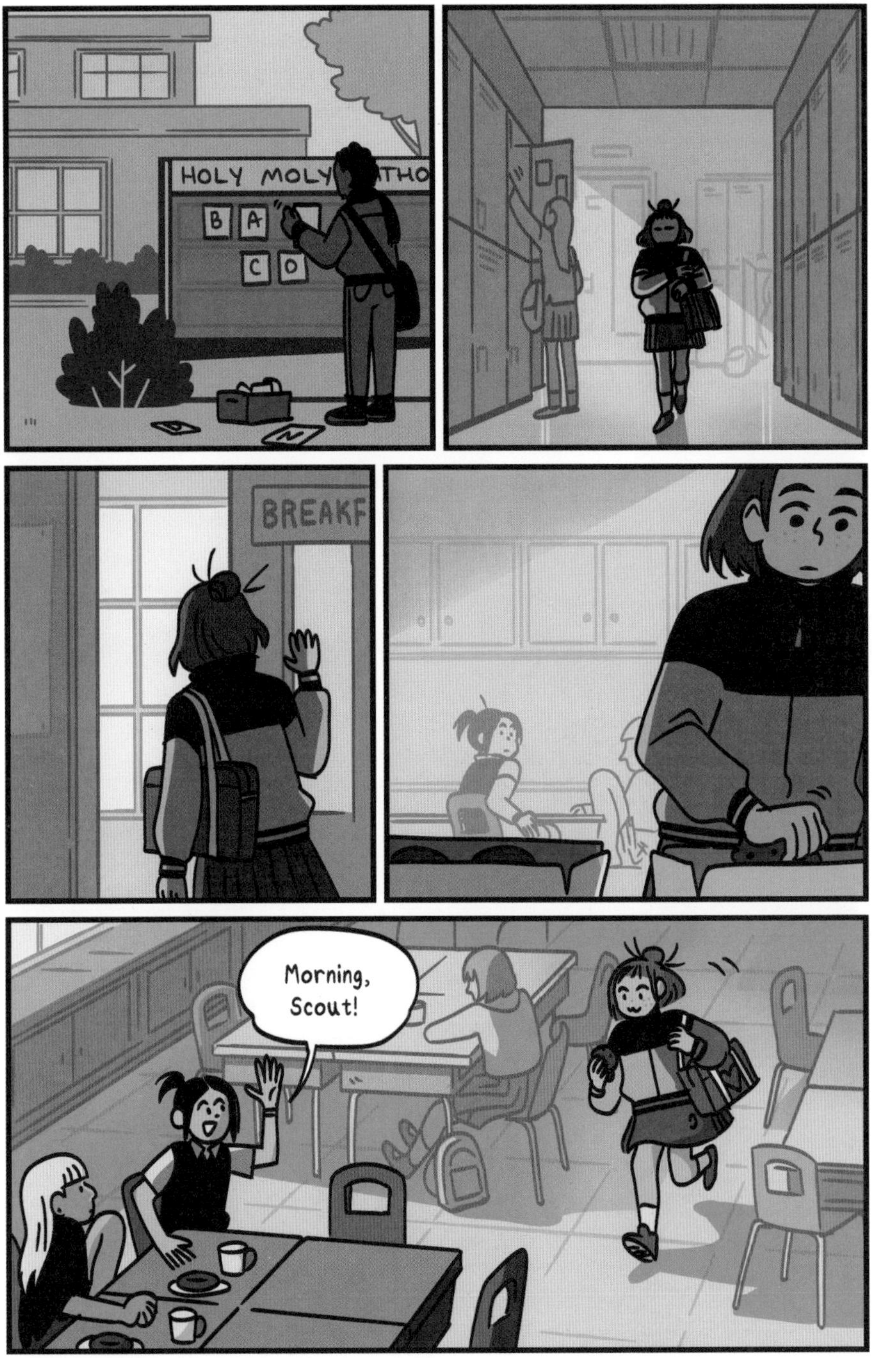
HOLY MOLY
THO
B A
C O
BREAKF
Morning, Scout!

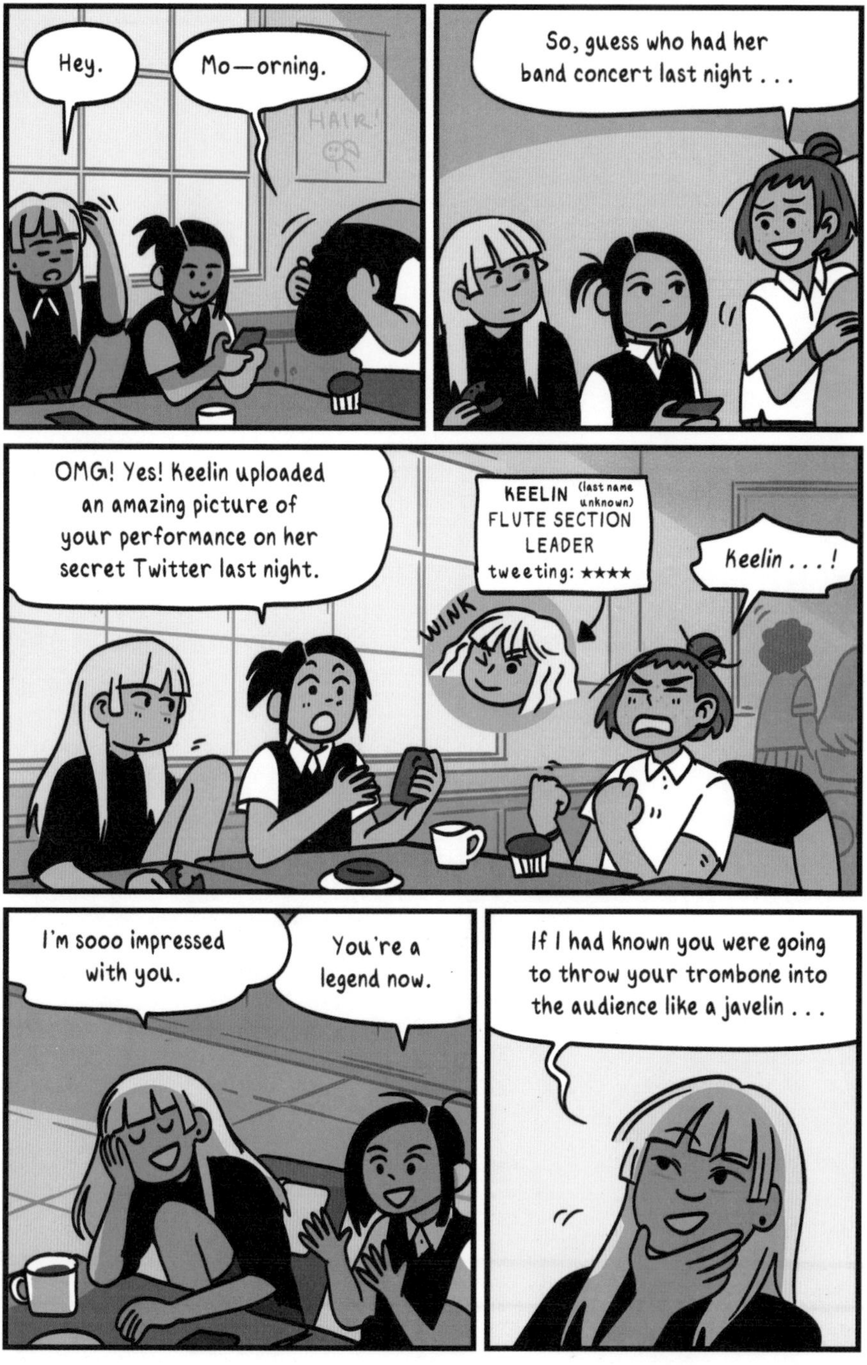
Hey.
Mo—orning.
HAIR!
So, guess who had her band concert last night . . .
OMG! Yes! Keelin uploaded an amazing picture of your performance on her secret Twitter last night.
KEELIN (last name unknown) FLUTE SECTION LEADER tweeting: ★★★★
WINK
Keelin . . . !
I'm sooo impressed with you.
You're a legend now.
If I had known you were going to throw your trombone into the audience like a javelin . . .

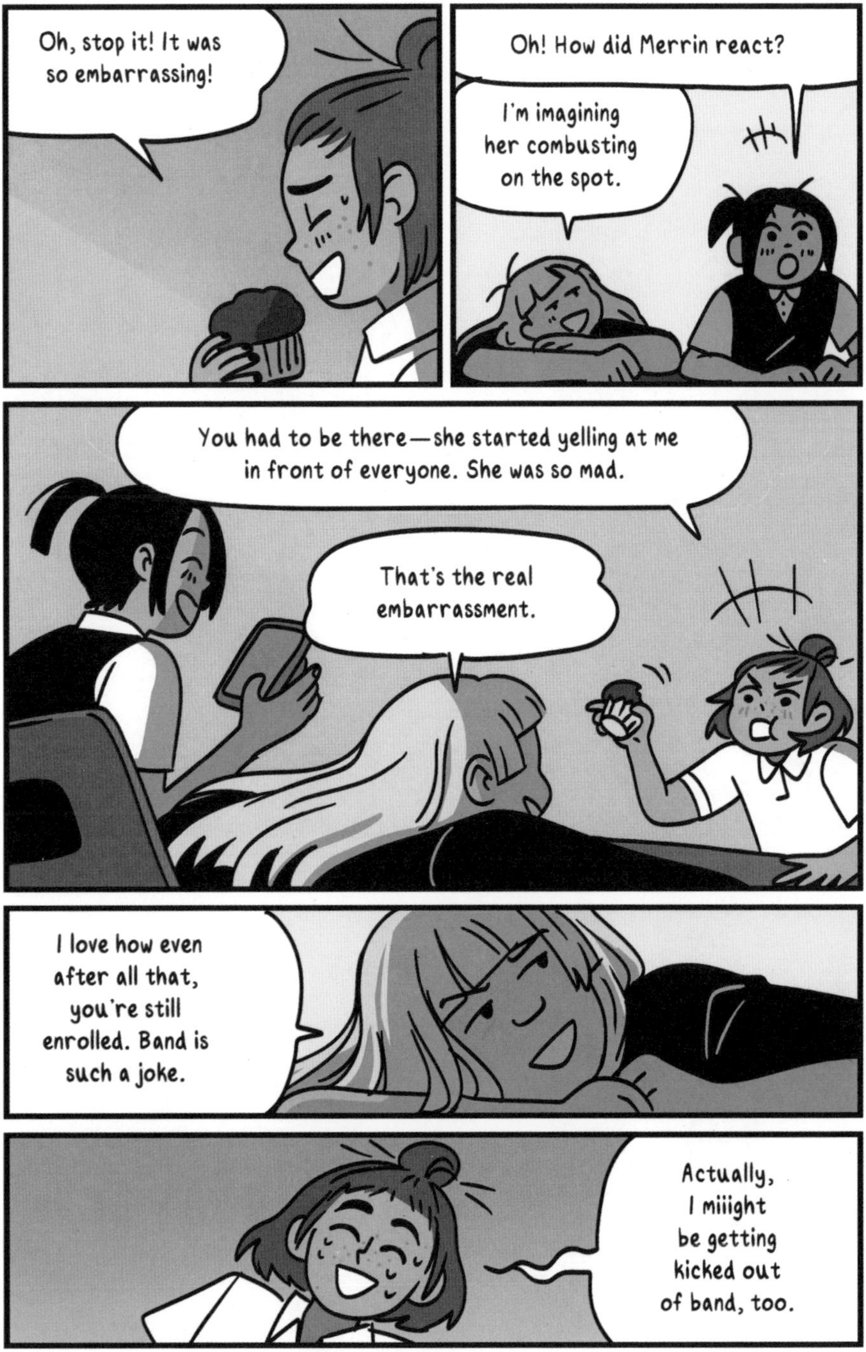
Oh, stop it! It was so embarrassing!
Oh! How did Merrin react?
I'm imagining her combusting on the spot.
You had to be there—she started yelling at me in front of everyone. She was so mad.
That's the real embarrassment.
I love how even after all that, you're still enrolled. Band is such a joke.
Actually, I miiight be getting kicked out of band, too.

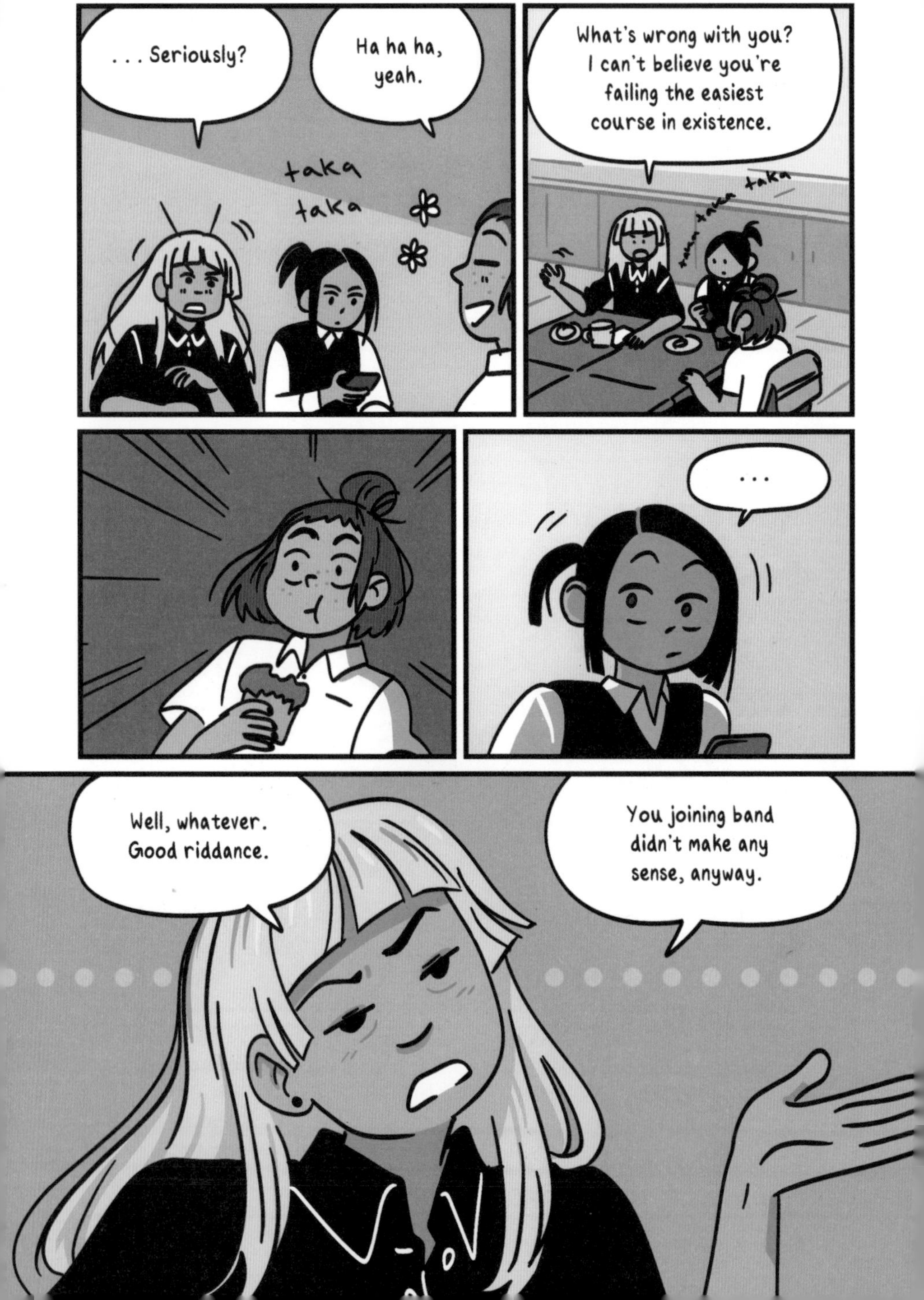
. . . Seriously?
Ha ha ha, yeah.
taka taka
What's wrong with you? I can't believe you're failing the easiest course in existence.
taka taka taka
. . .
Well, whatever. Good riddance.
You joining band didn't make any sense, anyway.

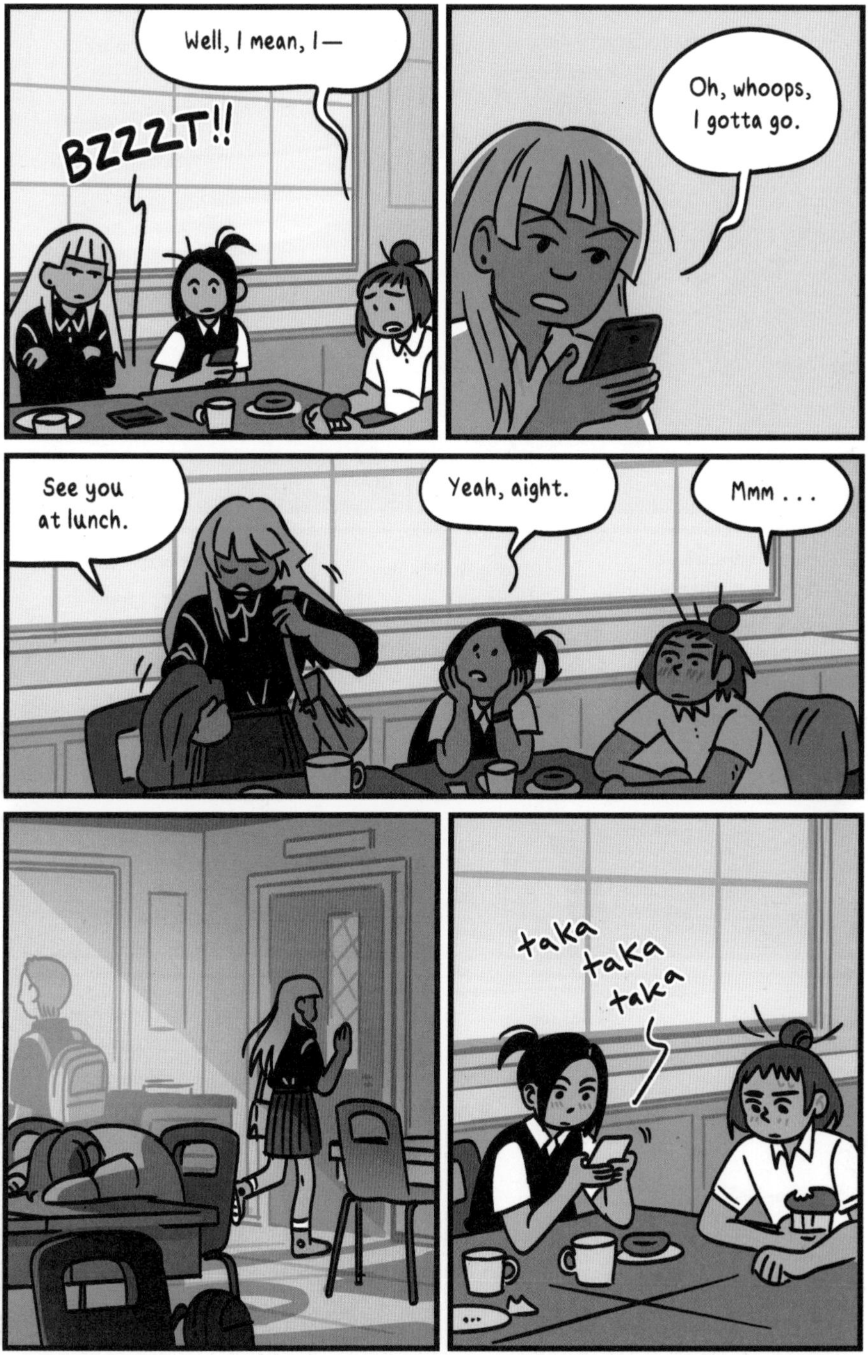
Well, I mean, I—
BZZZT!!
Oh, whoops, I gotta go.
See you at lunch.
Yeah, aight.
Mmm . . .
taka
taka
taka

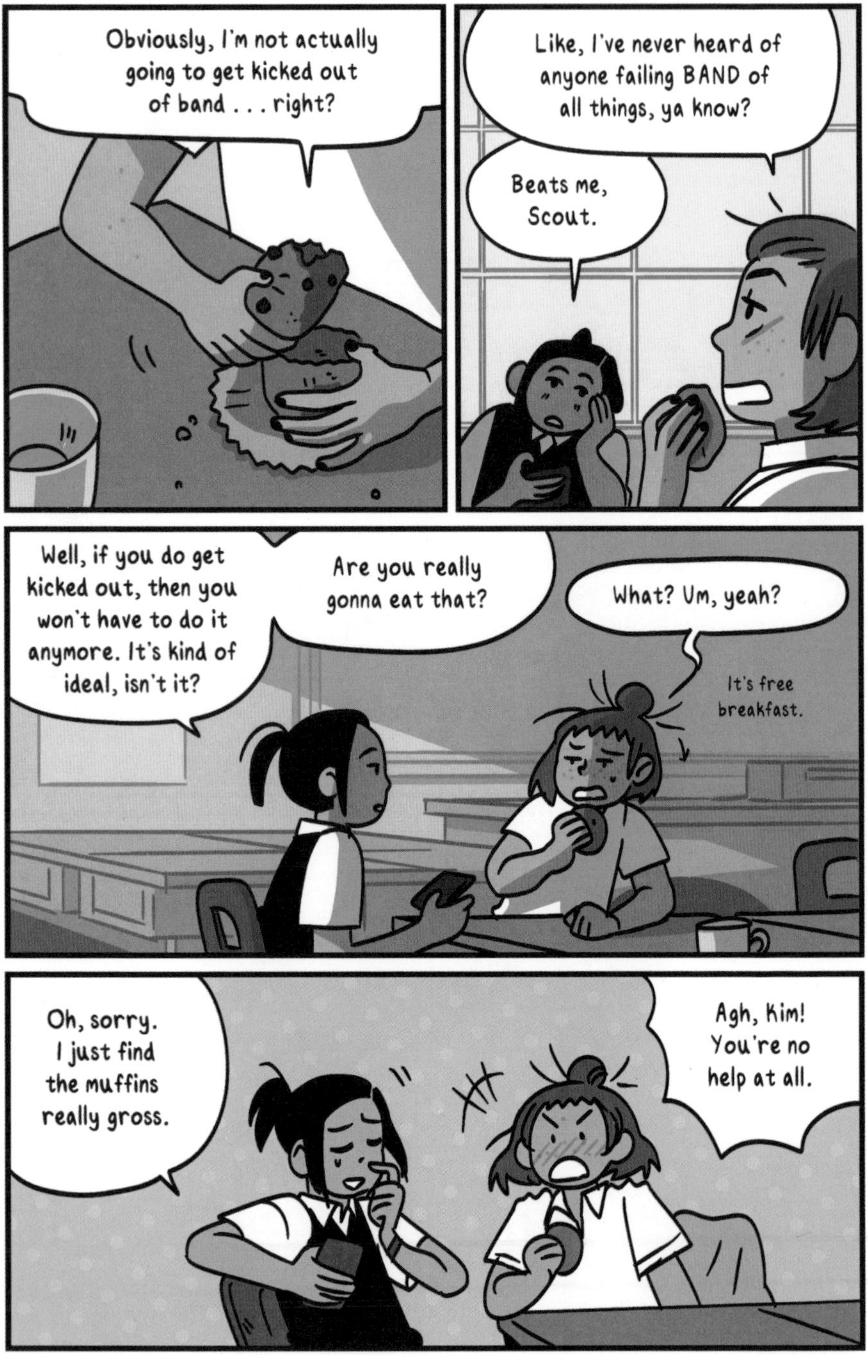

Obviously, I'm not actually going to get kicked out of band . . . right?
Like, I've never heard of anyone failing BAND of all things, ya know?
Beats me, Scout.
Well, if you do get kicked out, then you won't have to do it anymore. It's kind of ideal, isn't it?
Are you really gonna eat that?
What? Um, yeah?
It's free breakfast.
Oh, sorry. I just find the muffins really gross.
Agh, Kim! You're no help at all.

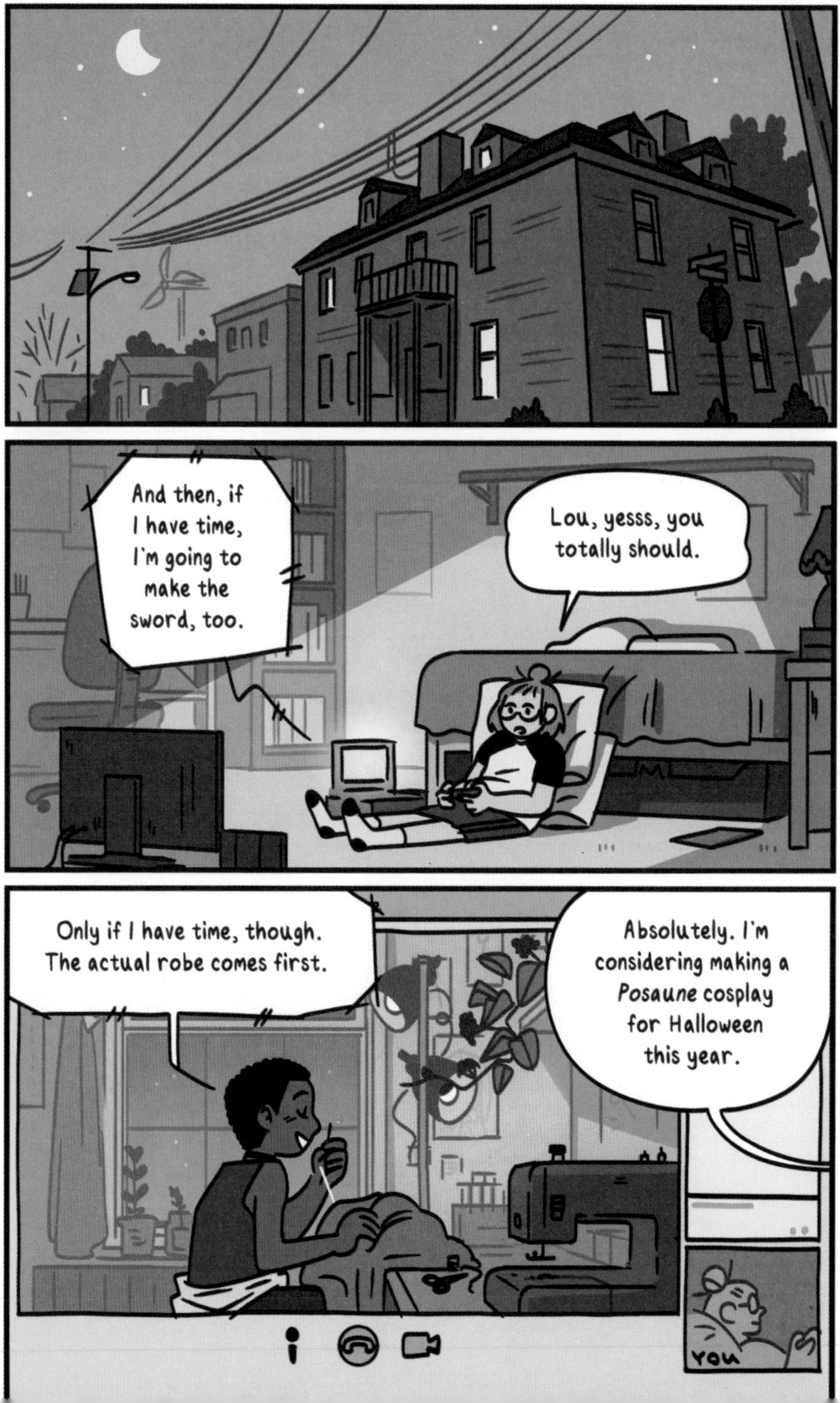
And then, if I have time, I'm going to make the sword, too.
Lou, yesss, you totally should.
Only if I have time, though. The actual robe comes first.
Absolutely. I'm considering making a *Posaune* cosplay for Halloween this year.
YOU

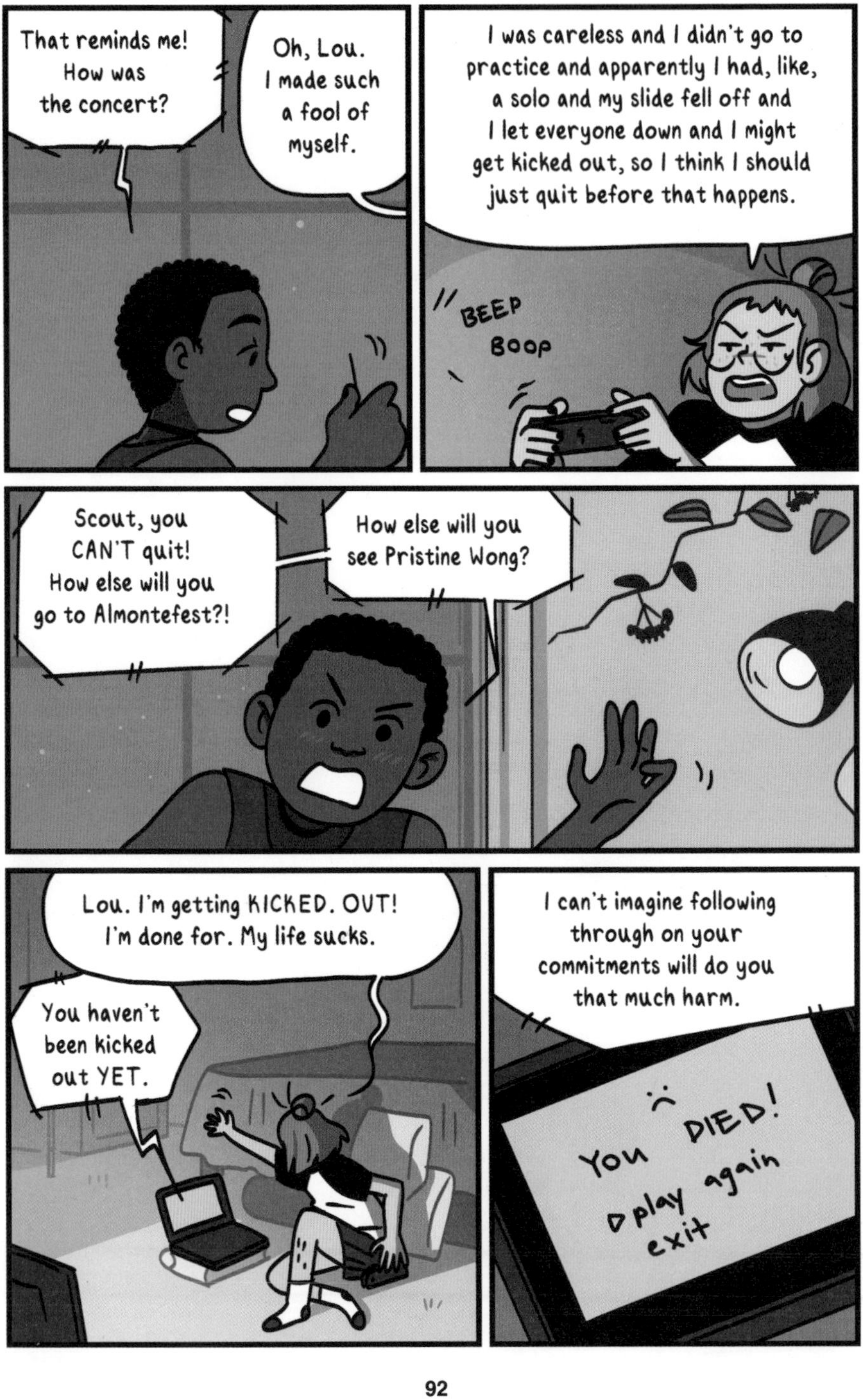
That reminds me! How was the concert?
Oh, Lou. I made such a fool of myself.
I was careless and I didn't go to practice and apparently I had, like, a solo and my slide fell off and I let everyone down and I might get kicked out, so I think I should just quit before that happens.
BEEP
BOOP
Scout, you CAN'T quit! How else will you go to Almontefest?!
How else will you see Pristine Wong?
Lou. I'm getting KICKED. OUT! I'm done for. My life sucks.
You haven't been kicked out YET.
I can't imagine following through on your commitments will do you that much harm.
You DIED!
play again
exit

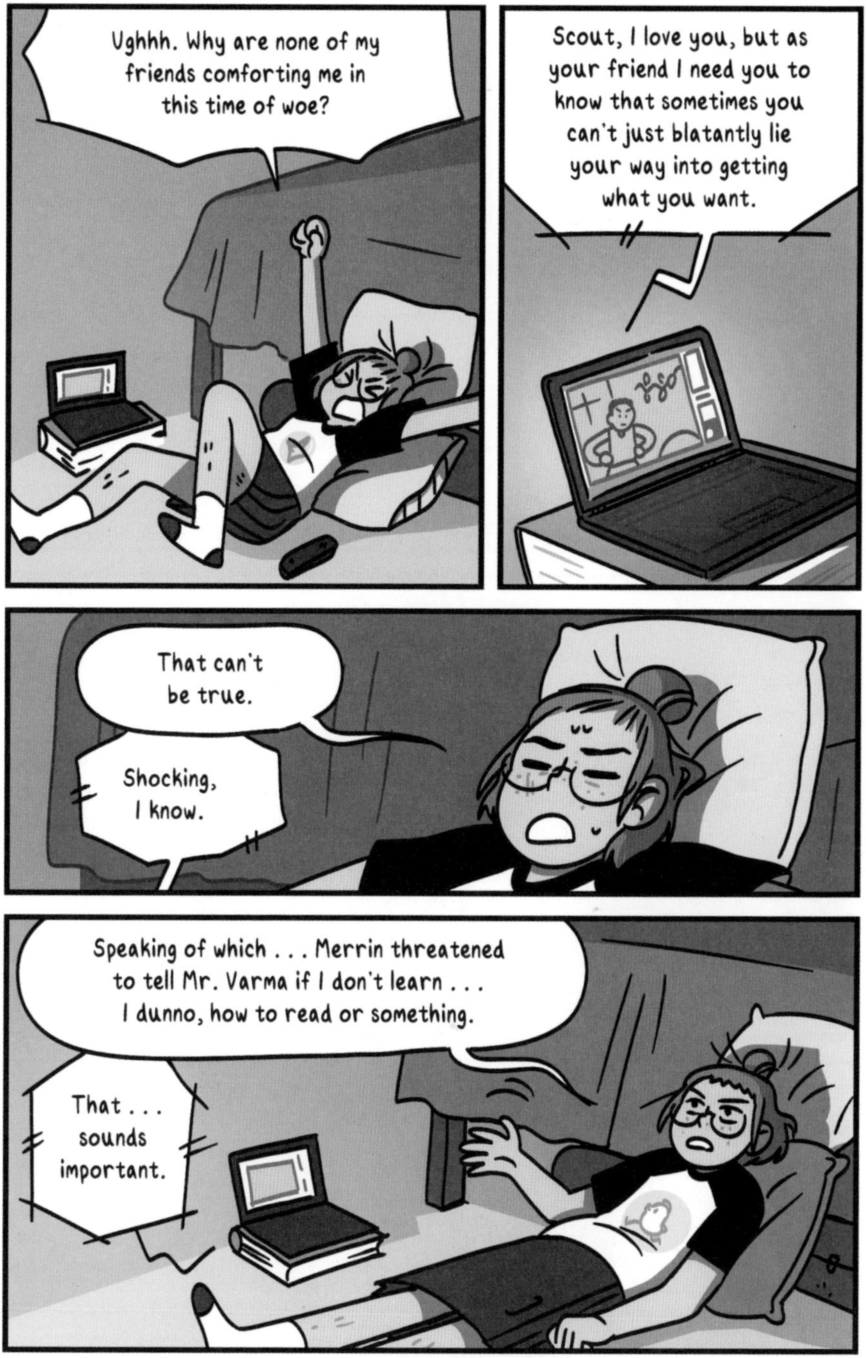
Ughhh. Why are none of my friends comforting me in this time of woe?
Scout, I love you, but as your friend I need you to know that sometimes you can't just blatantly lie your way into getting what you want.
That can't be true.
Shocking, I know.
Speaking of which . . . Merrin threatened to tell Mr. Varma if I don't learn . . . I dunno, how to read or something.
That . . . sounds important.

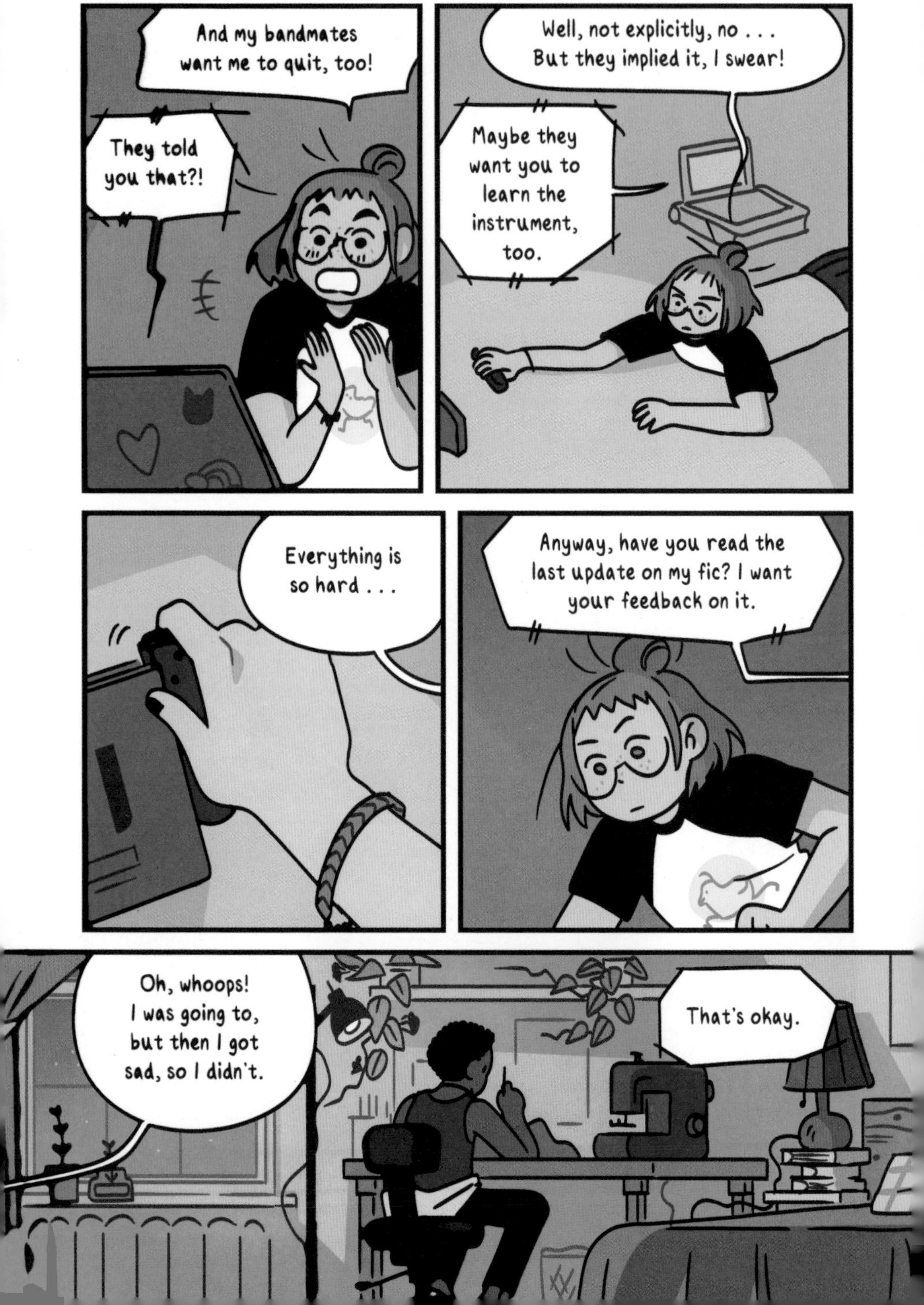
And my bandmates want me to quit, too!
They told you that?!
Well, not explicitly, no . . . But they implied it, I swear!
Maybe they want you to learn the instrument, too.
Everything is so hard . . .
Anyway, have you read the last update on my fic? I want your feedback on it.
Oh, whoops! I was going to, but then I got sad, so I didn't.
That's okay.

CLUNK!
shuffle
Oh dang, my dad's home. I gotta go. Love you!
'Ka—ay. Nighty nighty, Scout. Love you, too!
SLAM!
POSAUNE
pristine wong's
POSAUNE!!
FRIENDSH
is TEAMWORK!
. . .

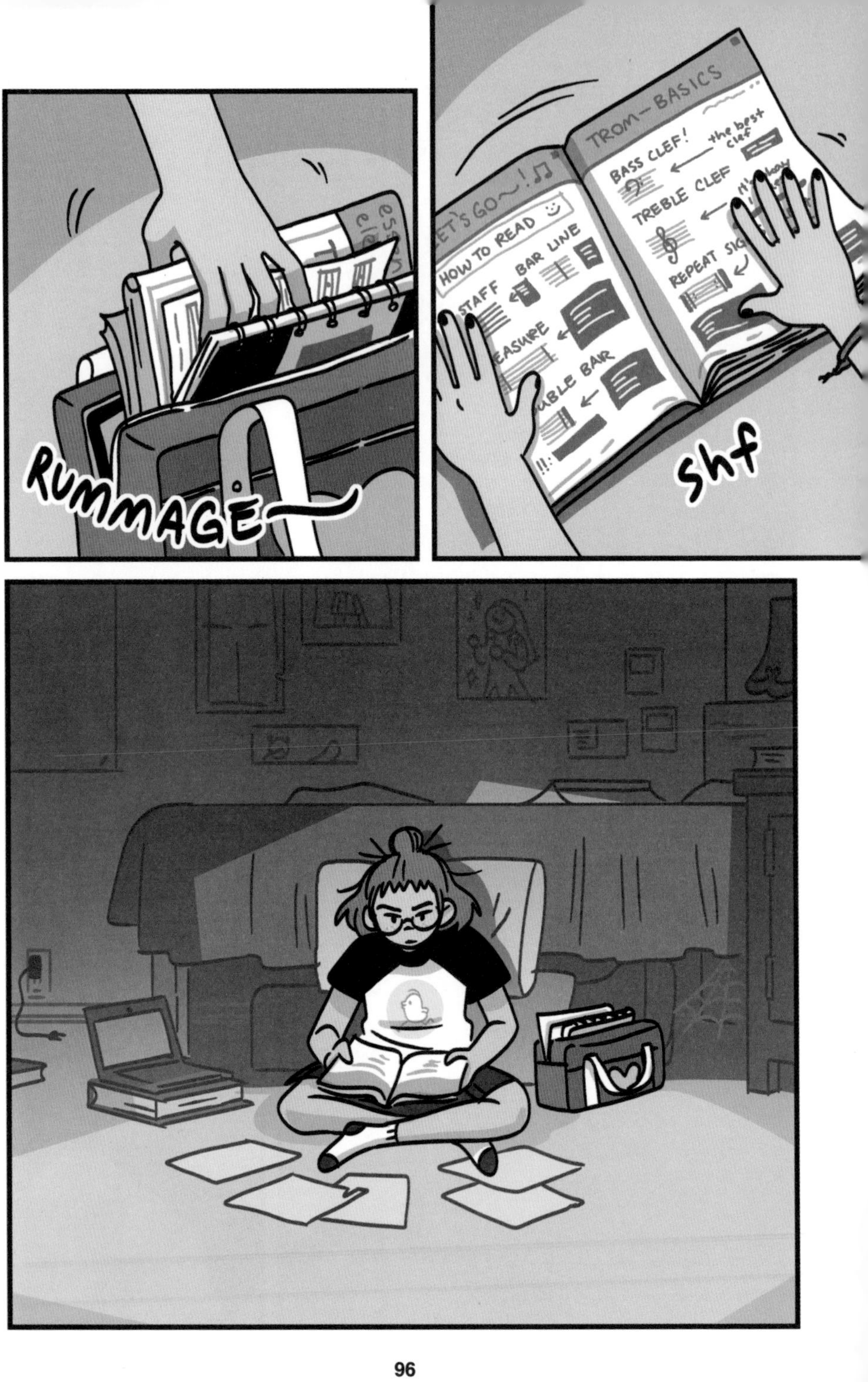
RUMMAGE—
TROM-BASICS
LET'S GO~!
HOW TO READ
STAFF
BAR LINE
EASURE
UBLE BAR
BASS CLEF!
the best clef
TREBLE CLEF
REPEAT SIG
Shf

Chapter 3

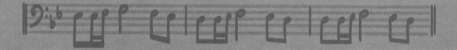

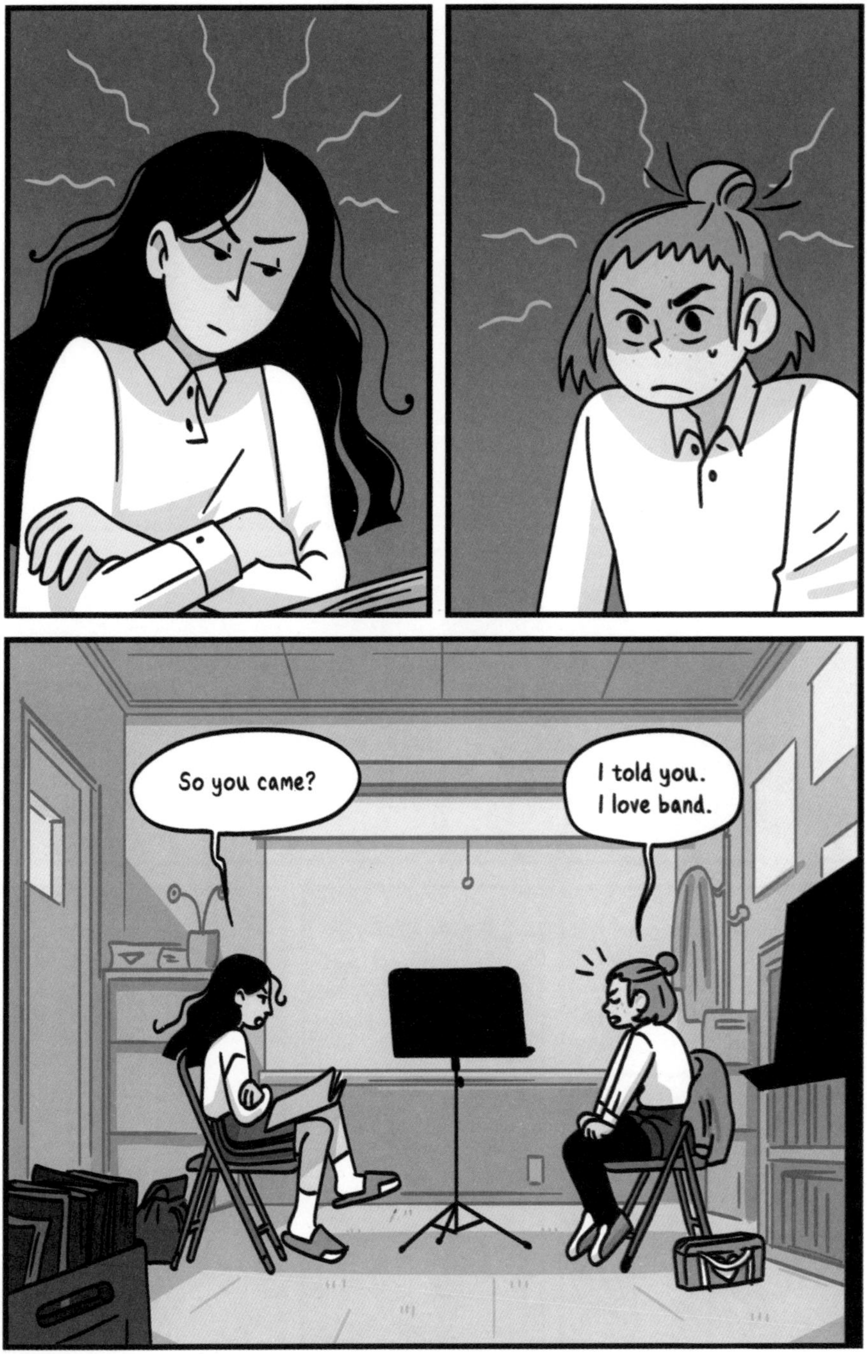
So you came?
I told you. I love band.

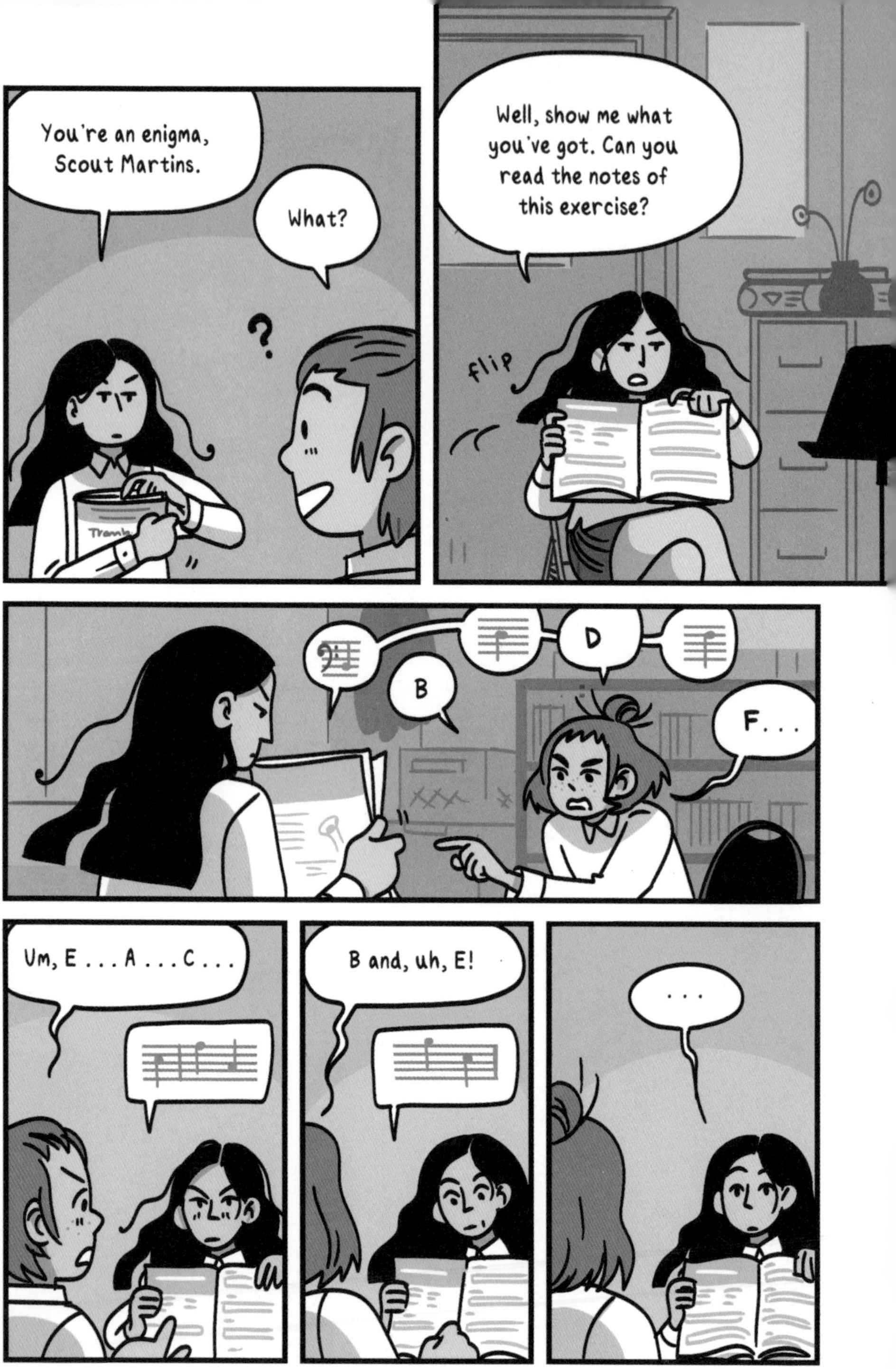
You're an enigma, Scout Martins.
What?
?
Well, show me what you've got. Can you read the notes of this exercise?
flip
B
D
F...
Um, E...A...C...
B and, uh, E!
...

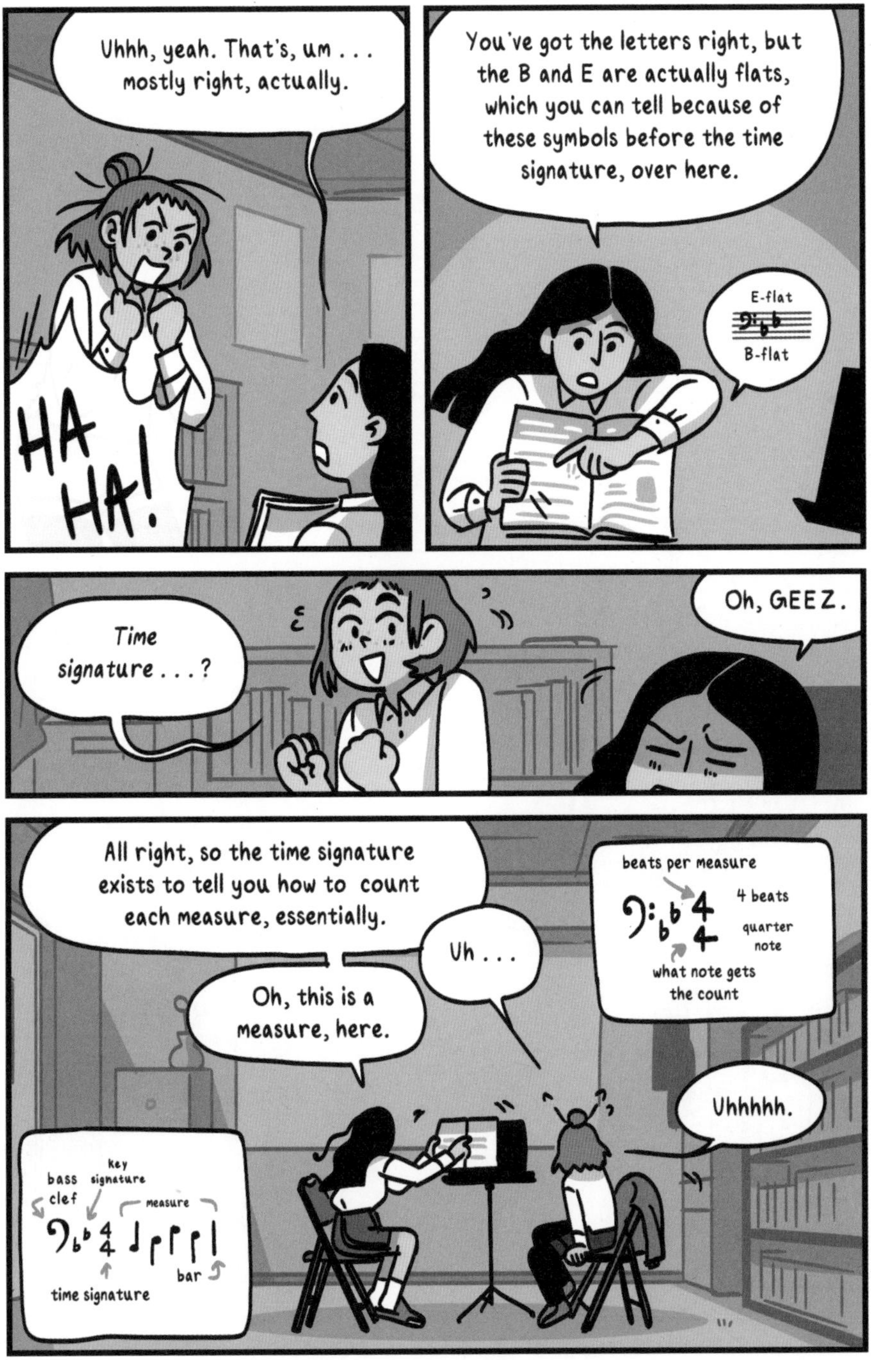

Uhhh, yeah. That's, um . . . mostly right, actually.
HA HA!
You've got the letters right, but the B and E are actually flats, which you can tell because of these symbols before the time signature, over here.
E-flat
B-flat
Time signature . . . ?
Oh, GEEZ.
All right, so the time signature exists to tell you how to count each measure, essentially.
beats per measure
4 beats
quarter note
what note gets the count
Uh . . .
Oh, this is a measure, here.
Uhhhh.
bass clef
key signature
measure
bar
time signature

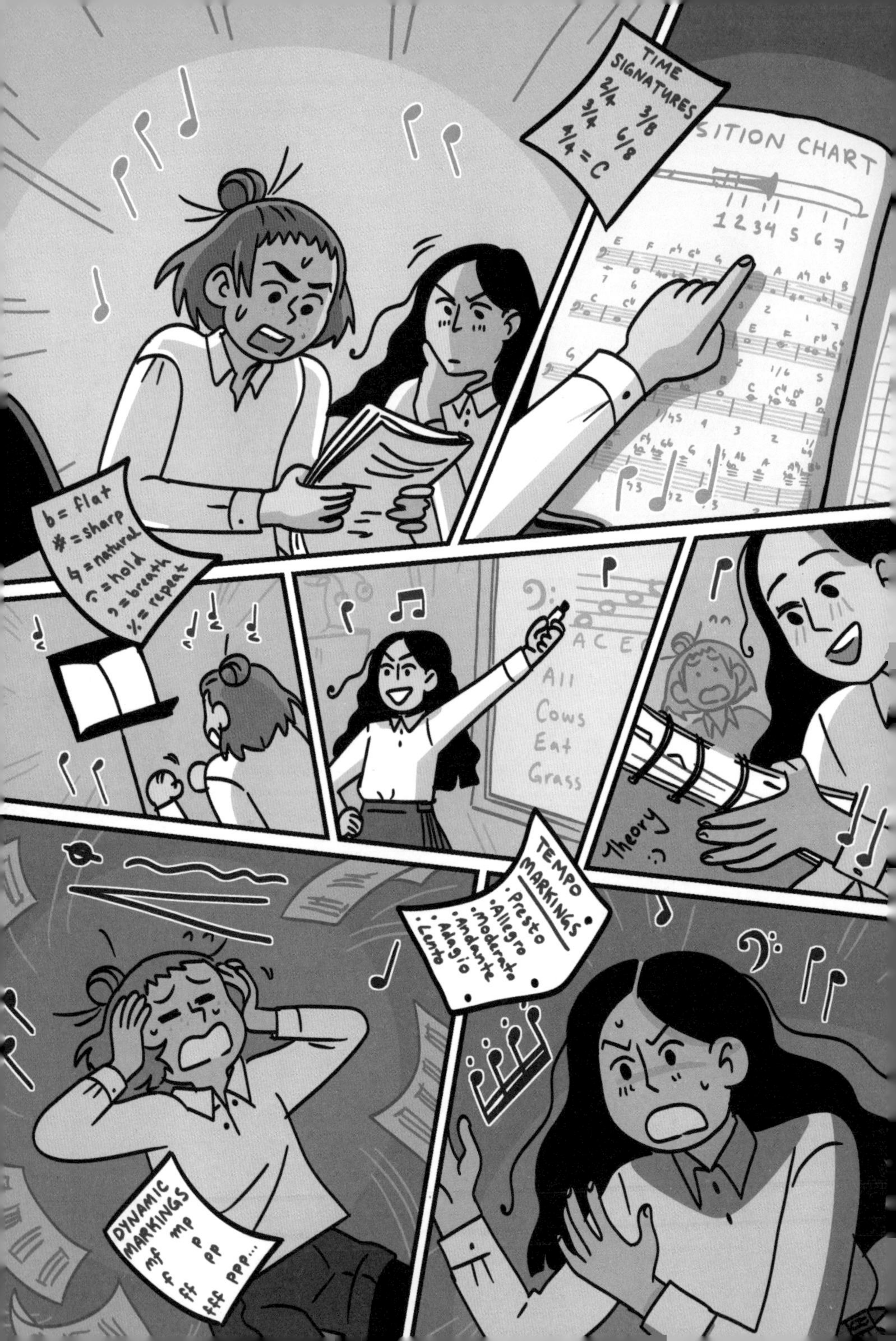
TIME SIGNATURES
2/4 3/8
3/4 6/8
4/4 = C
SITION CHART
1 2 3 4 5 6 7
b = flat
# = sharp
♮ = natural
𝄐 = hold
, = breath
% = repeat
A C E
All
Cows
Eat
Grass
Theory
TEMPO MARKINGS
.Presto
.Allegro
.Moderato
.Andante
.Adagio
.Lento
DYNAMIC MARKINGS
mf mp
f p
ff pp
fff ppp...

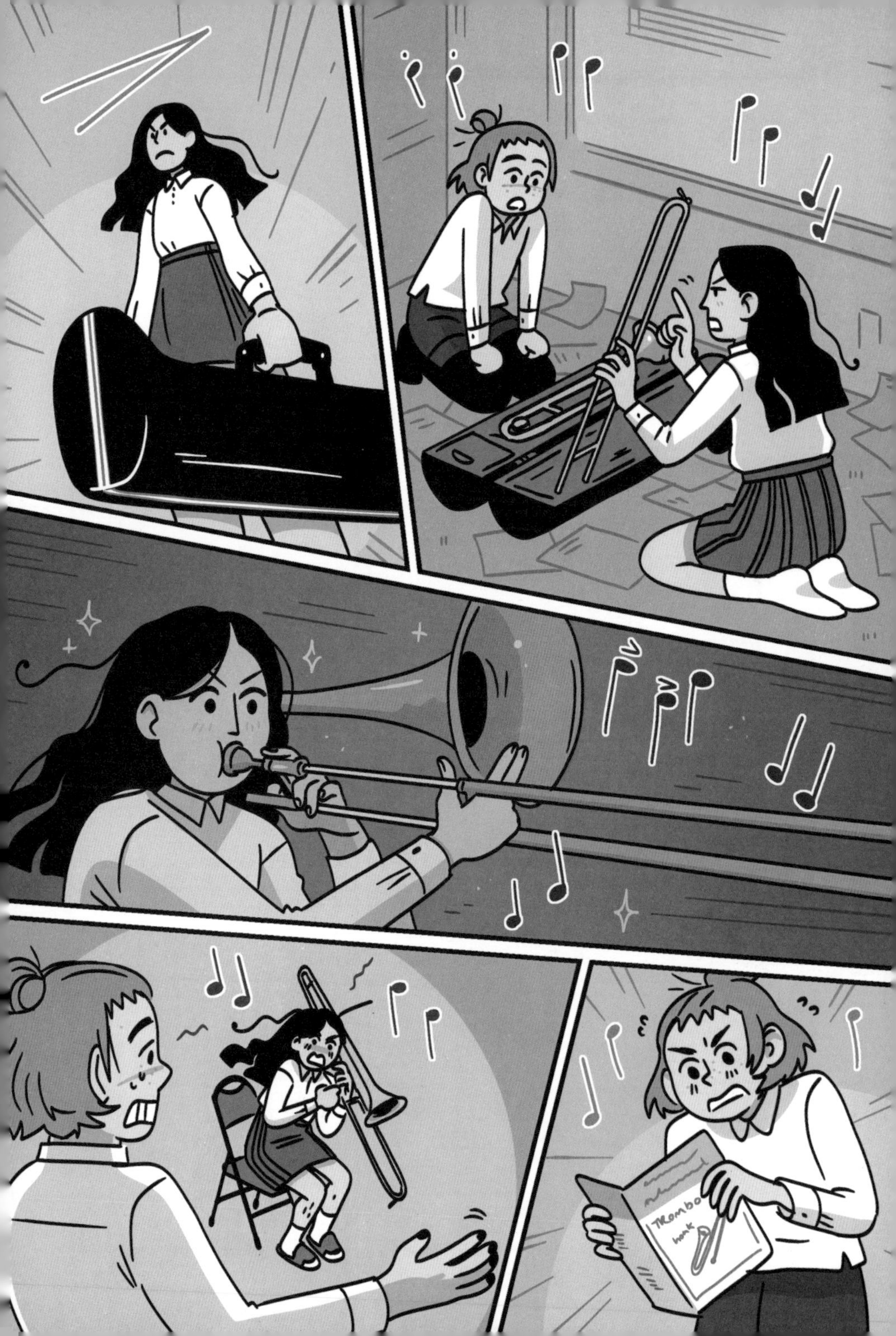
Trombo
honk

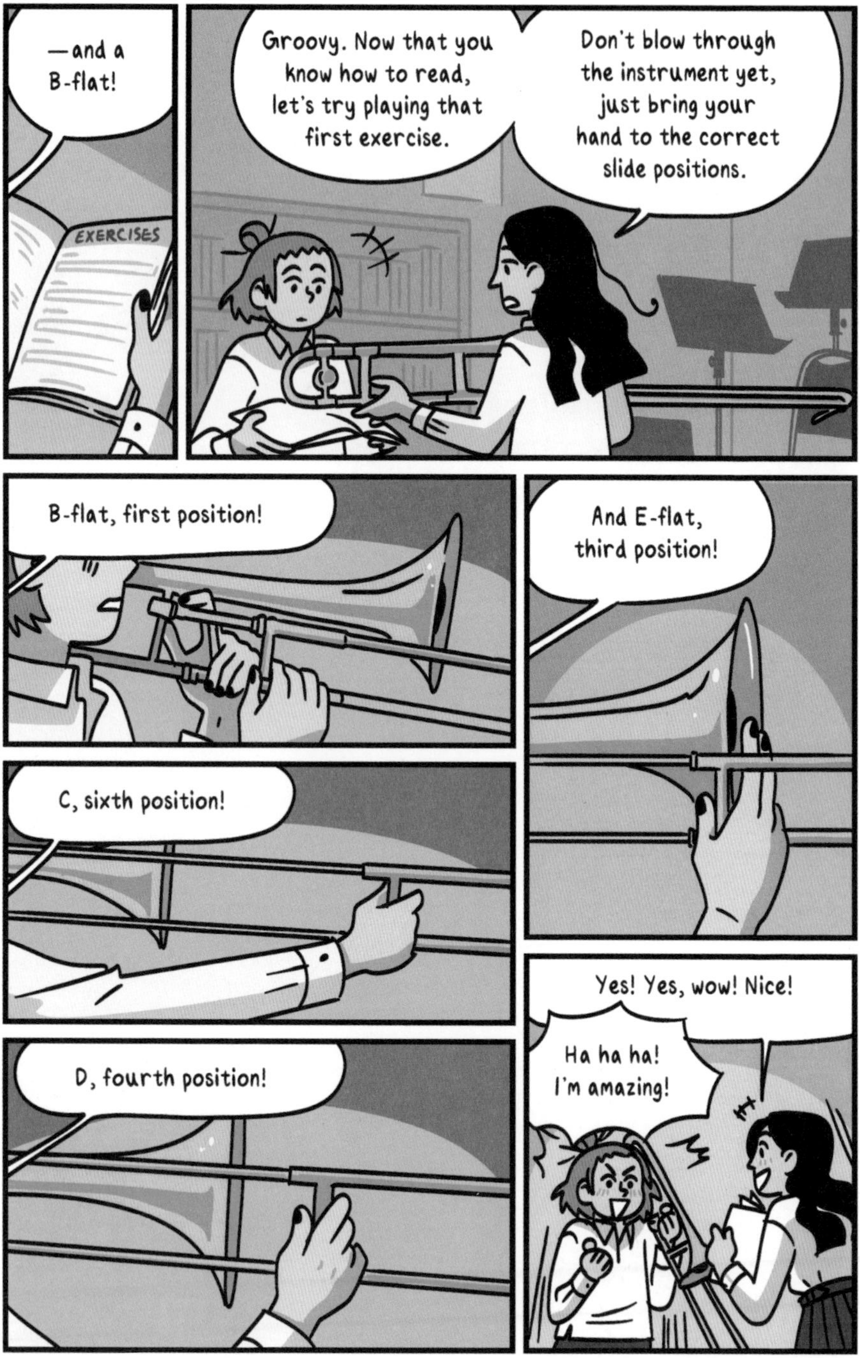
—and a B-flat!
Groovy. Now that you know how to read, let's try playing that first exercise.
Don't blow through the instrument yet, just bring your hand to the correct slide positions.
EXERCISES
B-flat, first position!
And E-flat, third position!
C, sixth position!
D, fourth position!
Yes! Yes, wow! Nice!
Ha ha ha! I'm amazing!

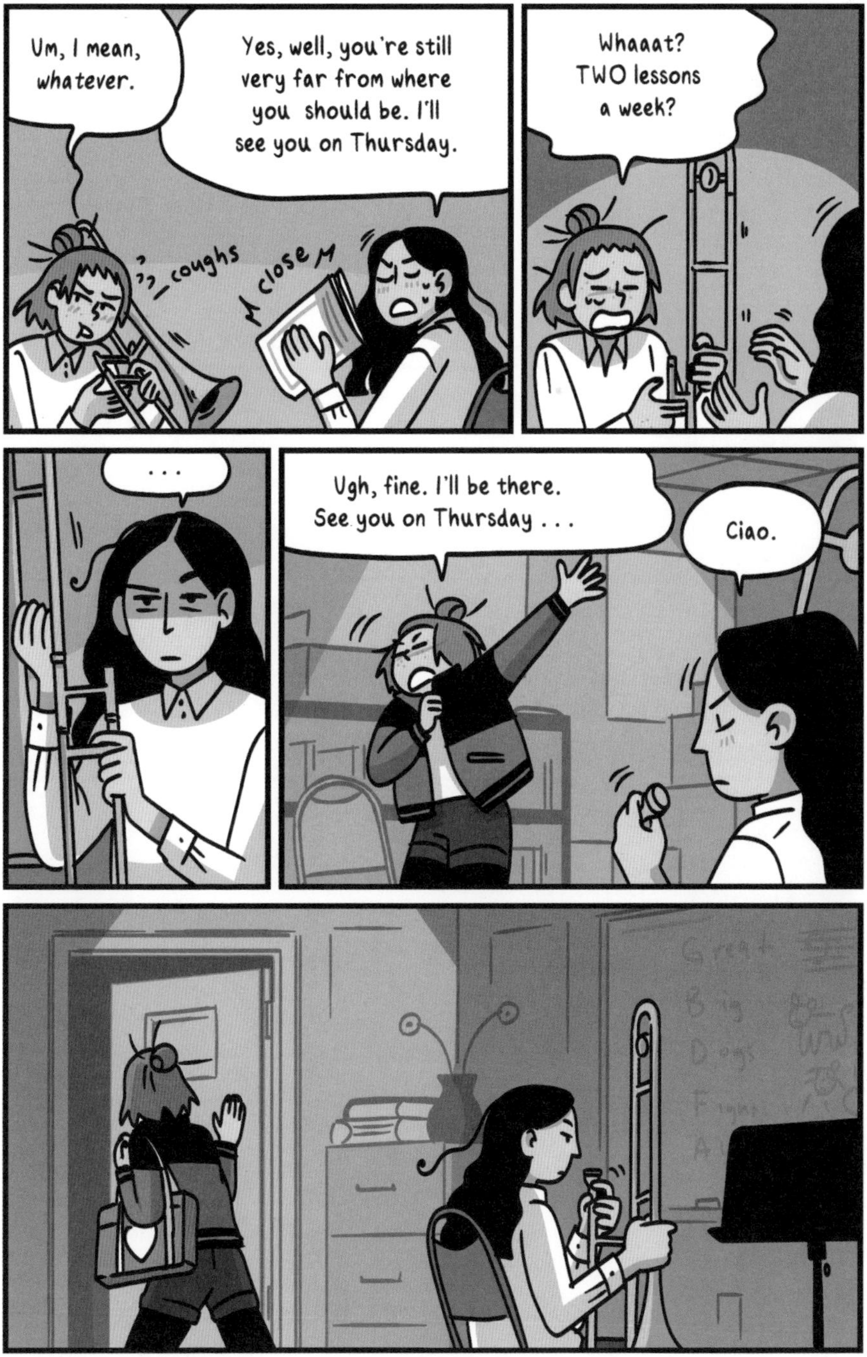

Um, I mean, whatever.
coughs
Yes, well, you're still very far from where you should be. I'll see you on Thursday.
close
Whaaat? TWO lessons a week?
. . .
Ugh, fine. I'll be there. See you on Thursday . . .
Ciao.

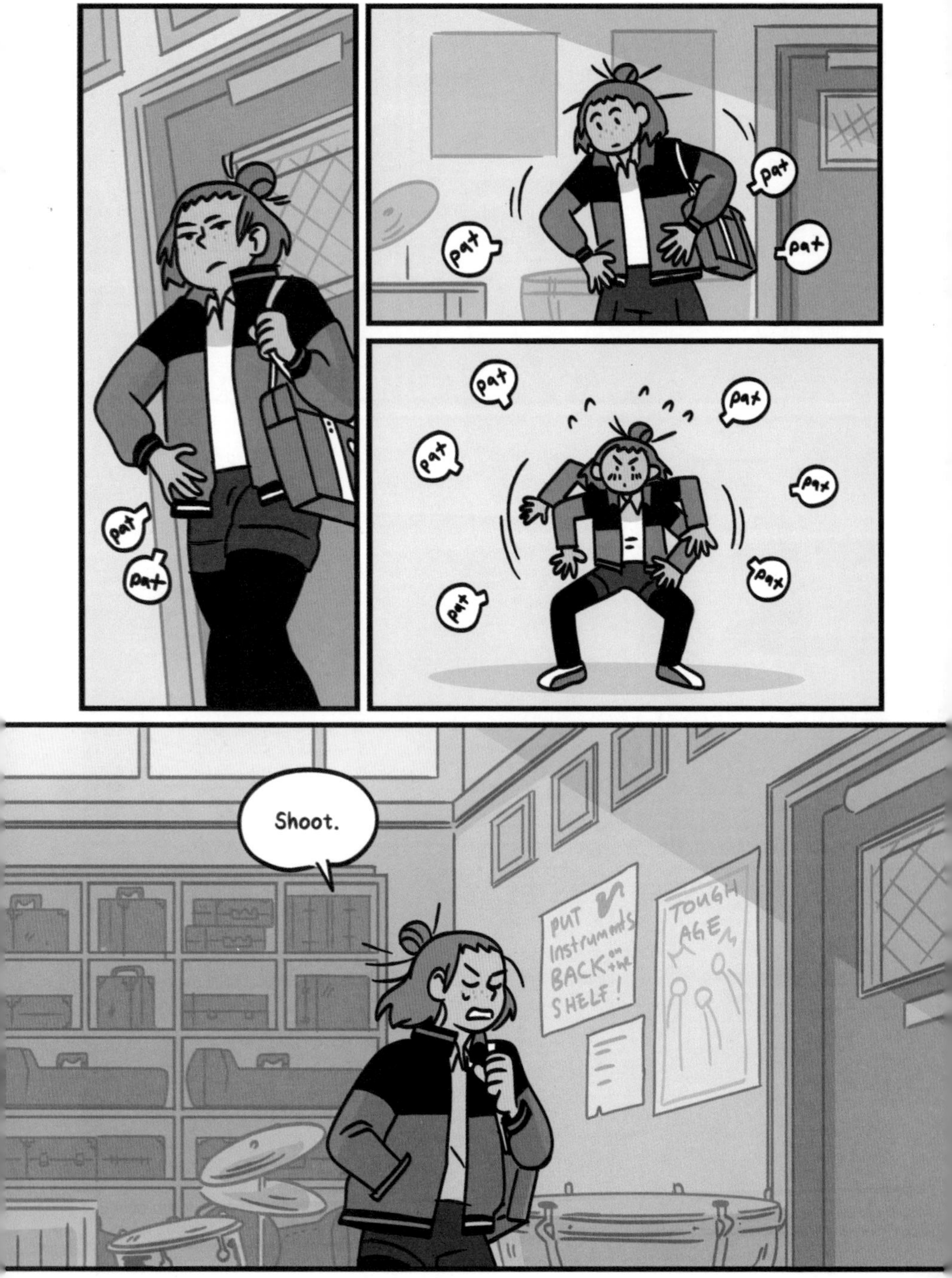

pat
pat
pat
pat
pat
pat
pat
pat
pat
pat
pat
pat
Shoot.
PUT instruments BACK on the SHELF!
TOUGH AGE

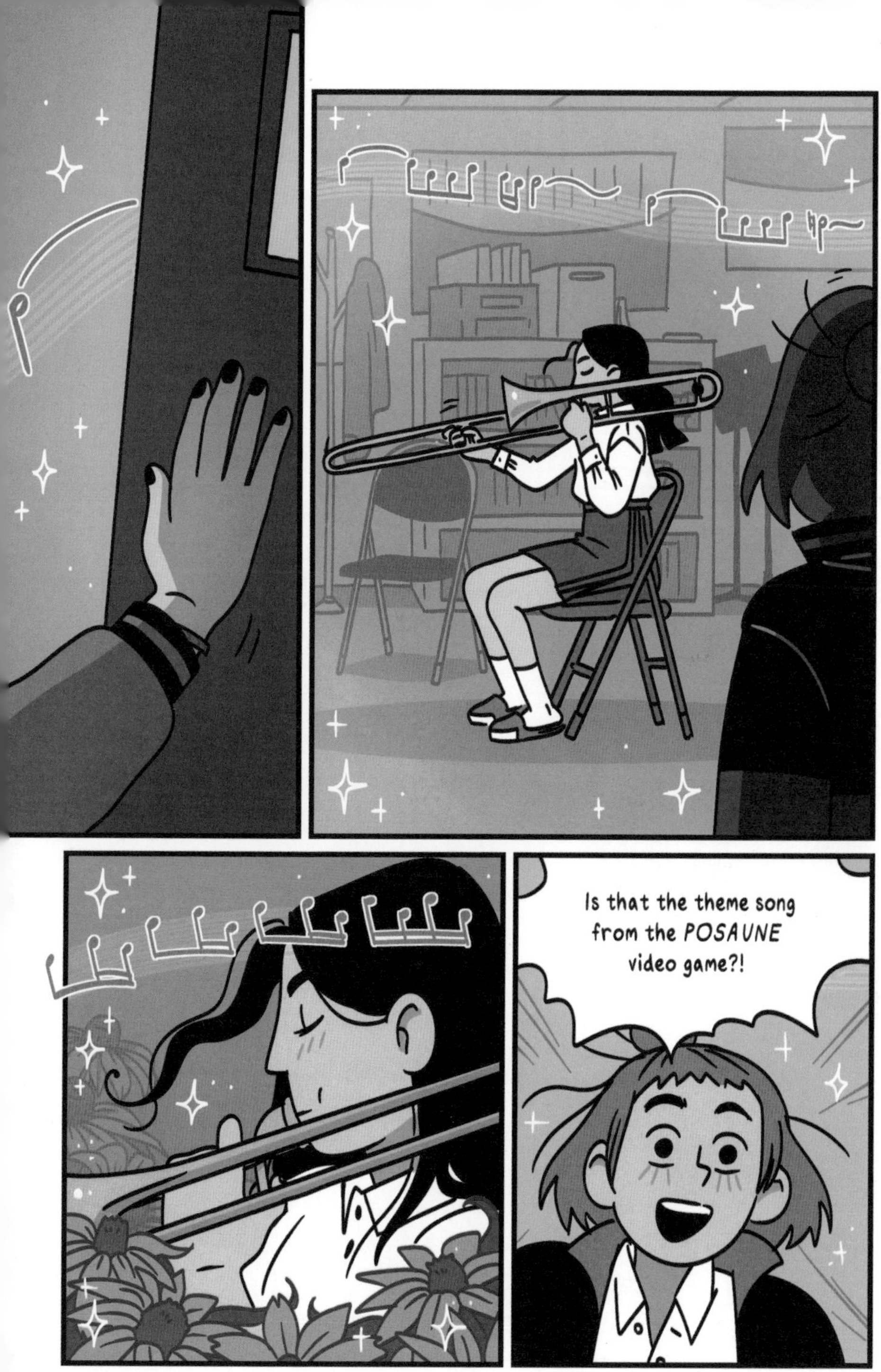
Is that the theme song from the POSAUNE video game?!

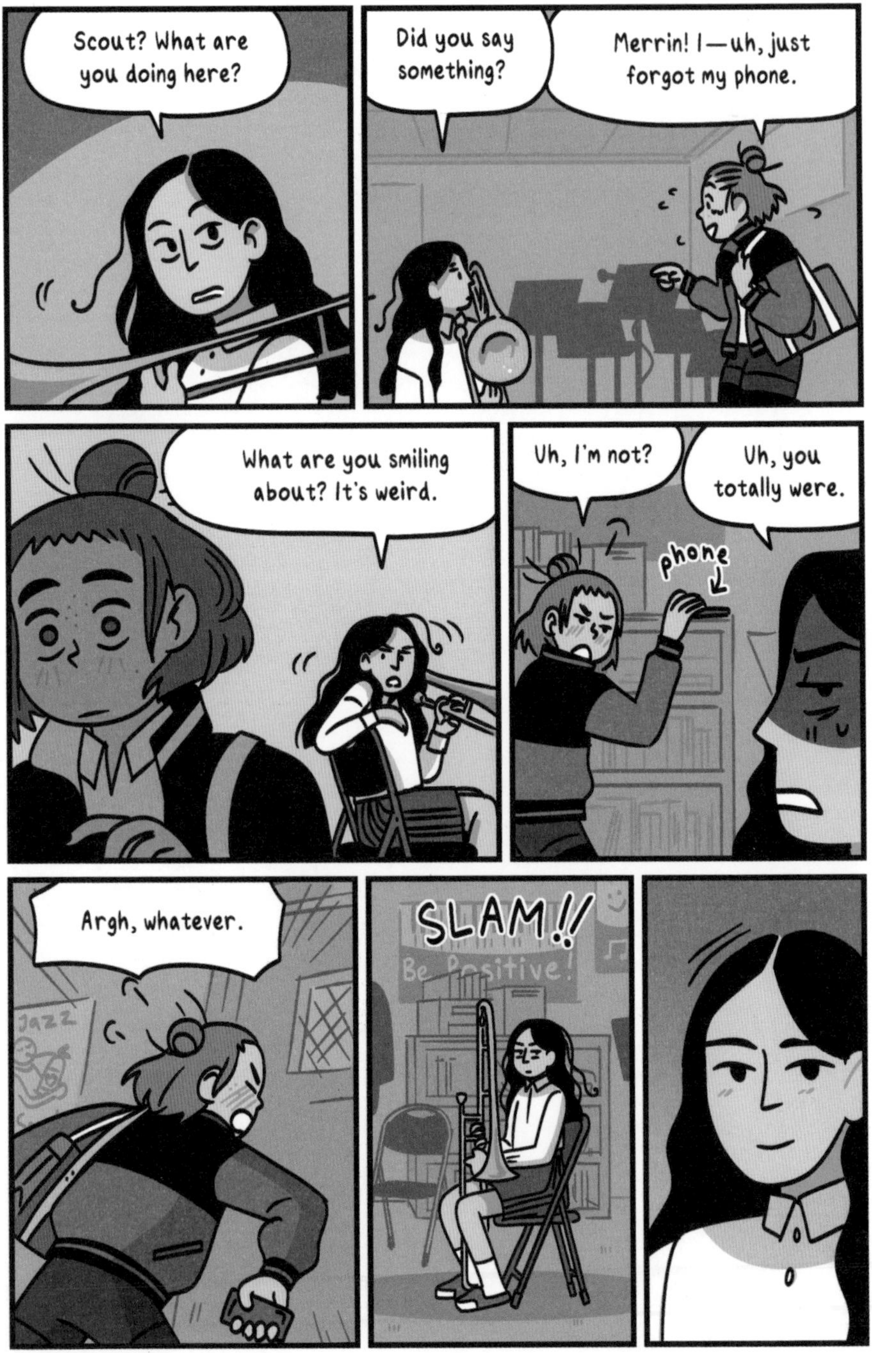
Scout? What are you doing here?
Did you say something?
Merrin! I—uh, just forgot my phone.
What are you smiling about? It's weird.
Uh, I'm not?
Uh, you totally were.
phone
Argh, whatever.
SLAM!!
Be Positive!
Jazz

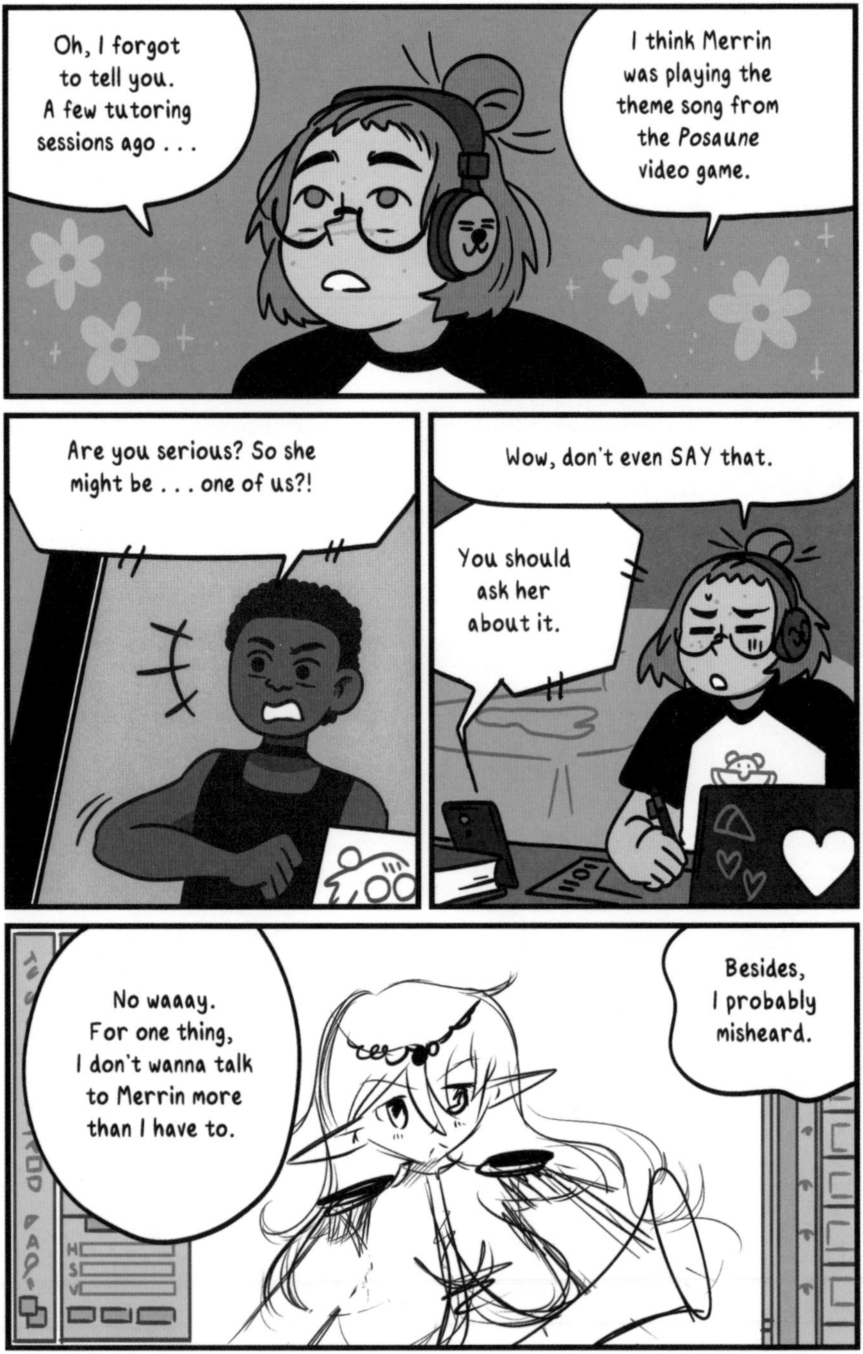
Oh, I forgot to tell you. A few tutoring sessions ago . . .
I think Merrin was playing the theme song from the *Posaune* video game.
Are you serious? So she might be . . . one of us?!
Wow, don't even SAY that.
You should ask her about it.
No waaay. For one thing, I don't wanna talk to Merrin more than I have to.
Besides, I probably misheard.

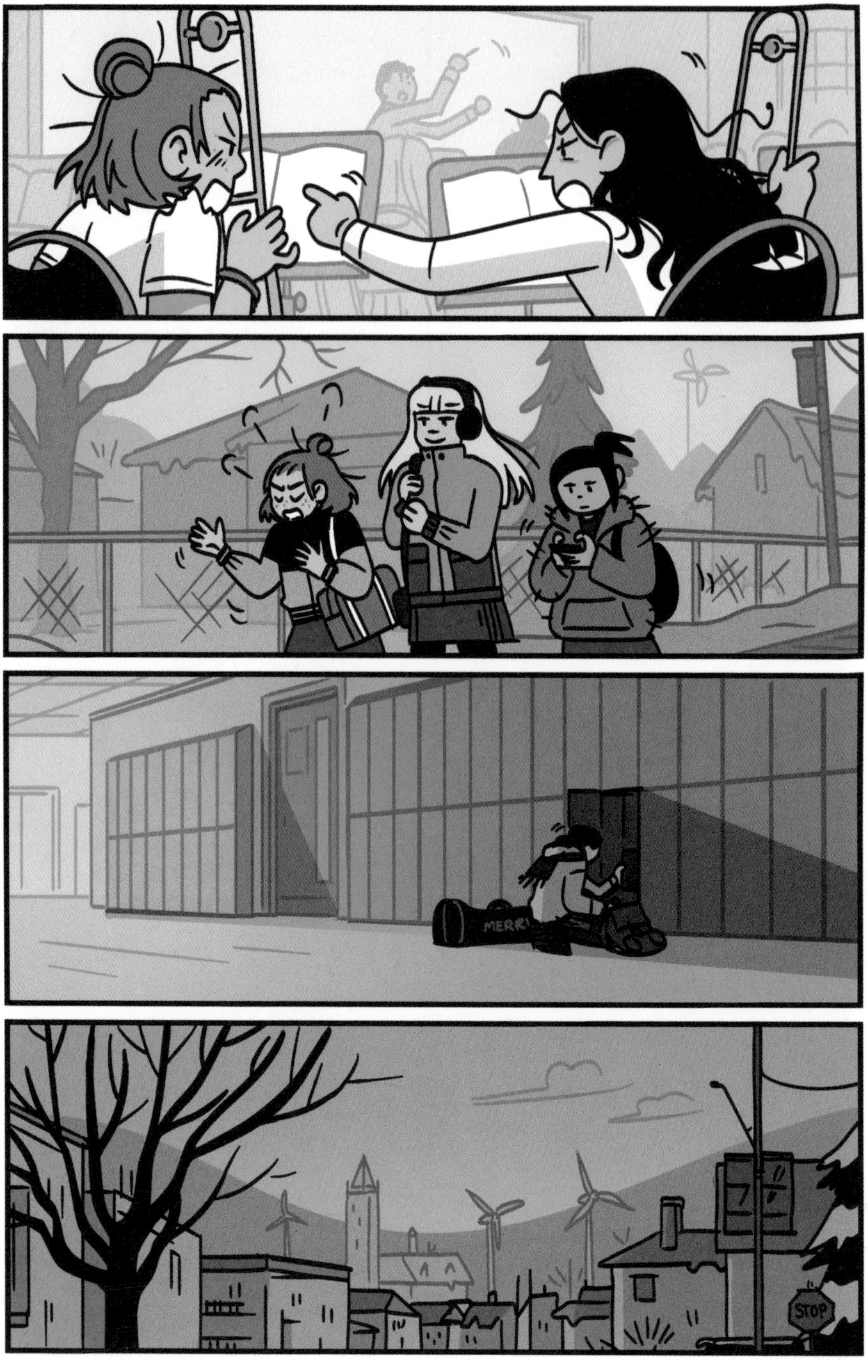
MERRI
STOP

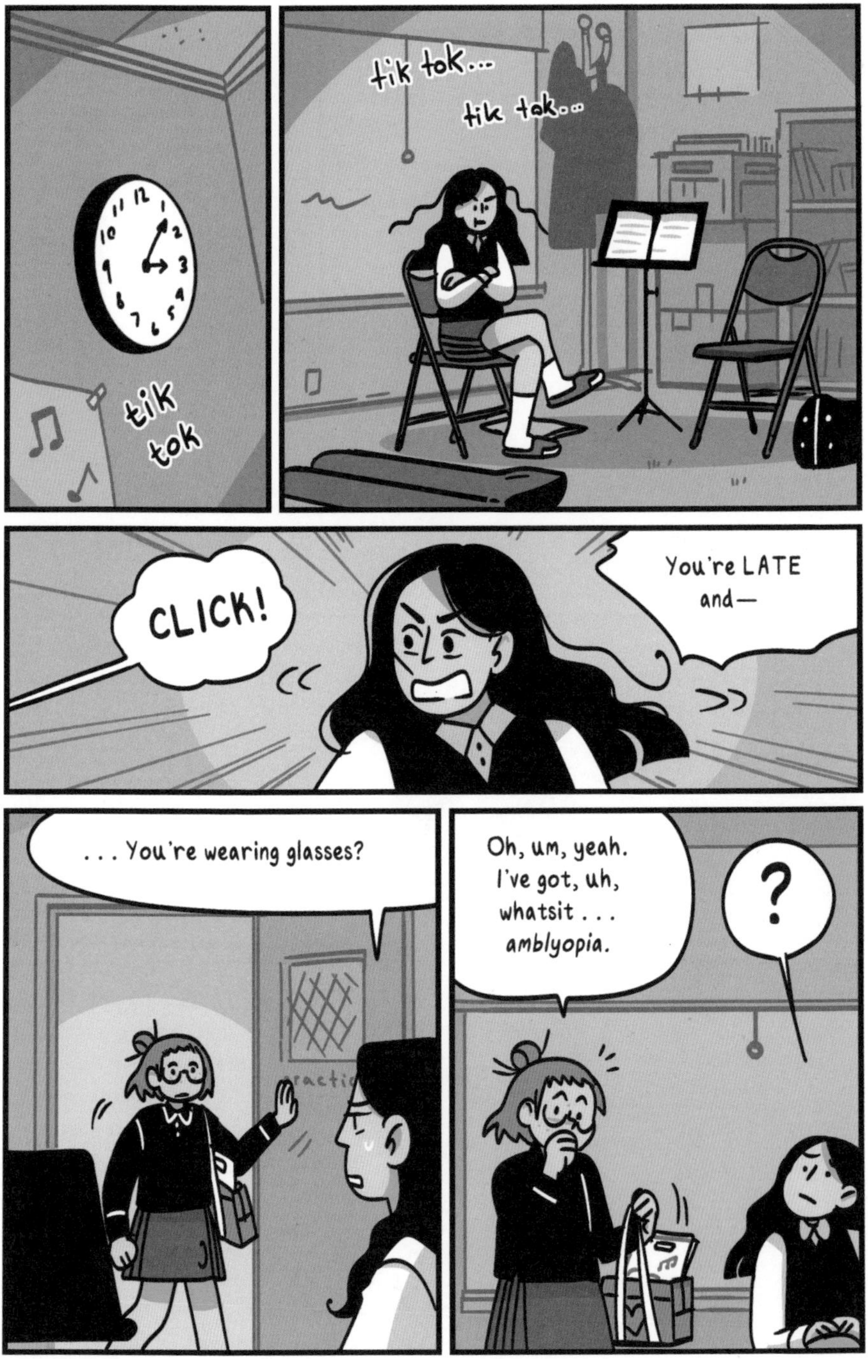
tik tok
tik tok...
tik tok...
CLICK!
You're LATE and—
. . . You're wearing glasses?
Oh, um, yeah. I've got, uh, whatsit . . . amblyopia.
?

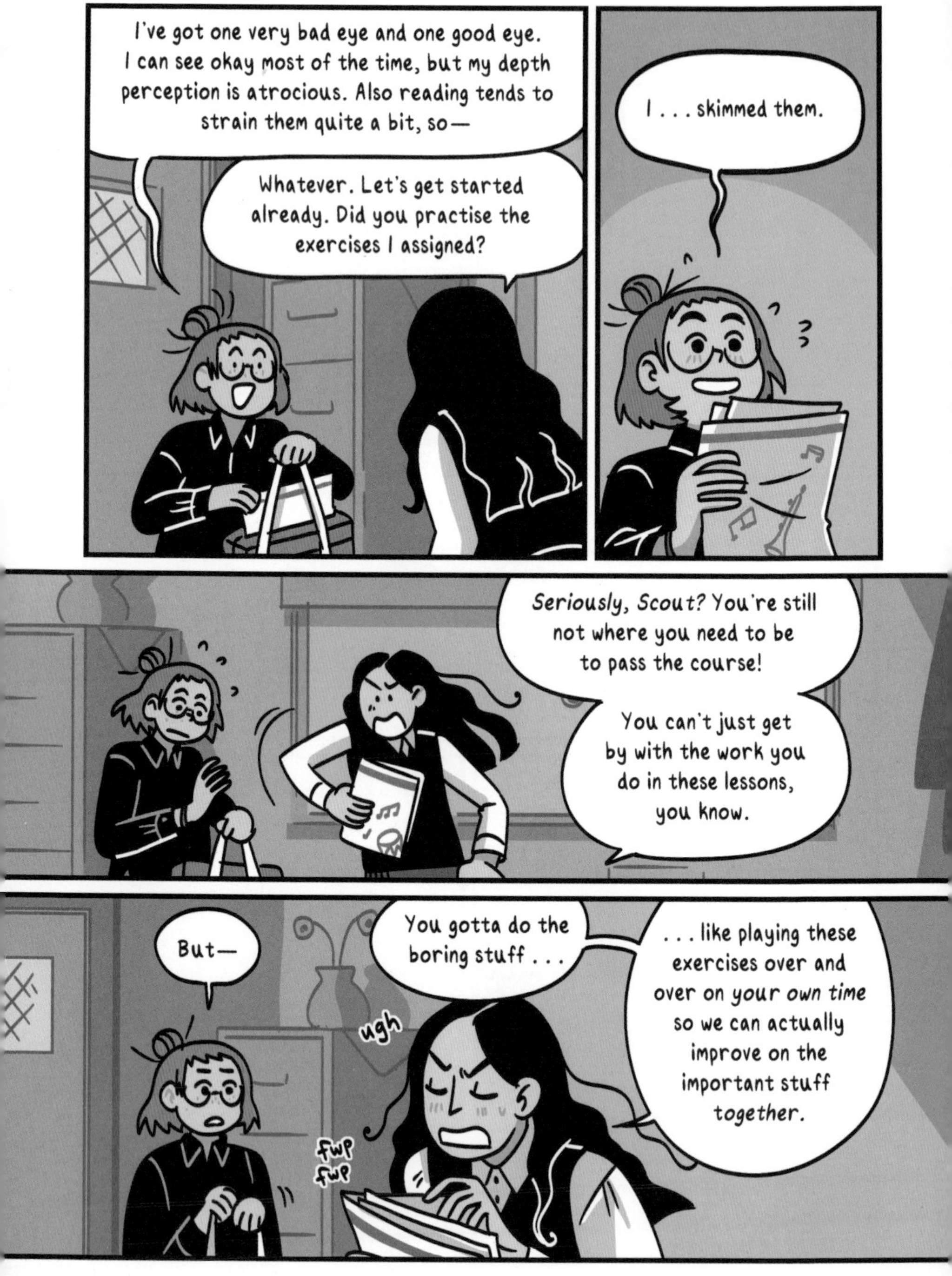
I've got one very bad eye and one good eye. I can see okay most of the time, but my depth perception is atrocious. Also reading tends to strain them quite a bit, so—
Whatever. Let's get started already. Did you practise the exercises I assigned?
I . . . skimmed them.
Seriously, Scout? You're still not where you need to be to pass the course!
You can't just get by with the work you do in these lessons, you know.
But—
You gotta do the boring stuff . . .
. . . like playing these exercises over and over on *your own time* so we can actually improve on the important stuff *together*.
ugh
fwp fwp

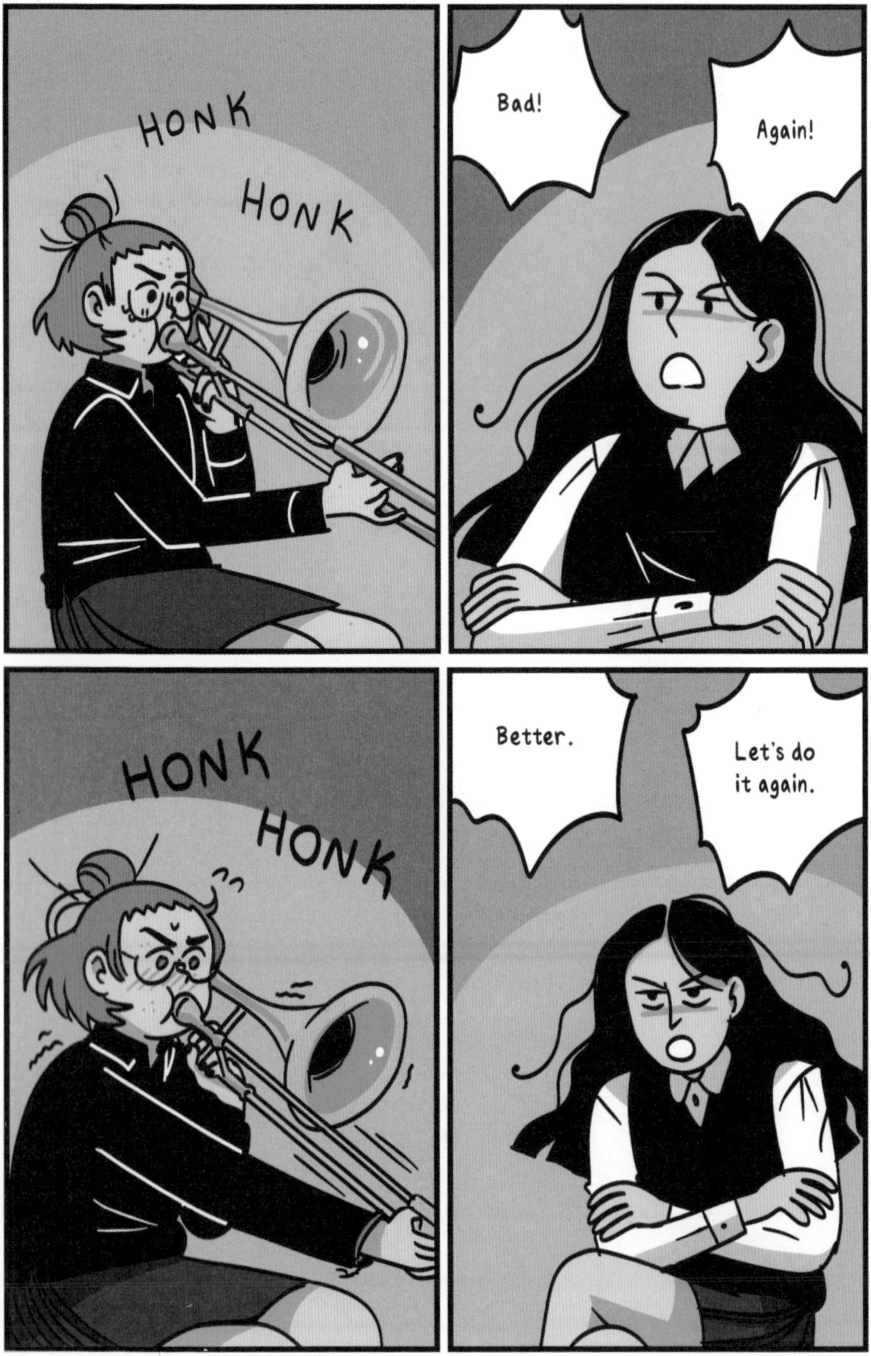
HONK
HONK
Bad!
Again!
HONK
HONK
Better.
Let's do it again.

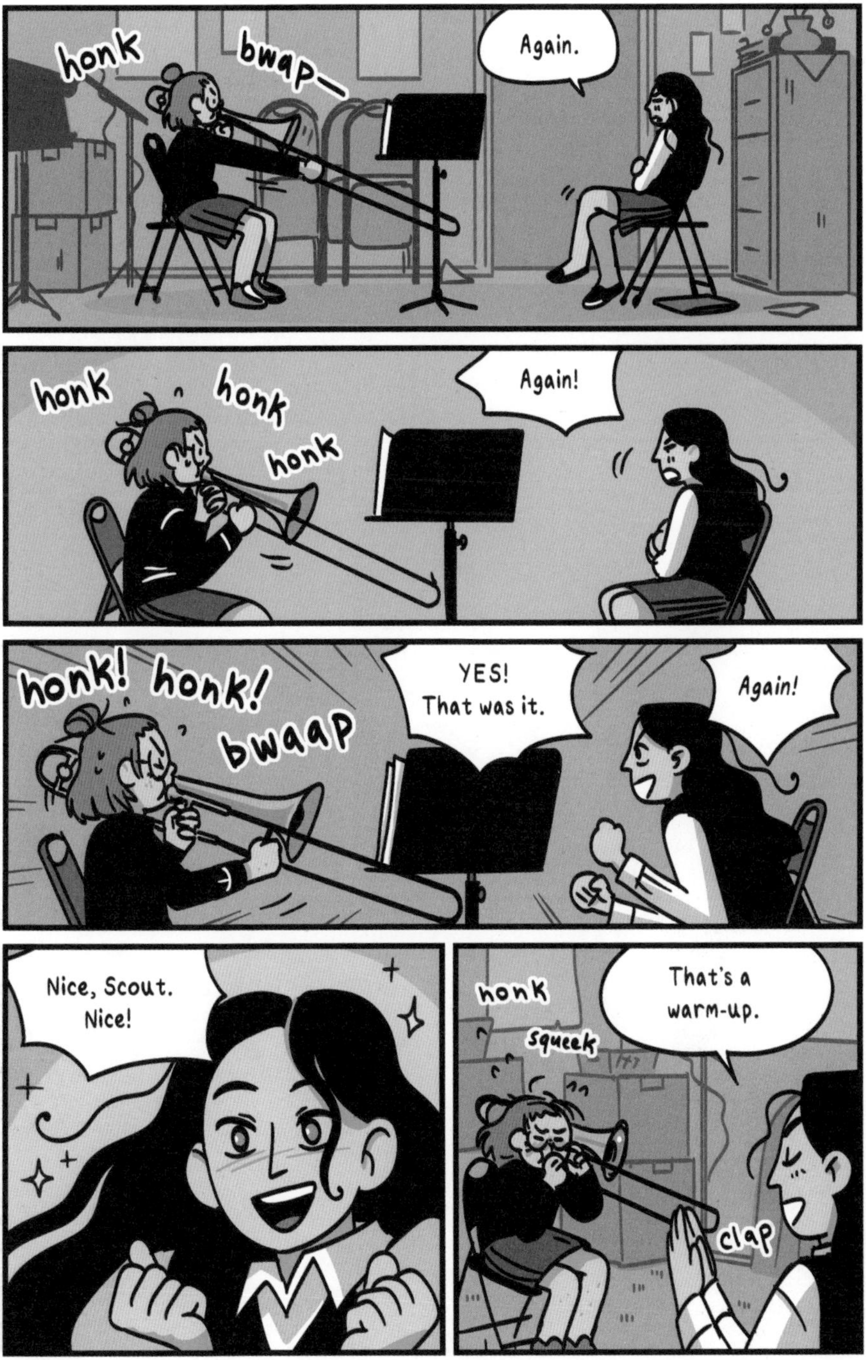
honk
bwap—
Again.
honk
honk
honk
Again!
honk! honk!
bwaap
YES!
That was it.
Again!
Nice, Scout.
Nice!
honk
squeek
That's a
warm-up.
clap

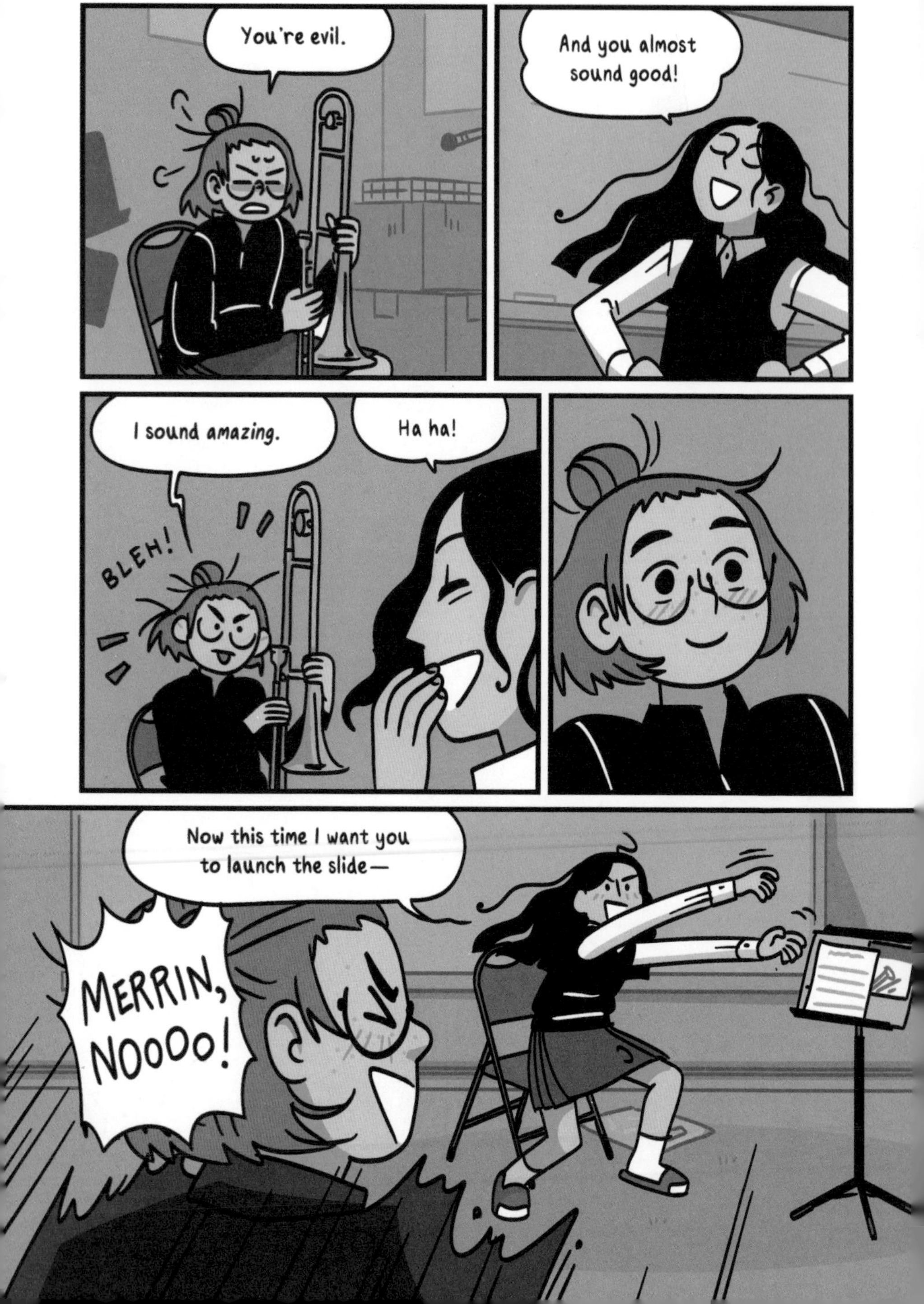
You're evil.
And you almost sound good!
I sound amazing.
BLEH!
Ha ha!
Now this time I want you to launch the slide—
MERRIN, NOOOo!

123

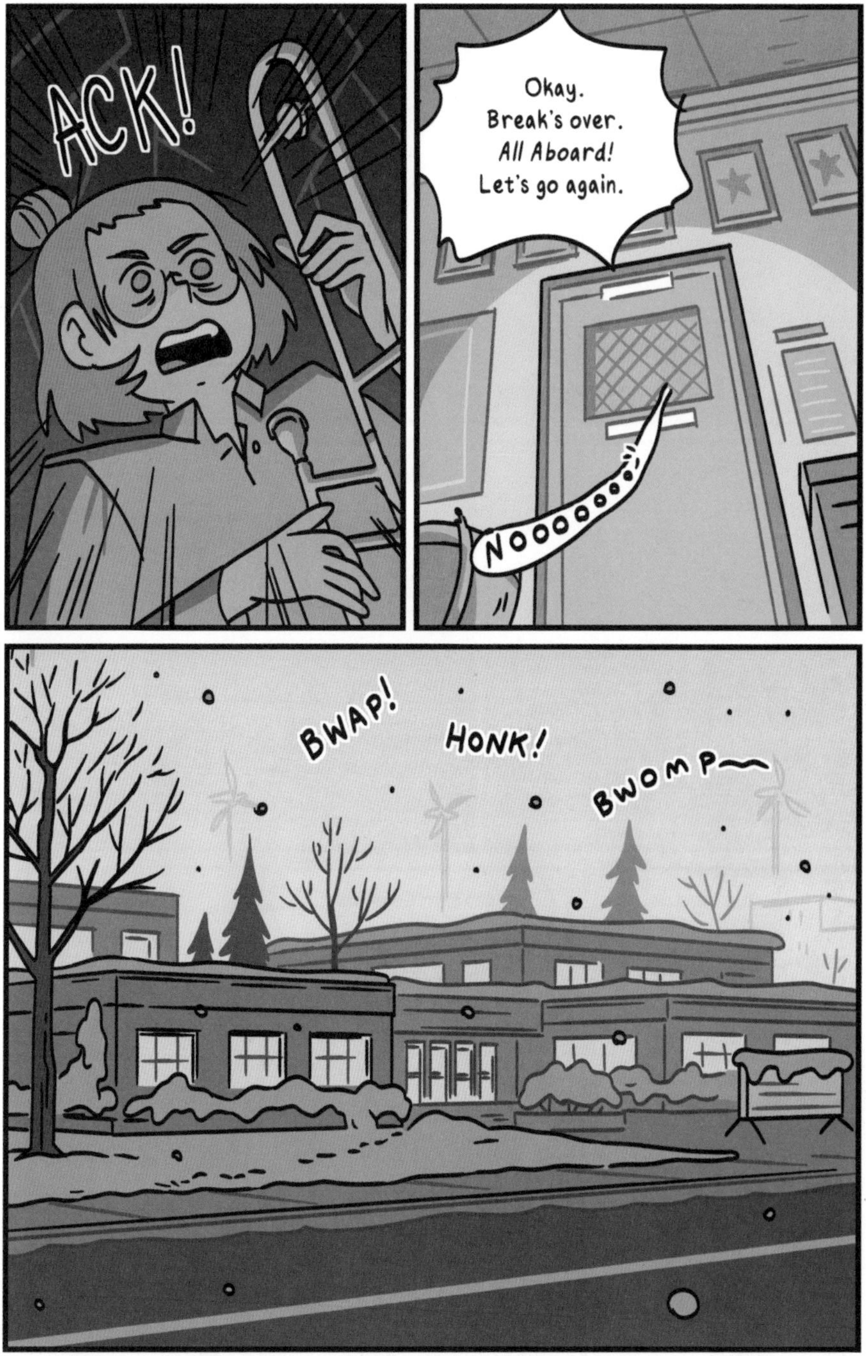
ACK!
Okay.
Break's over.
All Aboard!
Let's go again.
NOOOOOOOO
BWAP!
HONK!
BWOMP

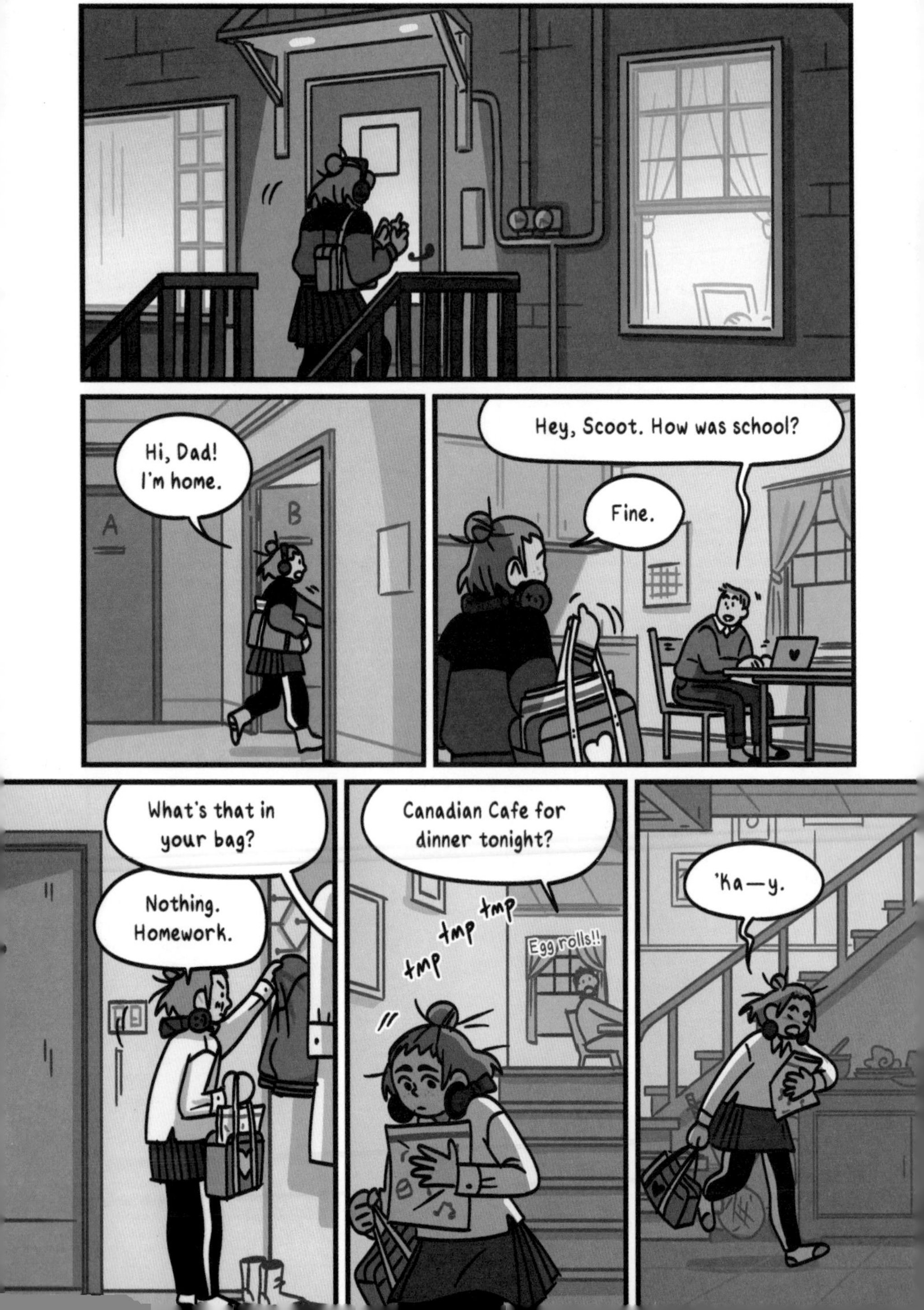
Hi, Dad!
I'm home.
A
B
Hey, Scoot. How was school?
Fine.
What's that in your bag?
Nothing. Homework.
Canadian Cafe for dinner tonight?
tmp tmp tmp
Egg rolls!!
'Ka—y.

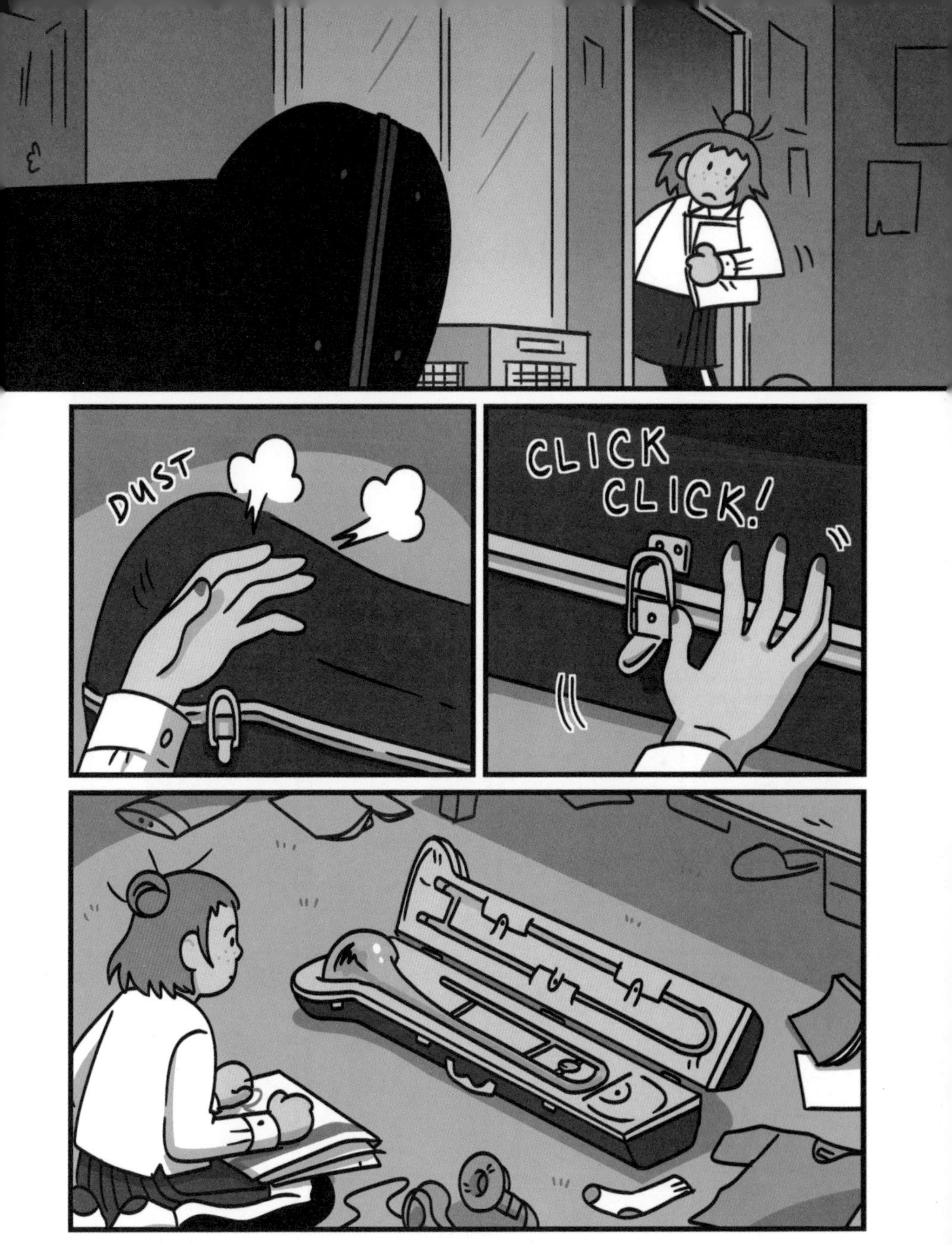
DUST
CLICK
CLICK!

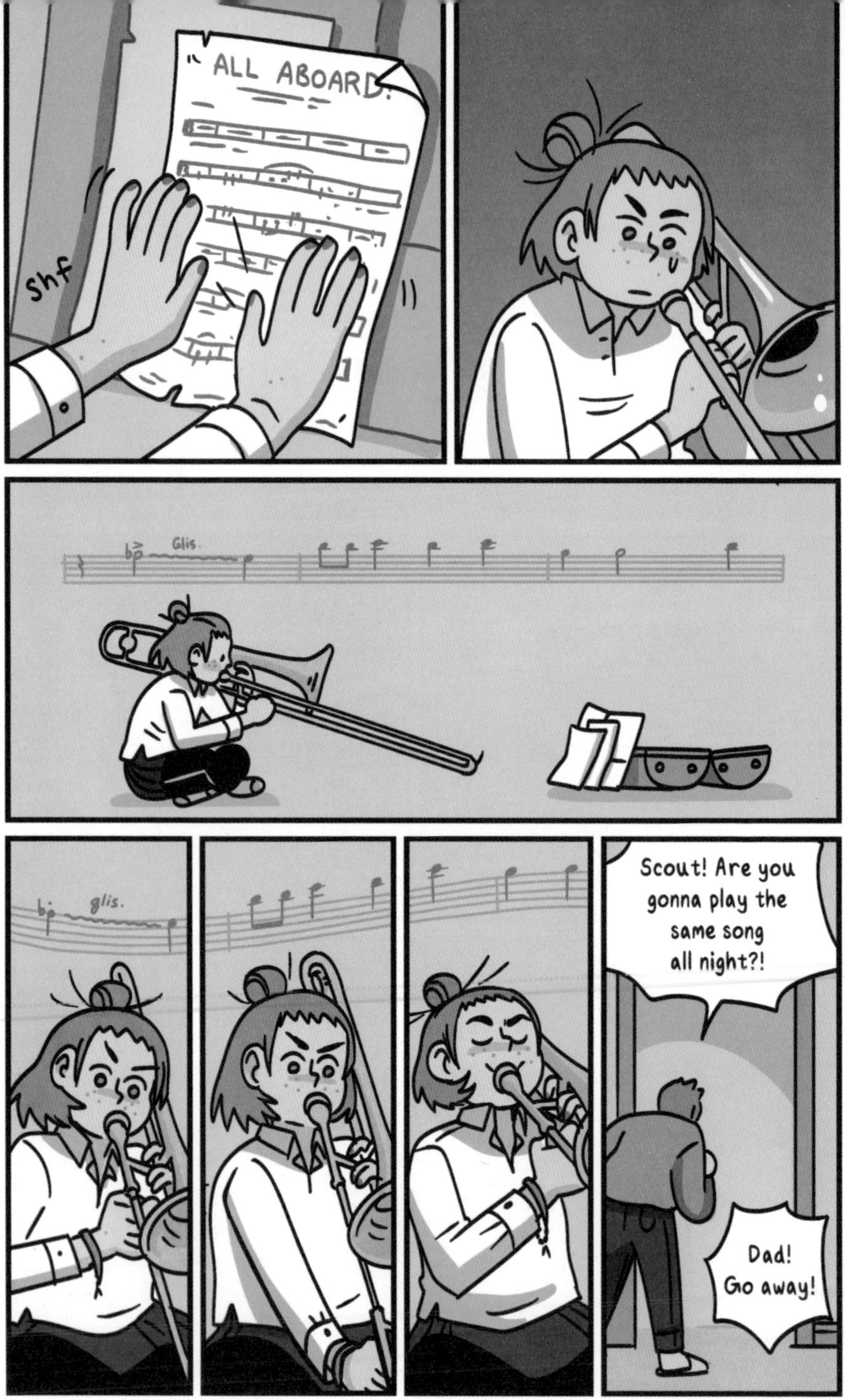

"ALL ABOARD!"
Shf
Glis.
glis.
Scout! Are you gonna play the same song all night?!
Dad! Go away!

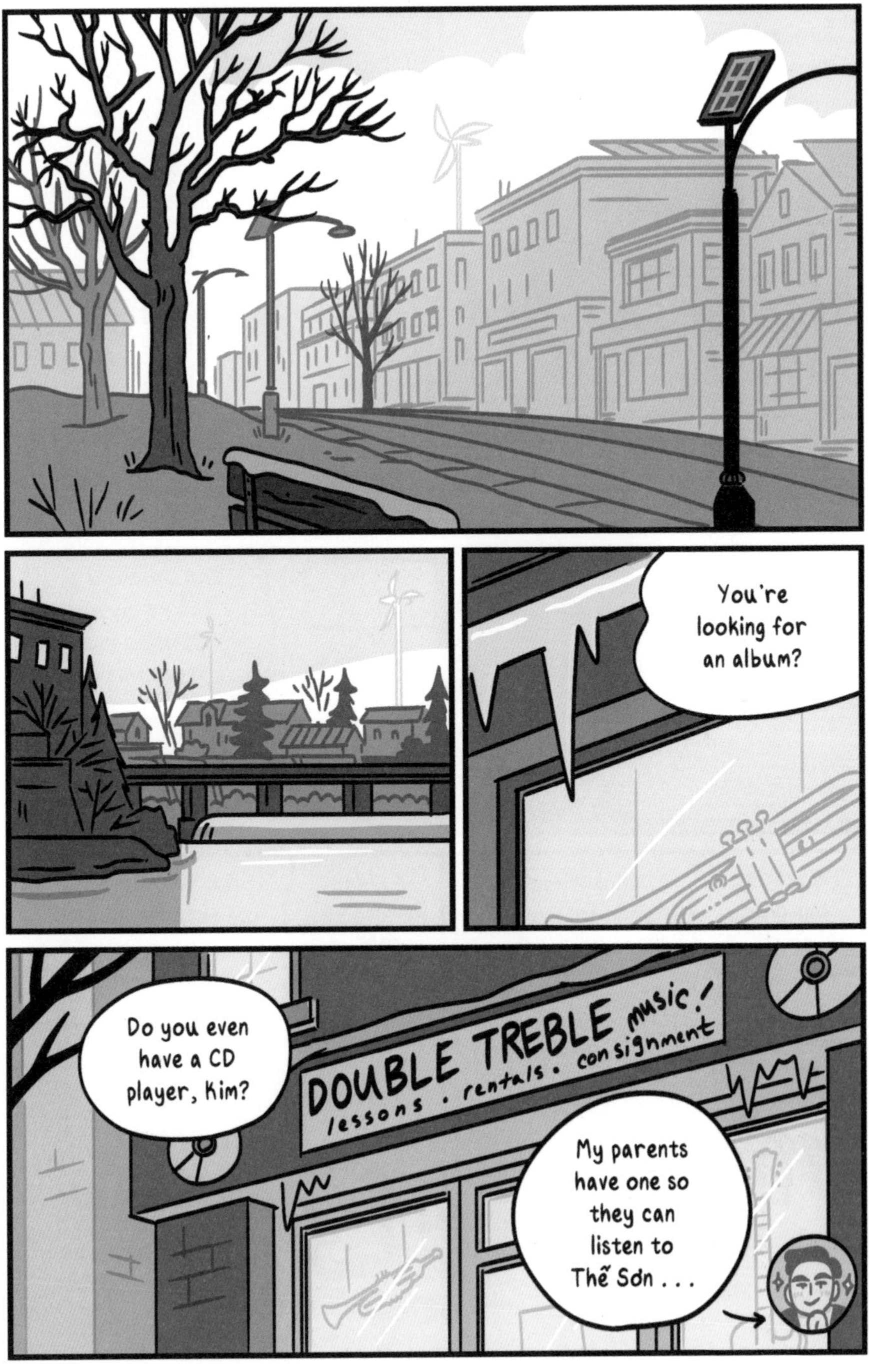
You're looking for an album?
Do you even have a CD player, Kim?
DOUBLE TREBLE music!
lessons . rentals . consignment
My parents have one so they can listen to Thế Sơn . . .

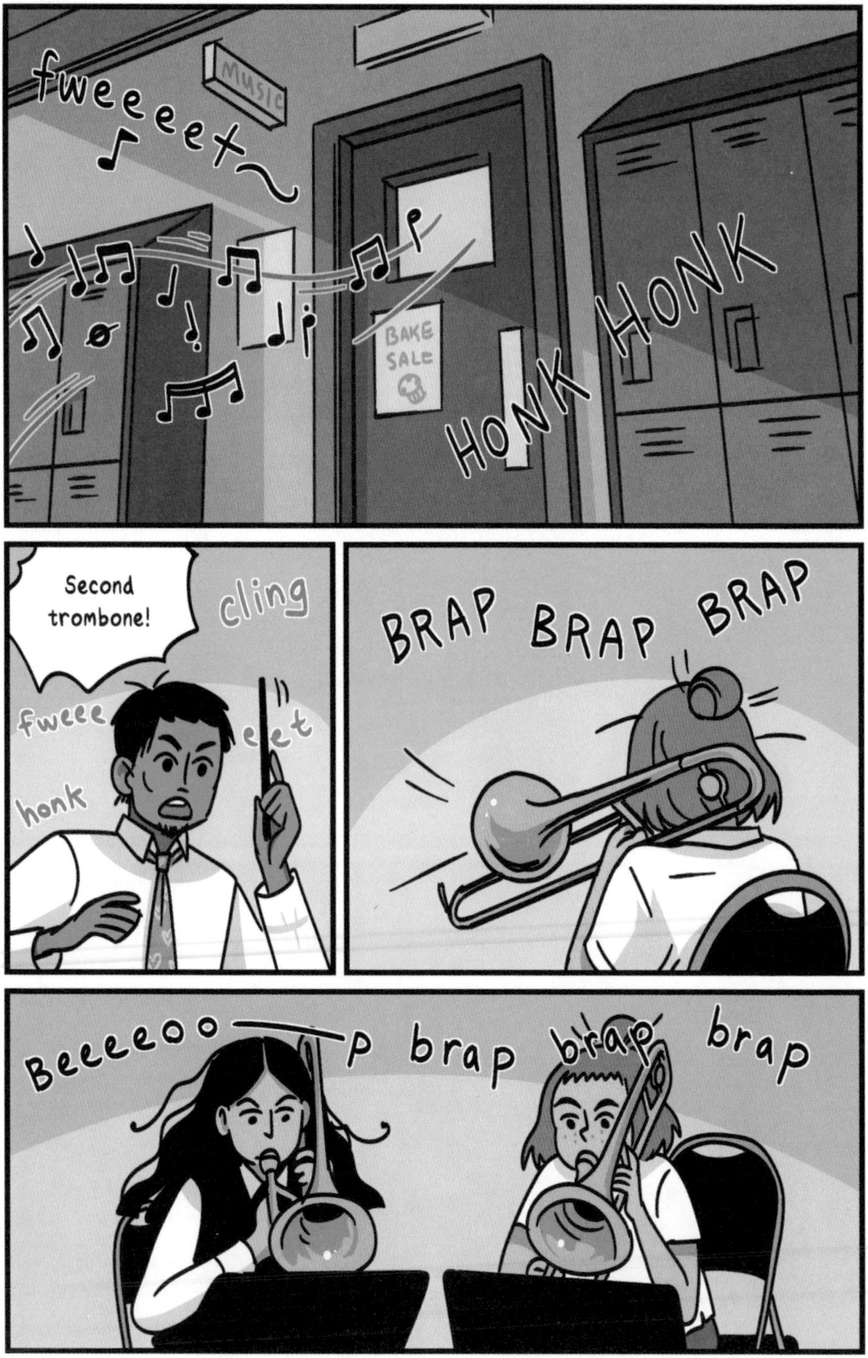
MUSIC
fweeeeet
BAKE SALE
HONK HONK
Second trombone!
cling
fweee
eet
honk
BRAP BRAP BRAP
Beeeeoo——p brap brap brap

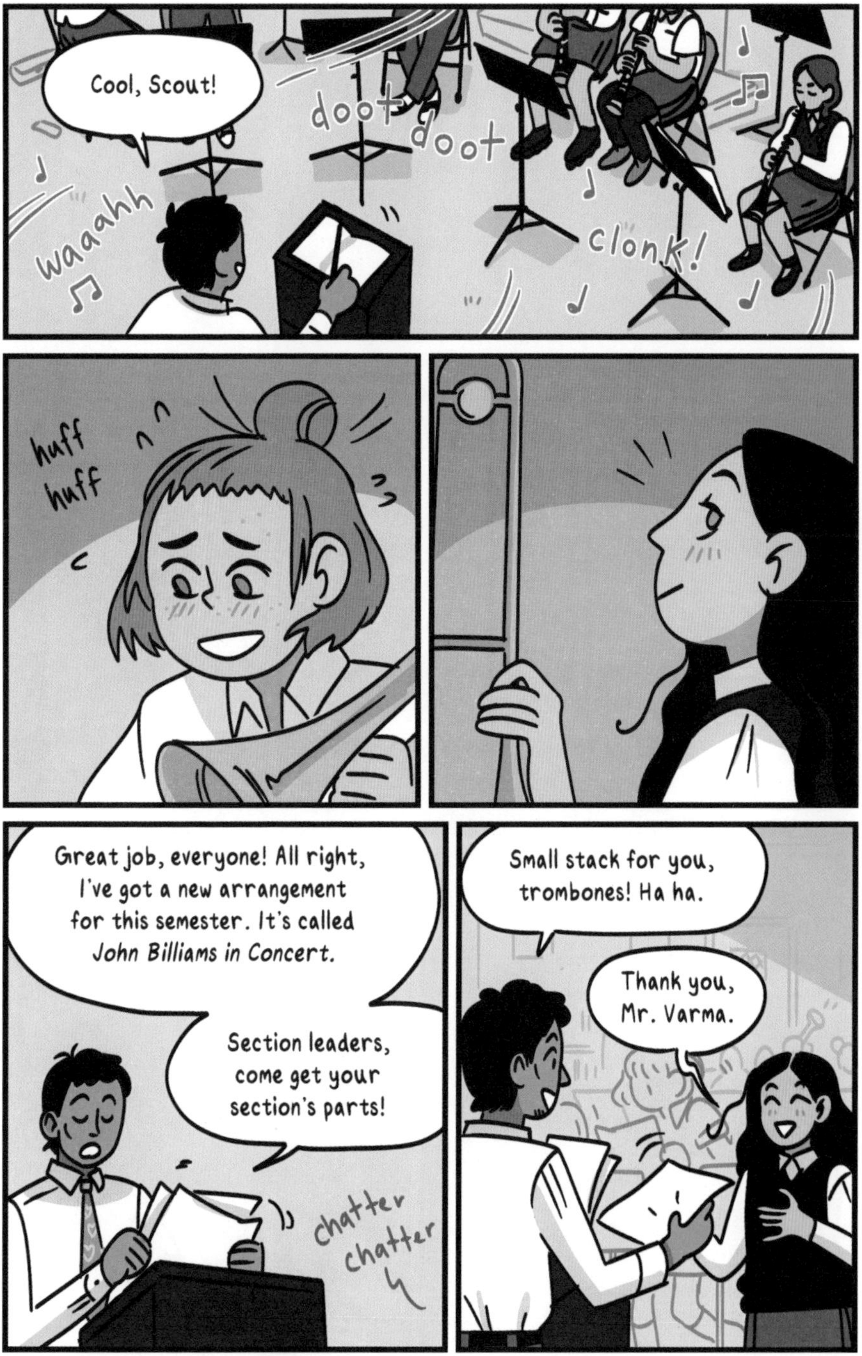
Cool, Scout!
doot doot
waaahh
clonk!
huff
huff
Great job, everyone! All right, I've got a new arrangement for this semester. It's called *John Billiams in Concert.*
Section leaders, come get your section's parts!
chatter chatter
Small stack for you, trombones! Ha ha.
Thank you, Mr. Varma.

*Canadian data plans are some of the most expensive and most limited in the world!

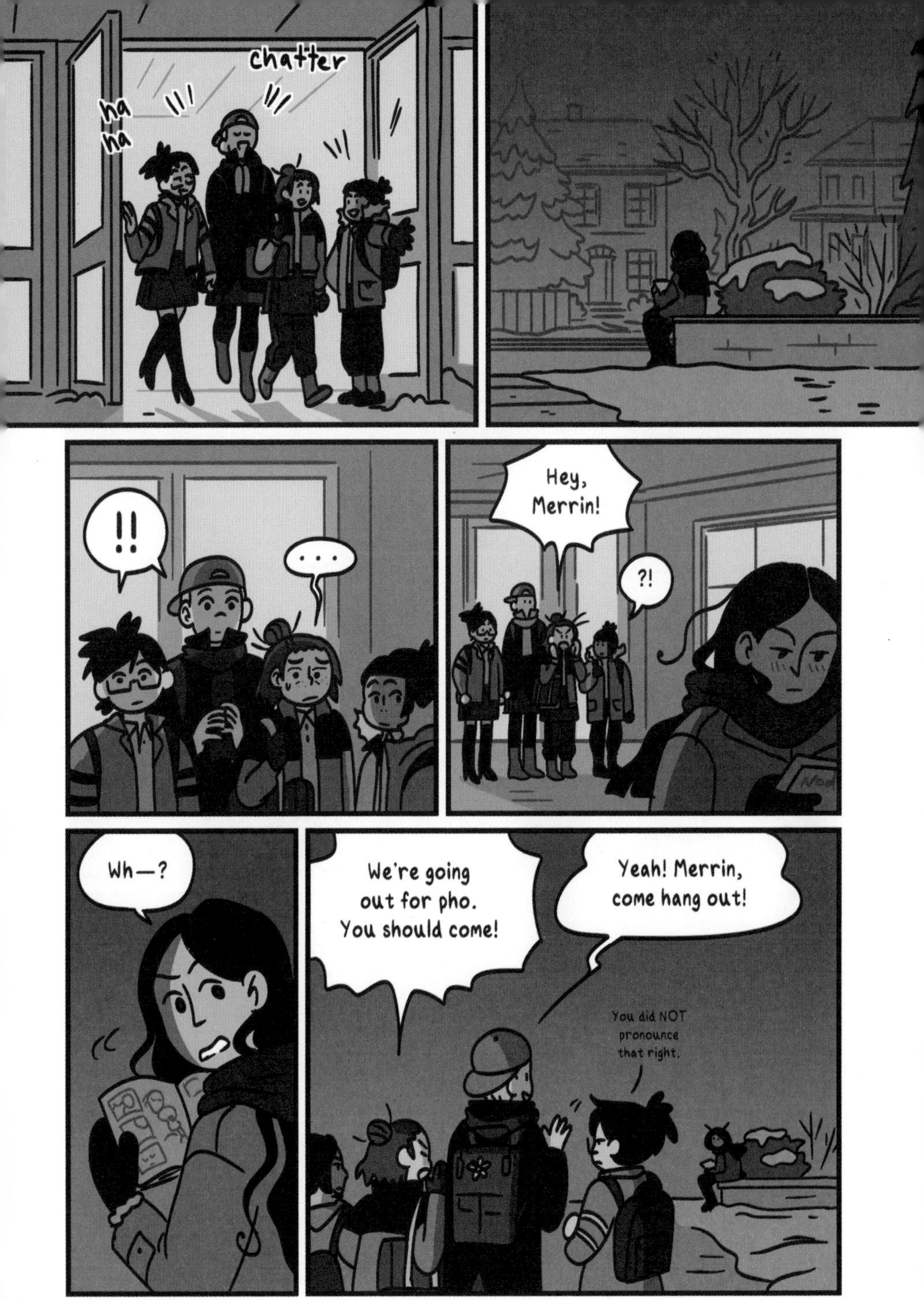
ha ha
chatter
!!
...
Hey, Merrin!
?!
Wh—?
We're going out for pho. You should come!
Yeah! Merrin, come hang out!
You did NOT pronounce that right.

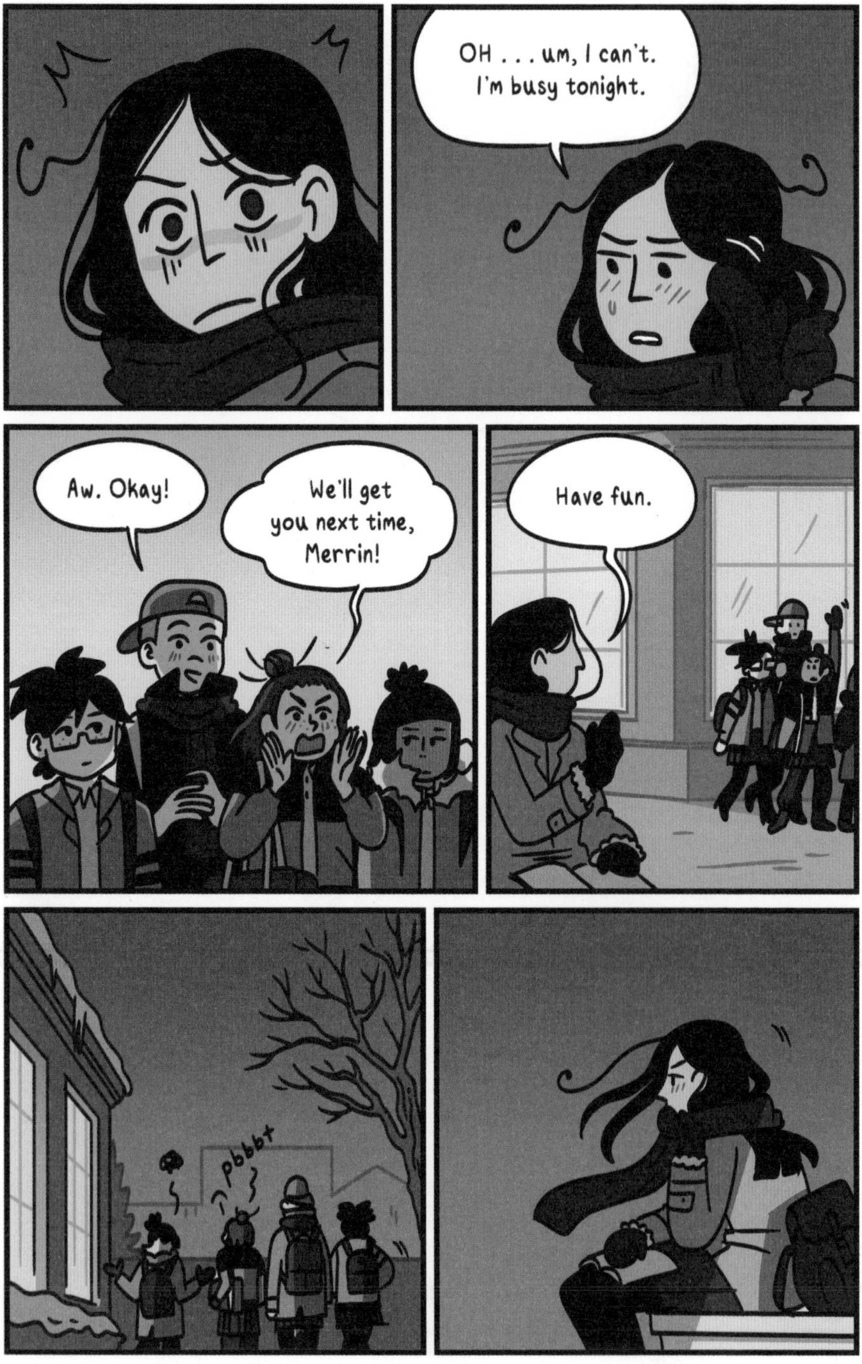
OH . . . um, I can't. I'm busy tonight.
Aw. Okay!
We'll get you next time, Merrin!
Have fun.
pbbbt

*Tsundere is a Japanese term for a character with an initially tough, cold, and moody personality who later changes over time to become someone warm and friendly.

Chapter 4

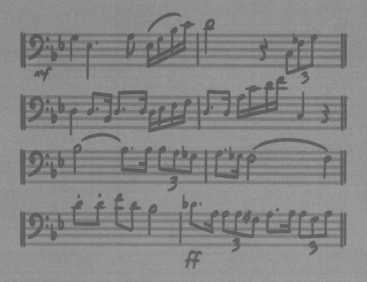

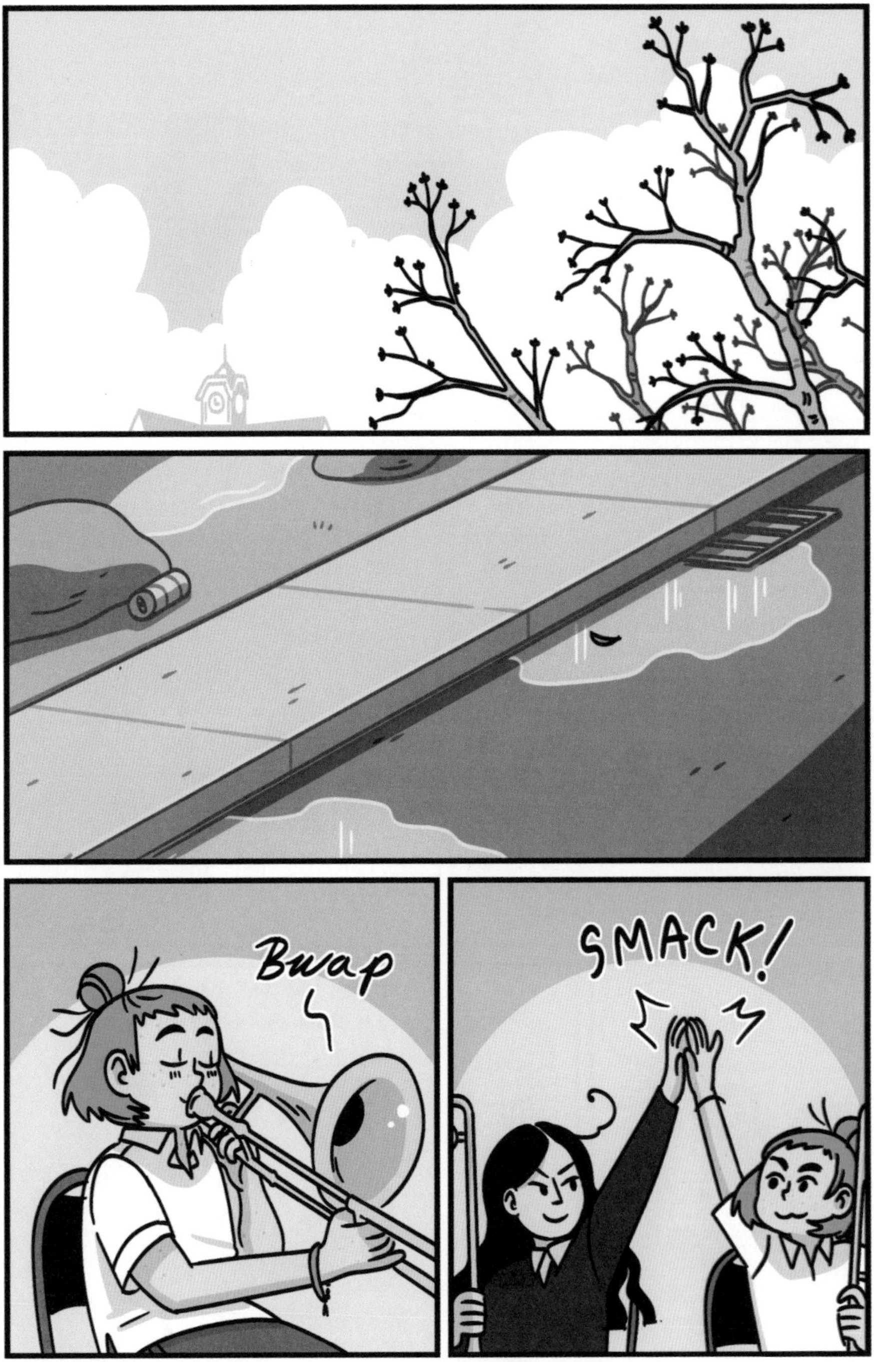
Bwap
SMACK!

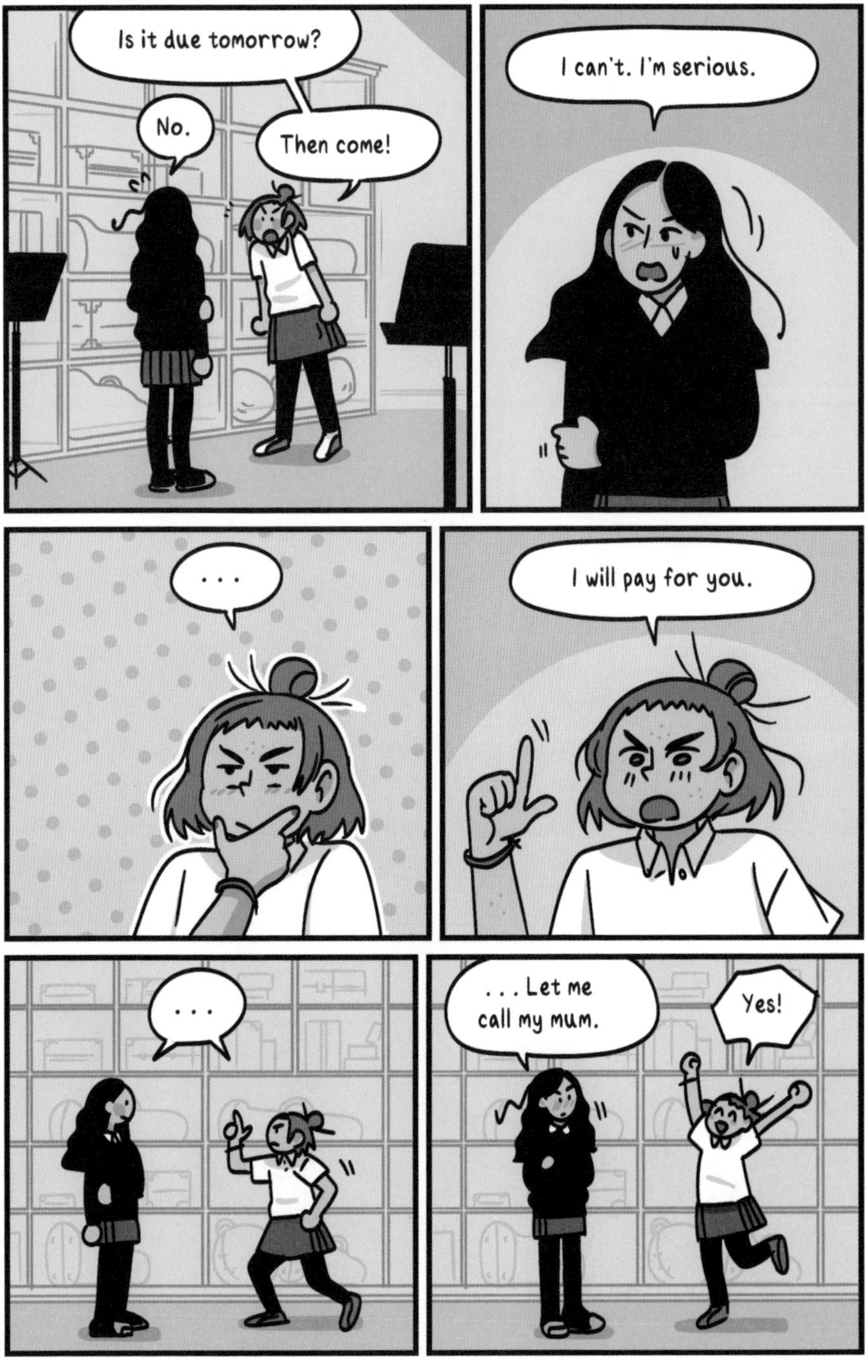
Is it due tomorrow?
No.
Then come!
I can't. I'm serious.
. . .
I will pay for you.
. . .
. . . Let me call my mum.
Yes!

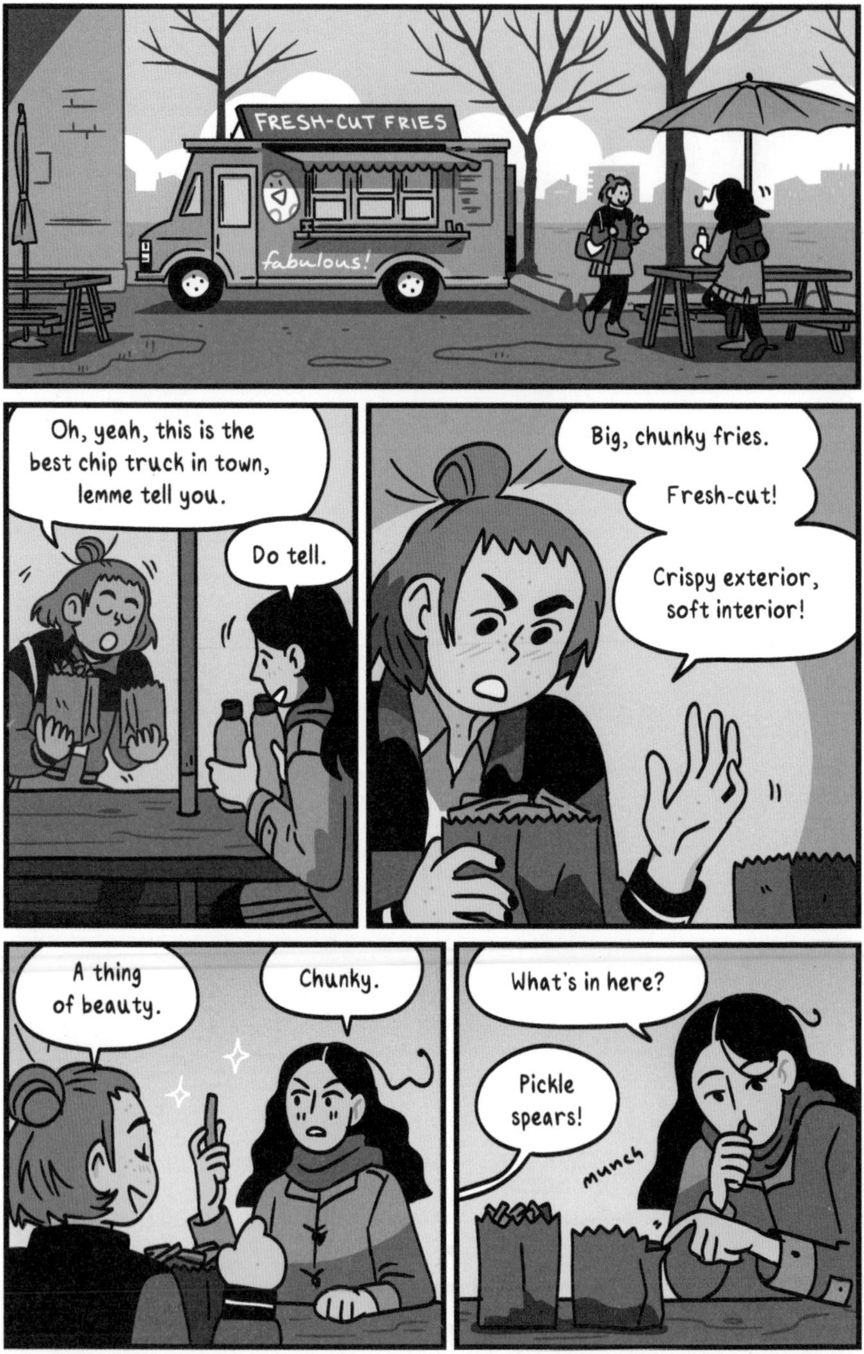
FRESH-CUT FRIES
fabulous!
Oh, yeah, this is the best chip truck in town, lemme tell you.
Do tell.
Big, chunky fries.
Fresh-cut!
Crispy exterior, soft interior!
A thing of beauty.
Chunky.
What's in here?
Pickle spears!
munch

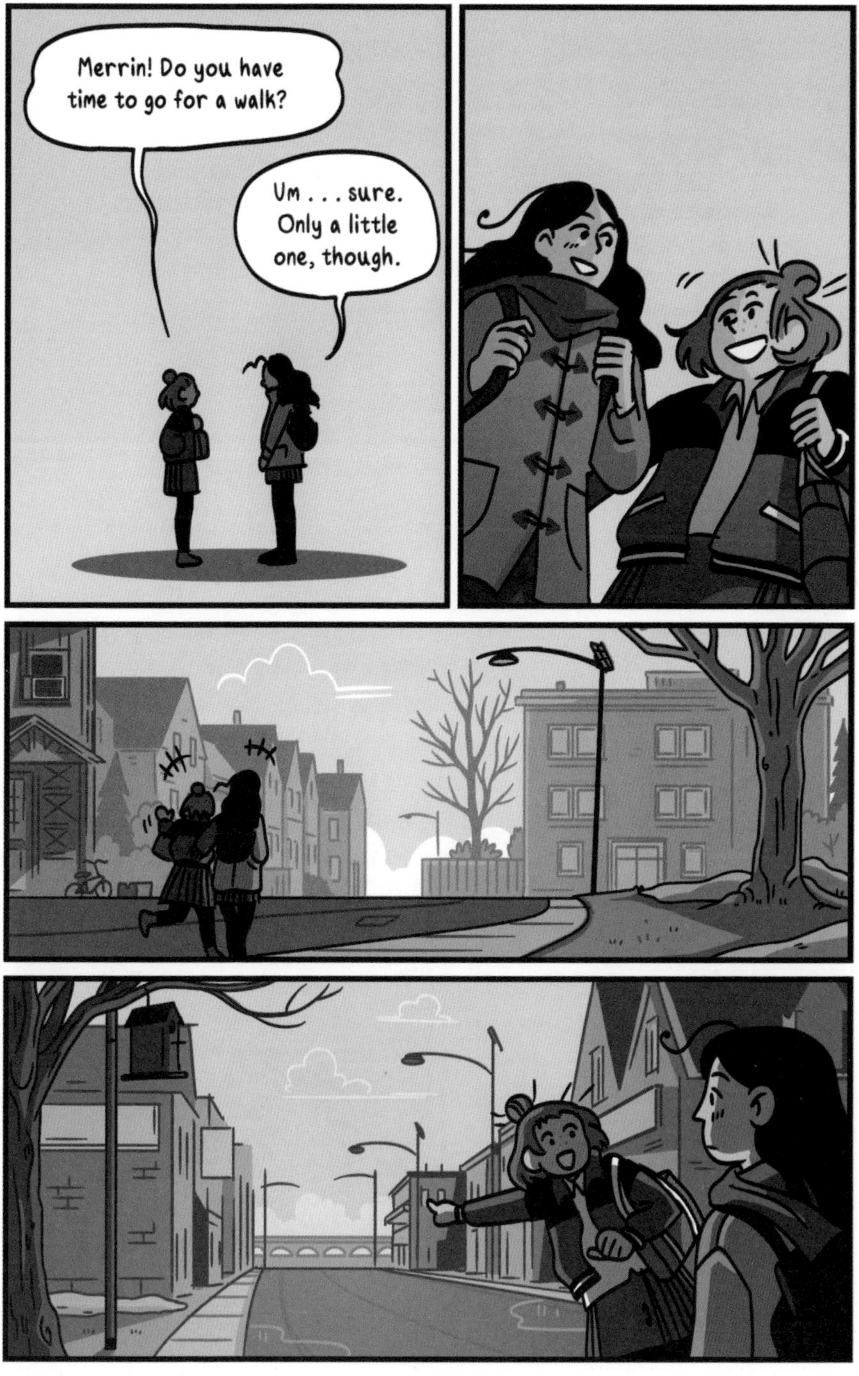
Merrin! Do you have time to go for a walk?
Um . . . sure. Only a little one, though.

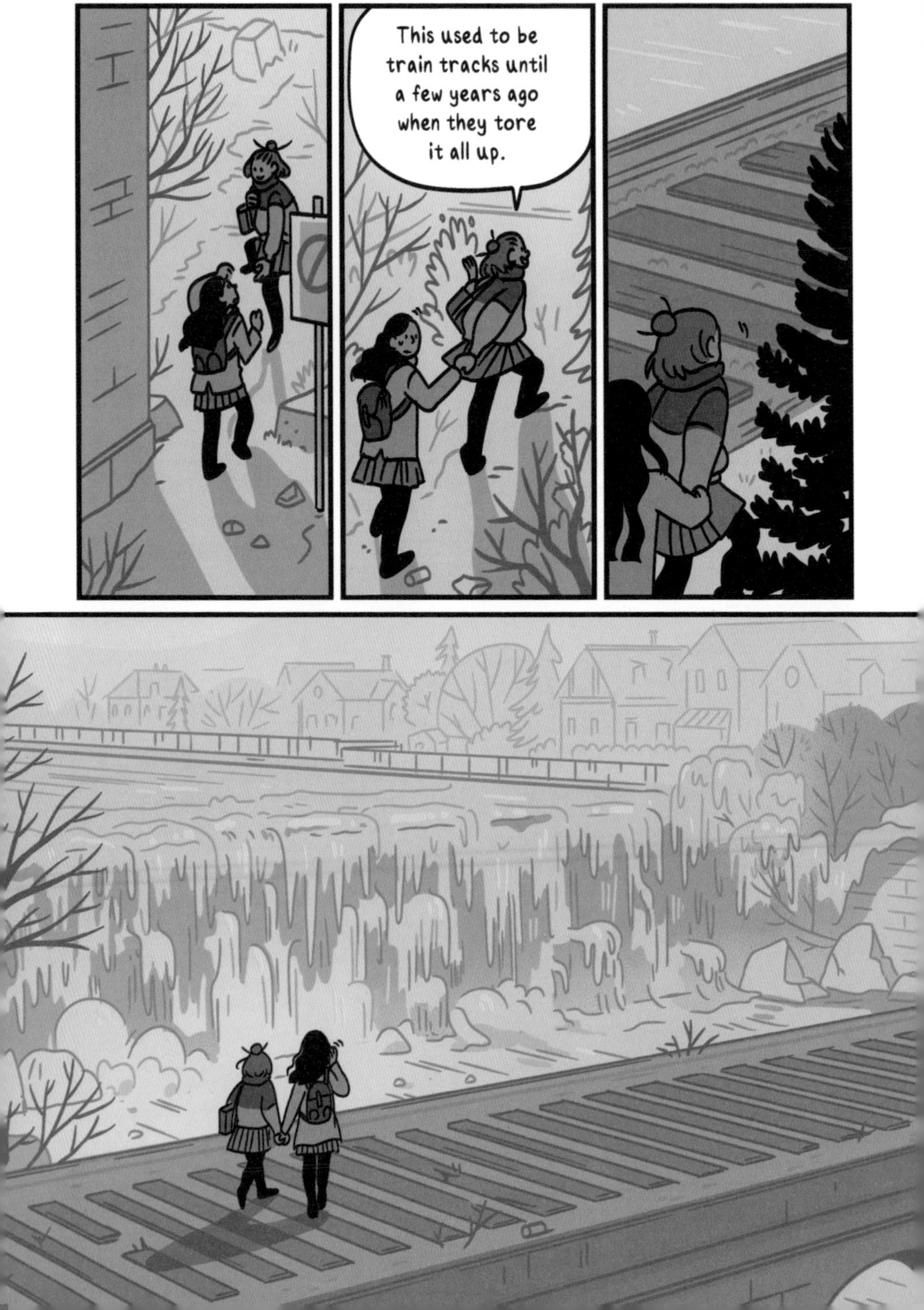
This used to be train tracks until a few years ago when they tore it all up.

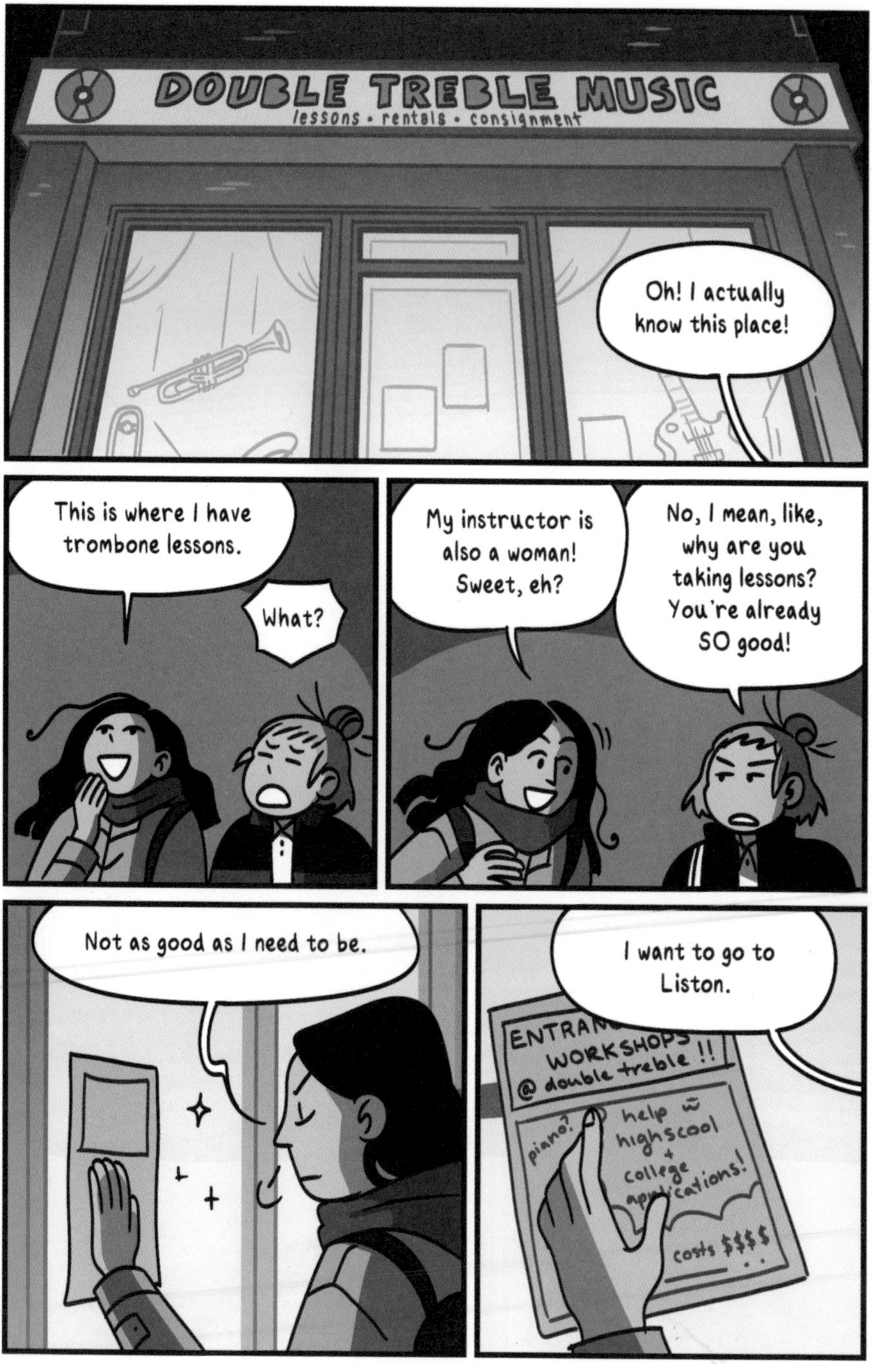
DOUBLE TREBLE MUSIC
lessons • rentals • consignment
Oh! I actually know this place!
This is where I have trombone lessons.
What?
My instructor is also a woman! Sweet, eh?
No, I mean, like, why are you taking lessons? You're already SO good!
Not as good as I need to be.
I want to go to Liston.
WORKSHOPS @ double treble !!
piano?
help w highscool + college applications!
costs $$$$

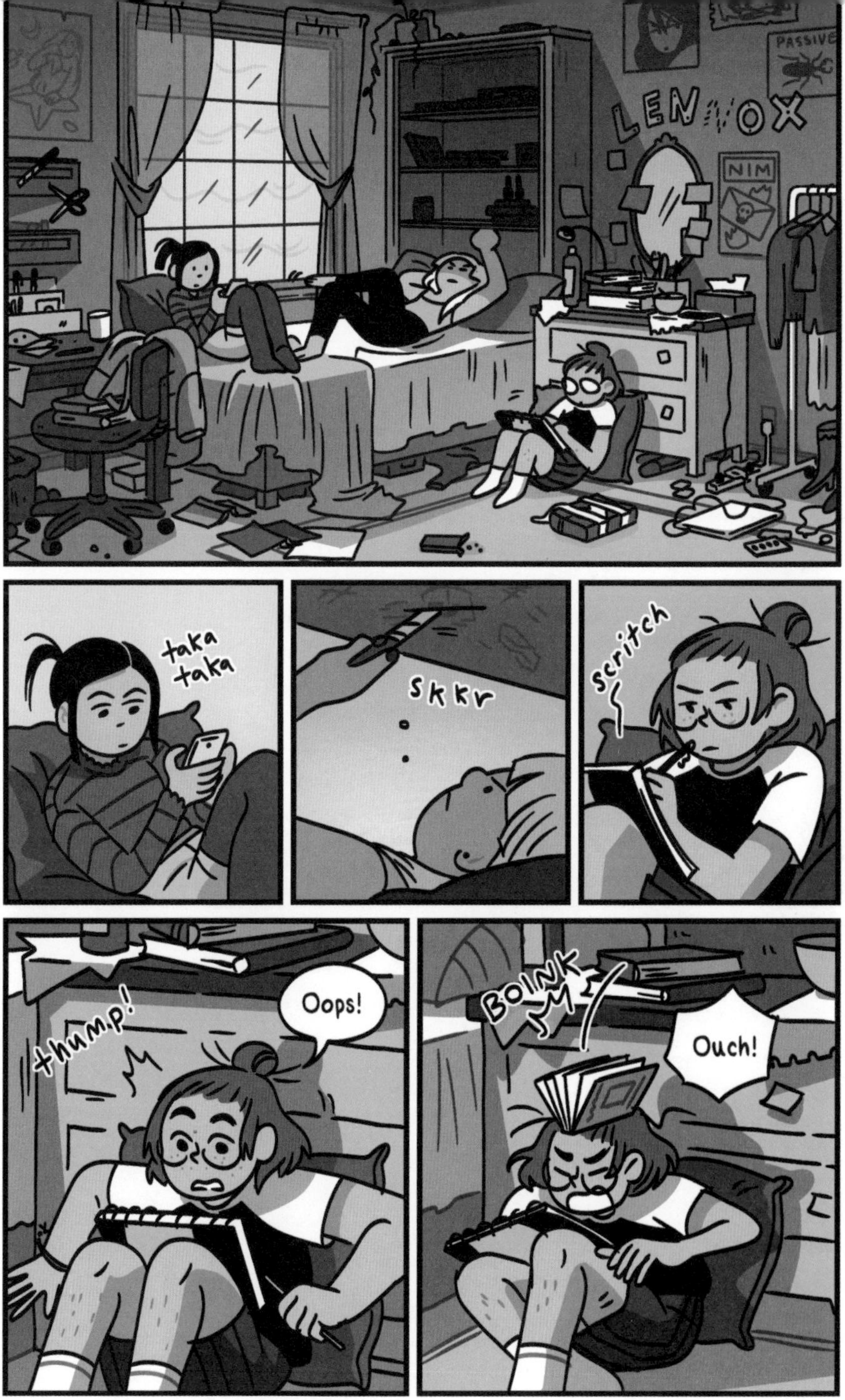

LENNOX
NIM
PASSIVE
taka taka
SKKR
scritch
thump!
Oops!
BOINK
Ouch!

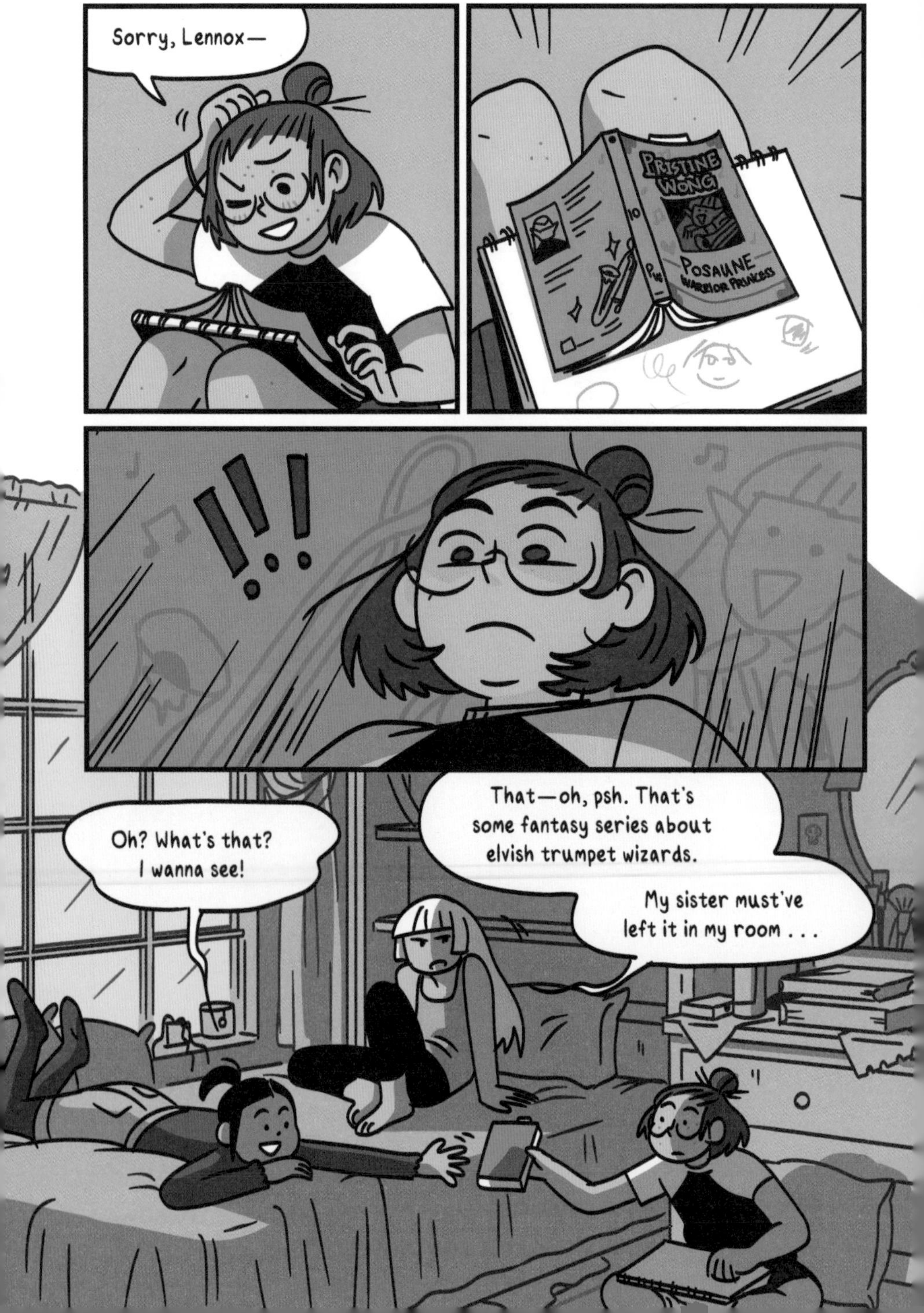
Sorry, Lennox—
PRISTINE WONG
POSAUNE WARRIOR PRINCESS
!!!
Oh? What's that? I wanna see!
That—oh, psh. That's some fantasy series about elvish trumpet wizards.
My sister must've left it in my room . . .

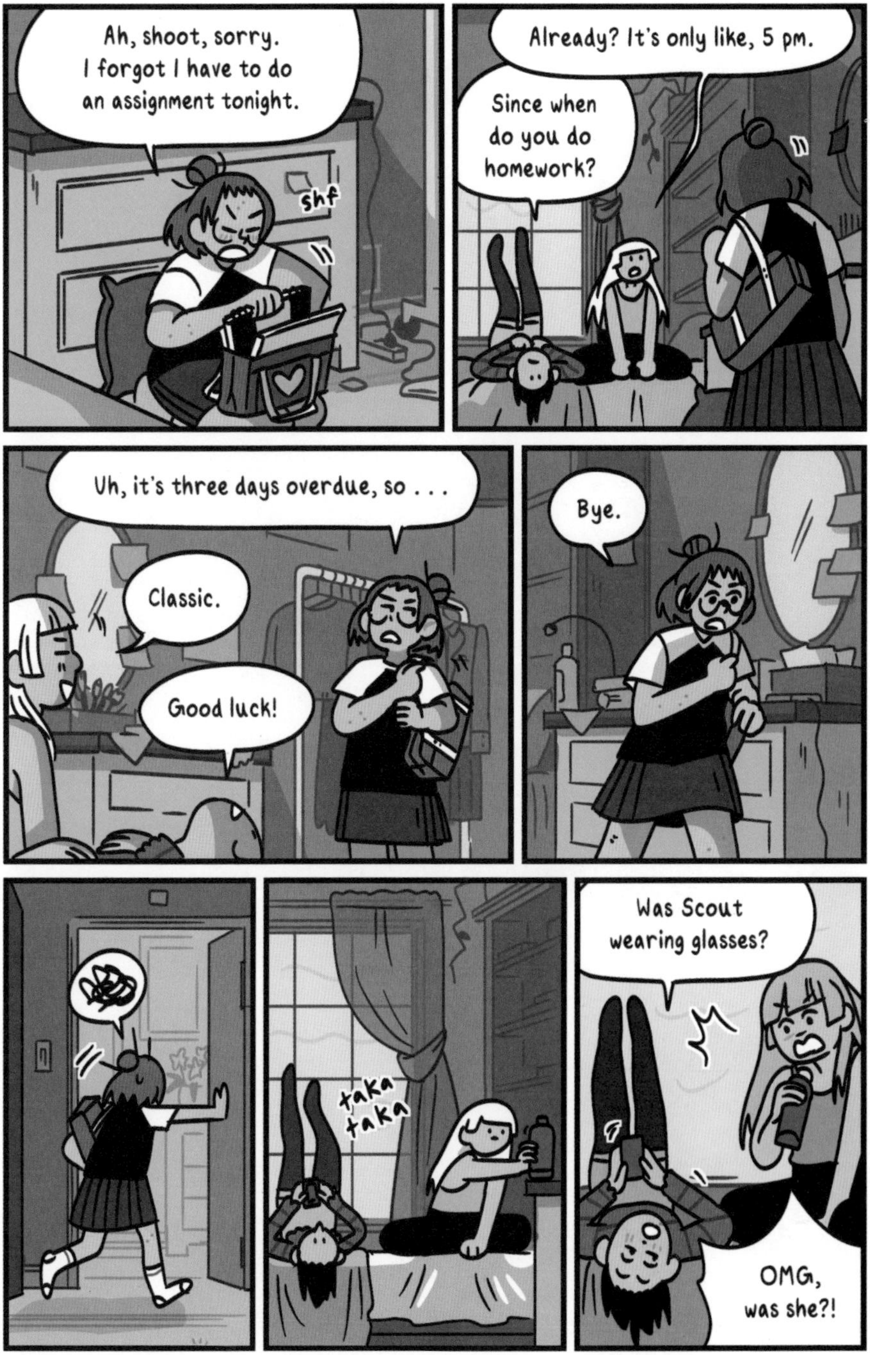
Ah, shoot, sorry. I forgot I have to do an assignment tonight.
shf
Already? It's only like, 5 pm.
Since when do you do homework?
Uh, it's three days overdue, so . . .
Classic.
Good luck!
Bye.
taka taka
Was Scout wearing glasses?
OMG, was she?!

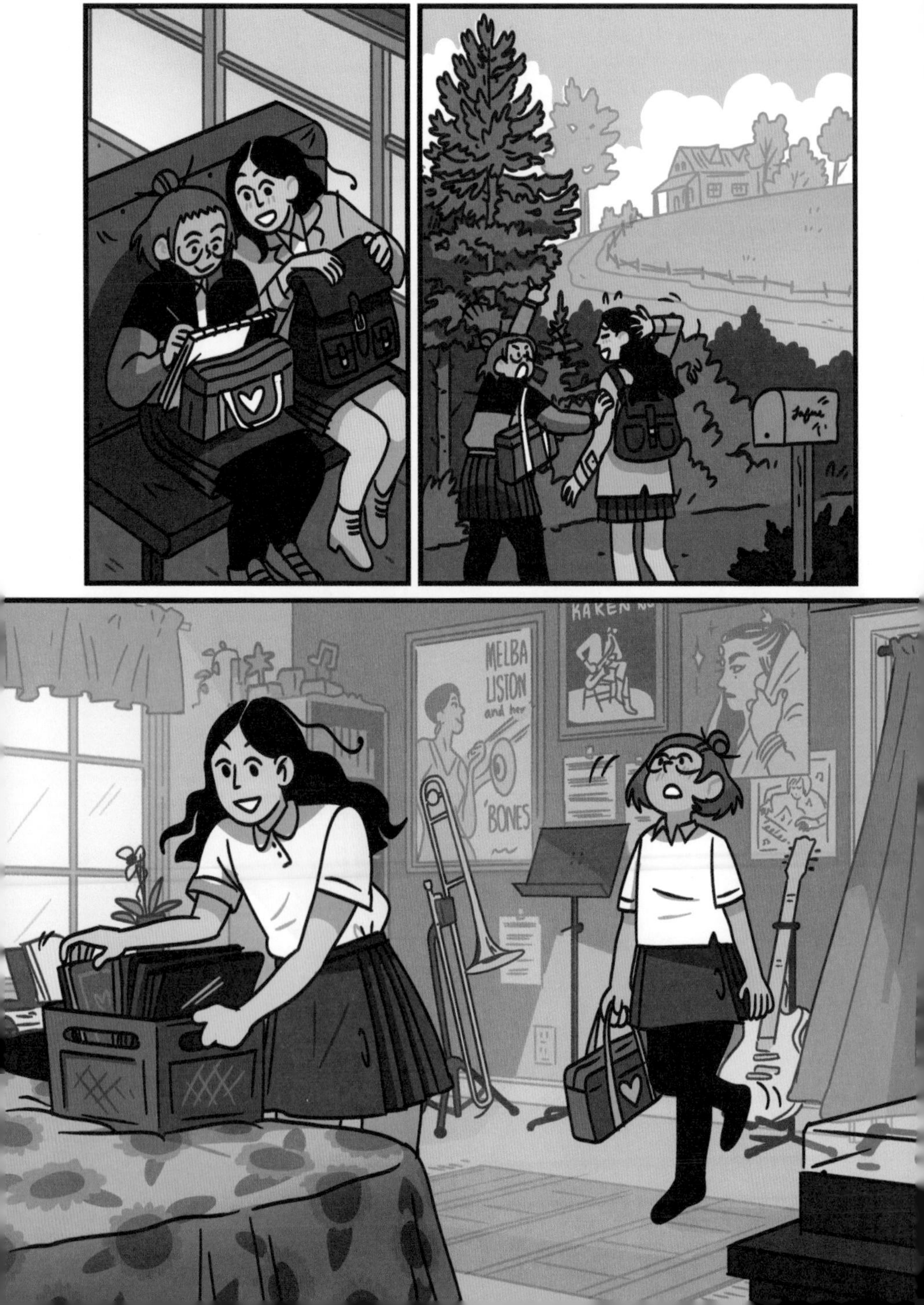
MELBA LISTON and her 'BONES

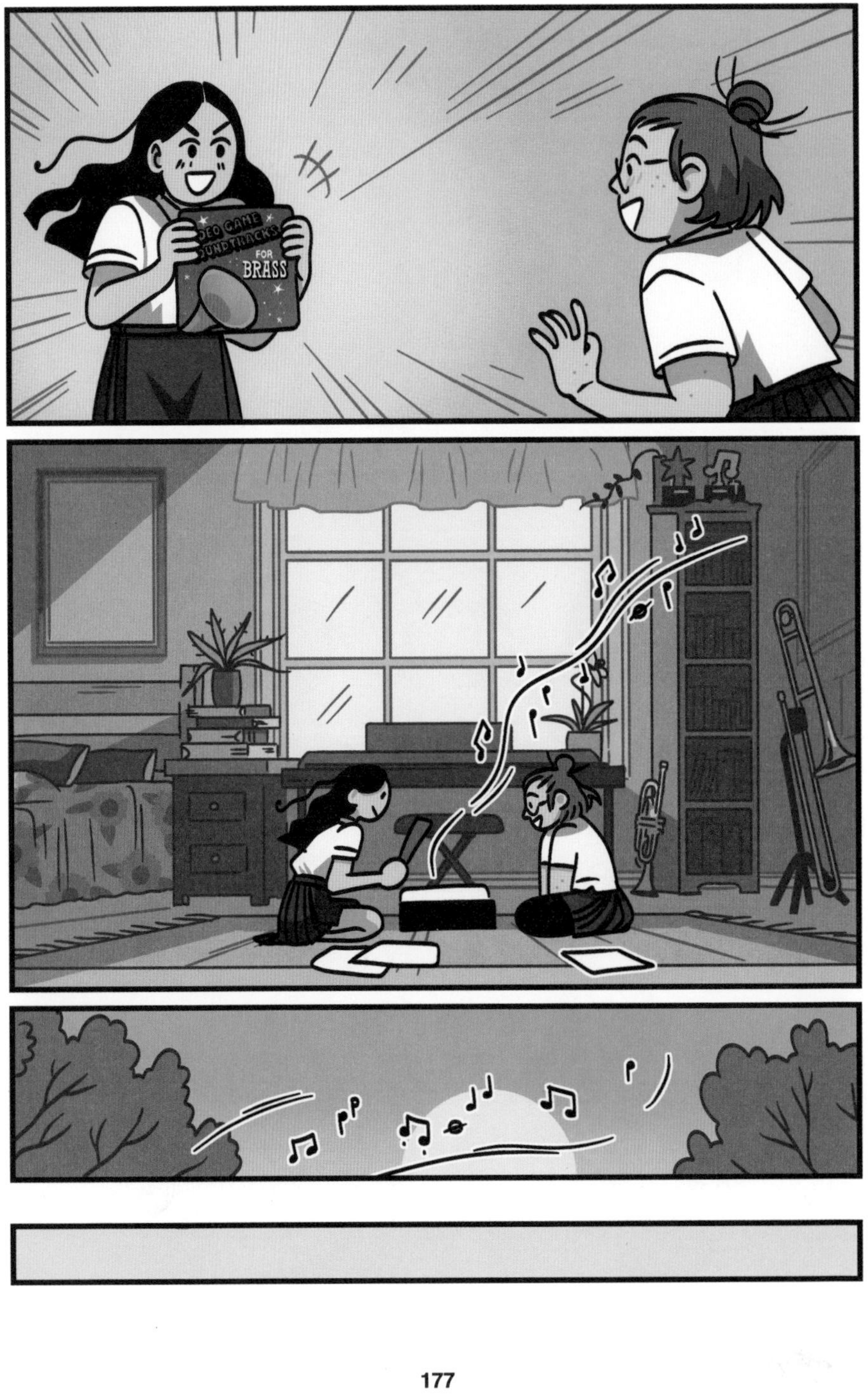
FOR
BRASS

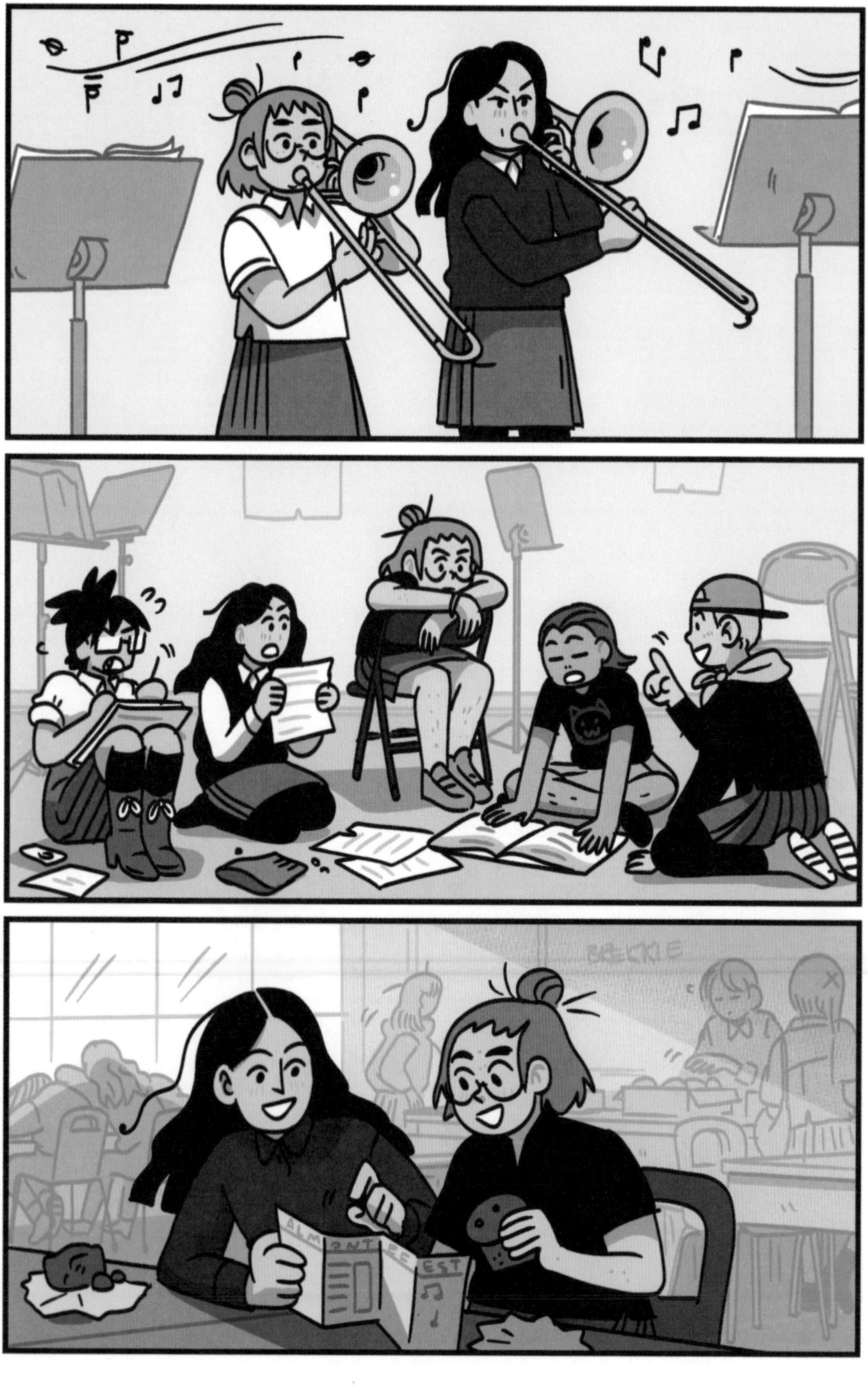
BREKKIE

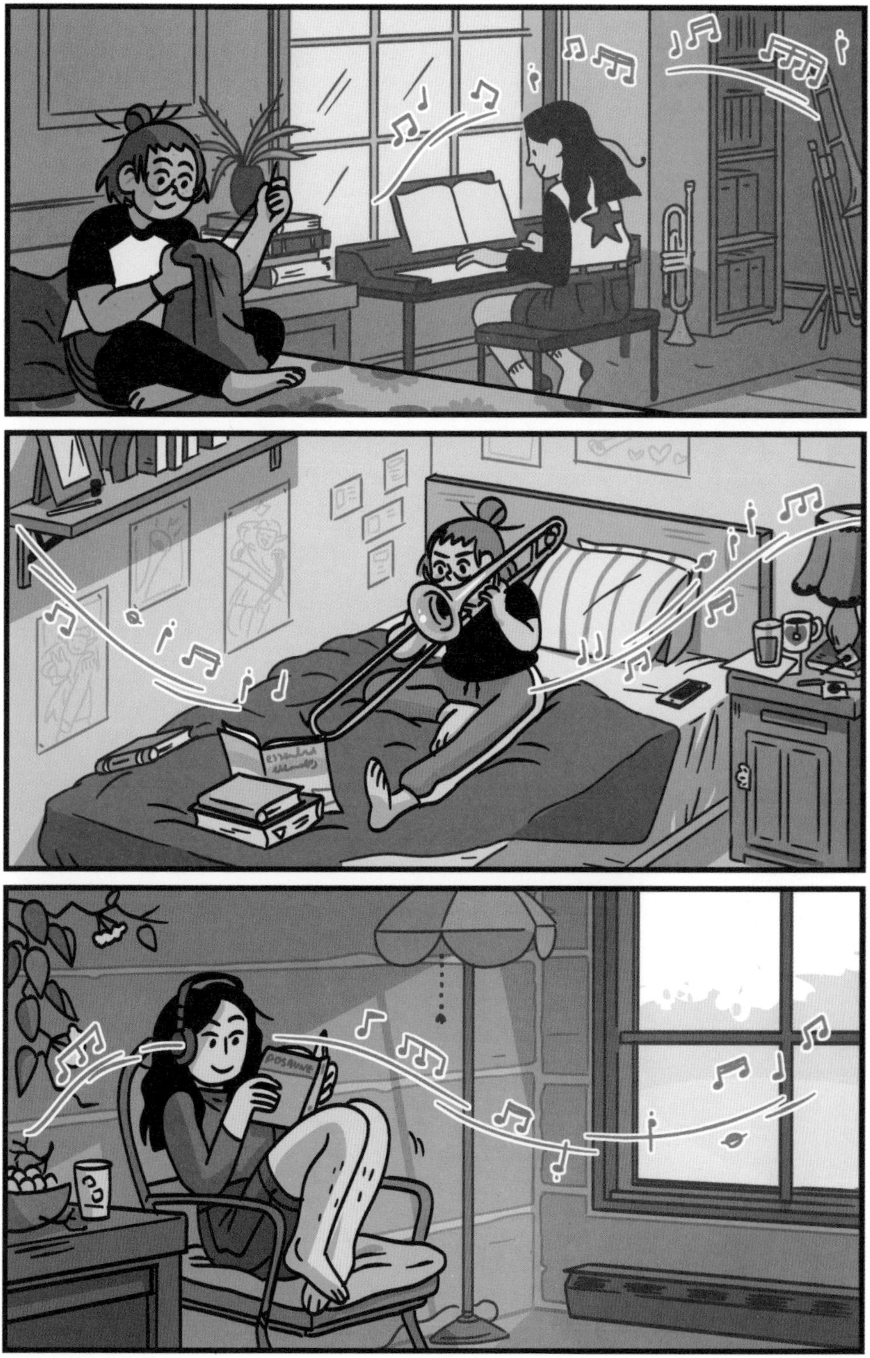
POSAUNE

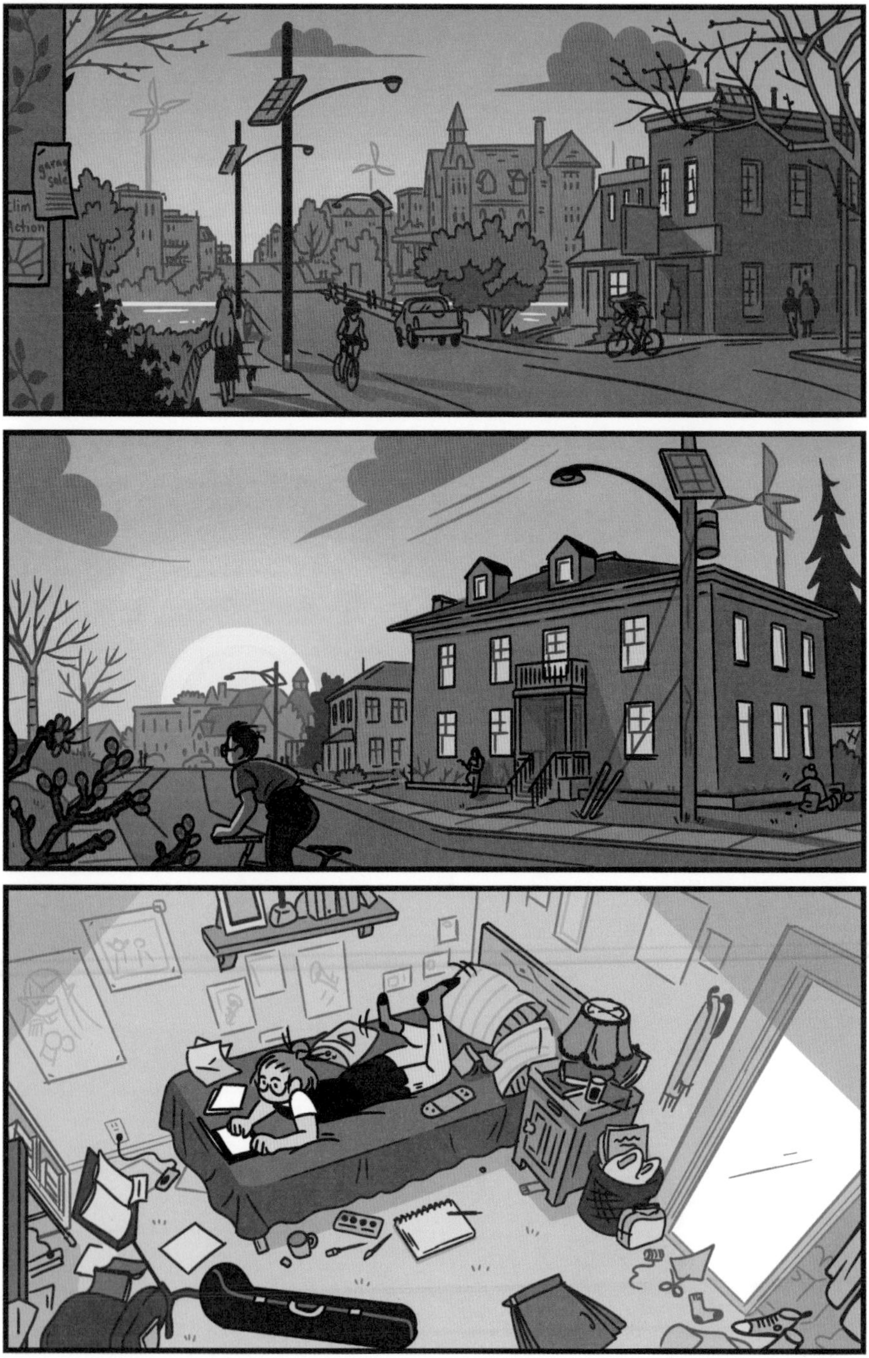

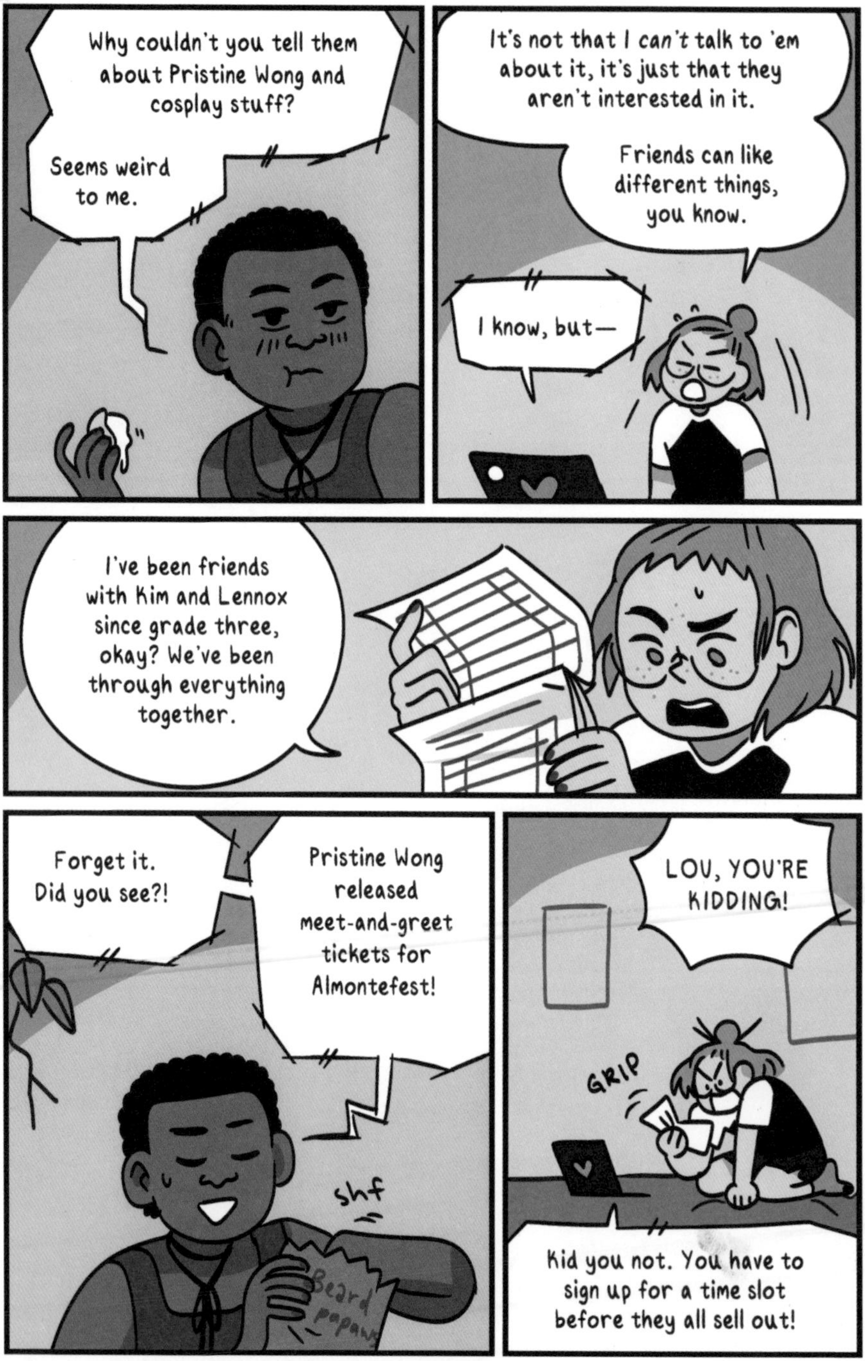
Why couldn't you tell them about Pristine Wong and cosplay stuff?
Seems weird to me.
It's not that I *can't* talk to 'em about it, it's just that they aren't interested in it.
Friends can like different things, you know.
I know, but—
I've been friends with Kim and Lennox since grade three, okay? We've been through everything together.
Forget it. Did you see?!
Pristine Wong released meet-and-greet tickets for Almontefest!
shf
Beard papa's
LOU, YOU'RE KIDDING!
GRIP
Kid you not. You have to sign up for a time slot before they all sell out!

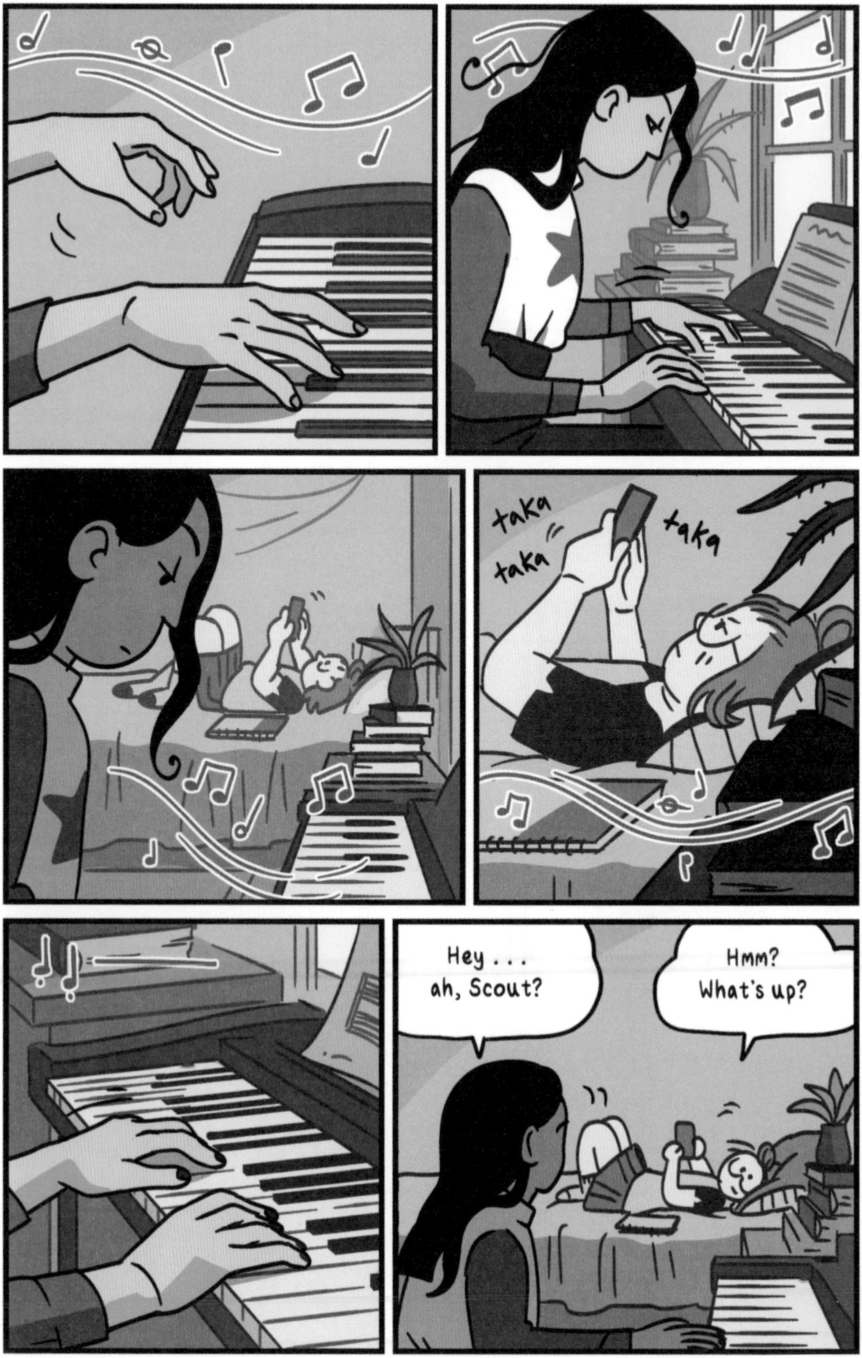
taka
taka
taka
Hey . . . ah, Scout?
Hmm? What's up?

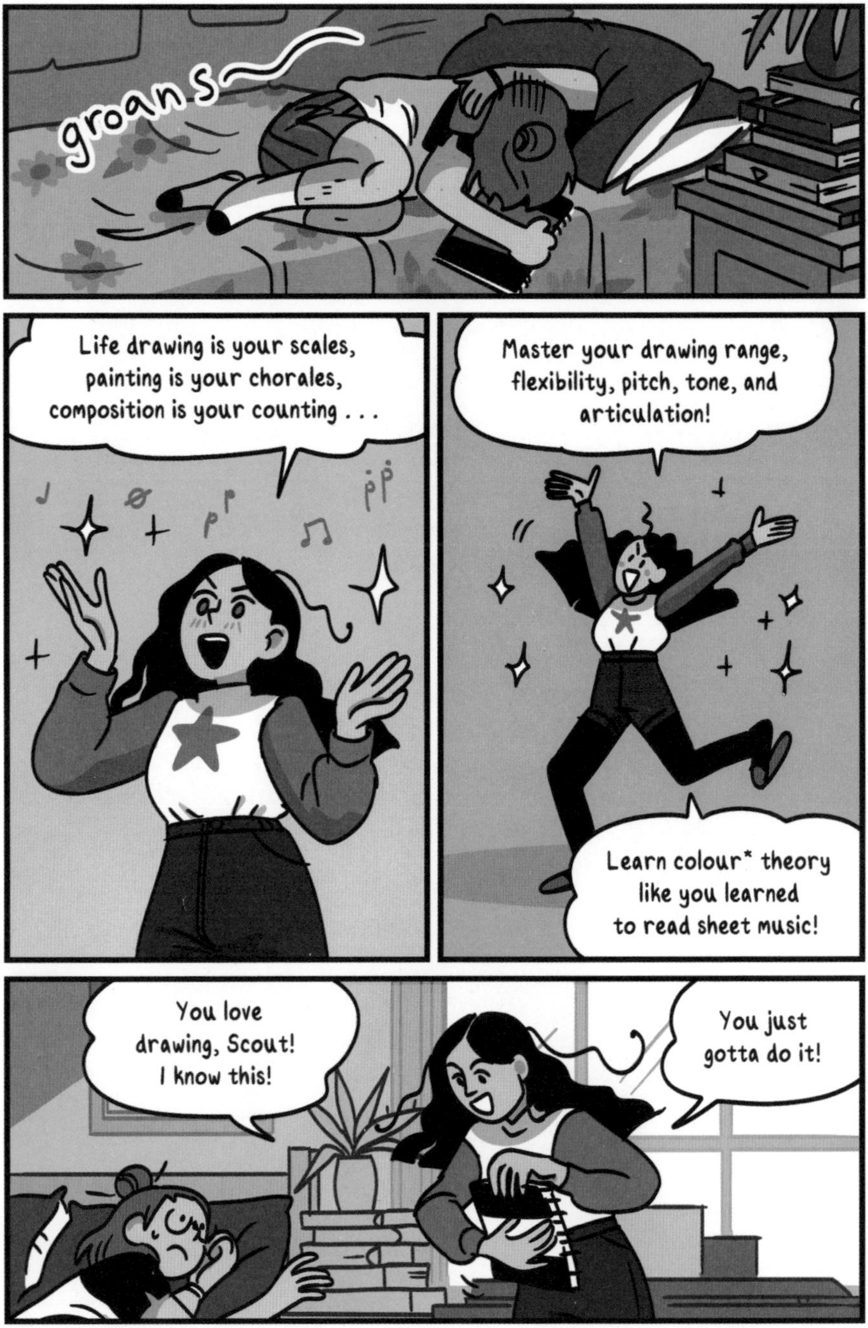
groans
Life drawing is your scales, painting is your chorales, composition is your counting . . .
Master your drawing range, flexibility, pitch, tone, and articulation!
Learn colour* theory like you learned to read sheet music!
You love drawing, Scout! I know this!
You just gotta do it!

*Color is spelt colour in Canadian English.

Chapter 5

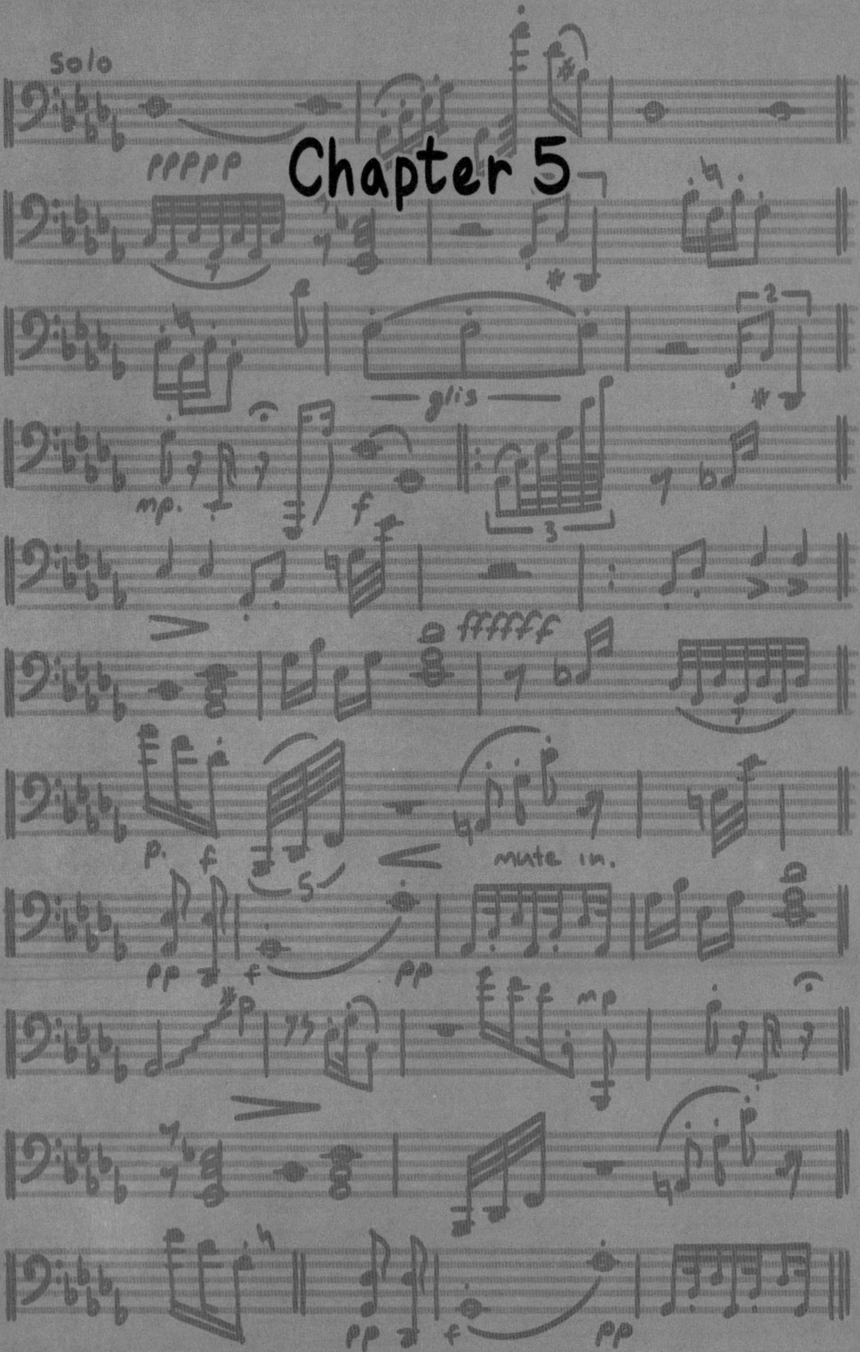

Solo
ppppp
gliss
mp.
f
ffffff
p.
f
mute in.
pp
f
pp
mp
pp
f
pp

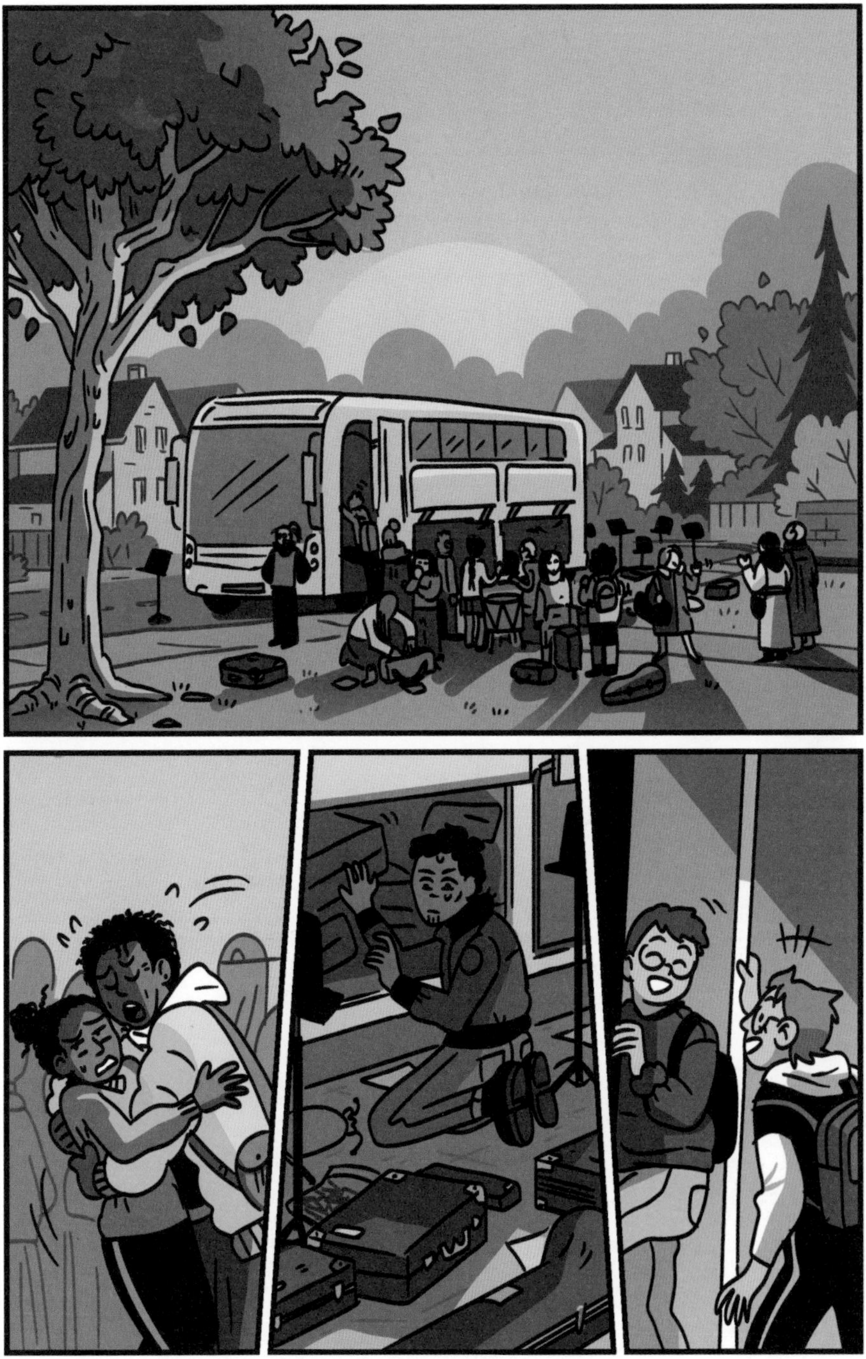

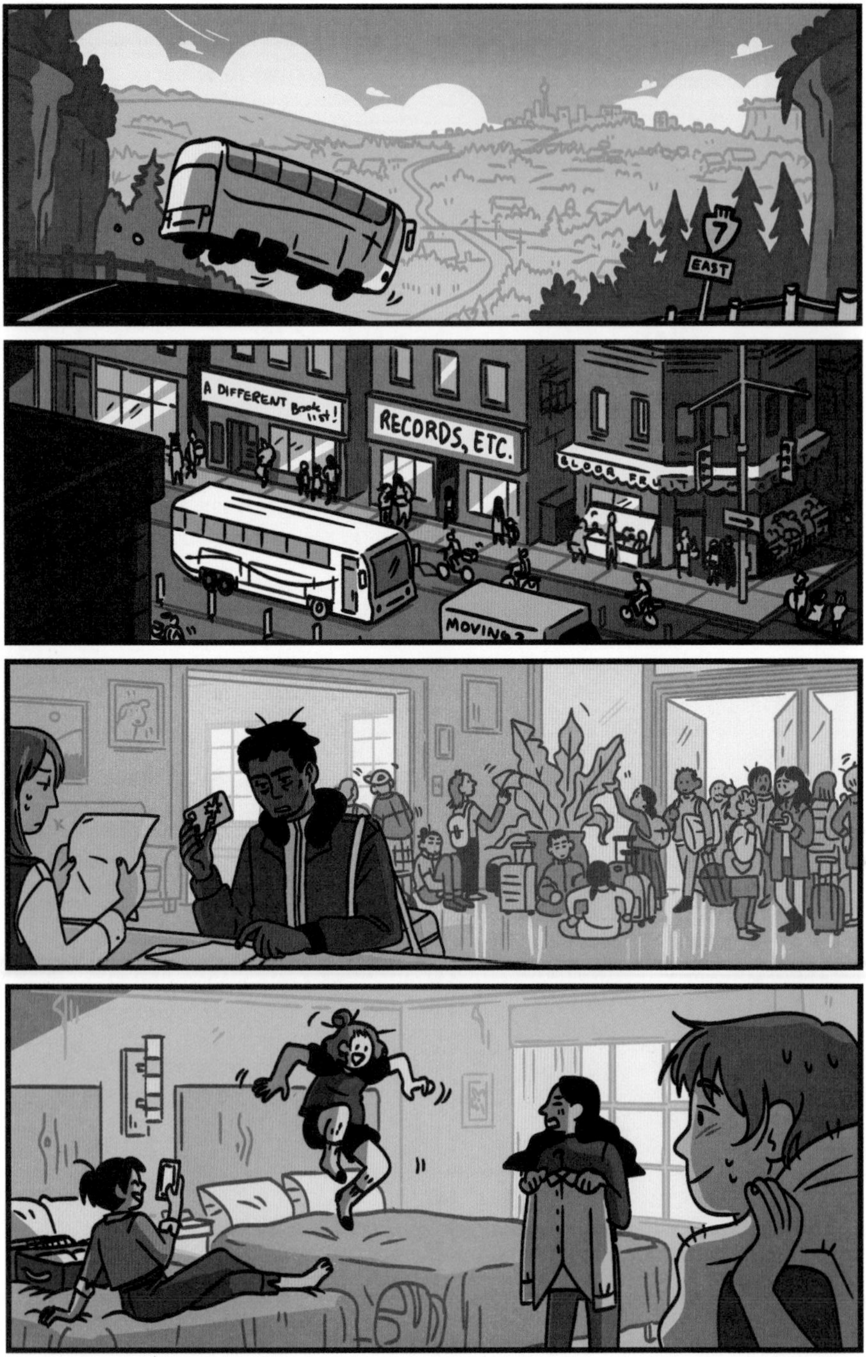
7
EAST
A DIFFERENT Book list!
RECORDS, ETC.

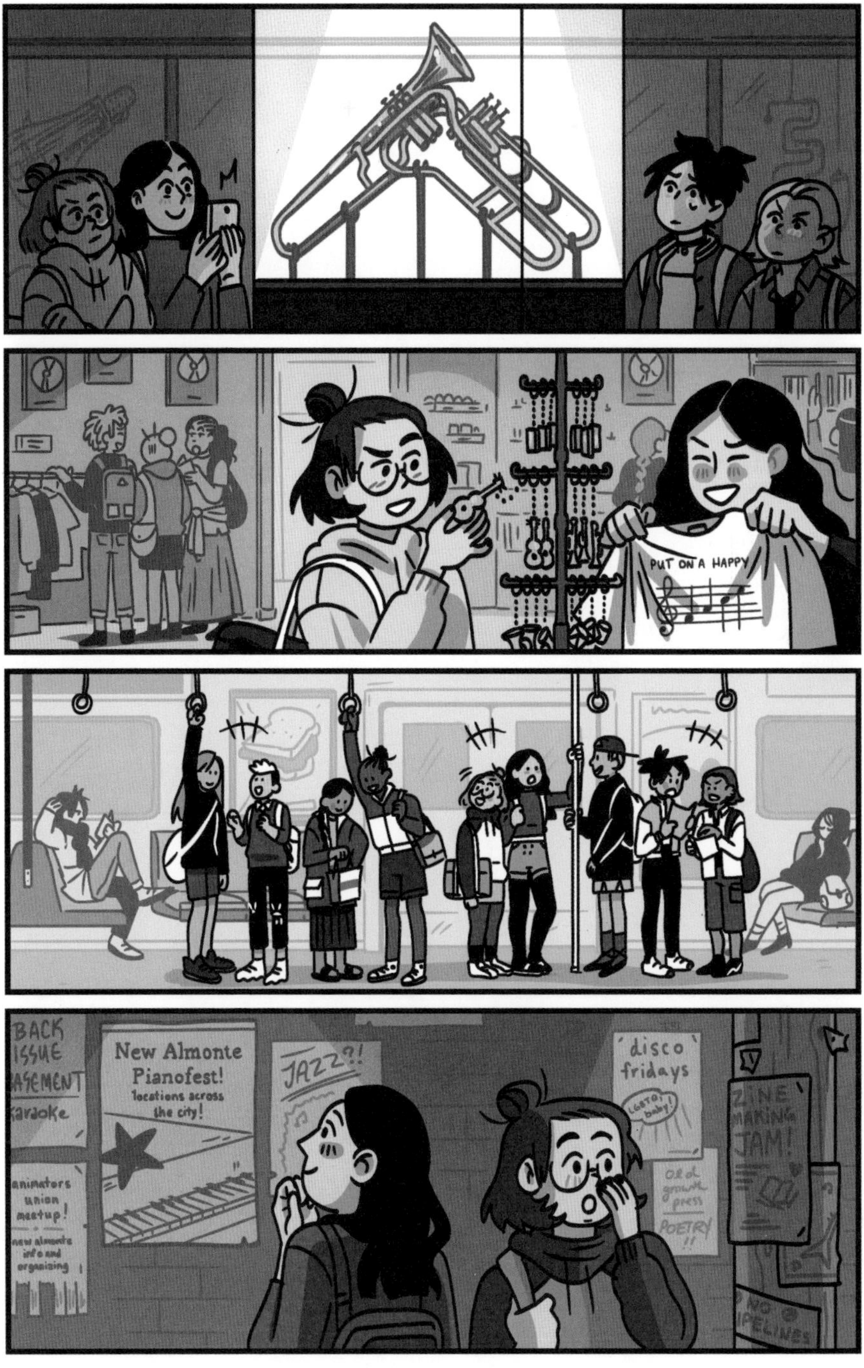
PUT ON A HAPPY
BACK ISSUE
New Almonte Pianofest!
locations across the city!
JAZZ?!
disco fridays
LGBTQ, baby!
animators union meetup!
new almonte info and organizing
POETRY !!
ZINE MAKING JAM!

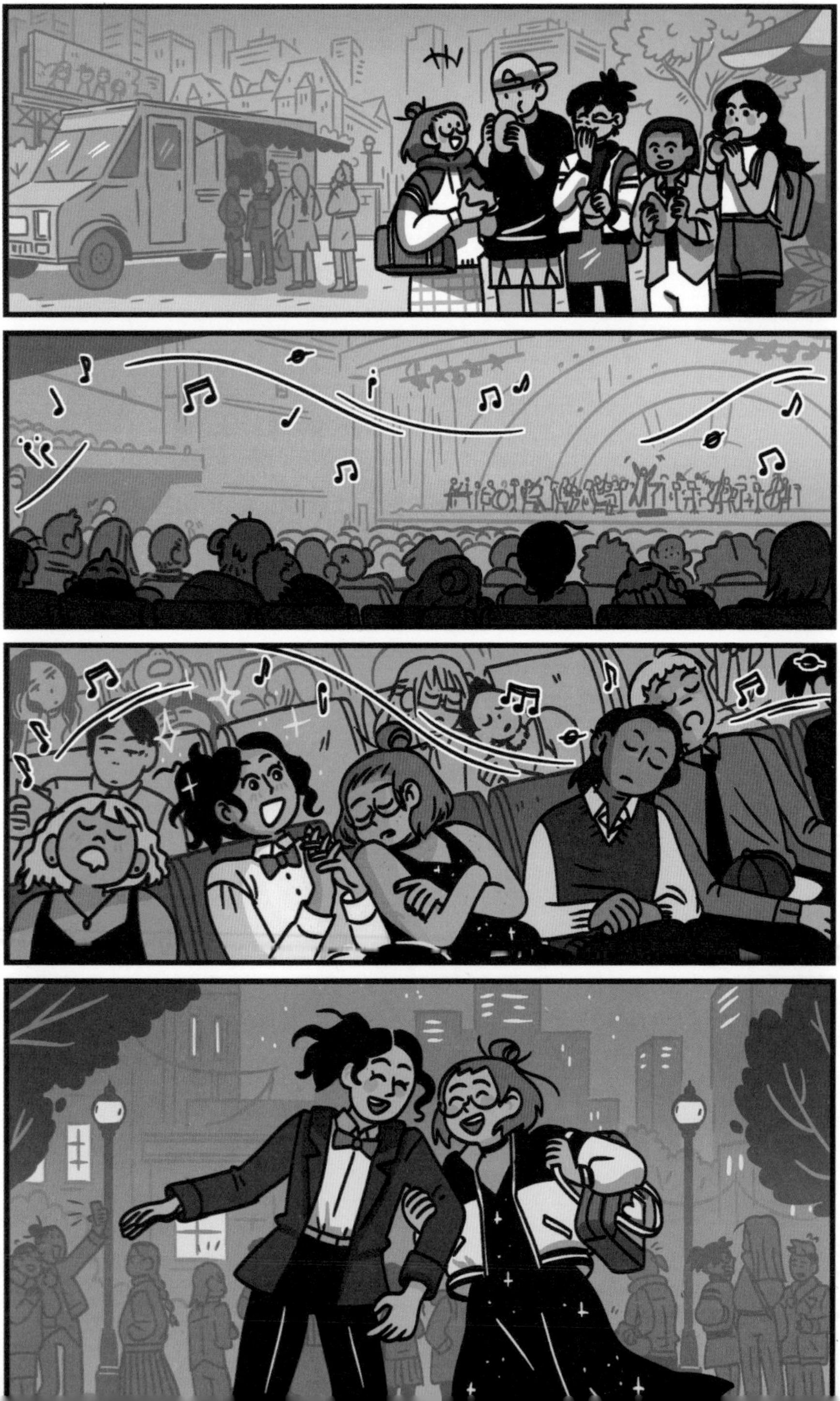

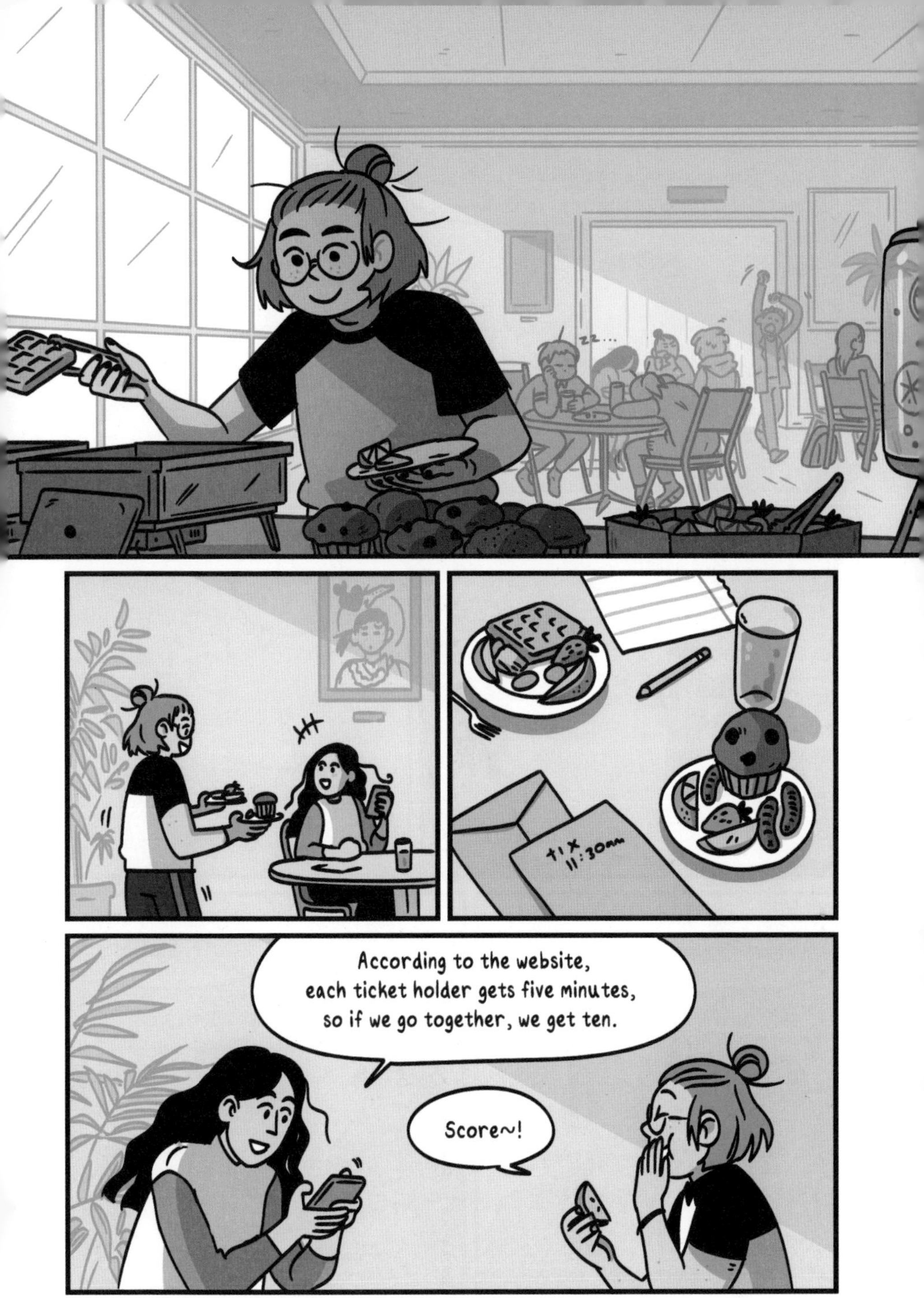
zz...
tix
11:30am
According to the website, each ticket holder gets five minutes, so if we go together, we get ten.
Score~!

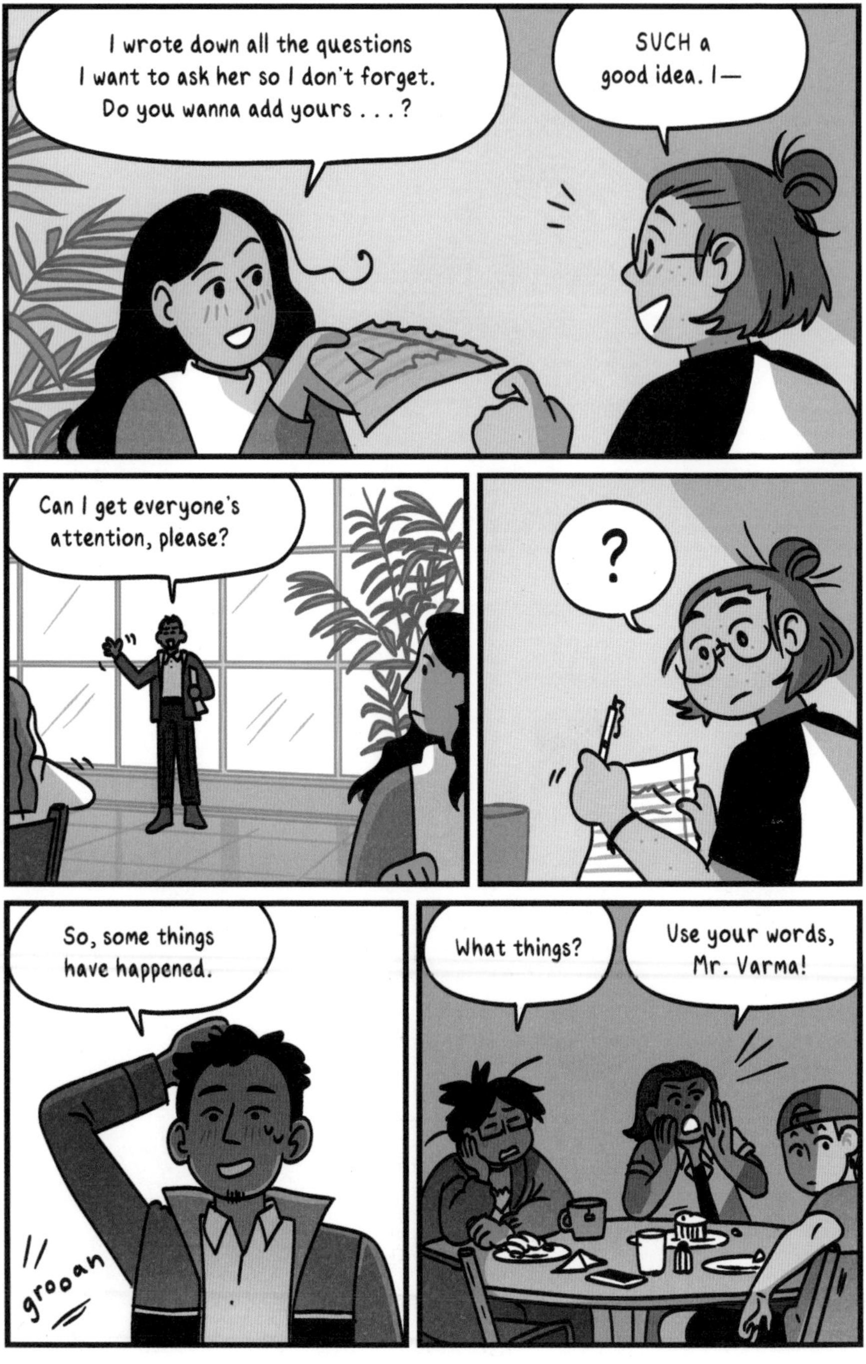
I wrote down all the questions I want to ask her so I don't forget. Do you wanna add yours . . . ?
SUCH a good idea. I—
Can I get everyone's attention, please?
?
So, some things have happened.
groan
What things?
Use your words, Mr. Varma!

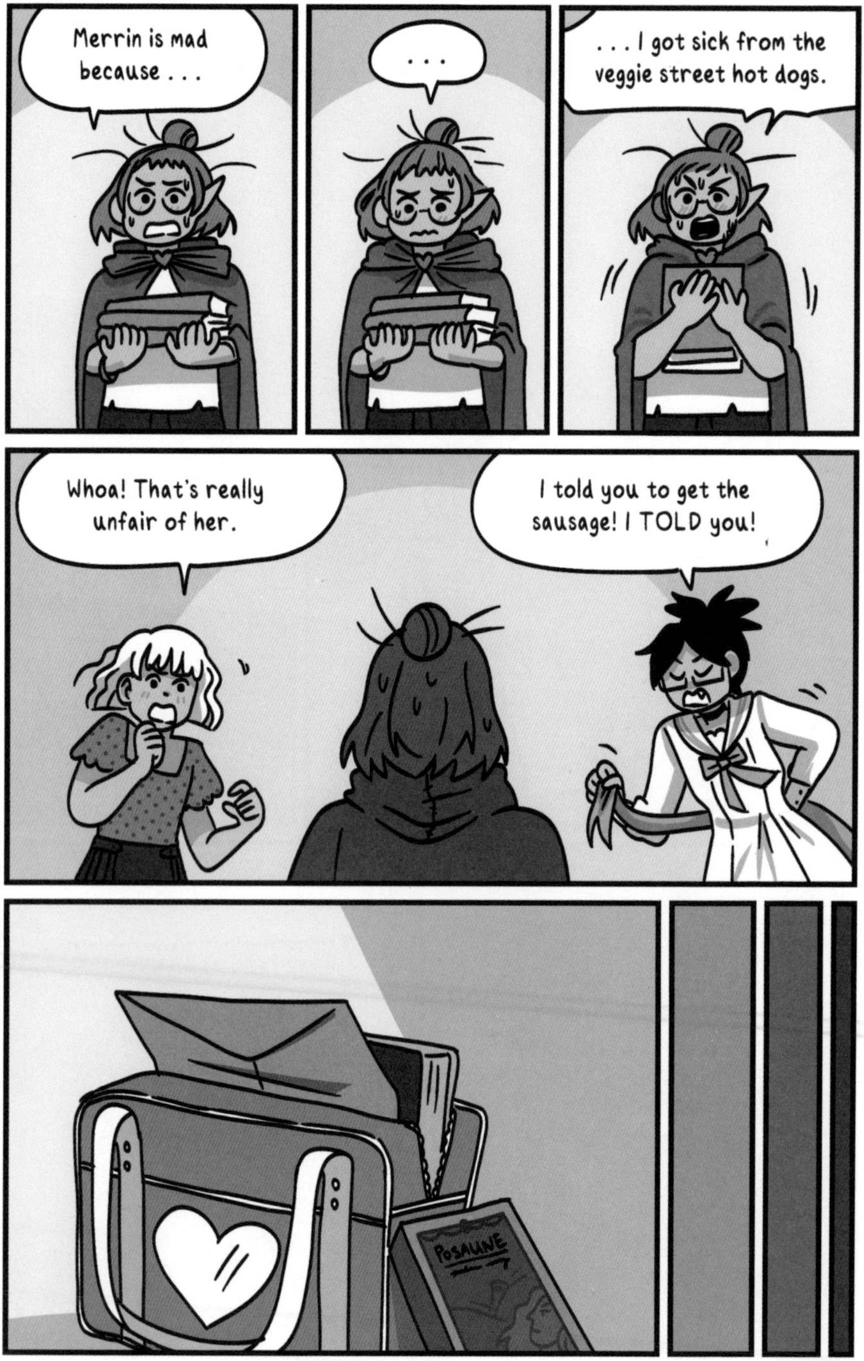
Merrin is mad
because . . .
. . .
. . . I got sick from the
veggie street hot dogs.
Whoa! That's really
unfair of her.
I told you to get the
sausage! I TOLD you!
POSAUNE

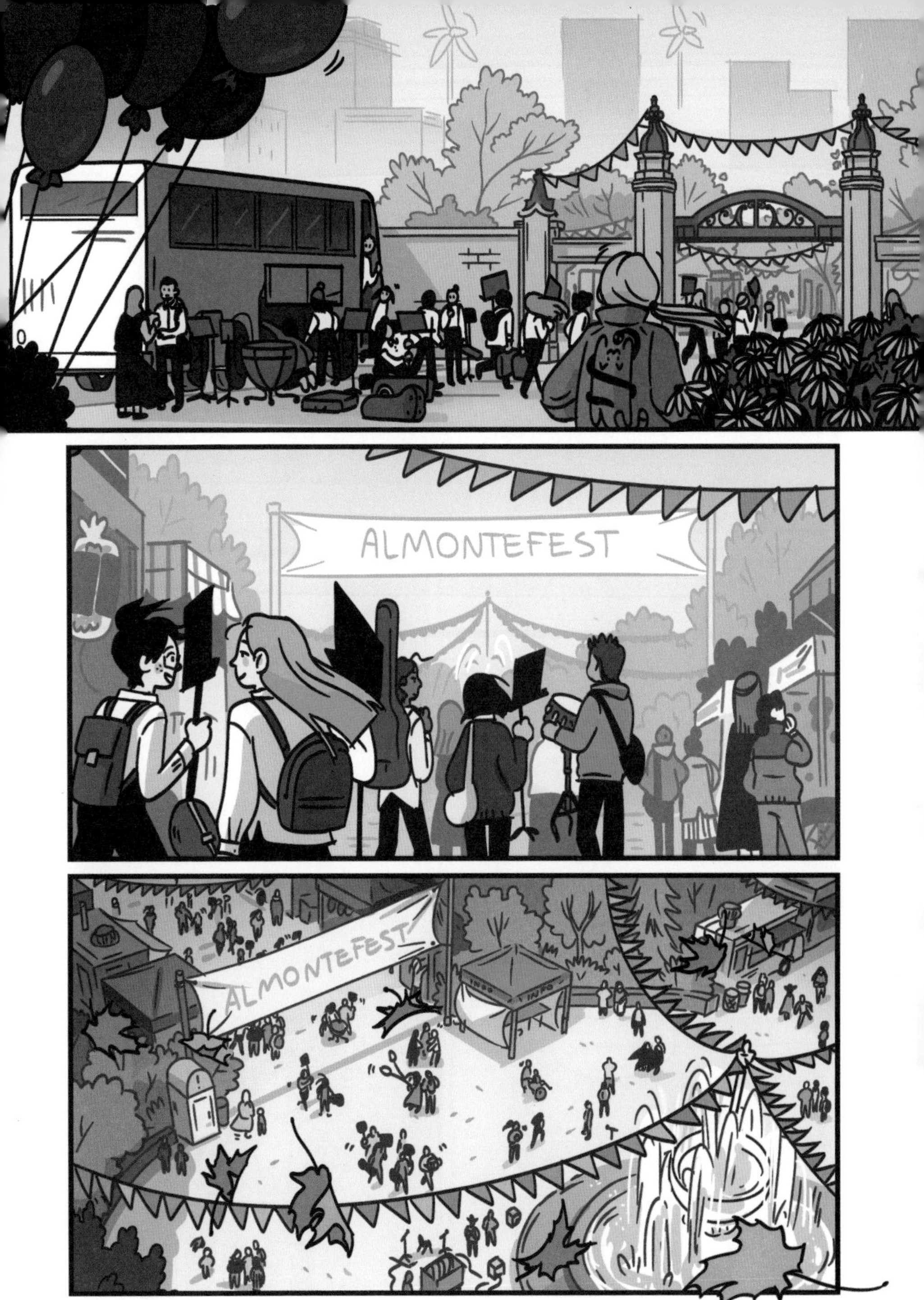
ALMONTEFEST
ALMONTEFEST

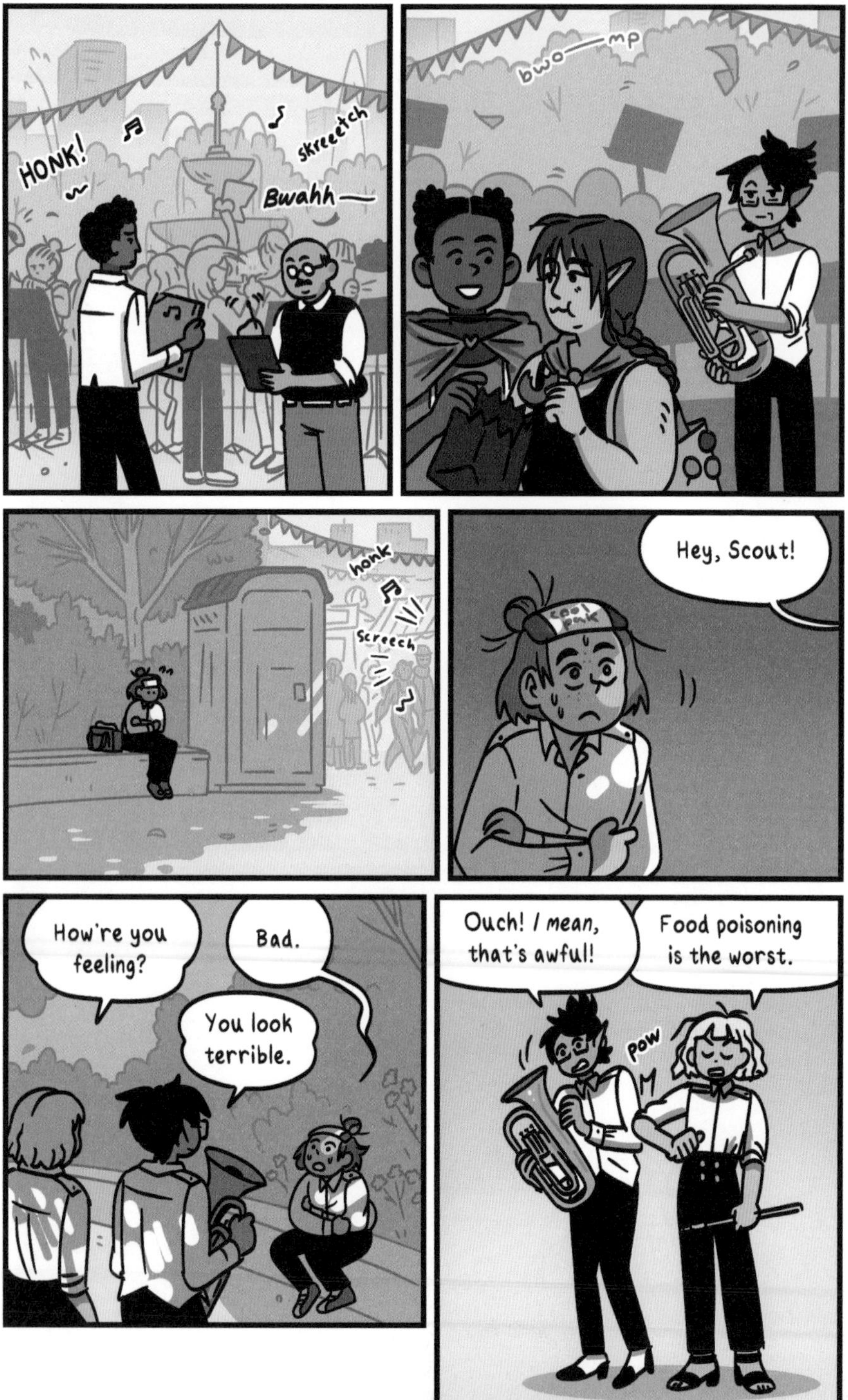
HONK!
Skreeetch
Bwahh—
bwo—mp
honk
Screech
Hey, Scout!
cool pak
How're you feeling?
Bad.
You look terrible.
Ouch! I mean, that's awful!
Food poisoning is the worst.
pow

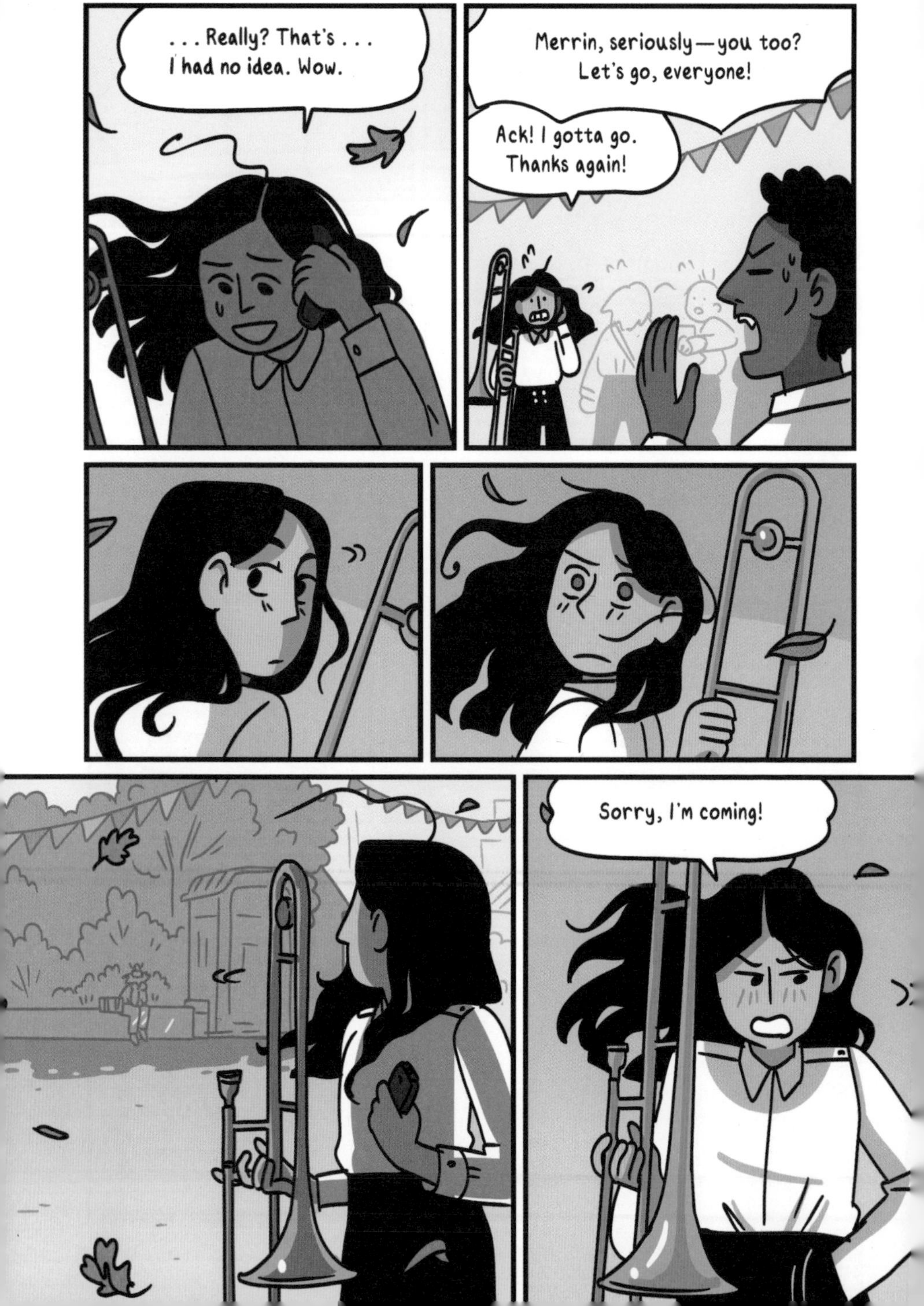
. . . Really? That's . . .
I had no idea. Wow.
Merrin, seriously—you too?
Let's go, everyone!
Ack! I gotta go.
Thanks again!
Sorry, I'm coming!

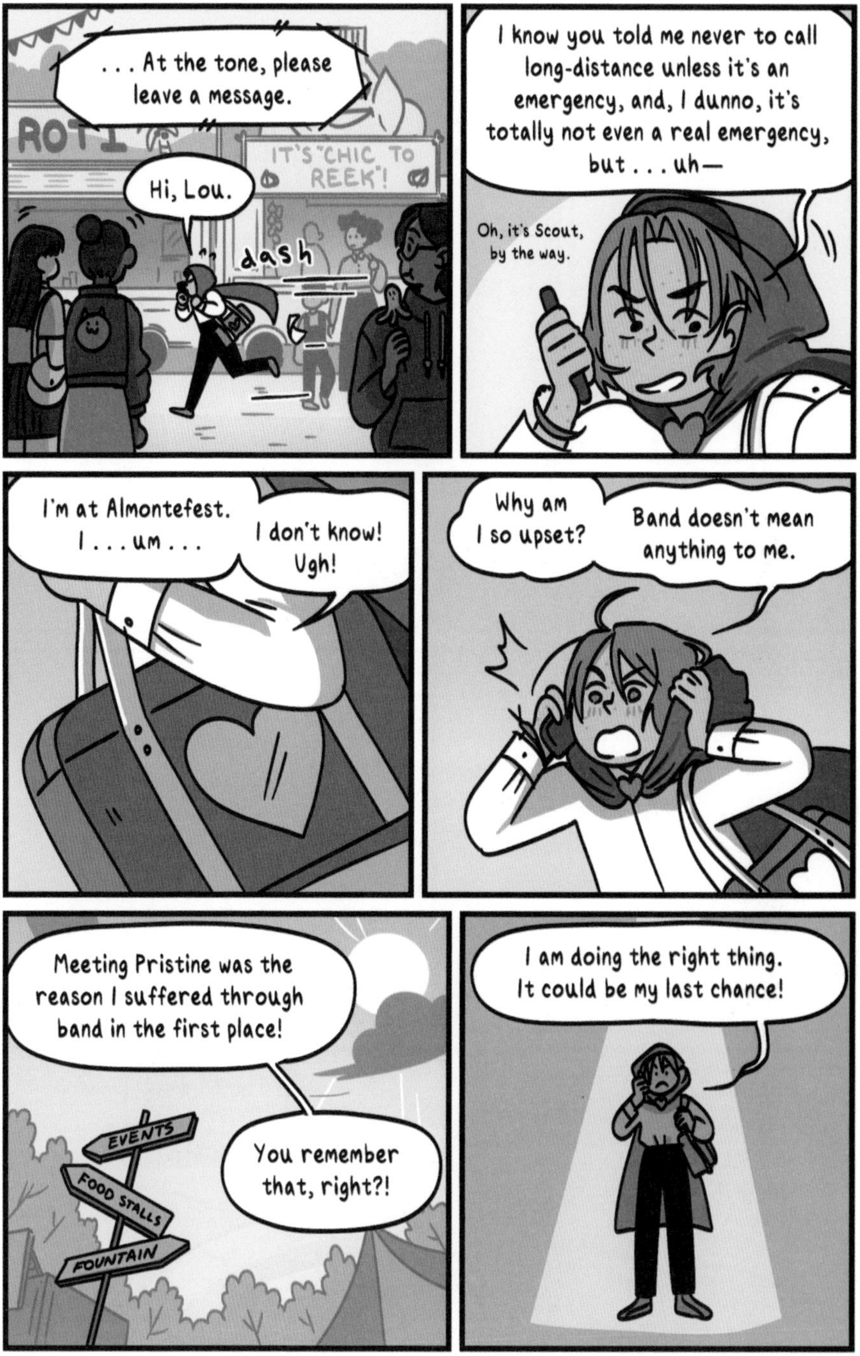
. . . At the tone, please leave a message.
ROTI
IT'S "CHIC TO REEK"!
Hi, Lou.
dash
I know you told me never to call long-distance unless it's an emergency, and, I dunno, it's totally not even a real emergency, but . . . uh—
Oh, it's Scout, by the way.
I'm at Almontefest. I . . . um . . .
I don't know! Ugh!
Why am I so upset?
Band doesn't mean anything to me.
Meeting Pristine was the reason I suffered through band in the first place!
You remember that, right?!
EVENTS
FOOD STALLS
FOUNTAIN
I am doing the right thing. It could be my last chance!

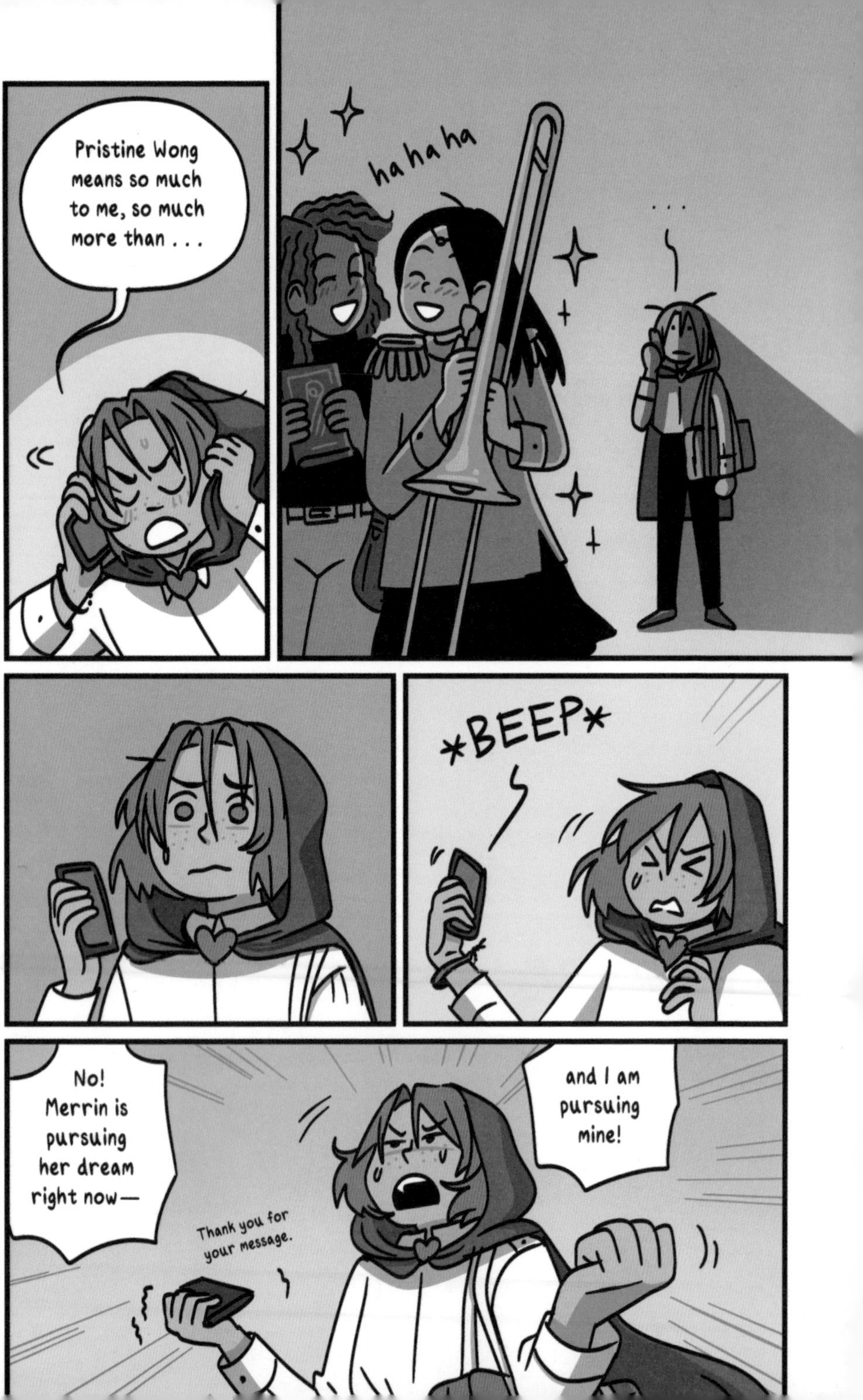

Pristine Wong means so much to me, so much more than . . .
ha ha ha
. . .
BEEP
No! Merrin is pursuing her dream right now—
and I am pursuing mine!
Thank you for your message.

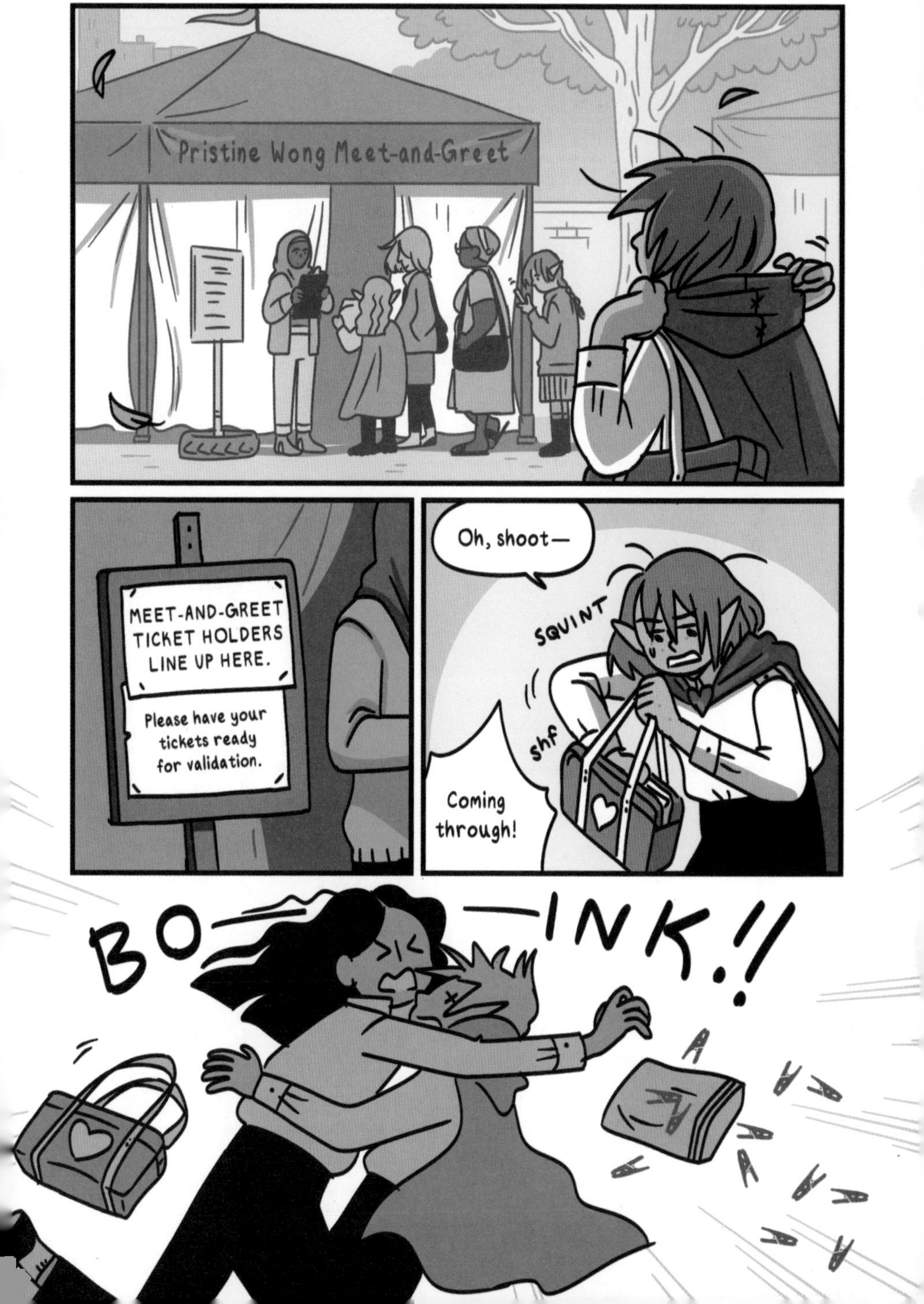
Pristine Wong Meet-and-Greet
MEET-AND-GREET TICKET HOLDERS LINE UP HERE.
Please have your tickets ready for validation.
Oh, shoot—
SQUINT
shf
Coming through!
BO——INK!!

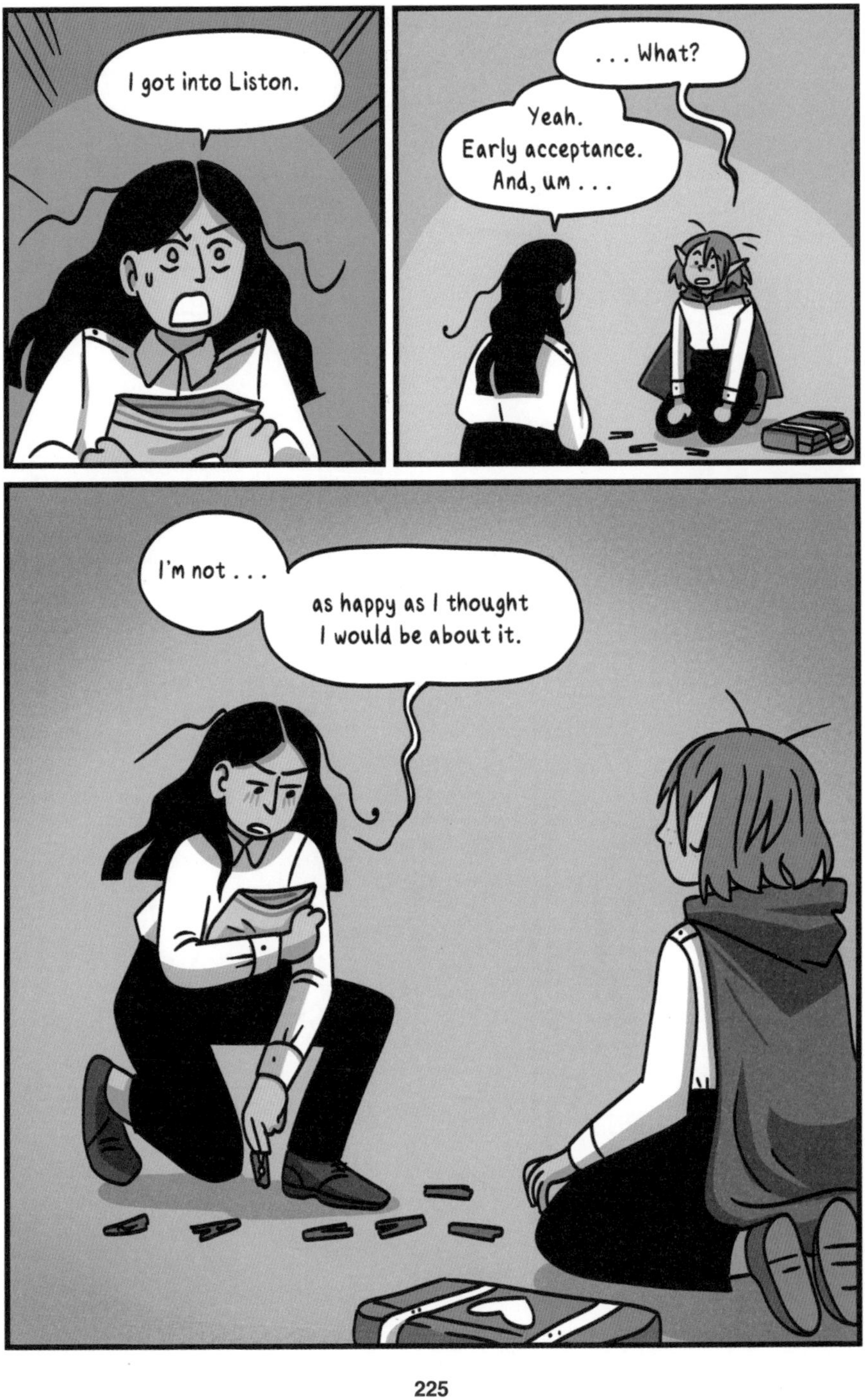
I got into Liston.
. . . What?
Yeah.
Early acceptance.
And, um . . .
I'm not . . .
as happy as I thought
I would be about it.

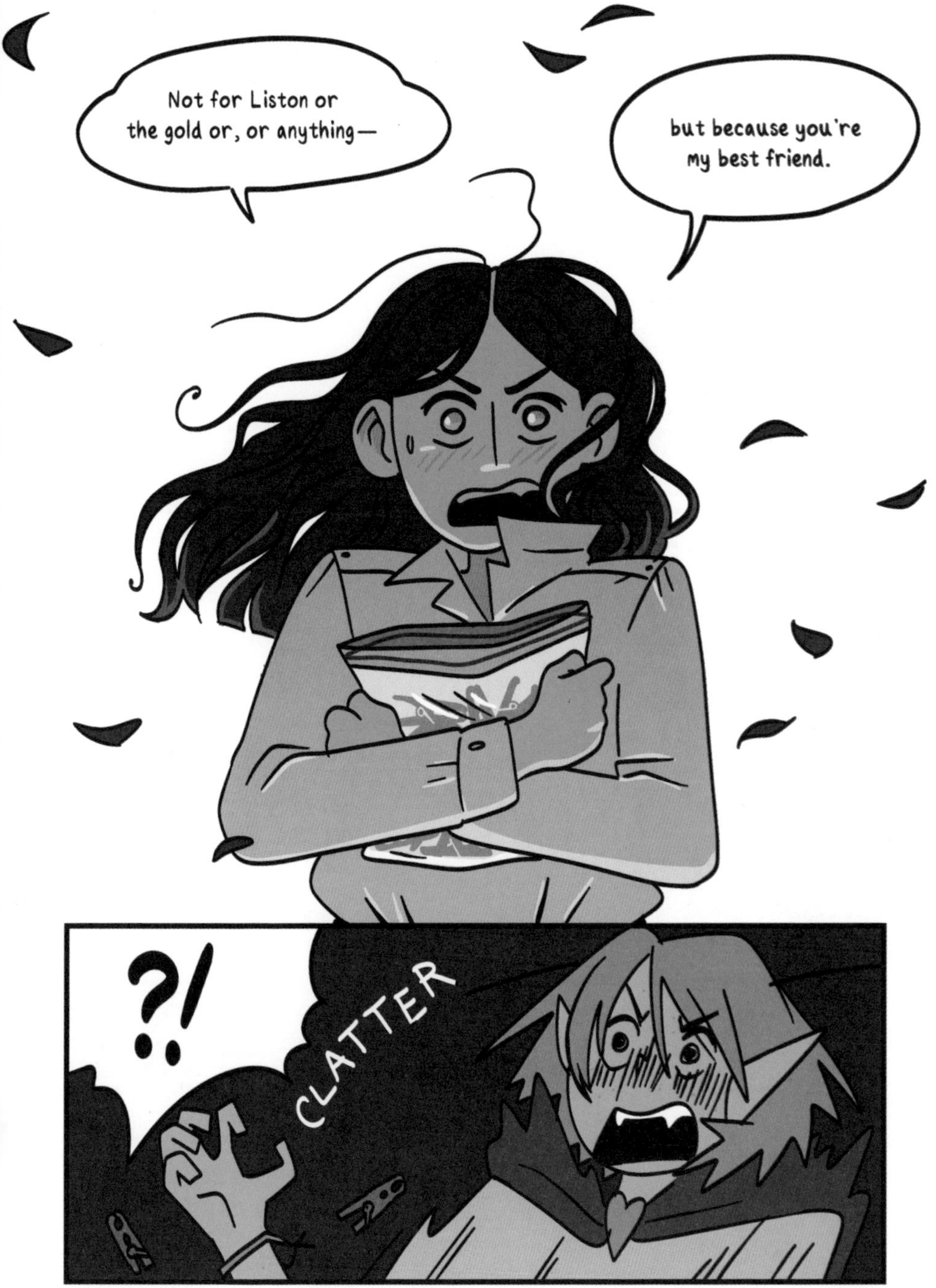
Not for Liston or the gold or, or anything—
but because you're my best friend.
?!
CLATTER

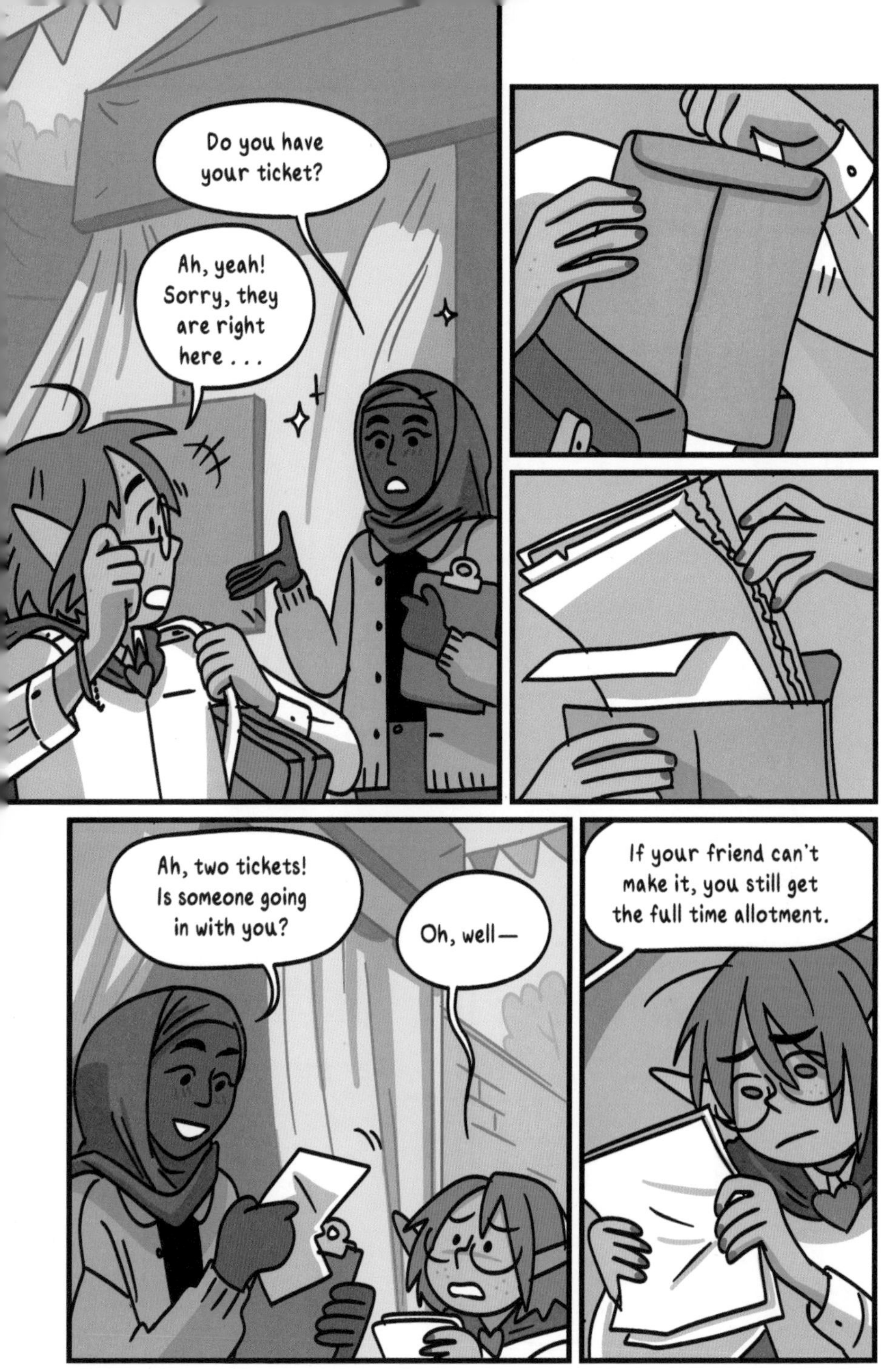
Do you have your ticket?
Ah, yeah! Sorry, they are right here . . .
Ah, two tickets! Is someone going in with you?
Oh, well—
If your friend can't make it, you still get the full time allotment.

questions
1) who is your
4.) i love your blog
for: Pristine
I'm sorry. I actually have to go.
Eh?
I—I got food poisoning from a street hot dog!
Bathrooms are by the pavilion!

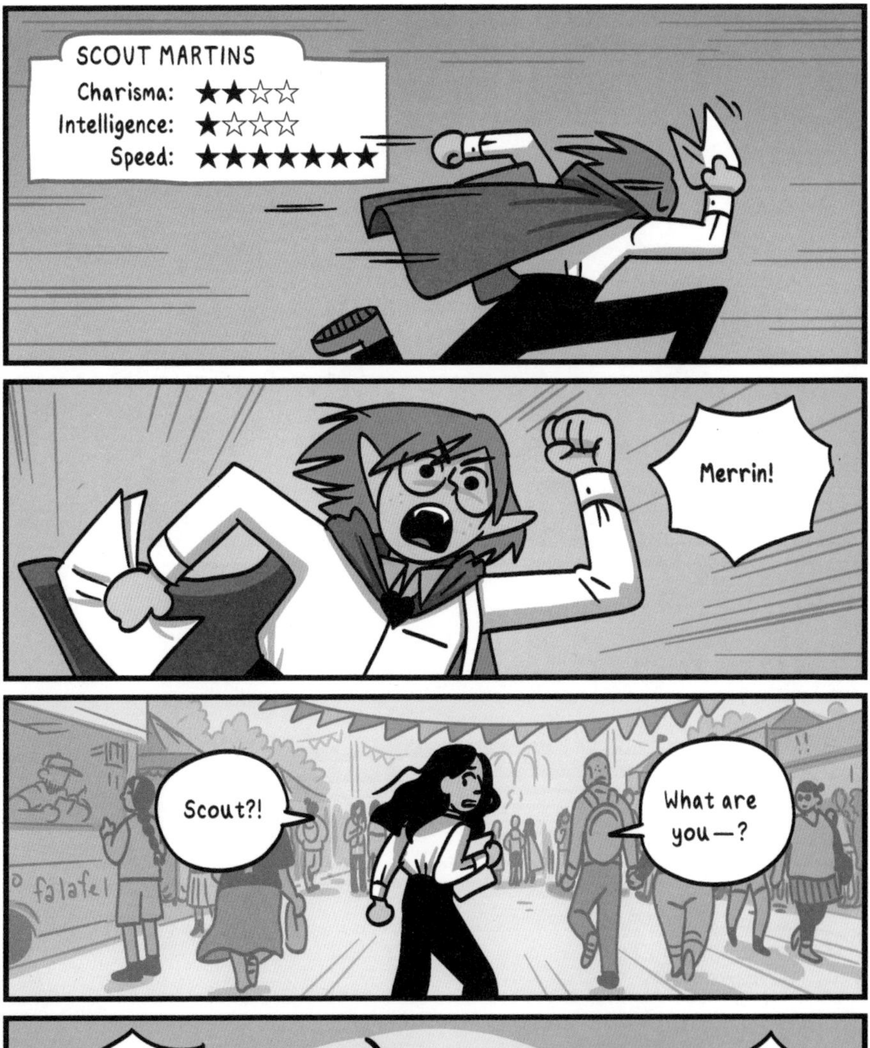
SCOUT MARTINS
Charisma: ★★☆☆
Intelligence: ★☆☆☆
Speed: ★★★★★★★
Merrin!
Scout?!
What are you—?
I'm sorry!
I'm sorry! I changed my mind!

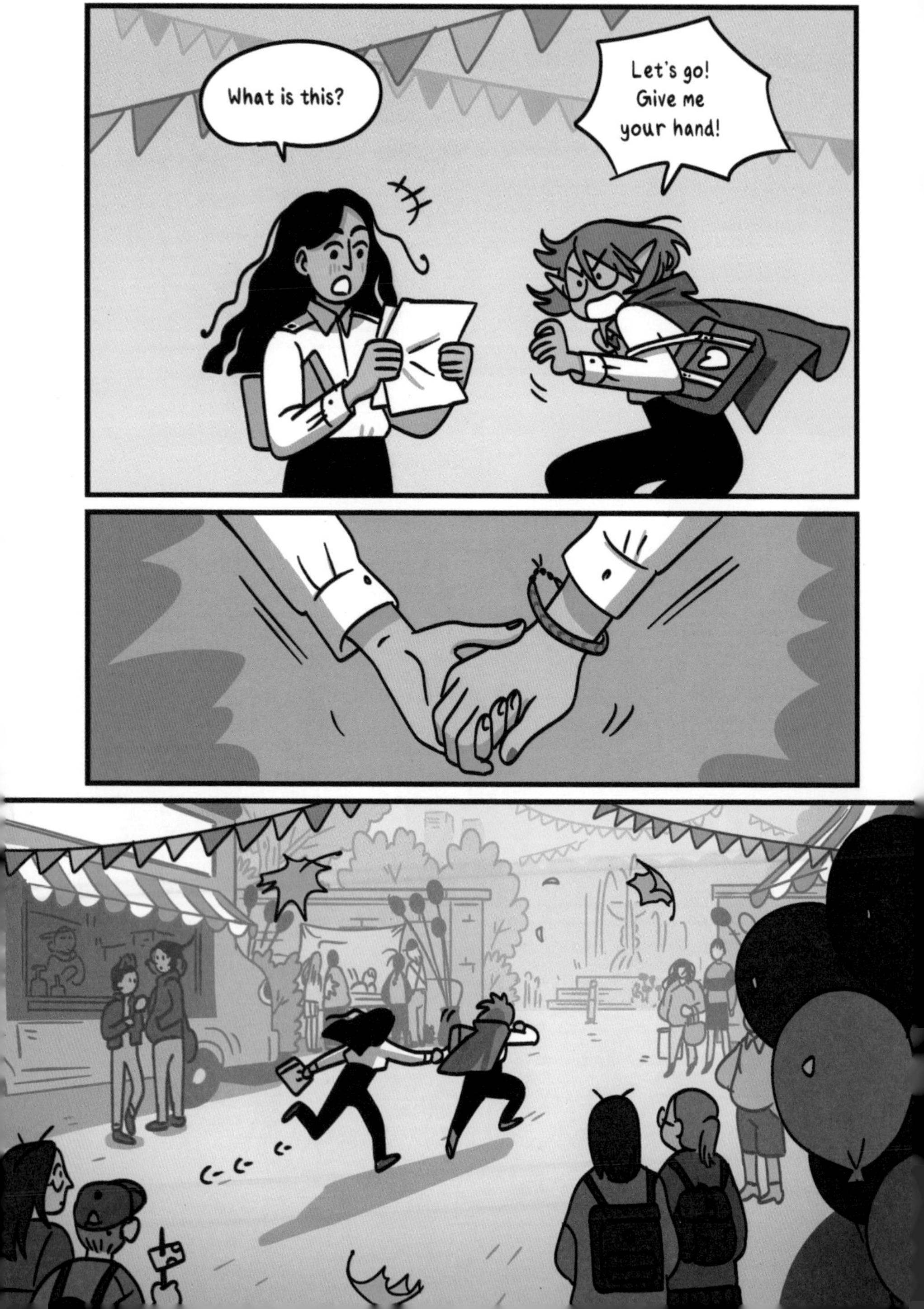
What is this?
Let's go! Give me your hand!

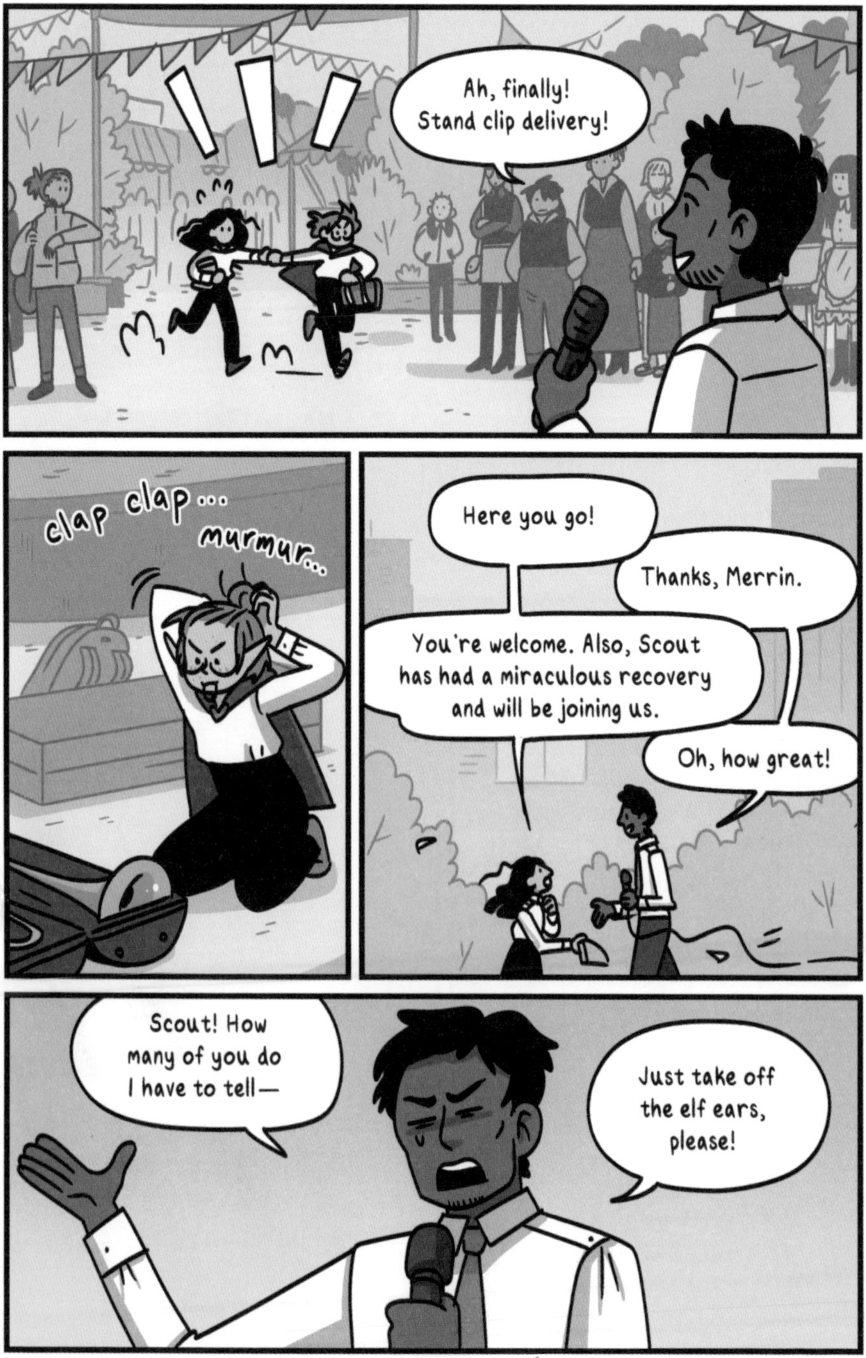
Ah, finally! Stand clip delivery!
clap clap...
murmur...
Here you go!
Thanks, Merrin.
You're welcome. Also, Scout has had a miraculous recovery and will be joining us.
Oh, how great!
Scout! How many of you do I have to tell—
Just take off the elf ears, please!

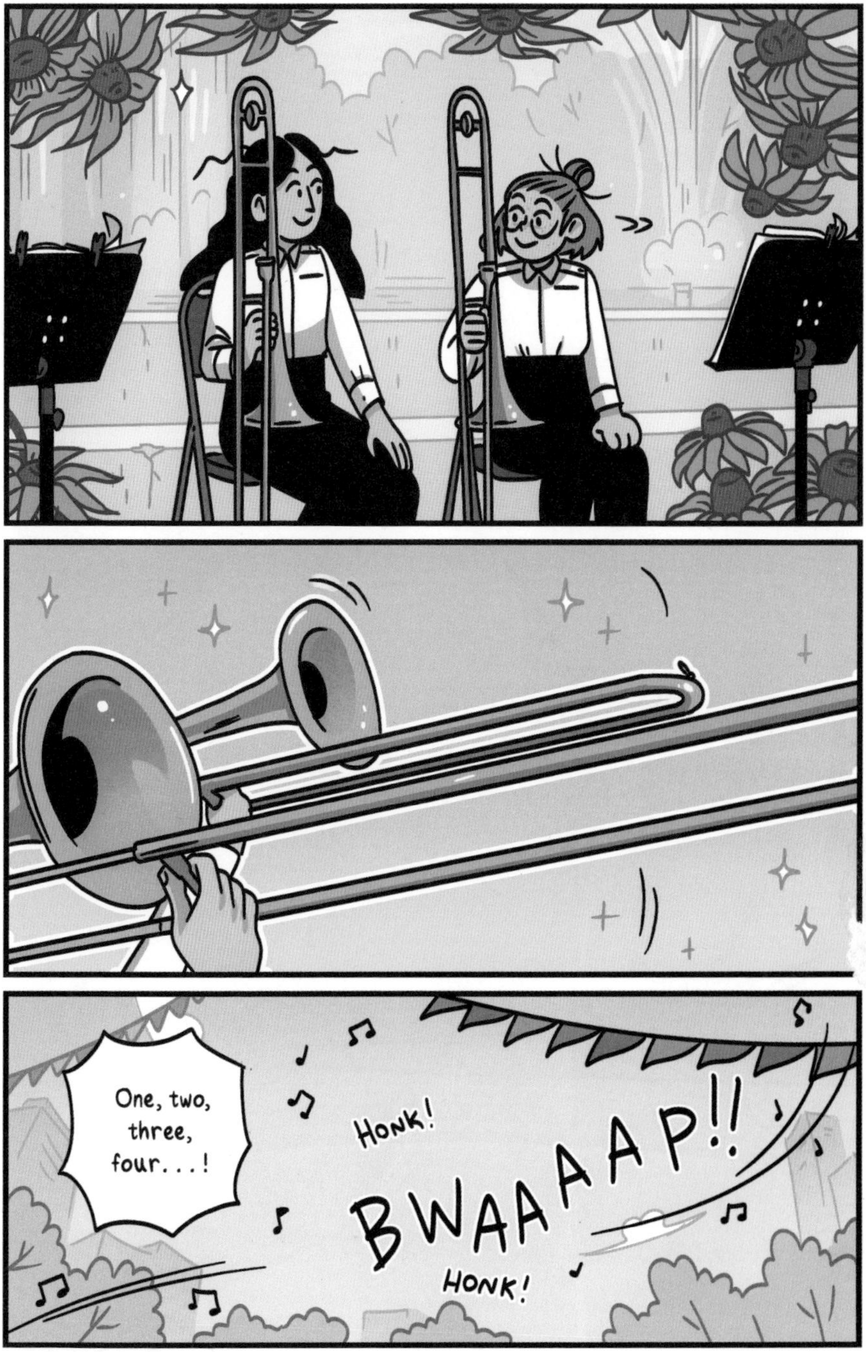
One, two, three, four...!
HONK!
BWAAAAP!!
HONK!

Chapter 6

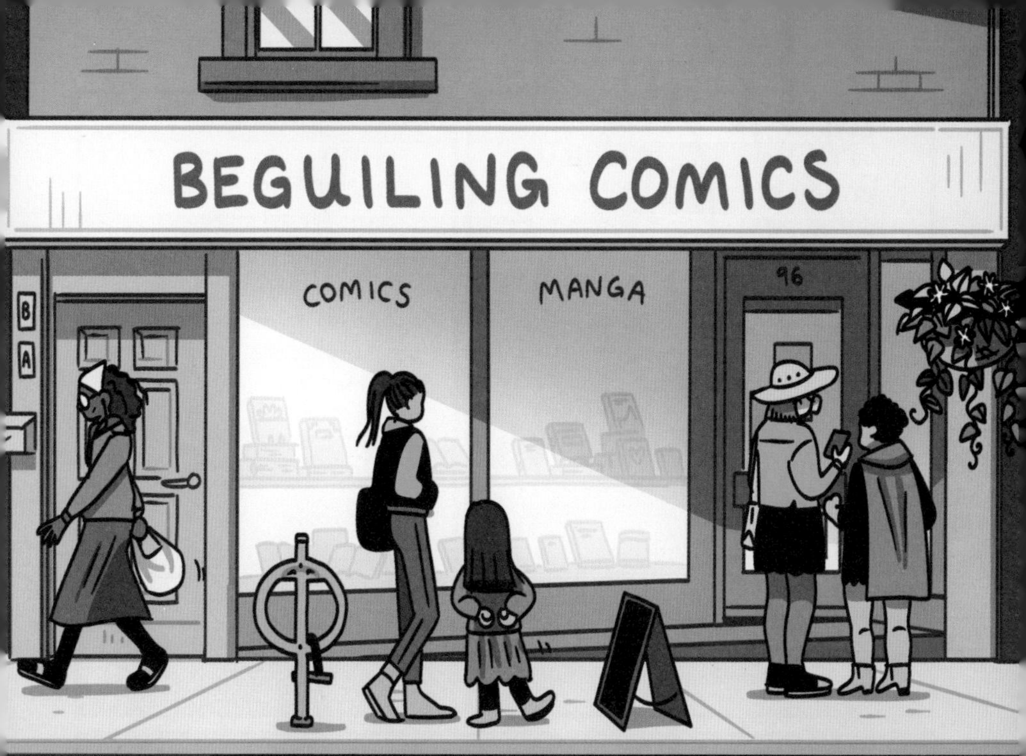
BEGUILING COMICS
COMICS
MANGA
96
B
A

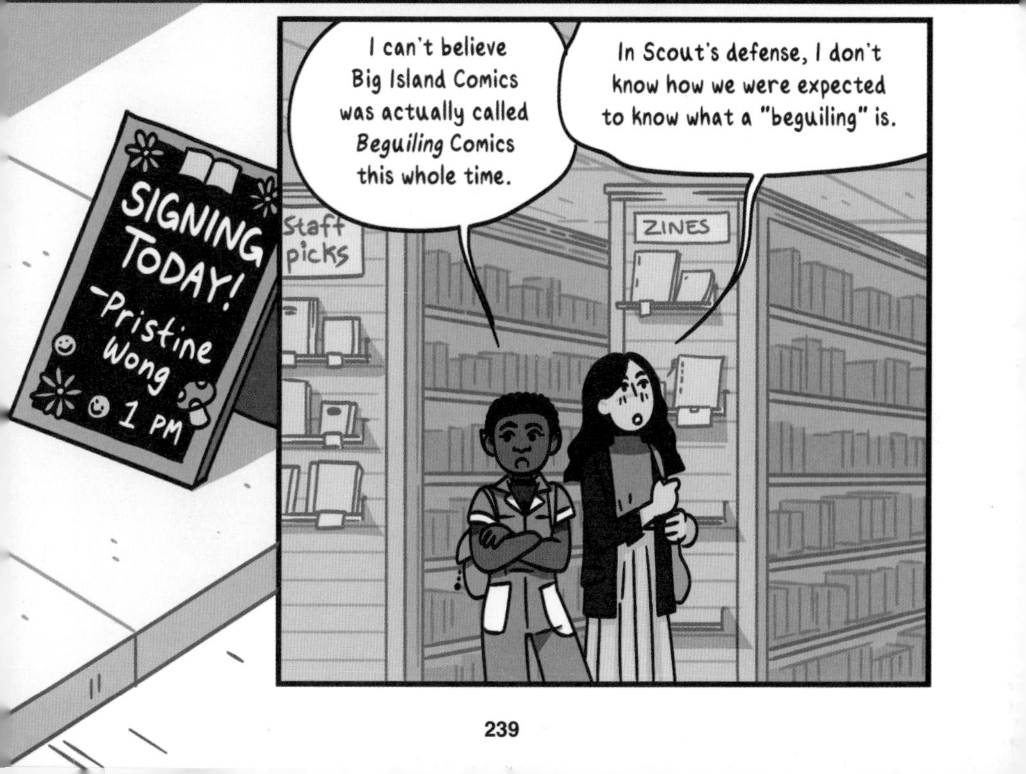
SIGNING TODAY! -Pristine Wong 1 PM
I can't believe Big Island Comics was actually called *Beguiling* Comics this whole time.
In Scout's defense, I don't know how we were expected to know what a "beguiling" is.
Staff picks
ZINES

*Chiaroscuro is an art technique that uses strong contrasts between light and dark.

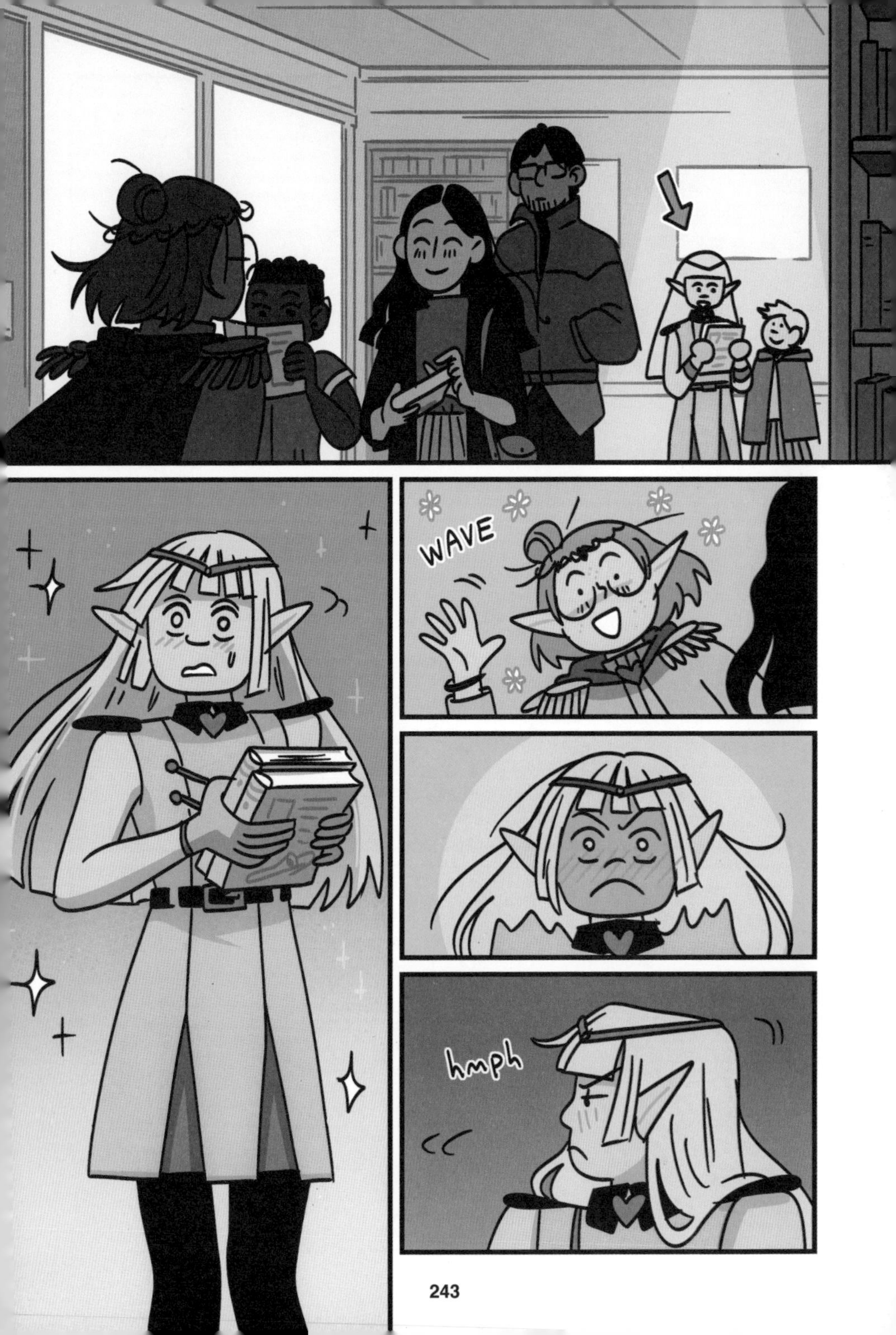
WAVE
hmph

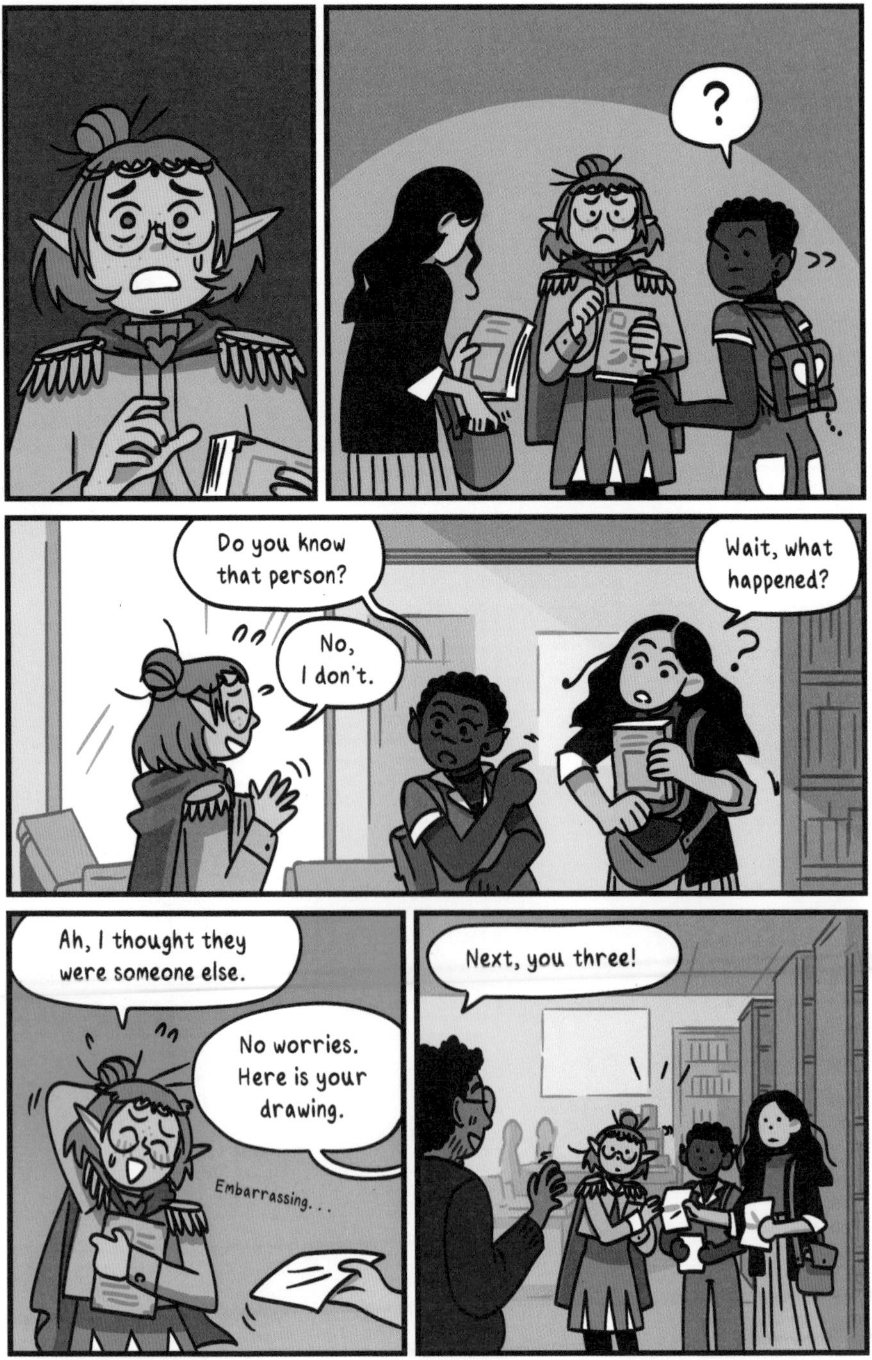
?
Do you know that person?
No, I don't.
Wait, what happened?
Ah, I thought they were someone else.
No worries. Here is your drawing.
Embarrassing...
Next, you three!

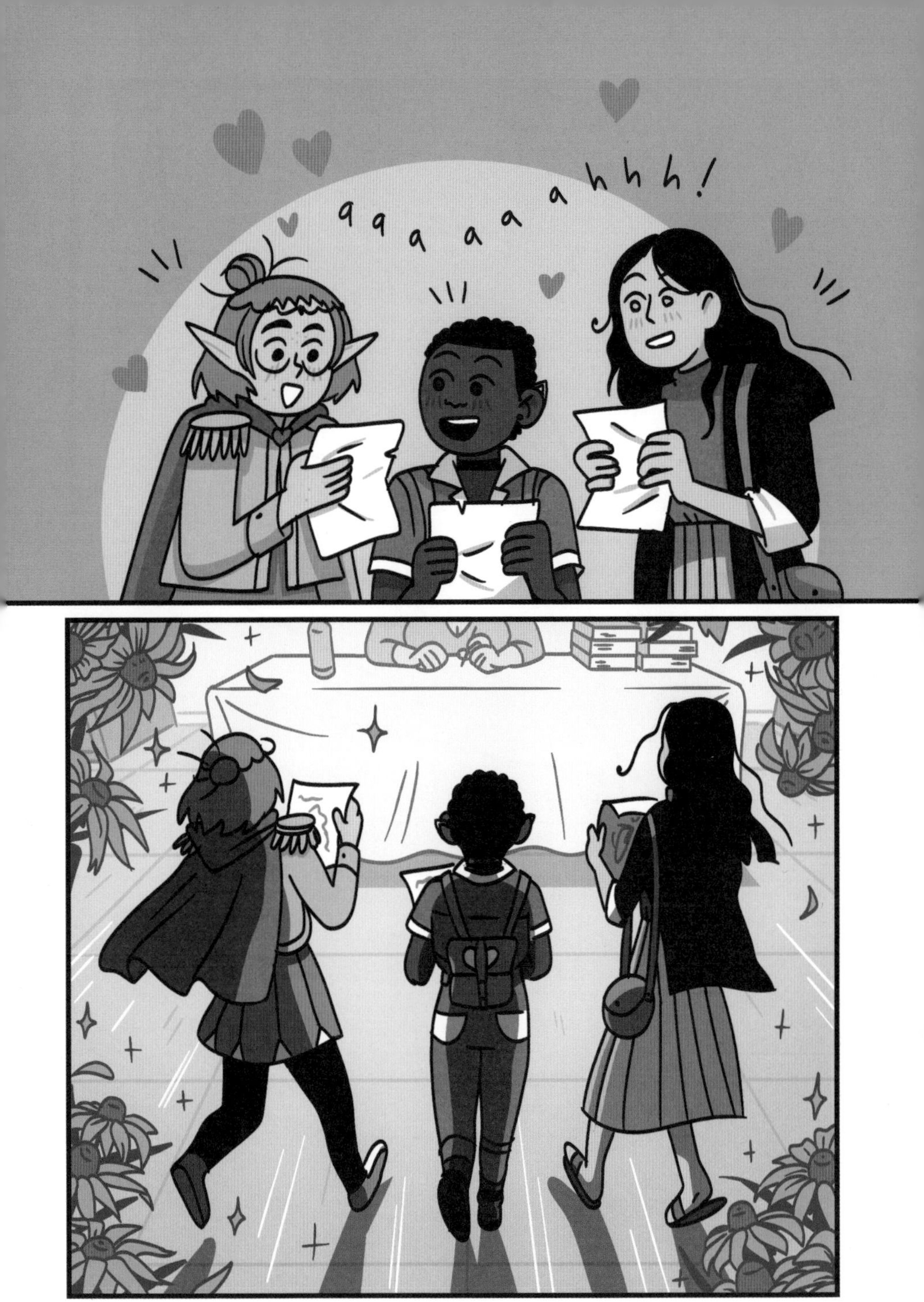
aaaaaaahhhh!

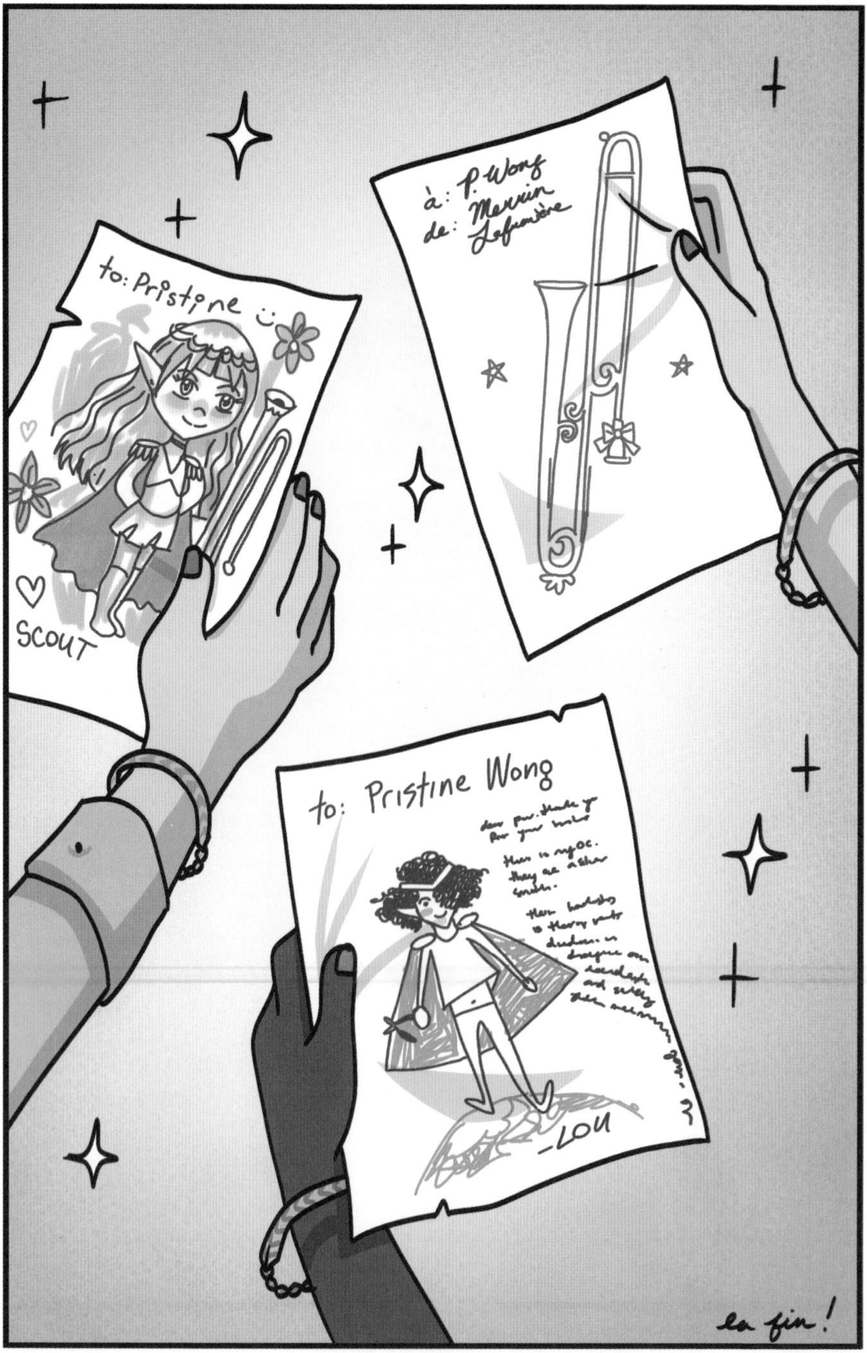

to: Pristine :)
SCOUT
à: P. Wong
de: Mervin
to: Pristine Wong
-LOU
la fin!

Scout!

these are some of the designs
i would reference when drawing
scout in this book.

i love her so much, but i struggled
a lot with drawing her in a way
i was happy with! as i was penciling,
i kept telling myself, "i'll figure it
out eventually!" but i don't think
i ever did (lol).

glasses

hair
above
shoulders →

coat
(thrifted
trucker
jacket)

bracelet

untuck
shirt
+
cute
belly

painted
nails
(always!)

bowling
lol →

bag

scout's bag.
i almost gave up
on this design
because it was
so hard for
me to draw.

scout's laptop

PRISTINE
WONG

POSAUNE
WARRIOR PRINCESS

i drew these prop designs
after inking 75 percent
of the book and had to
go back and change what
i drew originally.

VIDEO GAME
SOUNDTRACKS
FOR
BRASS

Merrin

merrin was easier for me to draw from the beginning. i think her hair length changes all throughout the book, but maybe we can pretend it grows really fast and she cuts it a lot?

the straight cut at the bottom makes me think she chops it off herself. her hair is very thick. when she braids it, the braid is so heavy it hurts her scalp! she absolutely can't put it up in a ponytail for too long for the same reason . . .

good posture

pointy chin?

like 𝄞

steps on the heels of her shoes

merrin's bag. based on the leather bag i had in high school that i "borrowed" without permission from my mum. (sorry ,mum.)

Merrin

merrin definitely has her own trombone. i bet she had one of those colourful novelty trombones at one point but then thought it wasn't "mature." (incorrect opinion. sorry, merrin.)

essential elements
TROMBONE
honk

music book

did she ever even wear these shoes . . . ?

music folder

Merrin

Lennox and Kim

rect. face

eye bags? idk...

round face

collar buttoned up

pierced

tall converse

lennox was my favourite girl to draw. while all the characters in the book are "very me," i feel like lennox is the most me. whenever lennox showed up in this book, i was like, "ah! here i am!" it's probably the bangs.

i loved writing kim a lot. i really wanted to bring the feeling of young crushes and how distracting and horrible they can be. kim is a girl with her head constantly in the clouds.

don't think i drew these shoes on her once.

Lou

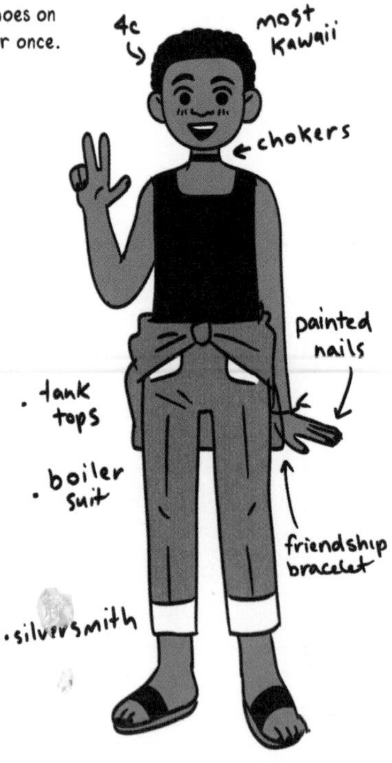

4c

most kawaii

chokers

painted nails

tank tops

boiler suit

friendship bracelet

silversmith

lou was named after mary lou williams, but apparently lou williams is also a professional basketball player?! that is kind of cool, too! i don't follow sports that much, obviously.

i had a few internet friends growing up who i still talk to and cherish to this day. one of which was my first non-cis friend, so i really wanted someone similar in the book!

Chris, Vic, and PB

square glasses

square face

no nose just freckle

round face

pierce

long

thicker brows

chris basically had the same design since day one, although putting together these pages i noticed i gave her a long kilt in the concept art? why did i change that? it's so cool.

rolled

long skirt

vic originally had a buzz cut hairstyle but i got bored of drawing it after pencils so i changed it to mid-length hair.

heels (always)

fun socks

these are all their coats.

i changed PB's name, like, probably six times in the course of writing this book. i'm very bad at naming characters.

i settled on PB because my deadline was coming up and I liked to think it was short for "peanut butter," which is very cute and funny.

251

the rest of the band

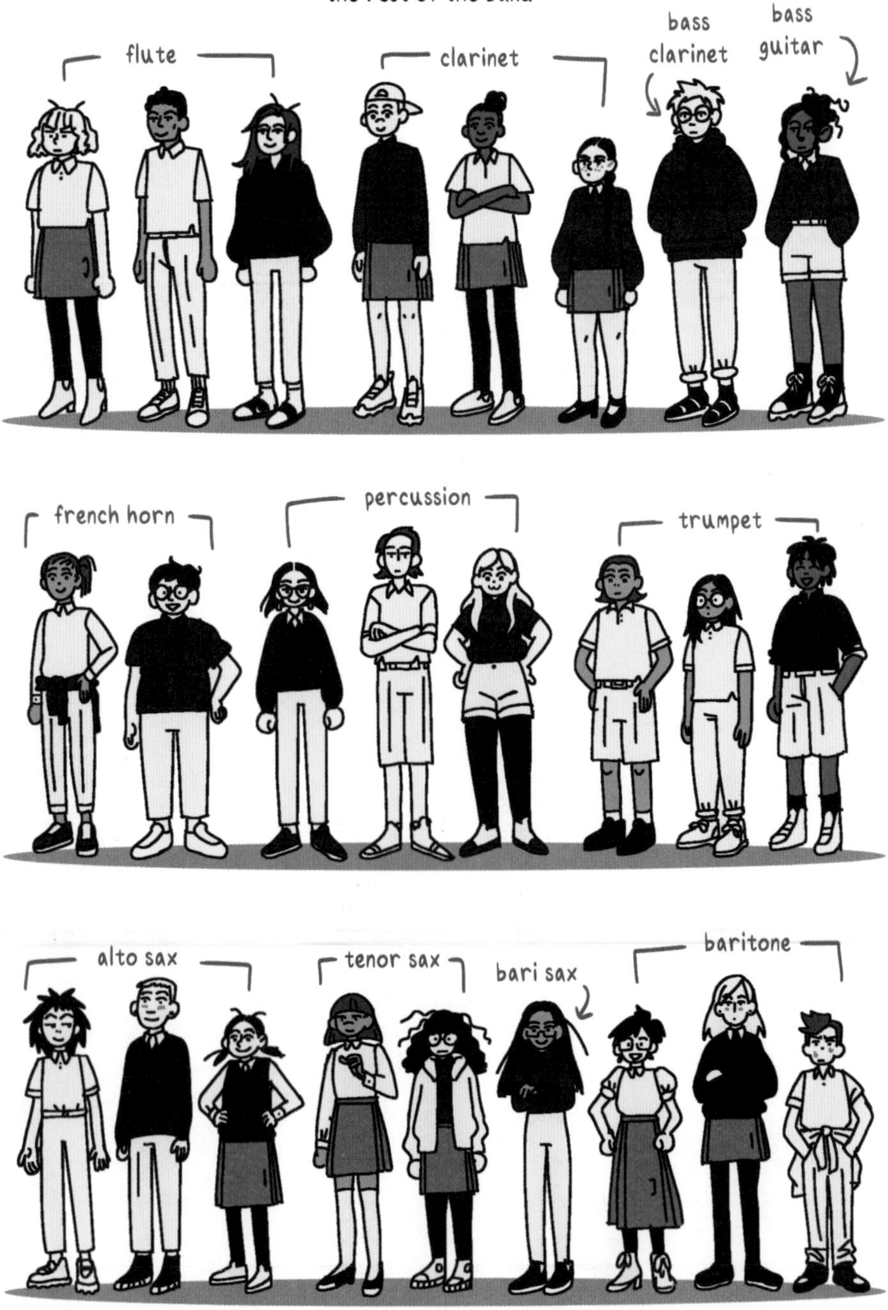

flute
clarinet
bass clarinet
bass guitar
french horn
percussion
trumpet
alto sax
tenor sax
bari sax
baritone

band uniform concepts

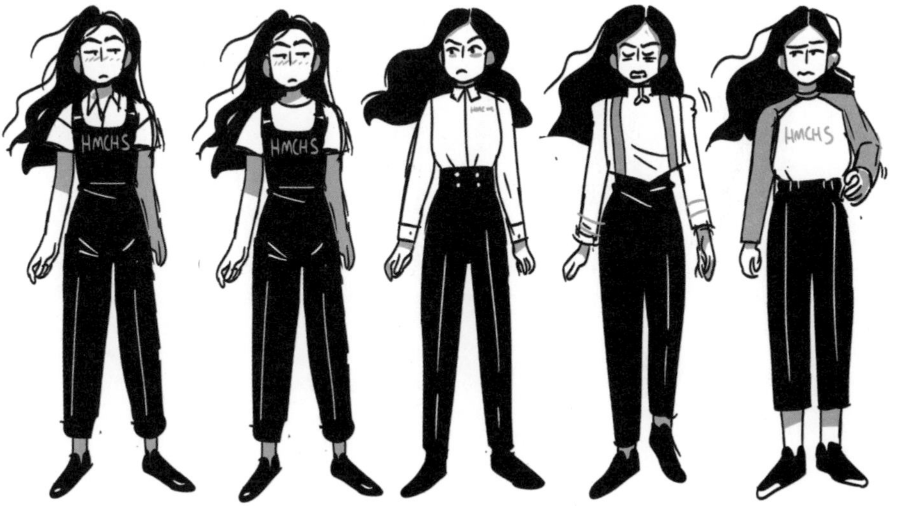
HMCHS
HMCHS
HMCHS

old *posaune* designs

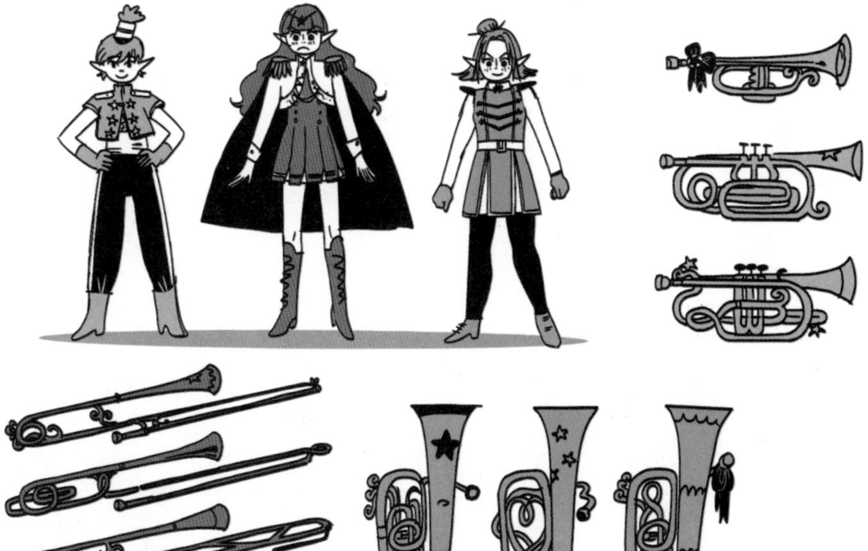

254

spit rug

spit cannon

mum means well

cat person

hey, mum, uh no problem if you can't but, um, could you pick me up in town tonight?

i get along better with animals than people . . .

sure, the truck is free tonight. everything ok?

oh. um. i'm, uh, hanging out with a friend, so . . .

meow meow! tch tch!

tch tch baby! meeeow meeeeow!!

HANGING OUT WITH A FRIEND?! OH OF COURSE! STAY AS LATE AS YOU WANT! WHO IS IT? DO I KNOW THEM? HAVE FUN!!!!!

MRYEW

. . . . .

great now i feel horrible

merrin must not do this very often

i see

i didn't say animals got along well with ME . . .

freetalk

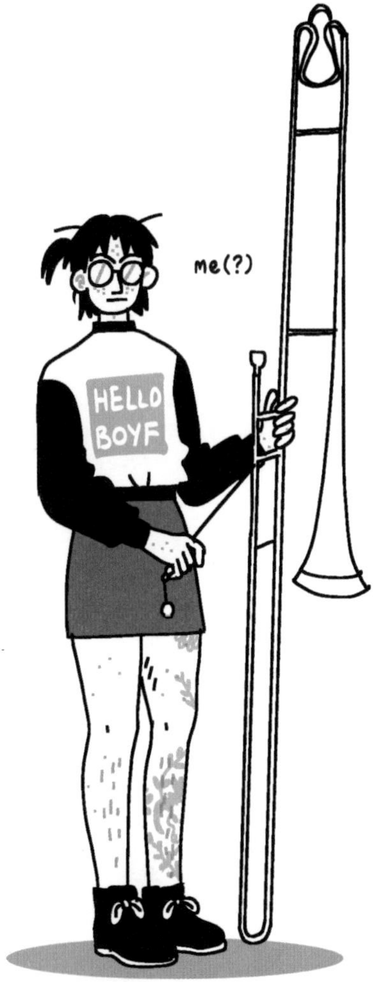
me(?)
HELLO BOYF

hello, everyone. 2021-05-14

thanks for coming to my freetalk. it's 11 am on a friday. i want a steamed pork bun and a soda and i am going to have a nice lil picnic in the park.

when i was 11 i switched from the local public school to a catholic school in the next town over, even though i knew nothing about religion nor knew anyone at the school. i did it because i wanted to wear a school uniform with a pleated skirt so badly.

my best friend and i met when i opened my locker and had my anime fanart taped up on the inside and she asked if i had a deviantart. we have been best friends ever since and talk to each other every day :)

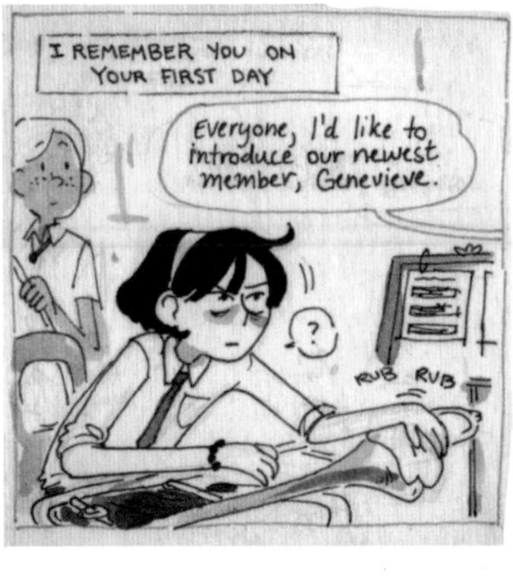
I REMEMBER YOU ON YOUR FIRST DAY
Everyone, I'd like to introduce our newest member, Genevieve.
?
RUB RUB

this book was inspired by a short comic i drew in 2018. it was about a trombone player who murders another trombone player for making fun of band (and being too pretty). i quickly realized i couldn't write a full-length book about murder so it eventually became this!

thank you from the bottom of my heart for reading.

love, jade

Special Thanks

Deep gratitude and appreciation to my family for their unwavering support and love. Thank you, Mom, Dad, Keely, and Selena. Thank you to Annabel Scott for being the best friend anyone could ever ask for. Thank you to my dearest friends and fellow collective members Victor Martins, Keelin Gorlewski, and Christine Wong, whose incredible comic work inspires me to no end and whose friendship I cherish. Special thanks to Rabeea S, D. Chouk, Jarrett S, Emma H, Kim + Serge, Beena M, Kristina L, the Luu Nguyen family, Sara C, Lis S, Anna K, Andrew T, my middle school music teacher Mr. Stuart, everyone in Friendo Art Share Jamboree, Gundam consultant Dan, colour consultant Killian Ng, longtime internet pals Alex and Lina, my agent Seth, designer extraordinaire P. Crotty, and my editor Whitney for taking a chance on me so long ago. Shout-out to Diskette Press and Koyama Press for their inspiring and wide support of the arts, and to Olivia at Pindot Press for printing all our zines so beautifully even when we don't format them correctly. Thanks to The Beguiling for letting me and HBF use their basement to work on comics and definitely not goof off. Shout-out to the broader support from the arts communities of Toronto, Montréal, and Almonte, and any person who has ever picked up a zine from me. Thank you so much!

Special thanks to my flatters Natalie Mark and Kristen Cooper for all their hard work and attention to detail, and for working with line art that had so many broken lines.

I would like to acknowledge the support of the Ontario Arts Council, an agency of the Government of Ontario, in the creation of this book.

I moved five times creating this graphic novel! Never doing that again. As such, I would like to acknowledge that this book was written on the unceded traditional territories of many nations including the Mississaugas of the Credit, the Anishinaabeg, the Ojibwa, the Haudenosaunee, the Mohawk, and the Wendat peoples. This book was written on and based upon unceded traditional Omàmìwininì (Algonquin) territory.

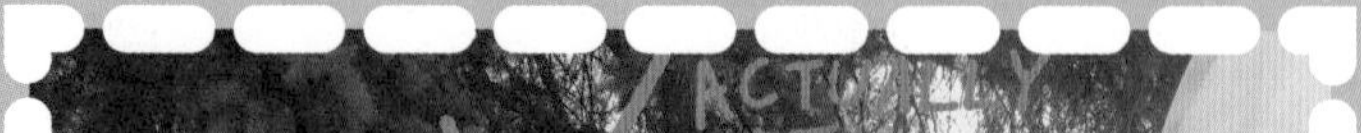
ACTUALLY
ME

Jade Armstrong is a Canadian comic artist and a member of the star-studded comics collective Hello Boyfriend. They played trombone pretty well in middle school but play bass guitar pretty badly now. *Scout Is Not a Band Kid* is their first graphic novel.

The artist at work :)

FIND YOUR VOICE
WITH ONE OF THESE EXCITING GRAPHIC NOVELS

PRESENTED BY RH GRAPHIC

f @RHKIDSGRAPHIC

A GRAPHIC NOVEL ON EVERY BOOKSHELF